# DOROTHY KOOMSON

**DOROTHY KOOMSON** is an award-winning, internationally bestselling author and journalist whose books have been translated into more than 30 languages, with sales that exceed 2 million copies in the UK alone.

Her third novel, *My Best Friend's Girl* (2006) was selected for the Richard & Judy Summer Reads Book Club, while a TV adaptation based on *The Ice Cream Girls* was shown on ITV1 in 2013.

Dorothy was featured on the 2021 Powerlist as one of the most influential Black people in Britain and appeared in *GQ Style* as a Black British trailblazer.

She loves reading and writing, and is passionate about supporting other writers no matter what stage they are at in their career.

For more information about Dorothy, check out her website www.dorothykoomson.co.uk where you'll find out about her podcasts, newsletters and latest events.

*Also by*

# DOROTHY
# KOOMSON

# DOROTHY
# KOOMSON

# My
# Other
# Husband

REVIEW

First published in 2022 by Headline Review
An imprint of HEADLINE PUBLISHING GROUP

First published in paperback in 2023 by Headline Review
An imprint of HEADLINE PUBLISHING GROUP

2

Cataloguing in Publication Data is available from the British Library

ISBN 978 1 4722 7742 8

Typeset in Times LT Std 10.25/15pt by Jouve (UK), Milton Keynes

Printed and bound in Great Britain by Clays Ltd, Elcograf S.p.A.

Headline's policy is to use papers that are natural, renewable and recyclable
products and made from wood grown in well-managed forests and other
controlled sources. The logging and manufacturing processes are expected
to conform to the environmental regulations of the country of origin.

HEADLINE PUBLISHING GROUP
An Hachette UK Company
Carmelite House
50 Victoria Embankment
London EC4Y 0DZ

www.headline.co.uk
www.hachette.co.uk

To you
wherever you are.

# Prologue

'Cleo Forsum Pryce, I am arresting you on the suspicion of attempted murder.'

*No. They can't do this. Not right now.*

'You do not have to say anything.'

*I need to find her before it's too late.*

'But it may harm your defence if you do not mention when questioned something which you later rely on in court.'

*Because if I don't do whatever I'm told, she's going to die. He's going to kill her.*

'Anything you do say may be given in evidence.'

'Please, I didn't do this. I promise you, I didn't do this. And you have to let me go.' *You have to let me go. It's a matter of life or death.*

# Part 1

# 1

'You really didn't have to come in to the office to see me about your divorce, you do realise that, don't you, Ms Forsum?'

I nod. 'I know. I know I could do it all online, that it'd be cheaper and probably quicker, but I didn't want a paper trail – or online trail.'

Jeff Burrfield frowns at me, confused all of a sudden. 'I thought you said your husband knows about this?' He starts flipping through his notes, probably scared now that he's wrongly attributed this nugget of information to the desperate woman in front of him who is checking out of her relationship. 'You said that he was on board and . . . ah, yes' – his finger runs along the line where he has made his initial observations – 'he couldn't wait to get rid of you. And he couldn't believe he'd spent so many years of his life with a heartless cow like you.' He raises his balding head and we lock gazes.

'To be fair to me, I did make it clear that he never actually said all that,' I offer in a pathetic voice. 'That was my interpretation of the situation as seen by him. Possibly.'

'But he does know you're divorcing him?'

'Yes, he does know.' *He doesn't know why but he does know*, I add in my head.

'Oh good,' Mr Burrfield murmurs, visibly relieved that there is no subterfuge. 'Things are always a *bit* less unpleasant if everyone involved is apprised of the situation.'

'My husband would never say anything like that, it's not his style or nature. He's very much a peace, love, hope-to-all-beings kind of person.'

'And you're not?'

'Yes, yes I am. Within reason.'

A ghost of a smile haunts Mr Burrfield's lips and I feel sorry for him. It can't be pleasant or even vaguely fun to be this close to human relationships as they disintegrate. Does it make you cynical? It must do. You can't sit on that side of this type of desk, listen to all those stories of things going awry and *NOT* wonder why people bother in the first place. His ring finger is bare so I'm assuming he hasn't married or, if he has, that it's gone awry. I don't get the feeling he is long-term attached, but I could be wrong. Either way, he gives the impression that he is someone who would prefer all of this 'unpleasantness' not to exist, but since it does, he'll continue on with the forbearance needed to guide lost, separating souls through it.

'Can I ask you something, off the books, as it were?' I say. I need to get a definitive answer to this, this question that has been circling my mind for many, many years. This question that I get a million different answers to whenever I'm brave enough to search the internet.

'What do you mean, "off the books"?' he replies, drawing back a little from me. Not very noticeably, just slightly. Just enough to let me know on an unconscious level that I won't be getting anything for nothing out of him.

'I mean, not something you should probably write down in my file there since it doesn't really relate to me.'

'Who does it relate to, then?'

Good question. Obvious question. So why don't I have a ready answer? Because every answer will sound fake, every reply will be a lie. 'I mean, well, a friend of mine. A close friend of mine.'

Mr Burrfield puts down his pen, shuts his file, removes his glasses. Now he is out from behind his glasses, he looks much younger but more mature. Much more worldly than the long-suffering, slightly bumbling solicitor I originally sat down with. I'd picked his name from the internet. Trawled through until I found one near enough to where I am currently working so I could base my break around this meeting, but also far enough away that no one will see me going in to these offices and find out before the rest of my family about the irretrievable breakdown of my marriage.

'What is it your close *friend* would like to ask?'

'Well, it's kind of awkward and she feels extremely silly, but what would happen if she'd . . . no, no, let me start again. What if my friend, at some point in the past, had gone to another country and just, on a whim, got married? If she didn't register that marriage when she came back to England all those years ago and then got married again to someone else, would it be OK or would she, potentially, be in trouble?'

Mr Burrfield looks like I have smacked him square in the face right after I've sworn at him. He doesn't move or even seem to breathe for a few seconds, he just sits with shock and horror drenching his face as he stares at me. Eventually, he looks down at the file in front of him, at its mottled beige cardboard that holds the early details of the dissolution of my marriage. 'Your *friend* would not be *potentially* in trouble, she would be in a huge amount of trouble. Bigamy, which this is, carries a prison sentence of up to seven years.'

*Seven years! SEVEN years.* Those words have turned my stomach, have made me want to vomit right here on his nice, neat desk. SEVEN years.

'But if it wasn't registered, does it count?'

'Assuming your *friend* followed all the legal requirements when getting married in whichever foreign country she chose for the ceremony to take place – that is, she had all the required documentation and then signed a marriage licence or register – then the marriage is considered legal and binding here in the United Kingdom.'

'Even if it wasn't registered?'

'Foreign marriages are not "registered" as such. What you're referring to is the commonly misunderstood situation where the foreign marriage is "recorded", almost a case of letting the Government know the marriage exists at the General Register Office and letting them keep a copy of the licence so that you can have access to it if you require for any reason – such as proof that you are indeed married. This would ensure that while your marriage would not be "registered" in the same way a marriage of UK citizens getting married here would be, there would be a record of it and you would be able to get a copy of your wedding certificate. However, this practice was discontinued in 2014. No foreign marriages are "recorded" at GRO any more. And in any case, whether the marriage occurred before or after 2014, your *friend* would still be married with or without the marriage being "recorded" at the GRO.'

Oh. *Oh.* 'Seven years you said, yes?'

His nostrils flare briefly before he nods gravely.

'OK, good. Fine. Thank you. I'll be sure to tell my friend to, you know, not get married until the old marriage is sorted out.'

'You do that,' he states before slipping his glasses back into place and picking up his short, stubby fountain pen. 'You should also warn her not to tell anyone about it. If she has indeed married while already married, that is a criminal offence. Not something to shout about.'

'She wasn't shouting about it, she was just asking . . . Me . . . Asking me to ask you.'

'Indeed,' he replies sourly. 'I'll make sure I'm in touch later this evening about the papers. I have a feeling this divorce needs to be expedited.'

I couldn't argue with that. At all.

## Horsforth, 1996

'That guy's staring at you,' Trina stated with a mixture of puzzlement and disdain.

The university common room where we sat often made me feel like we were sitting in the Colosseum – little groups of five or six gathered at small, low circular tables, waiting for the show to begin in the centre. Some groupings had more members and they spilled out, no matter how close they tried to fit themselves together. Other people had fewer companions, some were on their own – but all of us noisily crammed in here sat around the large expanse with its well-worn, shiny parquet floor, apart but together.

At the end of the canteen by the large glass doors, which opened out to the grass-and-concrete quad, was a serving hatch where cut-price teas and coffees, snacks and cold cans of pop were sold by the people who ran the Students' Union. Cut-price instant coffee in a Styrofoam cup and a bag of Maltesers had become my daily 'poison'.

Trina and I, first-year students who lived on campus, had one of the better seating areas. Our table and seats were wedged slightly behind one of the smooth stone circular pillars, creating a sort of nook where we could see everything.

'Which guy?' I asked distractedly. I was concentrating on watching the first Malteser of the pack disintegrate into my coffee, to which I'd already added five sugars. The Malteser bobbed along the surface, seemingly impervious to the heat, acting as if it could possibly survive the hot milky end that was fast approaching.

'First of all, that's disgusting,' Trina said, screwing up her beautiful face and pointing one of her glossy sea-blue nails at what I was doing to the chocolate and the coffee, 'and second of all, the guy with the jacket and the dimples.'

I knew who she meant. 'Oh, him.'

'You haven't even looked up.'

'Don't need to. Jacket and dimples – how you can see them from here I don't know – describes him perfectly. There's only one guy with a jacket of note who stares at me.'

'So you know he stares at you?' She was really puzzled now.

'Yes. He's in my Psychology class.'

'So you know him beyond the staring?'

'Yes, he's in my Psychology class.'

'And you know his name?'

'Yes, he's in my Psychology class. How many times do I need to say it?'

'And you know why he stares at you?'

I shrugged half-heartedly. I suspected I knew why, but to be honest, it wasn't something that happened to me on a regular basis. Or at all, really. Not unless the starer was a creepy older man who thought . . . well, actually, I tried to avoid wondering about creepy older men as much as I could.

'Have you spoken to him?' Trina asked.

'Don't make me say it, Trina,' I told my next-door-neighbour-in-halls.

'Oh shut up! You might be in the same class as him but never spoken to him. Like, have I spoken to half the freaks in my Maths classes? I think not.'

'Yes, I've spoken to him. We're working on a project together in class.'

'Oh . . .' she said knowingly. 'Ohhhhh . . . It's like *that*.'

'It's like what?' I asked, abandoning the disintegrating Malteser to its fate to look at her.

She flicked a few of her black-and-royal-blue plaits over her left shoulder, then smoothed her hand over them, twisting them together to sit over her right shoulder. 'You and him are making the beast with two backs.'

'What? No! NO. Absolutely not.'

'*Really?* Why not?'

'We're just not.'

'Well, with the way that man is staring, I guess you're RCing him.'

I side-eyed my friend. I had *NO* idea what she was on about. 'What is RCing?' Knowing Trina, we were about to go off on a tangent so sharp the original point would be completely forgotten.

'Oh please, like you don't know,' she scoffed.

'I totally do not know. You need to tell me what RCing is and tell me quick.'

'You're Romantic Comedying him. You know how it goes: you don't know he exists or you hate him and then you end up having to "work together" and you start to see a different side to him and decide to give him a chance. That chance turns into you falling for him. You have a few weeks or months of sickly, kissy-kissy bliss. And then something big happens which means he discovers that you didn't feel for him like he felt for you and you split up. You both mope around for a bit, then you have to make some huge, grand gesture to get him back.' To complete her soliloquy, she flicked her plaits back over her shoulder and then snatched up her coffee cup, took a gulp and realised too late she'd actually picked up my cup and now had a mouthful of sugary coffee and half-melted Malteser. Her gagging face was so funny it was almost worth having to buy a new coffee to start Malteser-melting again.

'I know what romantic comedies are, thank you,' I told her. Trina kept opening her mouth and sticking out her tongue, obviously trying to get rid of the taste. Trina and I had never discussed our mutual love for those movies and books, and I couldn't believe she was crowbarring the dude with the jacket into my tried-and-tested, loved-and-adored framework. It was a heinous act on her part as far as I was concerned. I pointed briefly in his direction. 'He is not and never will be the star of my rom-com life. All right?' I looked around the room. 'I can't see anyone in here who's going to be a part of it.' I returned to eyeing her distastefully again as she glugged water, trying to wash away the taste. Trina was being overdramatic – Malteser-flavoured coffee wasn't *that* bad. 'And if you keep going on about that guy, you're not going to be my sassy best friend.'

Trina stopped mid-gulp and slowly lowered her water as she spun on her seat to look at me. 'I am *no one's* sassy best friend. I am the main character. *Always.*'

'Well, I am too, so . . .'

'I've always wondered what happens when the two people who are traditional sidekick characters are friends? How do they negotiate the thorny subject of who gets to main character and who gets to sidekick?'

'The first one to get a long-term love interest, I guess.' I shrugged and rummaged in my pockets for change. I was careful with my coffee-and-Malteser money. I only brought out the exact amount of money so I wouldn't be tempted to spend too much. My grant and student loan had a long way to stretch but these two were my daytime luxury. Technically, Trina should be doing the coffee-buying, though. Like that was going to happen. She would simply tell me there was nothing wrong with the cup she had pretty much spat into. Like she wouldn't pour away a cup I had breathed too close to.

As I looked for any amount of money, my gaze scanned the room and snagged on the green gaze of the man who hadn't stopped staring at me. His expression didn't change when our gazes slotted together, stuck on each other like two vital pieces of a puzzle.

I didn't understand him.

When we were in class, when we worked together, he talked to me like he talked to everyone else. I didn't detect anything that might suggest he thought differently of me to anyone else. He was jokey and clever – always answering questions with the assurance of someone who did the extra reading and then some. Always ready with a joke or humorous observation that might have escaped most people. But when we were in other settings, when I wasn't directly interacting with him, he would stare at me. Only at me.

'Don't you start!' Trina said, nudging me and releasing me from the stare-hold that had taken over for a few moments.

'What do you mean?' I asked her.

'Don't start staring back at him. I literally just told you – I am no one's sidekick. You're not allowed to get with him or anyone else until I have someone.'

'I am not getting with him.'

'Yeah, pull the other one, it's got carnival bells on.'

I allowed myself another sneak look at him, and he wasn't staring at me. He was sitting back in his seat, a book in one hand, a hot drink in the other. It was almost as though, now he'd got my attention, as brief as it might have been, he could get on with his life. Now that he knew I knew he was there, he could go about his day.

And what about me? How was I meant to go back to normal knowing that any second now he could start staring at me again?

# 2

I'm juggling my bag, my laptop bag and a brown paper bag of my sleep medication, as well as my jacket, my hat and hand sanitiser, when I try to press the white rectangle of my pass with my name and a picture of my face against HoneyMay Productions' security panel.

It takes a couple of goes and I probably should just dump a couple of things on the floor to make it easier, but I don't. I'm the kind of stubborn that means I'll keep going, keep swinging my pass in the direction of the security panel until . . . until . . . until I can get the pass to dangle close enough and long enough to beep and flick from red to green.

As it beeps to let me in, I put my shoulder against the frosted glass door and push it open. I usually work from home, holed up in my office with my messy desk, draughty windows and very expensive ergonomic office chair that makes my coccyx hurt if I sit in it for more than twenty minutes. But for the past six months, I've been coming regularly to write at the offices of HoneyMay Productions, the production company who bought my books for TV adaptation seven years ago.

15

In the early days, when I was learning all about writing for TV, I also used to come here to meet with more experienced writers and script editors. I've been coming back recently because I can't be at home. I'm in the process of dismantling my life as I know it, and I have to focus. At home there is Wallace. And even when he's not there, he's there. In the pictures, in his scent on the bedding, in the way the furniture is arranged, the way the lights are placed. We moved into our house seven years ago, and every day has been spent making it ours. With all the stuff in front of me, the things I have to do, I have to focus on work and I can't do that if I'm getting sentimental and googly-eyed over belongings.

The office area they've found for me to work in is just off the main open-plan workspace. It's a smallish meeting room with a bank of four desks pushed together in the middle. Where I usually sit and plug in my laptop has the picture window to the right and the door to the left.

Most people ignore me as I bustle past with my belongings in my arms and my security pass dangling from my wrist. They didn't do a *Cheers*-style 'NORM!' greeting when I used to arrive, but some of them at least raised their heads and smiled at me. Now they all pretend they don't see me; they blanch and look away if they accidentally make eye contact and they absolutely do not want to say hello.

Everyone hates me at the moment. I'm learning to be OK with that.

I dump the tangle of my belongings on the desk beside the one I sit at and notice there's a laptop, a mobile charger and a reusable coffee cup on the desktop. Someone came in to work in here while I was out, obviously. I wonder if they'll stay or will come scuttling in, collect their belongings and leave.

'Oh,' Gail Brewster, one of the production assistants, says as she enters the room. 'Didn't realise you were back.' She stands just inside the doorway, looking on edge and unsure about whether to come in or just run for it.

'Yup,' I reply and dip my head as I start to sort out my belongings and set up my computer for work. I mean, yes, I've been telling myself that I'm fine with everyone hating me but, er, maybe I'm not as at ease with it as I thought.

'I'll just get out of your hair,' she says. She starts to gather up the items she's left on my desk.

'Cool,' I mumble.

'Are you OK?' Gail asks as I take a seat at 'my' desk.

'I'm fine,' I say.

'Are you sure? You seem . . .'

'I'm fine. Honestly, I'm fine.'

'If you're sure. How are the rewrites coming along?' Even though Gail smiles as she asks this, her concern has evaporated as quickly as droplets of water dripped into a hot pan. It seems like something a supportive colleague would ask another colleague, but we are behind and they need this script. They needed it yesterday but I haven't finished it. I'm finding it difficult to do that.

I'm finding it difficult to end this.

I mean, I have to. But it's not as easy as it should be.

Seven years ago, not long before I married Wallace, my agent, Antonia, sold my first novel, *The Baking Detective*, to HoneyMay Productions. It'd been a real dream-come-true moment. It took me a while to realise that things are rarely that simple. That despite all the heralding in the entertainment press and social media, 'optioned' meant pretty much nothing. Anyone could option anything if you had a few thou to hand. But this was different. This was one of the things that went beyond optioning and skated smoothly and deliciously into being

slated for development, to being greenlit for production. To being actually made.

And to actually appearing on a streaming network. Every step of
the way, I'd kind of stood on the outside myself a little, wondering
when it would all go wrong. Not only had it got on to the screens,
people liked it enough to keep tuning in. So much so, it was not only
commissioned for a second series, it stopped being shown in one
clump and was actually scheduled to run weekly. *The Baking Detective* was a hit because, apparently, everyone loved a woman who could
bake *and* solve crimes at the same time. Some of the crimes committed were hideously gruesome – but because Mira Woode solved the
mystery while finding time to bake at least one thing (the more the
better), people seemed to ignore the truly horrible nature of the murders. In fact, the more ghastly the murder, the more elaborate the cake
to balance the sensibilities, the more people seemed to love it.

Which led to where we are now.

Me in the middle of a divorce and dismantling my life as though I
were taking scaffolding down from the outside of a finished building.
And part of that dismantling meant leaving the show.

No one is happy.

No one wants this to end.

Once I'd handed the first *Baking Detective* novel over for adaptation, I had no power. They could do whatever they wanted, except the
two things I'd had written into the contract:

1.  The main character had to be played by a dark-skinned
    Black woman.
2.  Once I decided it was over, it was over, and HoneyMay
    Productions couldn't make any more.

What this meant in real terms was that when I decided the series was over, the character, the stories and pretty much the entire franchise stayed with me and they couldn't make any more. No one wanted to agree to that, of course. They offered me an eye-watering amount of money to get rid of that clause. When that didn't work, they went to the other end of the spectrum and threatened to walk away. But I wouldn't budge.

*'Fine!'* I could almost hear the HoneyMay team involved in this deal say. *'But we're lowering our offer and she'd better not think about trying to negotiate for more when she changes her mind further down the line.'*

I minded, of course, not getting as much money as I could potentially have got. But I cared more about having a woman who looked like me on the screen and being able to walk away cleanly.

So Gail's nice question was probably delivered through gritted teeth. She tosses her wavy blonde-brown hair, revealing the line of studs and mini-hoops that run from the top of her ear to her earlobe. All silver. All marking out her style. She is my age and a jeans, T-shirt-and-hoodie woman, but these earrings show that she has her own style, too. Since she started about six months ago, she's always been quite nice to me, but she, like everyone, is probably being nice to my face because we have to keep working together for now.

'The rewrites are going well,' I reply to Gail. 'I've nearly finished the latest draft for the penultimate episodes and then I'll get on with the final episode stuff.'

'Great, thank you.' She lets the mask slip for a moment and those three words come out forced, as though they've been squeezed out like toothpaste from an almost empty tube. Everyone gets like that when the final episodes are mentioned.

Ordinarily, I would care, it would eat me up that someone doesn't like me or is cross with me or is possibly upset with me, but right now, I don't mind.

I don't deserve friends, I don't even deserve people to be nice to me. I deserve . . . everything that's coming, I suppose. Every little thing.

'I'll leave you to it, then,' Gail says before she heads to the door with her stuff in her hands. 'Holler if you need anything.'

'I will.'

She shuts the white door behind her and I physically relax now I'm alone. Instead of allowing my fingers to move over the keyboard to get this work done, I drop them onto my lap. That doesn't feel enough somehow, I need to unravel some more. I lower my head to the table and rest my cheek on the desk, while my eyes stare outside. From this position, high up in a Brighton building, you get the most amazing views, the most incredible vistas.

What I wouldn't give to be one of the clouds that hangs over the city, part of the air that circulates, anything rather than being Cleo Forsum right now. Anything.

## Horsforth, 1996

'Cleo, I have a problem,' Heath stated.

Heath, the man who stared at me, and I were in a small space off the main area on the first floor of the library working on our project for the Philosophy of Science module of our Psychology degree. It was almost like an alcove, but with a door that could slide across to make it a cosy little room with a table and two chairs. We had the door open, but it still felt like we were cocooned here, cossetted and hugged by the smell of books and the reverential atmosphere of learning. Libraries had always been my happy place, somewhere to visit and disappear; to escape and just 'be'.

We'd been here a while and had been making steady progress, but suddenly he had made this statement – more of a quiet declaration, really – and I was sure it was not the sort of problem I wanted to deal with. I moistened my lips and said, 'If your problem is something along the lines of "How are we going to condense all of this essential information into a five-minute presentation?" then I share your pain. If it's anything else, then I don't think it's anything to do with me.'

Since Trina had initiated that 'Romantic Comedying' conversation, every interaction with Heath had become an issue. If I was friendly to him, I worried I was moving into the 'doe-eyed, soon-to-be-kissy-kissy' stage of the RC timeline. If I was blunt or short, I felt, rather acutely in every cell, that I was just extending the 'enemies-to-lovers' part of the story. If I tried to be nonchalant, it felt exactly that – I was trying too hard. Basically, Trina had rather expertly got into my head, messed around and ruined any chances of me and this guy being anything even resembling friends.

I mean, I heard the way those words just came out of my mouth and they weren't exactly pleasant. I liked to think of myself as a pleasant person, that I could get on with most people no matter how odious, but I was constantly on edge around him. If he could just stop staring at me, too, that would be helpful.

'I suppose it is kind of to do with the presentation and the philosophy of science,' Heath replied. 'And kind of not.'

I stared at the books and notebooks in front of us, the notes we'd both made, the highlighted sections and the sticky-note bookmarked sections. I wasn't sure if I should speak or if I should wait for him to elaborate.

'It's the kind of not that makes it related to the philosophy of science because it is and it isn't related to the philosophy of science, which invokes the quantum philosophy of things existing and not existing at the same time, which is hard to prove exists. A bit like trying to prove the mind exists as a separate construct to the physical brain.'

I squeezed shut my eyes. Frustration. Despair. Complete frustration. Trina had got right down into my head, hadn't she? Right deep down, past all the rational layers, past the places that control our actions, into the irrational areas, the places where little thoughts take hold and start to grow. Start to grow in stupid, stupid ways.

Usually, being in a library space, with the books and the atmosphere they created, acted like a shield to protect me from the excesses of being around other people. They absorbed the nonsense and made me not mind as much if they went off on random tangents that were nothing to do with me. But not this fella, it seemed. He was immune to the sponge-like powers of books.

'What are you talking about?' I asked, my eyes still closed, straining to not scream at him.

'I think . . . no, no . . . I *know* I have fallen in love with you.'

My eyes popped open in surprise, then slowly swivelled in his direction to look at him, before coming back to centre to stare at the notes and learning detritus in front of us. The theories of science applied to and about the study of the mind – finding out if the way we studied the physical world could be harnessed and deployed to study what goes on in the metaphysical space attached to the brain. That's what we were doing here, that's what I'd sat down to do.

'I'm going to be honest with you here, Heath. I'm not sure what I'm supposed to say to that so I'm going to pretend you didn't say anything.'

'And therein lies my problem. Problems. Because my problems are twofold. One, I am as certain as I can be that you are not even remotely interested in me. Two, I'm not sure I want to feel this way. I've always been led to believe that love is pleasurable, something that people pursue. This . . . this is not pleasurable. This . . . is not something I wish to experience. Quite the contrary. This . . . *these* emotions are very much unwanted.'

'Do you always speak like a robot?' I asked, conversationally. If Trina heard him speak, she'd know why – despite her mind-messing – nothing could happen with this guy.

'No. I have it on good authority that I speak more like a Vulcan.'

That made me laugh despite myself. 'OK, kudos for the *Star Trek* reference, but I have to ask – with the way you talk and all – did you get hassled in school?'

He conjured up a ghost of a smile, amused by the question, it seemed. 'No, no, I didn't actually.' He shook his head briefly. 'I had the living shit kicked out of me pretty much every day, but I was not really "hassled".'

I turned in my seat to stare at him in surprise and horror.

He stared back at me with an open face. 'I take it from your reaction you were not expecting that answer,' he said quietly, looking suddenly dubious about the way he had told me that he had been assaulted almost daily.

I shook my head. I was not expecting that answer at all.

'Oh. Maybe I should have sugar-coated it? I just assumed . . . you're a very straightforward person so I assumed you would prefer me to be direct about such matters.'

A wave of sadness almost submerged me as it crashed over and through me. There was such quiet acceptance in his voice, like it was something normal. He was weird and he knew it. And he'd suffered for it. I was weird, I knew it, but I had escaped that sort of suffering. 'I'm sorry you went through that,' I whispered, even though those words seemed insubstantial when weighed up against what they were trying to make up for.

'Thank you, I appreciate you saying that,' he replied.

We sat in an awkward silence, where I stared at the work in front of us, not really reading the open pages, not picking up our pens to make notes, not adding anything to the prompt cards, just staring at our work, wondering how we moved on from here.

Apparently, we moved on by him saying: 'About my problem?'

Yes. About his problem. What was I going to do about his problem that was clearly becoming partly my problem now that he'd gone beyond staring and had opened up? 'You know, Heath, when I was in fifth form, there was this guy who was really goofy, a bit weird. Not anything too weird, just a bit odd, like anyone really. But he still got hassled a lot and sometimes beaten up. And honestly, it was so sad, because he seemed nice enough. I suppose he stood out because he didn't seem to hide his weirdness, or even try to hide it, or even think he might need to hide it.'

'How does that relate to my problem?' Heath asked.

'I'm coming to that. Don't be so impatient. This guy from fifth form wanted to be my friend—'

'Just your friend?'

'Will you stop interrupting?! I'll never get to the end of this if you keep interrupting. Yes, just my friend. Well, at first. Cos I'm a bit gullible? No, that's not the right word. I'm a bit clueless, I suppose. All my friends were going – are you really going to hang out with him? – and I went, "why not, seems harmless enough". When I say "hang out" I literally mean we used to talk at the bus stop. He was the only one who lived on the same bus route as me so we'd talk as we walked to the bus stop, talk while we waited for the bus and then not even sit next to each other on the bus. Then out of the blue, he asked me if I would go to the cinema with him one weekend. And there I was, stuck.'

'Because you didn't like him?'

I glowered at Heath until he mumbled, 'Sorry.'

'And there I was, stuck, because I did not like him. And also, even if I *did* like him, how am I explaining going out with a boy to my African parents? Yes, I could have gone down the whole sneaking-around thing, but for me, that's all far too much hassle. So I did the next best thing.'

Heath stared at me.

I stared at him.

He stared at me.

I stared at him.

'Oh for pity's sake,' I snapped, when the staring was stretching into a minute, 'you decide to pick now to stop interrupting?'

'What was the next best thing?' he dutifully asked.

'I found him another girlfriend. Well, I found him an actual girlfriend because I wasn't in any way his girlfriend.'

'So you're saying you're going to find me a girlfriend instead of you?'

'Well, I am not your girlfriend, but I think if you met someone who was attracted to you . . .'

'I wouldn't want you?'

'If you want to put it like that.'

'But you seem like a nice, accepting person, and you still think I'm weird, therefore I am as certain as I can be that most people think I'm weird. How, pray tell, are you going to find me a companion who would even consider becoming my girlfriend?'

'Ah, you're not weird.' I obviously couldn't look at him when I said that. 'Not *that* weird, anyway.'

'How exactly are you going to make me not weird enough to find someone who might be interested in me?'

'Makeover, of course!' I said gleefully.

He physically drew back, horrified by the idea. 'I'm not sure that's the course of action either of us should be considering right now.'

'Nothing drastic, just a haircut, some grooming, some clothing rehoming.'

'What is wrong with my clothing?'

'Everything. That jacket . . .' I shook my head, not bothering to mask my disgust. 'That jacket . . . Heath, it's 1996, no one outside of Nashville wears a suede jacket – with tassels. I hate to break it to you in such a blunt way, but come on, mate, even the citizens of Vulcan must know it's time to retire the jacket.'

Heath stared at me and I thought for a moment he was going to say something else, to protest, but instead he sighed. 'You think it's best that I completely transform myself to make myself acceptable to the opposite sex? Haven't people advocated since time began for one to be oneself?'

'Yes. And I am completely on board with that message, it is why I myself wear a skull buckle belt with purple jeans so ripped my mother would have a nervous breakdown if she saw them, but I don't think this is the real you. I think the real you has yet to find expression, so me sprucing you up is going to do wonders for your confidence.' I clapped my hands together in delight. 'I can't wait to upgrade you – this is like *Pretty Woman* . . . without the prostitution element, of course.'

'Do you honestly believe you can make me irresistible to women?'

'Erm . . . I didn't actually say that. And let's not get ahead of ourselves. We're just going to make you a bit more eligible, looks-wise. Which will help people get to know the real you.'

Unusually, he didn't say anything. Maybe I upset him with the idea that he had to change. Maybe he liked his jacket that looked all sad and bedraggled, maybe it was bequeathed to him by a favourite uncle or aunt and he'd been saving up to get some cowboy boots and a hat to match. Maybe I had mortally wounded poor Heath Sawyer and this was where everything went wrong and instead of just staring at me, he started to actively hate me. 'Erm,' I began, leaping in to do some serious damage limitation, 'you know, you don't have to do any of this, right? You can carry on as you are because you're perfectly fine as you are. You don't have to do anything.'

'I know I don't, but I want to. I want to do everything I can to be worthy.'

'Worthy? No, no. This honestly isn't about changing who you are so you live up to some impossible standard. It's literally just sprucing you up, making the best of what the Lord gave you.'

'I want to be worthy of you.'

'Again, you are worthy. But you and me is not up for grabs.'

'It's not up for consideration at all?'

'I knew you weren't listening when I was talking earlier. If you want a girlfriend, you're going to have to learn to listen.'

'I was listening. I am simply confirming that you helping me make these changes won't facilitate the establishment of a relationship or liaison with you.'

27

'You are correct, it will not facilitate any such contact between us. The mission is to find you someone suitable. Someone more right for you.'

'More right for me . . . more right for me,' he said, as though musing over the points. 'I suppose, in the absence of anything else, that will have to do.'

# 3

Gail sticks her head around the door when the world outside is darkening and people are thinking of heading home. I've made good progress but I've still got so much left to do. So much. It's one of those 'so much to do' situations where I want to throw my computer out the window, climb into bed and cry while drowning Maltesers in sugary coffee.

'We're all heading off now. Are you coming?' she says, back in nice mode.

Behind her in the open-plan space outside the room where I work, Clarissa, the runner, and Amy, the junior script editor, are both lurking with their coats and bags on. I suspect they're not paid enough to properly hate me, they just have to work in a negative environment created by my decision to end a successful show.

'I might just stay—'

'OK, when I asked if you were coming, I meant, come on, let's all get out of here. It's not good to stay here when everyone else has gone. It is über creepy in here.'

'Yeah, come on, get your coat, you've pulled,' Amy adds in a broad South London accent.

29

'How can I resist?' I reply and set my work to back-up on my computer while I clean up my workspace. I'm messy – in so many iterations of that word – so I make sure to put my inhaler into my rucksack along with the hand sanitiser. I push my black hat onto my head and slip on my black jacket. When the laptop says it has safely backed up everything I've done this afternoon, I zip it up into its black carrying bag before I start shoving everything else – notebooks, pens, Post-its, mints, notecards, sleep medication, security pass, highlighters, keys and my earrings – into my main bag. At one point, I take so long that first Gail then Amy come to assist me. They help me gather up my belongings like I'm incapable of doing anything for myself.

As we let ourselves out of the building, they make small talk about going to the pub over the next weekend, and in their own ways they all try to include me in that chat – suggesting places they might go to and asking if I like them, asking if I could be tempted to get a train to London one evening since Gail and Amy live up there and commute down to Brighton. Clarissa makes a case for going to a restaurant so we can eat while we drink and says us Brighton-based folk will be able to find something nice but easy on the pocket, too. All of us know I won't be joining them, that I'm not one of them on any level, but I'm grateful that they're trying. It takes the sharp edges off the bleakness of ending my marriage and leaving my job and knowing I'm going to have to move away soon as well.

We part ways after climbing the long, steep stone steps behind Brighton station and walking through past the new taxi rank (that isn't so new but will always be new in my mind), along the walkway parallel to the platforms and onto the concourse. Gail and Amy go to get trains to their different parts of London and Clarissa heads down towards the seafront. I stand at the grand entrance to Brighton station feeling enchanted by the beauty of another day drawing to a close, another day becoming so rich and dark and studded with the jewel-like lights of shops, cars and street lights. I also stand there, people bumping into me as they hurry on with their lives, knowing that I don't actually *deserve* to have anyone be nice to me, but appreciating it all the same.

## Leeds City Centre, 1996

Heath and I met outside the bus station in Leeds city centre on an October Saturday afternoon.

Thankfully, he'd had to go into town a little earlier, otherwise we might have had to get the bus down together, which would have been thirty minutes of awkwardness I could do without.

'Where do you want to go?' he asked. He waved his arm around, trying to take in the expanse of Leeds. 'There's a whole city full of clothes that will transform me into a suitable, dare I say, eligible, life form.'

*Eligible life form.* I gave him a very hard stare from the sides of my eyes and frowned, thinking, *Where does he get this stuff from? Who is this person?* He didn't notice – he was apparently oblivious to my response to the things he said. 'Let's go to the markets,' I told him. 'We can get some decent stuff for a good price.'

'That sounds just the ticket.' I chose to let that one go unside-eyed.

I hadn't lived in Leeds for long, but I'd got to know the streets by walking and walking. When Trina, the only person I would call a proper friend at this stage, was off taking part in her extra-curricular activities, I would get the bus into town and walk. I would go up and down roads and side roads, taking in shops and emporiums, second-hand treasure troves and out-of-the-way restaurants. I would see where the cafés were, the takeaways, the electronic shops. I would note the areas that were a bit too shady for me to go any closer to. I'd also found the quickest bus route out of the city centre to Chapeltown where I could buy my Black magazines and newspapers and hair products. I immersed myself in the city by walking its streets and unearthing the secrets you usually found by living somewhere for a long time.

Heath followed me as I led us on a short walk to the markets. We wandered past the rotund Corn Exchange, across the double road, and joined the groups of people moving like shoals of fish towards the big glass entrance above which was emblazoned: LEEDS CITY MARKETS.

As soon as we stepped through the doors, I felt the atmosphere change, almost like the moment you step outside an airport in a differ-ent country – the air changes, the pressure changes, your body experiences this new place in so many visceral ways. I felt like I had stepped into a microcosm, a planet that was contained in this historic building. The glass roof was striped with intricate ironwork, the walls above the stalls were moulded with white masonry and beautiful black iron cornicing, creating the effect of a palace dropped right in the centre of a busy city.

Heath and I navigated our way through the slightly-too-close-together stalls, all overflowing with their wares. The people talking, mingling happily, the bright colours of piled-high fruit, veg, sweets, fabrics, the smells of the food, fish, meat, perfumes – all created a comforting, buzzy backdrop.

'I'm thinking the Zack-from-*Saved-by-the-Bell* look for you,' I told Heath above the sound of the market. 'You've got the blond hair and innocent looks already, we just need to add jeans, a white T-shirt and a lumberjack shirt. A couple of other shirts. Nice jacket – either black leather or one of the jackets with white arms and a letter on the front.'

'I have no idea who Zack from saved by the whatever you said is.'

I stopped walking and pulled him to a halt, too. 'You what? You haven't heard of *Saved by the Bell*?'

'I am extremely sad to say I have not.'

Having stopped so suddenly, I became an obstruction in the lane we were walking in and the person behind me, clearly having no time to ask me to move, simply shoved me aside, forcing me up against Heath's body. His hands instinctively reached out to steady me and we stood for a second or two, him holding me, me mortified. Extremely embarrassed, I stepped away and started walking again at speed, trying to put that moment as far behind me as I could. 'I can't believe you haven't heard of *Saved by the Bell*.' I started talking again – loudly, to try to drown out the embarrassment that was still raging in my head – without checking he was walking with me. 'Wow, have you been living under rock or something? How can you not know *Saved by the Bell*. Heathen.'

'No, it's Heath,' he said.

'What?' I said and turned to him.

'You called me Heathen. My name is Heath. I have no "e" or "n" on the end.'

'I meant—'

He grinned at me, the action a little breathtaking because I'd never seen him smile like that before. His eyes danced, his dimples deepened and he seemed to be staring right into my soul.

'Can't believe I fell for that,' I said and carried on walking.

'I can't believe you fell for it, either,' he laughed, keeping pace. 'I am sorry I disappoint you so about this programme.'

We arrived at the first circular clothes stall, run by a man with bushy brown eyebrows whose neck seemed to blend into his head and shoulders without any clear demarcation. Men's clothes – band T-shirts, white T-shirts, normal button shirts, denim jackets, leather jackets and all types of jeans – hung from hangers the full 360 of the stall.

'I take it this is where the transformation is to take place?' Heath said.

'The start of it,' I replied. 'Now, do you like any of those T-shirts?'

'Not a Motorhead or heavy metal fan,' he stated.

'As I suspected, you're going to be a good Zack.'

'From *The Bell Saved Me?*'

'*Saved by the Bell*, but near enough, I suppose.' We chose white T-shirts, a couple of lumberjack shirts in blue and green – red would have been too much this soon. A couple of pairs of jeans – black and blue – and the all-important jacket. I wanted to go for a grey jacket with cream arms and a large letter Y, but I could see Heath was trying – and failing – to control his revulsion at the idea, so I went for a black leather blazer instead. He looked cool when he slipped it on over his usual clothes. Cooler than I actually thought possible. I'd nodded my approval at him. He held out his arms and spun in a slow circle so I could get a full look at him. 'You like?' he said when we were facing each other.

'I like. The jacket,' I added quickly. 'I like the jacket.'

Heath gave me a wry smile as he broke eye contact and took the jacket off. We'd been having too much fun, I realised. Too much fun and we'd both inadvertently forgotten what this was all about – finding him a girlfriend who wasn't me.

*Stop this*, I told myself sternly. *Don't start thinking that Trina might have a point about you and him. Because honestly, it's not as if you're capable of feeling anything for anyone, is it? It's not as if you have any idea what love or anything close to love is all about, is it?*

We'd been to almost every clothes stall in the market, collecting bags of clothes for him – obviously I stayed well away when he found a stall for his socks and underwear – and now we were laden with a whole new wardrobe.

'The trick to keeping these clothes in good condition is to wash them carefully,' I said to Heath as we headed for the exit, nearly a dozen bulging bags between us. I'd started being a bit cooler, a bit more removed, because I did not want either of us to forget what we were doing and why we were doing this. 'They last longer if you wash them at the right temperature, reshape them while wet, hang them out to dry.'

'I did not realise I would be receiving life lessons as well as purchasing a new wardrobe collection,' he said.

His accent and phraseology was off the scale today. The weird thing was, it wasn't his natural way of speaking. I had heard him speak in class, in the canteen, in the common room, sometimes even when he was talking to me – and he wasn't verbose and almost painfully 'proper'. I was going to have to bring it up with him sometime.

'Life lessons are always included,' I said as we reached the pavement outside.

'What about washing lessons? Are they included? Would you come over to my halls and show me what to do?'

'Do it *for* you, you mean? I think not,' I replied.

'Worth a try,' he chuckled.

When we arrived at the bus stop, I handed over his bags. 'I'm meeting Trina and a few other friends to go to the pictures, so I guess I'll see you around?'

'You are definitely not going to accompany me to the barbers to get a cut?' he asked hopefully.

'I do not need to experience that. Just get it cut short all over and

35

leave the front long, so you get the full Zack effect. I can't remember his surname. Urgh, I was only watching it last year and all that revision has knocked out these vital pieces of information. This is a travesty, you know? That exam prep has replaced important stuff. I mean, what if I end up on *Mastermind* and "what is Zack from *Saved by the Bell*'s surname" is the deciding question? Can you imagine the pain?'

'I understand your concern about a very-likely-to-occur situation. That is why I suggest you quit college, reacquaint yourself with *Save My Bell* and all would be well in the world.'

'Oh you'd like that, wouldn't you?' I shot back at him. I gave him a beady-eyed look. 'You've clearly got issues with me being top in our Psychology department, so you'd prefer it if I left to concentrate on the important things, wouldn't you?'

He laughed, his eyes crinkling and his face creasing. 'Yes, you caught me out. I am, indeed, trying to get to first place in class.'

'Good on you, admitting that,' I laughed. 'Anyway, look, down on the Headrow there are a couple of barbers, think there's a hairdresser, too. Someone will sort you out.'

'Thank you,' he said with meaning, sounding genuinely touched. 'I really appreciate it.'

'I'll see you around,' I told him and began to walk away. I stopped, turned back. 'And by the way, it's called *Saved by the Bell*, not *Save My Bell*.'

'I'll remember that,' he called after me. And I knew, even without looking around this time, that he stood and watched me walk away until I was out of sight.

# 4

Keys returned to pocket. That's the first thing I do when I shut the front door behind me. Laptop on wooden box seat, hat in hat box, mask in small wicker wash basket, coat on hook, shoes in shoe cubbies. I'm not sure when my life became about boxes, but that's what coming home is like.

'Hello?' I call as I go through the routine. 'Hello?'

At the turn at the end of our long, tiled hallway, a head appears. I have to pause to assess that face: close-shaved head, dark brown skin, big black eyes, long eyelashes, full, kissable mouth . . . And at first glance, I still can't be sure. I mean, could be my husband, could be his twin. From here, without my glasses, I can't see the chicken pox scar close to the hairline on the left-hand side of his forehead, which is usually the clue as to whether I'm speaking to Wallace or his twin brother.

'Hello,' he says without emotion. Wallace.

I know it's taken him a huge amount of effort to strip any kind of feeling from showing in his voice. He is – and has been since I've known him – an emotional person. But since his wife decided to

37

divorce him, he's tried to be less expressive until, I assume, he understands what is going on.

'Hello,' I reply. 'How are you?'

His face twitches for a second like he wants to scream at me: *How the hell do you think I am?* 'I've just finished making dinner, if you want some?' he replies, avoiding my question.

I do not want dinner. Everything I eat nowadays, when I do actually eat, tastes like nothing. My tastebuds have been blunted and there is a solid and immoveable rock that sits at the back of my throat. I have to swallow hard several times to get saliva or water past it and every bite of food feels like I am pushing a bowling ball down a plughole. I love my food, as well. I love to eat and I love to drink, and I especially love Wallace's food. He pours so much love into every dish – he uses the best ingredients, he takes his time and the results are always out of this world. Before Wallace, when people talked about the languages of love, I would wonder if they had nothing better to do with themselves. But then I met a man who could cook, who would seem to tell me how he felt by making elaborate meals and I, too, became someone with nothing better to do with myself.

'Since when do you call it dinner?' I tease. 'I thought it was breakfast, dinner and tea?'

'Well, you've obviously got in my brain. I meant tea, of course.'

'Nah, I'm not having that! You've finally realised that it's breakfast, lunch and dinner.'

'Really? So those women at school who served you your daytime meal, what did you call them?'

'Well, di—'

'Sorry, what was that?' Wallace says with raised eyebrows and a big grin spread right across his face.

I clear my throat, uncomfortably.

Waiting for me to reply, Wallace moves into the part of the corridor where I can still see him but he stays a good distance away.

'You know what, I haven't washed my hands yet.'

'Come now, don't be difficult, Cleo, what did you call the women at school who served your daytime meal?'

I roll my eyes and try not to smile, no, grin at him. 'I don't remember.'

'Shall I prompt your memory?' he says, coming a little closer. 'Seeing as you've forgotten.'

'If you must,' I reply. I can't look at him. Sometimes he's like the sun, too luminous, and ultimately dangerous if I stare too long – mainly because I will want to fall into him and never leave. I will fall into him and forget what all of this is about.

'Dinner ladies,' he says with a small, triumphant smile.

'All right,' I concede. 'They were called dinner ladies.'

'So what does that mean about the meal they were serving?'

'That it's called lunch and they were confused about what time they should be doing their jobs?'

He grins again and I feel my knees go funny as my stomach flips. I'm pretty sure a woman of my age and experience shouldn't have those sorts of things happen to her. She should be stoic and unflinching in the face of the smiles of the man she's divorcing.

'Is that sore loserism, Miss Cleo?'

'No,' I say brusquely, trying to get control of this. Remind us both that we're not those people any more. 'No, that is a woman who needs to wash her hands, change her clothes.'

The smile stays in place as I march down the corridor on shaky legs, skirt around him and go to the toilet under the stairs. I shut and lock the door behind me, take my time to wet my hands, lather them with soap and then rinse them clean before drying them on the towel hanging through the metal ring. I remember when we put that towel holder up, how it'd been such a big deal, us having this big house all to ourselves, us doing DIY. Me letting him use my drill to make holes in the wall to hang the chrome circle.

It all seems so . . . trivial now. Pointless. I've done that. I've made our life together pointless. I can't look in the mirror while I wash my hands. I can't look in any reflective surface for too long because I will see who I am.

And I do not want to see the truth reflected back at me.

Wallace is outside the bathroom, leaning against the wall, arms folded across his chest. There are so many things I want to say to him, so many words that I know would explain everything and take away the distress that defines our relationship. But I can't say any of them. I can't remove or alleviate any of this agony. Not now. Not yet.

I open my mouth to say something, knowing the right words will find their place in my throat, on my tongue and then out of my mouth. Maybe a return to our messing around earlier, maybe to ask what's for dinner, maybe to find out how his day has gone because he didn't answer me earlier. Nothing. Nothing comes out, even though my mouth is there agape, ready and willing to say something my brain has not provided. I close my mouth, feeling more than a little foolish. Wallace seems to understand that there is something I want to say but can't and he decides to close the gap between us. And then he is standing right in front of me, too close for me to do anything but stare at him, feel his body heat, inhale his scent and long for him. Suddenly he scoops me up and kisses me with all the drama that is usually missing from our everyday lives.

We're normal, see? We're people who give each other the odd peck, who cuddle and hug, drop the odd kiss onto each other's heads or the soft space on the back of the other's neck, but not the big snogs. Not the grandiose pashes. Sometimes not even as a prelude to sex. Normal is as normal kisses. Until . . . his grip on me becomes firm, holding me tight in case I slip away. In case I realise this is the last thing we should be doing. That in actual fact, we're doing divorce all wrong. We haven't argued yet, not about the divorce, we haven't started tearing strips off each other, we haven't even started on the snide looks, passive-aggressive sighs and irritated tuts.

I don't hesitate in kissing him back. I don't even think to. He presses his body against mine and I do the same. I feel his fingers on the bottom of my top and the tugging sensation of him pulling it from the waistband of my jeans. I kiss him more urgently. His fingers go to my jeans, freeing the button from its buttonhole. I reach for his trousers, opening his button and unzipping him, running my hand up and down the thick shaft of his erection. And then his fingers are inside my knickers and I sigh as they brush over my pubic hair. I moan softly, feel my body convulse a little as two of his fingers slip inside me. The kissing is more intense and I want nothing more than to undress him right now, have him undress me and for us to—

A key is inserted in the front door and it swings open almost immediately. 'Yo, who's in?' Franklyn calls from the doormat where he's going through the process that I went through earlier. Only he's quicker, *much quicker*. 'Smells good in here, so I'm guessing Wals is back,' he continues at the same volume as he progresses down the corridor. Franklyn is not quiet at the best of times. 'No disrespect, though, Cleo, cos your food is top notch. Could eat your yam and chofi till kingdom come, not forgetting fufu and soup, but when it comes to—'

41

Franklyn stops talking when he turns the corner and finds us standing close together outside the kitchen door looking extremely guilty. I'd only managed to do up my trousers, not properly pull down my top, Wallace only managed to pull up the zip from where I'd opened his trousers and hadn't got the button done up again.

Franklyn looks from his twin to me, then back again at his twin, but his final gaze – glare – lands on me. Because he knows that the divorce is all on me. He wants to know what the hell I'm doing to his brother; he wants to know what the hell his brother is doing even giving me the time of day. (I know that's what he thinks because I've heard him tell Wallace exactly this – more than once – in his not-very-quiet tones.)

'You two are messy,' he says with disgust coating every word, every syllable. 'Proper, proper messy.' He kisses his teeth so hard I'm surprised his mouth doesn't cave in on itself. He shakes his head to underline his feelings, then opens the door beside the kitchen to the back of the house. 'I'm washing my hands down the back,' he throws over his shoulder as the door shuts behind him, but it sounds very much like, 'I can't stand to look at either of you right now.'

I drop my face into my hands; part of me wants to cry with the humiliation and the look that Franklyn just fired at me, but most of me wants to laugh. I want to double over and laugh, because being caught having sex, or almost having sex, with your ex by his brother will never not be funny to me. But it's not funny. I shouldn't be doing this, I shouldn't be giving him hope. Less importantly, I shouldn't be giving myself that same hope.

'I'm going for a shower,' I say without raising my face from my hands.

'Can I join you?' Wallace jokes. I don't need to look at my husband to know he has the cheeky smile on his face that made me fall for him, and possibly one eyebrow raised at the thought of what we could do in or out of the shower.

'And further traumatise your brother and make him hate me even more than he already does?'

I feel the grin disappear, and an emotional and physical distance land with a thud between us. 'I'm sorry, Wallace, I shouldn't have done that. We need to keep our distance. Not do that again.'

He shrugs. 'If that's what you want,' he states and I turn to the stairs. He opens the door to the understairs toilet, I presume to wash his hands, but pauses. 'Franklyn doesn't hate you,' he says as I climb the stairs. 'He could never hate you . . . Just like I could never hate you.'

*You both would. If you knew the truth, you would both hate me with a fury that would never, ever end.*

## Horsforth, 1997

'I'm thinking of trying it on with your Romantic Comedy mate,' Trina said to me. We were back in our usual place in the common room, slightly shielded. I had stopped torturing Maltesers in coffee and had moved on to Minstrels. They took longer to disintegrate and left a thick, syrupy sludge on top of the sugar at the bottom of the cup that took an age to edge onto my tongue.

I wasn't looking at Trina, but I guessed she was looking over at Heath, who was sitting where he used to sit when he stared at me, but he was not alone now. He was very rarely alone these days and he very, very rarely stared at me.

'Go for it,' I told her without looking over at him. 'Although you're going to have to get in line. I mean, the guy is never without female company nowadays. Homeboy is on everyone's list at the moment.'

'And you don't mind?'

That did make me refocus my attention on her. Every part of her was saying she suspected I minded. In fact, she looked like she thought I minded very, very much.

'Why would I mind? This was the plan and the best possible outcome.'

'The plan, huh?'

'Yes, the plan. I told you that I was going to spruce him up. Turn him from Nashville reject to Zack from *Saved by the Bell*. And there we have it. He gets lots of female company and I get to sit here without him staring at me. Win. Win. Win.'

'And you're not even a little bit jealous? Not even a little bit?' Trina pressed as she wound one of the red locks from her newly installed curly extensions around her fingers. She'd taken to wearing lots of gold rings on her fingers and painting her nails to match the colour highlight of her hair. Trina was so beautiful and stylish I often felt like I didn't make enough of an effort. Well, to be fair, I didn't make much of an effort, but Trina's immaculate looks meant I *noticed* that I didn't make much of an effort and I wondered if I should. My signature baggy jeans (sometimes so ripped I had to wear leggings underneath), comic-book-character T-shirt and longline black cardigan with plain black extensions pulled back into a ponytail were so laid-back next to my best friend's looks. I usually comforted myself with the fact that we were all different and some of us needed to fade into the background to allow others to shine. 'Not even an ickle bit jealous?'

I did look at Heath then, my attention sweeping over him like it would a stranger I'd been asked to assess. He was certainly good-looking now you could see his face and his clothes didn't make you baulk.

44

'No jealousy,' I confirmed to Trina. 'Not even the slightest bit of it.'

'Don't believe you,' she said, affecting a Trinidadian accent for a moment to emphasise how much I was deluding myself. Having known her for six months now, I knew she only deployed this accent when she wanted me to know she was serious.

'Fine, don't believe me. I have no interest in Heath. Our project was done a million years ago, and he's stopped staring at me . . . mostly. It's all good.'

'He is kinda cute, though,' Trina said. She was obviously trying a different tactic.

'Trina, my love, my best friend, the path is open. I can introduce you, if you like? I will not mind at all.'

'Nah, I'm good. I've got other *tings* distracting me.'

'Oh yeah? Who?'

'That, I cannot tell you right now. But all I can say is that my RC is in full swing.'

Outraged, horrified and completely shocked, I revolved in my seat until I was facing her properly. 'You cow!' I hissed. 'You absolute cow! You've made me the sassy best friend. The Sassy *Black* Best Friend. It's not right. And it's not fair.'

She shrugged her shoulders at me, before tipping her head in Heath's direction. 'You could climb out of Sassy Black Best Friend hell really easily. I'm sure if you gave homeboy even the tiniest indication that you're interested, he would be here like that!' She made a circle with one hand and then was about to do something crude with the other hand, so I snatched my gaze away from her.

'No need for any of that,' I said.

She laughed out loud at my horror. 'How come you don't like him?' she asked when she'd calmed down.

45

I risked looking in her direction and thankfully she'd stopped what she'd been going to do with her hands. 'Dunno, just don't.'

'Do you like guys?' she asked.

'Yes.'

'Do you only like guys?'

'Yes.'

'Do you like white guys?'

'I think so,' I replied.

'You think so?'

'Yes. I think so.'

'So you've only been out with Black men?'

'No.'

'You've been out with Black men and white men?'

'No.'

'You've only been out with Asian men? Pacific South Islander men? Middle Eastern men?'

'No. No. And no.'

'Come on, girl, give me a clue here . . .' Her voice petered away as it finally dawned on her. 'Have you been out with *any* men?'

I paused before I admitted: 'No. I have not.'

'Oh, *ohhhhhh*. So you're still a—?'

'Yes, yes I am.'

'I thought we were close – why am I only hearing about this now?'

'Not something I ever talk about. Like ever.'

'Fair enough, but hey, how come when that idiot the other day said you looked like you'd been around a bit you didn't say anything? I mean, I was going to tump him down but you stopped me. Why didn't you say anything?'

'What was I supposed to say? Oh, actually, random-man-who-means-nothing, I'm a virgin. In fact, I've never even kissed anyone. Oh, and, random-man-who-means-nothing, I'm starting to think there's something wrong with me because I don't feel anything for anyone? Is that what I should have said?'

'Well, when you put it like that . . . so you really don't like that guy at all?'

'Who, Heath? No. I don't.'

'Is there anyone you like?'

I shook my head. 'I mean, guys off the telly and movies and stuff. But the ones in real life? No. I can't seem to jump over that line. I can't feel stuff. I don't know if that makes sense to you?' It didn't make sense to me. Not really. When I was helping Heath with changing his image, I had enjoyed myself. We'd had fun together, and if I was in one of the movies or books I devoured, our eyes should have met, I should have felt a tingle deep inside, stars exploding, feelings amassing. And none of that had happened. None of it. *Maybe I'm broken*, I thought for the umpteenth time. *Maybe I am broken. Maybe there is something wrong with me.*

'We need to get you laid,' Trina stated. She said this with the authority of someone who knew what was what.

'Maybe.'

'No maybe about it, babe. We need to find you a man and burst that cherry and then you'll see that there's nothing wrong with you.'

'Hmm, maybe. But I don't think I can jump into bed with just anyone, though.'

'You won't have to,' she reassured me. 'We'll find you someone. Someone nice.'

I watched my best friend; she was holding her head in a rigid position where she could only look at me, which told me quite clearly she wanted to look over at Heath.

'Not him,' I told her. 'Someone else. Anyone else. Not him.'

She seemed to deflate at that, resigning herself to possibly having to work a little harder at finding me a man who I might want to kiss. 'OK. Not him,' she grumbled.

*Definitely not him.*

# 5

The three of us eat dinner sitting at the round wooden table in the kitchen, acting as though what happened before didn't happen. We are good at that, I've noticed – good at pretending nothing untoward has occurred.

'Down the back', where Franklyn disappeared off to earlier, is on the other side of the kitchen wall that runs the length of our house and is actually where Franklyn now lives. His 'living room' runs the length of our large open-plan kitchen, and at the other end there is a small extension that cuts into the garden. The living-room area we have kitted out with a sofabed, TV, book cases and music system. He also has a desk and chair he keeps in the bay window as well as a large beanbag I know he likes to read on. At the back of the living area, in the extension, is a small kitchenette – a four-ring burner, small oven, sink as well as a washing machine and dryer – which had been our 'laundry'. And at the back of that, also in the extension, is the small, functional but very nice shower room, sink and toilet. To the side of the 'laundry' are steep carpeted stairs that lead up to what had been Wallace's office and now has a double bed that Franklyn uses as his bedroom.

49

Franklyn's wife, Valerie, threw him out nine months ago. He keeps changing the reason why, 'just stress, man, stress' or 'she's never happy' or 'the woman's not right', though I suspect he's told Wallace the real reason. No one can accuse Franklyn of not being a good-hearted person and I actually adore Valerie. But she won't speak to either Wallace or me now because we took Franklyn in. I'm not sure what she expected us to do, especially since she won't tell us what actually happened, but she does always send me texts to check how their thirteen-year-old, Lola, is when she comes to stay, and to thank me for taking care of her.

Wallace has prepared a feast. Not sure why on a Monday night, but we're being treated to vegan jerk 'chicken', rice'n'peas, callaloo, cara-melised plantain and mango salad.

'Lola is coming to stay this weekend,' Franklyn says when he is right in the middle of a story about something completely different.

'It'll be nice to see her,' I say.

'Yeah, well, I don't want her to see you, if you know what I mean.'

'I don't know what you mean,' I reply, scooping some food into my mouth. I've forgotten that I can't eat properly. I've been picking at my food, swallowing small mouthfuls like the boulders they are. Now I have a mouth full of food and I'm going to struggle to push it down.

'You two . . . your mess . . . you want to . . . go for it. But behind closed doors.'

'Come on, man—' Wallace begins.

'Nah, nah, I'm serious. What if I'd come back with Lola in tow? She would have walked into that mess. You two were barely dressed. A few minutes later and I would have seen things no man needs to see. Control yourselves. Especially since . . . Look, what is this all about? Why are you splitting up?'

Maybe it's a good thing I have a mouthful that I can't swallow because I also can't speak to answer his question.

'I don't get you two. Valerie was always on about your relationship. Wallace and Cleo this, Wallace and Cleo that. All, "You think Wallace talks to Cleo like that?" "You think Cleo would put up with that?" And now look at you.' He uses his fork to point at me. 'Mess.' Uses it to point at Wallace. 'Double-dose, super-size mess.'

'You're one to talk,' Wallace replies. 'At least I've got my own address.'

'You got someone else?' Franklyn asks me. 'Another man? Another woman? Another person? What? What is it? Why you checking out on my brother like he's some cheap motel that always gets one star on Tripadvisor?' He waggles his fork at me. 'Cos I know Wals isn't the one behind this.'

I'm still chewing so I can't – won't – answer and just stare back at Franklyn.

'Lay off her,' Wallace interjects. 'We don't need to justify ourselves to you. Our relationship doesn't work any more. Let's just leave it at that.'

'Speak your truth,' Franklyn says, still focused on me. 'Tell me why.'

With effort, I force the last of the callaloo down past the mountain in my throat. I push out my chair, stand up.

'I'm sorry about earlier,' I say to Wallace. 'It won't happen again.'

Three weeks ago, I sat him down and told him we needed to talk.

*'Oh no, what?' he said with the jokey laugh we always gave when one of us went serious.*

*'I don't see myself in this relationship for ever,' I said. It was all I could think to say. I couldn't tell him I didn't love him because that wasn't true. I couldn't tell him I had found someone else because that wasn't true, either. And I couldn't tell him the real reason we'd met in*

*the first place. Nor why I was doing this. In fact, there wasn't much I* could *tell him that he would understand, so I had to make stuff up, just like when I wrote my stories.*

*I pictured myself as Mira Woode, my famous character, saying what needed to be said, doing what needed to be done to get to the end of the episode.*

*'I don't see myself in this relationship for ever and I don't think it's fair on you to stick around when I'm not in this for ever, so I think . . .' I paused to gather all the main character strength I could reach for. 'I think it's best if we split up. Get divorced.'*

*'What?' he'd replied, crinkling up his nose. 'What?'*

*'I think we can live amicably here until I find somewhere else and I'm sure, eventually, we can be friends if you want to. I'll understand if you don't want to.'*

*'What?'*

*'I'm sorry. I know this is a bit of a shock. So I'll just leave you so you can digest the information and then at some point we can discuss the division of assets and what next.'*

'I'll say goodnight to both of you now. Thank you for the chat and reality check, Franklyn,' I say. 'And thanks for the great dinner, Wallace.'

I have to get out of here. Now. Before I start confessing and don't stop.


## Horsforth, 1997

Heath stopped in front of Trina and me in our part of the common room and smiled.

'Hello?' I ventured when he didn't say anything.

'Would you like to gofordinnerwithme?' he said in such a rush,

52

most of his words came out jumbled together like a pile of badly stored hangers.

'You asking me or Cleo?' Trina said. 'Cos a little bit more clarity is needed, bud.'

'Sounding a bit SBBF there,' I said to Trina from the corner of my mouth.

'You take that back,' she replied, completely affronted.

'SBBF is as SBBF does.'

'What's an SBBF?' Heath asked.

'Nothing for you to worry about,' I told him.

'OK. Will you do me the absolute honour of coming to dinner with me, Cleo? I will book a table somewhere non-studenty, with proper food on the menu. Proper wine. Cloth napkins. The whole works.'

'I can't afford that,' I replied.

'My treat.'

I responded with silence. My silence came from contemplating whether it would be a good idea to say yes to this guy. It'd been three weeks since the conversation with Trina; I hadn't had a kiss or anything else yet, and I honestly didn't want him to be the one. I wanted it to be forgettable. No big deal. Something I would remember in later years fondly, but not as a 'BIG MOMENT'. And I got the impression that if I did get involved with him, it would definitely be a big deal. And not only for me. For him, too.

My silence also came from glancing over his shoulder to the young women who sat at his table. Only three today, all pretty, all sitting there pretending they didn't mind the others being there, too. All scowling over at Trina and me because Heath couldn't see them. Heath's reputation as Mr Popularity meant that if I did go out with him – even platonically – I could be opening myself up to being hated by those women and others.

'If you don't say yes, I will,' Trina stated.

My head cranked round to look at her. 'OK, SBBF.'

'You take that back.'

I returned my gaze to Heath. 'All right, then.'

His face lit up with the most beatific grin. He looked so genuinely happy and relieved, I did a double-take. 'Shall I pick you up at seven o'clock on Saturday night?' he asked.

'Yes.'

His grin widened, showing off his straight white teeth, creasing his eyes. 'Can't wait,' he said, 'honestly, I can't wait.' He backed away from us, the grin still overtaking his face. He gave us a little wave as he continued to back away, until he had to turn away and face the direction he was heading in.

'Erm—' Trina began.

'Not him,' I cut in. 'Just not him.'

'Fine,' she huffed. I didn't even need to look at her to know she was screwing up her face at me. 'Not him.'


8 AUGUST, 2022
CLEO & WALLACE'S HOUSE, HOVE—BRIGHTON BORDER
LATE EVENING

*Dear Sidney,*

*How are you? I haven't heard from you in a while. Are you OK?*

*I know I say this every time, but I miss you. It's strange to write that when I haven't seen you or heard your voice in so long. Please change your mind. Please see me. Like I say, I miss you. And there are some things that can only be said face to face.*

*The writing is going as well as can be expected. I was about to draw an emoji then. Remembered how much you hate them.*

*Please write back to me. Please let me come and see you.*

*Miss you.*

*All my love*
*Cleo*

## Leeds City Centre, 1997

Hidden away down a side street in Leeds town centre, away from the main throng, Heath had chosen a quiet little Italian restaurant with low lighting, small intimate tables, white tablecloths, candles, soft music. We were the youngest in there by a mile and I knew why – the menu had no prices on it. Menus without prices meant food that would eat up my limited student finances in two bites.

I stared at everything with my eyes slightly widened. I wouldn't dream of letting him pay for all of it and had come along fully expecting to pay my share but . . . my eyes ran frantically up and down the menu, my heartbeat speeding like an out-of-control train in my chest. I could not afford this. I would have to pick a starter and make it last the whole meal.

'Please don't worry,' Heath said suddenly, obviously sensing my mounting panic. 'I meant it when I said I was paying. I want to thank you for all you've done for me, so please have whatever you would like from the menu. Honestly.'

The white-shirted, black-bow-tied waiter arrived to take our order, pen nib resting on the white notepad in his hand. He had fixed his face – which had been a picture of horror when he originally saw us – and was now valiantly battling with his disgust at our presence, and anger at having been duped into allowing us to stay even though Heath had booked a table. The waiter's greased-back fawn-brown hair made his angry eyes seem huge and his bunched-up lips seem even thinner.

My gaze continued to run up and down the page, frantically trying to work out which dishes seemed the lowest cost and I eventually settled for garlic bread because it was at the top and I figured it would be the cheapest, then a pasta puttanesca because that was near the top, too; Heath ordered bruschetta and spaghetti alle vongole. 'We'll also have the vintage Rioja Blanco,' Heath said, handing back the wine menu.

My hurtling heart stopped and dipped in utter dismay – vintage? Where was this guy getting his money? Because I was not getting it in the same place. 'Honestly,' Heath said quietly as the waiter practically snatched the menus out of our hands and stormed off, 'you have nothing to worry about. This is absolutely my pleasure.'

That didn't make me relax. I did not like being beholden to anyone, especially not a man I was on what could be construed as a date with. I had heard other female students discussing how they'd felt almost guilt-tripped into sex, oral action or at the very least a kiss because a guy had bought her drinks/dinner/tickets to a gig. What was this man going to want in return for bringing me here, to a place so expensive I would not know how much each bite cost until the bill arrived.

'When you said nice, I thought maybe somewhere with thicker paper napkins, not somewhere with high-thread-count napkins and real flowers,' I said just as quietly. 'Not sure what this is all about.'

'It's about me treating you to something refined. As a token of my appreciation for all the help you gave me.'

'That was months ago.'

'It doesn't feel like months ago; it feels like your assistance – as invaluable and generous as it was – was mere moments ago.'

All right, that was it. Enough already. 'What's with the Vulcan speak, Heath?'

'What do you mean?'

'I mean, why do you talk like that? I've heard you talk normally. And then you'll open your mouth and it sounds like you've got five plums jammed in your mouth while you read from the thesaurus. It's really unsettling.'

He flushed a little, glanced down at his napkin for so long I began to think I'd offended him. He rubbed at his eye for a moment with his left hand, then pinched the bridge of his nose between his forefinger and thumb. 'It's all really embarrassing,' he said before dragging his gaze up to meet mine. 'I . . . It's a bit like when you suddenly adopt a Brummie accent when you speak to people from the North – when I'm around you, my brain goes into panic mode and my voice does that.'

'Hang on a minute, I do *what*?'

'You adopt a Brummie accent. As though you're from Birmingham.'

'I don't.'

'You do. It's not intentional, and most people realise that. But when you speak to someone from up North, doesn't matter if it's Manchester, Newcastle, Liverpool or Leeds, your voice changes.'

'I don't do that. If I did, Trina would have told me.'

'But she's from London, so you don't do it with her. And her London accent seems to act like an anchor.'

57

I was pretty sure I didn't do that, but it *would* explain why people gave me odd looks all the time. It would explain a lot of things, actually . . . 'Anyway, that aside. Why would your voice change around me?'

Heath sighed, his whole body moving with the action. 'Because I want you to think well of me. I want you to think I'm intelligent and witty and, yes, like I can look after myself. I don't normally care what other people think about me. All water off a duck's back, but with you, I want, no – *need* – you to think well of me.'

I sat back in my seat, not sure what to say for a moment or two. It'd been three months; he was surrounded by other women constantly. He couldn't still be interested in me. Surely not. 'You must care what people think of you,' I said to him. 'We bought all those clothes, you got your hair done, you dress like a very different person, and as a result you are never short of female company, as you would say.'

'I only did all that because I thought . . . well, I thought it would give me a chance with you.'

'*What?*'

'I got to spend time with you. And I changed myself to look how you wanted me to—'

'I didn't want you to look like that!'

'So you don't find the Zack Morris look attractive?'

'Not especially. I mean, I don't find him unattractive but—Hey, is that his surname? Morris?'

'Yes.'

'How did you find out?'

'I looked him up. Had to find out what this guy you wanted me to emulate looked like. It wasn't so bad. At least you weren't hunkering after that Screech character.'

58

'He was kinda my favourite, actually,' I mumbled.

'Oh.'

'But not fancying-wise. I just watched the show for the drama and the impossibly beautiful people.'

'Why did you try to recreate me in Zack's image if you weren't attracted to him?'

'For you. You had a bit of a look of him, and I know how popular the show is still, so I figured quite a few women in college would like you. Win–win.'

The waiter arrived with two plates: my garlic bread was browned to perfection, oozing with butter and tiny pearls of garlic, Heath's bruschetta was an oval flatbread, smothered in a vibrant green pesto, topped with little cubes of bright red tomato. After placing the plates in front of us, he positioned our napkins on our laps with an elabor-ate, showy flourish. He offered pepper from a large black grinder, which we both refused, and then practically melted away into the background. Once we were alone, I stared at my food. I was trying not to calculate how much each tiny piece of garlic cost and how hard it would be to force it down if I didn't like it. But I was mostly thinking how I had led Heath on. Not intentionally, of course.

'I really was trying to transform you for you. I thought it would do you a lot of good, increase your confidence.'

'It has,' he replied, looking especially confused. 'It really boosted my confidence. As evidenced by who my lovely dinner partner is this fine evening.'

'Don't start.'

'Sorry. But I am serious. The shopping trip, the change of image. It worked like a charm. I don't even have to think about approaching women, they come to me. I have so many friends now. My confidence has been well and truly boosted. If you hadn't boosted my confidence, I would not be here right now. I wouldn't have had the courage to ask you out for a proper meal.'

'I'm not really sure what to say to all of this.'

'Say nothing. Enjoy your meal.'

'Well, I can't really, not if I think you're thinking this could go anywhere other than a deep and meaningful friendship. And it may not even be that deep or meaningful. Or much of a friendship, although you did look up *Saved by the Bell*, which shows the friendship side of things could work out.'

'I'll take "shallow and meaningless" over nothing at all.'

That made me laugh, the sound spilling over to him and causing him to laugh, too.

'Let's just enjoy the evening,' I said, because I couldn't think what else to say.

'It's all right, Cleo,' he said, 'this is sim—I mean, this is just a thank-you meal from one friend to another. No pressure.'

'Are you sure?' I asked him.

'One hundred per cent.'

'If you are sure, then I can breathe again. And I can make sure I concentrate on enjoying every single tiny part of the most expensive garlic bread I am ever likely to get this close and personal with again.'

'How do you know it's expensive?'

I leant forwards, lowered my voice. 'No prices. Anywhere that doesn't put the prices on the menu is—you just need a lot of money to pay for it.'

He blanched in horror. 'Is that true?'

I lowered the garlic bread from where it had been heading for my mouth onto the plate. Maybe if I didn't eat it I could send it back and they wouldn't charge me. Same with the puttanesca – if I cancelled it now, before they made it, maybe it would be OK and I wouldn't be charged.

'I didn't know that,' he said quietly. 'I just saw it and thought it looked nice. Oh hell. I didn't realise it'd be really expensive. What are you wearing on your feet?'

'Boots, why?'

'Can you run in them?'

'I suppose but why—?' It was my turn to look horrified. My horror was doused in huge doses of terror, though. He was talking about us doing a runner. A runner! They'd probably chase us down the street with big knives and meat cleavers. My lungs couldn't handle a runner, my conscience couldn't handle a runner, never mind my feet.

'I'm joking, I'm joking,' Heath said. 'My parents sent me a lot of money for my birthday. I've got all of this covered.'

'Never do that again!' I said and flicked my napkin at him.

'Your face,' he laughed.

And that laughter was so genuine and easy, it carried me through the rest of the meal.

8 AUGUST, 2022
CLEO & WALLACE'S HOUSE, HOVE—BRIGHTON BORDER
LATE EVENING

*Tap, tap.*

The knock on my door isn't completely unexpected. We've been sleeping in separate rooms and been mindful of giving each other space. I had moved out of the main bedroom – too many memories. Too much Wallace.

*Tap, tap* comes again. I sit on my hands. I need to ignore it. Ignore him. If I don't, we'll end up where we were before. And I will hurt him. I will really hurt him. Yes, it'll hurt me, too, but I can stand a little pain. At this moment in time, I'd say I deserve it.

*Tap, tap* again. Less confident this time. I do not move, I do not breathe. I wait for the moment to pass. I wait until he taps one last time, then listen to the soft pad of his footsteps walking away.

Once I hear his bedroom door shut behind him, I pull one of my pillows into my lap, I lean forwards so I can bury my face in it and then scream. Scream and scream and scream.

I do not want to be doing this. But I have no choice. No choice.


## Leeds City Centre, 1997

We finished dinner, all the while aware of the waiter quietly shooting his disapproval of us across the room. The waiter – and the waitress who had joined him to smoulder at us, too – were openly relieved when Heath decided he didn't want another espresso after all and just asked for the bill.

When it arrived on a little white dish, my eyes nearly popped out of my head – nearly ninety pounds for two starters, two mains, a bottle of wine and a coffee. Ninety pounds. Ninety pounds. While I tried to act cool, to keep my horror in check, Heath didn't even flinch. He simply pulled out a wodge of money, peeled off two fifty-pound notes and lay them on the plate. And as I squirmed with embarrassment and anger as the waiter openly checked they were real notes while standing at our table, Heath didn't even acknowledge him. The longer he lifted the notes, held them to the light so he could scruti-nise the money, the more my whole body burned with shame because the other diners in there – the older people who knew they belonged in a place like this while we didn't – were watching us. They were waiting for the drama of us being discovered to be forgers and fakes to explode; for us to be publicly denounced, for the police to be called, for us to be led out in handcuffs. It was mortifying. The food, the wine and the chat with Heath had been so nice, but everything else – not so much. When the waiter, satisfied the notes were real, took the little porcelain dish with the money on away and then failed to return, Heath called him over.

'I'd like my change, please,' Heath told him.

'Sorry, sir? There was no change,' he had the temerity to reply, somehow finding the 'sir' for Heath for the first time that evening.

'Yes, there was. In fact, there was £12.35 left over. I'd like it back. And then I can decide if I'd like to pay you a tip or not.' Nineteen-year-old Heath was staring right at this man who was probably twice his age, willing him to argue.

The waiter, with his head held high, went to the till, removed Heath's exact change and returned it to him – all in coins – on the white porcelain dish, this time accompanied by two small white mint spheres. 'Thank you,' Heath said, leaving the mints and pocketing the money. 'My tip is "be nice to all your customers, not just the ones you like the look of".'

That completely threw me. I'd never seen anyone do that before. People, grown adults, were rude to me all the time, but I'd never had the power or self-possession to actually get back at them.

The waiter's sallow skin pinked up almost immediately, the tips of his ears filling with dark red blood. He wanted to react, to respond, but he knew it would look terrible on him; would out him to the rest of the diners in the restaurant and would probably put this tip – and the other tips – at risk. So instead of grabbing Heath by the front of his jacket and calling him a little shit like he obviously wanted to, he stepped away before he forgot himself.

Heath and I left the restaurant in silence, me still a little shaken. Where did Heath get the confidence to do that? Because I could never . . . not on my own behalf. With other people, no problem, but for me? Nah. As we passed a cashpoint, we saw a man sitting on the floor, a blanket over his raised knees, his grubby overcoat zipped up to the top, a scarf wrapped tightly around his neck and a thick woolly hat pulled right down, covering his forehead, trying to protect himself from the late-January air. It often felt like there was a special kind of cold up here, one the winters in London could never touch.

'Spare some change?' the man asked us.

I was about to reach into my pocket, when Heath pulled the mound of one-pound and fifty-pence coins that the waiter had returned and said, 'Here you go, mate,' and slowly dropped his stash into the man's cupped hands.

He did a double-take at how much there was. 'Cheers,' he said, suspiciously at first, obviously wondering what Heath wanted in return, and then: 'Cheers, cheers!' he called when we carried on walking without asking anything of him. 'Cheers! Cheers!'

I side-eyed Heath. 'That's the sort of thing a guy does in a Rom-Com when he's trying to get the girl,' I said to him, loading my voice with all the suspicion that I felt.

'Is it?'

'Yes, big gesture designed to show how generous you are.'

'I see. Well, you know I don't watch those movies, so I do not know what the format is, but I am more than willing to give all of that a try if it gives me any type of advantage.' He grinned sideways at me.

'No advantage whatsoever,' I shot down. 'I tend not to be impressed by big public gestures just to show off.'

'Interesting that you think I was showing off.'

'Weren't you? You made a big deal of taking that money off a guy who relies on tips to top up his wages, and gave it to a homeless person. Big show-off gesture.'

'If that waiter relies on tips – which is not my fault, by the way – then maybe he should be nicer to people he sees as beneath him. And just because I didn't want him to have it because he was rude and condescending, doesn't mean I wanted to keep the money for myself. I was actually going to drop it into one of the charity boxes on the counter of a shop, but then I saw that man and thought he should have it. No showing-off intended.

'Besides, it's a bit of a rubbish way for me to show off when I know you aren't even the slightest bit interested in me.'

'This is true.'

The night buzzed around us with expectation as we walked through the city – most people were dressed up and heading into town for late-night drinking and clubbing. We were surrounded by the excited, emotional vibrations of people who been hibernating for most of the month. We walked mostly in silence and soon we were far away from the bright lights and buildings. We crossed the road to Hyde Park, a patchwork of shades of black against the black-blue inkiness of the sky.

'When was your birthday?'

'About three months ago,' he said.

'Oh . . . And you've still got money from back then?'

'I have a lot of money from my birthdays,' he replied. 'Since I was born, my parents have, between them, put aside ten pounds a week. No matter what, they put a tenner into an account for my birthday. And then, on the day, I get a card and five hundred and twenty pounds.'

'Wow, that's a huge amount of money!'

'I know. And I very rarely spend it all. So I have this money in my account for new clothes and taking people I like out for dinner.'

'Do you mind not getting presents?' I asked as we neared the end of the park. We were walking at quite a brisk pace. 'I mean, half the fun of birthdays is to have something to open on the day. Do you mind not getting something to open?'

He frowned, I could see that in the dark, as he thought it through. 'I don't think so. It's never occurred to me to mind. I can do whatever I like with the money – they never ever tell me how to spend it – so if there's something big that I want, I know I can get it, no worries. I don't have to beg my parents for it and they don't have to find extra money for it. I mean, I always got the top range of anything I wanted because I had the cash to buy it. My parents gave me the power and freedom to be in charge of my own destiny, and I think I much prefer that to unwrapping things.'

'I didn't think of it like that. I suppose in a way your parents gave you whatever you wanted for your birthday, so no disappointment.'

He stopped walking for a moment, then turned to me. I stopped, too, knowing that this was going to be one of those moments that I would look back on and regret in some shape or form.

'Cleo, I'm going to ask you something,' he said, rather dramatically I felt.

'OK,' I replied.

'I want you to keep an open mind.'

'OK.'

'I know there's no going back after I ask and I know it'll change how you see me.' He sighed. 'Can . . . well . . . can we . . .?'

I held my breath, waiting for him to say it.

'I can't walk any more, and I have some birthday money left, so can we get a taxi back to halls from here? I don't want you to think badly of me, or think I'm not having a good time. I'm just tired.'

'Sure,' I replied, suppressing a laugh. Heath was entertaining if nothing else. And I liked that. I liked that a lot.

# 6

The man sitting behind the desk is enjoying this too much. In the grand scheme of things, for how low level this is as a power trip, he seems to be deriving a hell of a lot of pleasure from it.

'Are you really saying that I have to go all the way home to get my security pass?' I say to him, and I swear a jolt of pleasure shivers through him at those words.

'Wasn't me who forgot it, was it?' he replies, barely suppressing his smile.

I have a sudden urge to grab him by the lanyard and shout in his face. My second urge is to burst into noisy tears that may or may not embarrass him and the other two security guards sitting with him. I suspect, though, my tears might just give him the happy ending he wasn't expecting but would very much welcome. Both urges are most unlike me, but 'unlike me' is pretty on-brand at the moment.

'Can't I just sign in as a visitor?' I ask evenly.

'I don't make the rules,' he says with a small smile that says he doesn't make the rules, but he does make sure they're enforced in as many petty and unnecessarily punitive ways as possible.

68

'But I used to sign in as a visitor all the time.'

'That was *before* you were given a proper pass. Once you are in possession of a proper pass, you cease to be a visitor and become someone who needs said proper pass to get into the building.'

I hear the clacking of high heels across the marble floor from the glass front doors to the security desk and know without looking round that it's Sandy Burton, Chief Operating Officer of HoneyMay Productions. When she marches into view, she's wearing the tightest-fitting black leather jacket I've ever seen, sprayed-on black trousers and the highest pink stiletto boots. She has slicked her short, white-blonde crop off her face so her expert make-up job is clear for all to see.

'Morning, Cleo,' she says, barely throwing her gaze in my direction because she is also VERY PISSED OFF with me for ending the show. She instead focuses on the man I have been verbally tussling with. 'Philip, I've left my pass in the car, buzz me through, there's a chap.'

Without even hesitating, 'Philip' flicks the switch and she click-clacks her way through glass turnstiles to the bank of lifts. She doesn't even bother to pretend to care why I'm not joining her. That gives 'Philip' an extra thrill. I can see that.

I am stuck here with this 'man', though, because Tuesdays, Wallace works from home. I can't be there even for a little while. I left early so I wouldn't see him this morning, I'm not going back there now to get my stupid pass.

I hear people approaching the reception desk in front of which I'm standing. 'Cleo, hi,' Gail says when she spots me. She's about to put her pass onto the glowing red rectangle to the side of the glass turnstile when she pauses. 'You coming?' she asks me.

'Apparently not; I don't have my pass so I'm not allowed in.'

'What, literally, "your name's not down, you're not coming in"?' Gail says with a smirk. Only someone my age would understand that reference.

'Yup.'

'Don't be difficult now, Phil,' Anouk, the senior script editor, says from somewhere near me. 'You know who she is, just give her a visitor's pass.'

'Philip' raises himself up to his full height, folds his arms across his puffed-out chest and moves his mouth to quote something, I'm sure.

'Oh, stop being so pathetic!' Gail snaps suddenly. 'Give her a pass, you petty individual.' I swear the guards on either side of him curl their lips in to stop laughing. And Philip, so flushed with embarrassment the tips of his ears turn pink, jumps to attention, grabs a visitor's pass and slides it towards me along with a pen. Once I've filled it in, he pushes the paper into a plastic holder and hands it back.

'Thank you,' I say to him. I'm too taken aback to find any pleasure in his mortification.

'Shoulda just given her the pass,' Anouk says, voicing what we are all thinking.

While we wait for the lift, Gail says to me, 'You know, when people used to say that phrase, "your name's not down, you're not coming in", I was convinced they were saying, "if your name's not Dan, you're not coming in". For ages.'

Anouk and I burst out laughing, and I'm aware 'Philip' is staring daggers into my back.

'Don't laugh!' Gail giggles. 'It was all those London accents, that's how "down" sounded.'

We all continue to laugh as the lift doors slide open. It's almost like having two work mates again. And even though I know I don't deserve it, I like it.

## Horsforth, 1997

'This really is the best part of the whole common room,' Heath said. 'I know I've said it before, but wow, it really is.'

Since we'd gone to dinner, Heath had taken this as an invitation to join Trina and me. We didn't mind, we quite liked it actually. Trina and I were quite laid-back about our twosome – if anyone wanted to join, they literally just had to pull up a chair and we'd talk to them. I wanted to say that to the women who felt slighted now Heath had crossed the floor. They really liked hanging around with him and they did not like him hiding away in the corner with two lasses. They didn't need to sit there glowering at us, they could come and join me and my pursuit of the best chocolate-to-coffee combo – but obviously not if they were going to talk about the Revels debacle – or they could try to rival Trina in her quest to be the most striking woman in Yorkshire. But the evil looks, the killer lip gloss and angrily flicked hair meant any offers that might have been extended remained in our heads.

Heath was very pleasant to be around – he was funny and interesting. Anything we talked about he took great interest in and sometimes tried to offer some insight that we often gently ribbed him about and he didn't mind. He was also first up to get the coffees and snacks. I could see why the people who hung around with him liked him so much.

'It really is the best part,' Trina agreed. She was currently sporting gold-and-black hair, but with silver nails. 'Cleo found it. We used to watch you stalking her from here. Good times, good times.'

'I didn't stalk her,' Heath responded. 'I just used to stare at her. I stopped short of showing up in places she was going to be that I shouldn't have been.'

'Oh, thank you, I suppose, for not stalking me properly,' I said, rolling my eyes.

'God, you're so dramatic,' Trina said. She paused, raised her eyes to the heavens. 'Sorry, Lord, for taking your name in vain.' She returned her gaze to me. 'You are so dramatic! Can he help it if he found you so incredibly beautiful? No, I do not think he could.'

'Erm . . . Think you'll find he didn't stare at me because he thought I was beautiful. He stared at me because he was trying to work out if there was something wrong with his brain. He was trying to work out what it was about me that he liked so he could solve the "problem" of liking me.'

Slowly Trina lowered her legs that she had crossed beneath herself and sat upright. She smoothed her hands over her hair and with very few movements wrapped a couple of plaits around the rest of her plaits into what could only be described as a fighting ponytail. Even more slowly, more dangerously, my best friend turned to Heath. 'You had better tell me that she is exaggerating, and you had better tell me fast.'

Heath stopped lounging against the seat and sat up, too. 'She is not exaggerating, she is misrepresenting what I said,' he replied. 'I liked her. A lot. In fact, I told her that I thought I'd fallen in love with her. But I knew she didn't like me, which meant what I felt was pointless, which made the whole experience of liking – loving – her really unpleasant and a bit painful. I told her how I felt as a last-ditch attempt to see if she might possibly change her mind. Instead, she came up with the plan of finding me a girlfriend. That is what happened and that is what she has extrapolated into that jumble she just told you.'

'Do you still like her?' Trina asked suspiciously. Thankfully she didn't use the other L word.

'Of course.'

'What about the Heathettes?'

'The what?'

'That's what Trina calls the women you hang out with. The Heathettes.'

'Right. Interesting. What about them?'

'Are you screwing any of them?'

'Yes.'

'More than one?'

'Yes.'

'But you still like this one?'

'Yes. Still feel like I love her, if you must know.'

'How does that work?'

'She—'

'I'd appreciate it if you lot would stop talking about me as if I'm not here,' I interjected. This conversation was making me slightly nauseous and a lot nervous. I could see this taking a sharp turn in a wrong direction, and them trying to analyse why I didn't like Heath when he was, on paper and in real life, quite eligible. And that conversation would inevitably lead to Trina telling – or even hinting to – Heath that I'd never kissed anyone, that I was still a virgin and there was still no one around that I was interested enough in to think about doing that with. I didn't want her 'outing' my sexual history status to him or anyone.

Things were often tense between us as it was. Heath and I regularly went for a drink or a meal on our own – just like I did with Trina, just like he did with a couple of the Heathettes – but sometimes there'd be a moment between us. There would be a moment where we were so obviously meant to get physically closer – a hug or a kiss or a linking of hands – and we would both freeze. We wouldn't know what to do – how to navigate the moment in the safest way possible, so one of us would make a smart-mouth remark and we'd both laugh it off. When I'd tell Trina about those moments, she would always say: 'Oh just jump him and put us all out of his misery.' I could feel her gearing up to say as much to me in front of him. 'Actually,' I added, 'how about you stop talking about me as though I'm not here *AND* we change the subject.'

'No!' they both emphatically replied.

'Come on, then, Heathie boy, tell me how you can be knocking off two or more Heathettes and still like this one here?'

'Cleo has made it abundantly clear she has no interest in me in that way at all. I'm more than happy to hang around with her like this. I just get my other kicks elsewhere.'

'But if she changed her mind . . . ?'

He stood up suddenly, stretched the top half of his body so hard his white T-shirt rode up, showing the soft brown hairs along the bottom of his stomach, leading down into his jeans. Quite a few eyes were on him then, taking in his body, being impressed or otherwise. I saw the three 'Heathettes' who were sitting at his previous table staring at him, then immediately glaring at us because we were near him and they weren't. They didn't get to hang out with him like they used to any more. Instead of offering a friendly smile like I usually did, I glanced away, embarrassed at what we'd been talking about, what we were still talking about.

Heath came out of his stretch as suddenly as he went into it and fixed Trina to the spot with those green eyes of his. 'She isn't changing her mind any time soon,' he told her. 'And that means, I don't think about it.' He moved his lips into a smile that was so bereft, I had to look away.

I didn't know why he liked me so much. Still. It'd been months. What was it exactly that he wanted from me? We hung out together all the time, we had fun, why did he still want something else? Was sex really so important that it would make him feel like this? 'Who wants a coffee and who wants a tea and who wants something hot to drown – what is it at the moment – Crunchies in?'

'Coffee,' I said, avoiding his gaze. 'Five sugars.'

'Same,' Trina said. 'Apart from the sugars. My round next.'

We sat in silence while he walked to the serving hatch, pausing to laugh and chat with a few people on the way. 'He's proper in love with you,' Trina stated. 'I mean, I'll admit I thought he was just a bit keen, like, wanting a bit of sweet Cleo *ting*, but no, he's proper in love with you. You know you can't ever do it with him, don't you? Not unless you mean it.'

I knew that. I hadn't articulated it in quite that way before, not even in the privacy of my own head, but what Trina said was true: I couldn't mess with Heath. Not even remotely. If I kissed him, then I had to mean it. For ever.

9 AUGUST, 2022
CLEO & WALLACE'S HOUSE, HOVE—BRIGHTON BORDER
EARLY EVENING

'Cleo, I need to talk to you,' Wallace says after knocking loudly on my bedroom door.

I've been holed up here since sneaking in earlier. I can't talk to him without wanting to explain everything and I don't have the words to do that. And if I try . . . well, it's likely to end up like it did yesterday.

I open the door and peek out. He's standing a way away down the corridor in front of the door to the box room, which is for the best. I feel able to step out into the corridor, too.

'Trina called me earlier,' he states. 'She said you've been ducking her calls and texts.'

I can't speak to Trina. I can't communicate with her. Because then I'd have to tell her about Wallace and me getting divorced. And that I cannot do. She has an affection for Wallace almost as deep as mine. She will not forgive me. She will not understand. And she will start to ask uncomfortable questions. Questions that I can't answer without telling her everything. And there is no way I'm doing that. If I did that, she'd be over on the next plane to slap several shades of sense into me.

'Right,' I say to Wallace. 'I'll, um . . . yeah.'

'She was asking about the holiday.' I must look like I have no idea what he's talking about because he adds: 'About us going to see her? She wants to book a couple of other trips and wants to check if we'd be up for them.'

'Right.'

'I'm guessing you haven't told her about—'

'No, I haven't,' I cut in before he says the words. I can think them but I don't want him to say them.

'Well, you'll have to.'

'I know.'

'Is it what you want?' he asks, perceptive as always. Of course it's not. It's the last thing I want. But I have to. It's as simple and as complex as that. I have to.

I nod in response to his question. Convincing I am not.

'Fine.' He turns to go back into his room, then stops, as though he's changed his mind and *will* ask me another question after all. 'Is it the baby thing?' he asks boldly.

I'm taken aback, but I immediately answer: 'No, no, absolutely not.'

'Cos I'd understand if that was why. If you wanted to find someone to give yourself a chance—'

'No,' I almost shout. 'It is not that. We don't know why it's turned out this way, and we both know it's more likely that it's because of me than you, but even if we did know, I wouldn't leave you because of it. It's not that.'

'Then why? Because "I don't see myself being in this relationship for ever" is not a proper reason.'

'It's the only one I've got.' If he knew – all of it, even a little of it – he would not be asking me if I was sure I wanted to end our marriage, he would be marching me to the nearest police station for my part in murder. If he didn't turn me in to the police, he would be unceremoniously chucking me out of his house, not trying to get me to stay.

'Look, C, why don't we put everything on hold? Take more time. Go see Trina, decide when we come back where we are?' he suggests.

I shake my head. 'No, we can't do that.'

'Why not?'

'Because we're getting divorced.'

'Just like that?'

'No, not just like that. Just . . . look, I meant it yesterday when I said that we should keep our distance.'

'I thought you meant it when you said "till death us do part", too,' he bites back. I know he wants to say more, to be nastier, but he's restraining himself. He's trying not to say anything that can't be taken back, that will cast an unpleasant shadow on 'us' if we decide not to get divorced. If *I* decide not to get a divorce.

'I did mean it,' I reply. 'And I changed my mind. I'm allowed to change my mind.'

Furious, frustrated, *hurt*, Wallace watches me, looking for a sign that I am in any way the person he thinks he knows.

I'm not, of course. I never have been.

With a shake of his head, he enters our bedroom, shutting the door behind him. The sound of the door closing is like a punch right at the centre of my being. I rush towards it, and press my hands against it. 'I love you. Always,' I mouth into the grain of the wood, hoping that when he touches it tomorrow, these words will diffuse through his skin and end up nestled in his heart.

# 7

10 AUGUST, 2022
4TH FLOOR, HONEYMAY PRODUCTIONS OFFICE, BRIGHTON
AFTERNOON

'Welcome to Burrfield and Co., Solicitors at law. We're sorry that there is no one here to take your call right now, please leave us a message with your name and number and the nature of your business and one of our associates will get back to you as soon as possible.'

I've tried calling at various times during the morning and lunch and there seems to be no one at Mr Burrfield's offices. Considering he said he would expedite things, I'm surprised I haven't heard from him. I haven't left any messages on their answermachine because, well, I do not want to leave a record of my 'friend's' problem that could get 'her' up to seven years in prison.

Seven years.

The thought of that still makes me want to throw up.

Seven years for doing something stupid. Am I being honest, here, though? If it wasn't for that stupid mistake, would I be getting divorced from Wallace? Would I be ending the television show that was a dream to have created, have had commissioned and shown on television? Would I be eventually moving away from the place where I've wanted to live since I was sixteen? Would I be inextricably tied up with the cover-up of a murder? No, no, no and no. So maybe seven years in jail is not enough. Maybe I should be looking at life.

I hang up the phone and clatter it onto the desk beside my laptop. I snuck out this morning again to avoid Wallace, and forgot my security pass *again*, but this time 'Philip' had given me no trouble. Franklyn's words from Monday evening echoed in my ears for most of last night. I know I have to stay away from Wallace; I have to keep my distance until everything I'm doing to untangle myself from this life comes together.

'What's spooky about it is that it looks exactly like one of our sets,' Amy, the junior script editor, is saying to Gail as they pass the doorway to the conference room where I'm working. Amy notices that I'm looking at them and stops. 'Up the road, there's a police cordon,' she explains. 'There's still quite a few police milling around in white overalls and whatnot. It's so much like the sets for *The Baking Detective*.'

'You think there was a murder up the road?' I ask, horrified and fascinated in equal measure. 'I didn't see anything online or in the papers.'

'Dunno, that's just what it looked like to me.'

'Where was it?' I ask.

'On the way to the race course. There's this little Ethiopian restaurant where I like to get my lunch and it was near there. Really spooky. I mean, it looks exactly like one of our sets.'

'I suppose it would do with all the trillions of police advisers we have on the show,' I respond. *Had* on the show, I suppose I should say.

'Your face,' Gail says. 'You look horrified. A bit weird considering what you write.'

'I used to write romantic comedies, believe it or not,' I reply.

'What, like the ripping bodices and stuff?' Amy asks.

'Not quite. Actually, let's be honest, they were the more modern version of those. Then I kind of got sucked into murder.'

Gail and Amy both laugh at that. 'Never say that outside of these four walls,' Amy says, still giggling. 'It sounds so dodgy.'

I pull a face when I mentally play it back. 'So dodgy.' So true, though, on many levels.

Again, it hits Amy and Gail that I've ended the show so they're not meant to have that much goodwill towards me – almost in unison their faces fall and they mumble, 'See you,' before moving on.

'See you,' I say softly and pick up my phone to try Jeff Burrfield again.

## Headingley, 1999

'I have wine, I have pizza, I have a spare pair of hands to clean with,' Heath said when I opened the door to him. He did indeed have a bottle of fizz peeking out of the top of the black cloth messenger bag slung across his body, he had two large pizza boxes in his arms and he had a familiar, comforting smile on his face.

'Sure, H, turn up to help when the cleaning has been done and this woman has been pretty much broken by doing said cleaning.'

'I'm here, aren't I? I may be late for the cleaning, but I am on time for the pizza and fun, which is so much better.'

'For you maybe, not for me.' I stepped back to let him walk in. He kicked off his shoes immediately, just like I'd trained him to. This had been a challenge in our student house, but Trina and I had held the line – reminding our housemates to take off their shoes and wash their hands every time they came home until it was easier for them to give in and do it as standard.

I'd lived in this five-bedroom house in Headingley with Trina and three other people from the Business and Management element of her degree course. She had been studying Maths with Business and Management as her professional option, I had studied Psychology with Media as my professional option. Heath had been studying Psychology with Public Administration as his professional but had swapped halfway through our first term to Media. (The three of us pretended that he hadn't done that to spend more time with me, but that had obviously been the case and I'd erased it from my mind because it was another thing that made me feel odd.)

We'd mostly got along living in our house, had mostly been a happy bunch, and the two years had actually been fun. Now finals and graduation were over, they had all managed to get jobs and departed at various points over the last few days. Trina had been the last to go, staying until last night before she moved in with her boyfriend, Steadman, over in Roundhay. He was actually one of the junior lecturers from our uni but hadn't had any teaching contact with Trina at all. Their eyes had met over congealed shepherd's pie one lunchtime when we were in first year and they had been together – on the down-low – ever since. Now college was over, they could flaunt their relationship by moving straight in together.

Before she left, Trina had helped clean one of the bathrooms as well as her room. My other flatmates had 'cleaned' their rooms, which in reality meant I'd spent most of the day with my hands in yellow rubber gloves, utilising various sponges, brushes, bin bags and cleaning implements. I was T-I-R-E-D. When I'd spoken to Heath at lunchtime, he'd said he was going to come over to help me.

'Where are we eating?' he asked.

'Bedroom. My bedroom. Only place with furniture. Everything else is gone.'

'Gone? Gone where?'

'Long story, but one of the people I was renting with did a deal with the landlord to sell the furniture because said landlord is now selling the property and couldn't be bothered with the hassle of clearing it. So it's all gone, hence the extra cleaning. When you take away furniture you find new, undiscovered types of debris and junk and trash. I kept my bed and bedside table and television, which is going back to the rental shop tomorrow, in exchange for cleaning. Suppose it's not that long a story, really.'

'Bedroom it is.' He led the way upstairs, the bag with the bottle banging against his hip as he moved, while I stopped by the kitchen and picked up the two mugs that I was taking home with me. I wasn't looking forward to making the journey back to London, to then go and stay with my parents and my younger sister until I started my Masters in Magazine Publishing in September. I loved my parents, adored my sister, but three years away had transformed my relationship with myself. I saw myself as an adult now, and my parents . . . I was pretty sure they were always going to see me as ten years old.

'Veggie feast for the lady, plain old cheese and tomato for myself,' Heath said when I entered my bedroom. He was on the bed – mattress, really, since the base had been sold from under me and my negotiation skills had garnered the mattress only – balancing the boxes on his lap so the grease didn't stain my duvet cover. He'd flicked on the television, and had put on my two desk lamps instead of the big light.

'Thank you, kind sir,' I said. 'I'm going to miss . . . this.' I'd almost said 'you' but stopped myself.

'You're going to miss "this" and not "you",' he replied, smirking. 'Don't worry, I've got the message, Cleo – I don't feature in the things you'll "miss".'

'Come on now, H, don't be like that,' I said. 'You know what I was saying.' I removed the bottle from his bag and ripped the foil top off. I started to unwind the wire, aware suddenly of him watching me intently. Once the wire was off, I gripped the cork.

'Twist the bottle, not the cork,' Heath said. He always said that on the occasions we had fizz.

And I always said: 'I'm going to twist the cork now just to spite you.'

The cork came out with a louder-than-expected pop and a little fizz rushed up to bubble over the side and dribble down the neck of the bottle. Judge Dredd and Incredible Hulk mugs filled, I handed one to Heath, took my pizza and settled down beside him on the bed.

'What is it that you're doing after college, H? You've been oddly quiet about it? Every time I ask, you change the subject.'

'That's because I didn't know and I didn't want to jinx it by talking about it. But today I got notification, hence the fizz. I am going to train to become a clinical psychologist.'

'Clinical psychology, huh? OK, OK, I am impressed. Where?'

'London. I was investigating psychiatry, but I'd have to do medical training and I don't have that in me. So clinical psychology it is, and I'm looking forward to it.'

'Look at us – academia here we come.'

We clinked cups, the sound of them hitting together ridiculously loud in my pretty much emptied-out room. Our eyes met over the mugs of cheapish champagne and unopened pizza boxes and in rushed another one of those moments; a complexity of emotion bubbling up to consume us. We should kiss. Everything around us was saying we should kiss.

Over the past three years we'd had many, many more of these

interludes, where it felt like everything in the universe was pushing for us to be together. And we hadn't. Not even close.

I'd kissed a few people, had even got to the hands-exploring-bodies-over-clothes stage, but I hadn't gone all the way. And although the Heathettes changed, dwindled in numbers and then swelled in numbers and then dwindled again, Heath was never short of people to get his 'kicks' with, as he called it. We never talked about this complexity, this thing that wasn't going to happen between us. I could tell sometimes, when he was over at our house and we were all having a laugh, that Trina wanted to encourage us together, but after that conversation in the common room, when she realised how close to obsessed he was with me, she never overtly brought it up again.

And here we were again. At that line, at that crossroads, at that moment.

*I might never see him again*, I realised. *It's highly likely I* won't *see him ever again.*

We all knew you made promises to keep in touch, you had good intentions and a will to stay connected. But I was on a part-time, two-year course in London and I had to get a job to support myself while doing it. Trina was going to be busy training in accountancy to eventually become a forensic accountant, and now Heath was going to be training, too. We had the next stage of our lives opening up ahead of us and we wouldn't keep in touch in any meaningful way. We would think about it, talk about it, but not do it.

The interlude stretched, elongated for far longer than usual. Far longer.

The tension started to ignite the air between us: the longing, the heat, the need. Without breaking eye contact, I moved the pizza off my lap onto the floor, I placed my mug on top of the pizza box. Without breaking eye contact he did the same. We both moved until we were kneeling in front of each other, staring at each other, neither of us brave enough to make the first move.

'I'm not gonna—' he began. 'I've got to know that you want to do this so I'm not going to make the first—'

'I've never done this before,' I interrupted in a rush.

'You've never made the first move before?'

'I've never done this before,' I said again, nervous and slightly sick that I had to tell him this. I didn't ever imagine telling him this, nor how he would respond.

'Never done . . . ?'

'Don't make me say it again, H. Please can you just use your big clever brain to understand what I'm telling you.'

He frowned, scrunching up his eyes and face as he did so. Then, *ping*! He got it. He understood. '*Ohhhh*, you've never done *this* before.'

'Yes.'

'And you want to?'

'Yes.'

'With me?'

'Well, not if you're go—'

He closed the gap between us and covered my mouth with his while his hands pulled me closer. I didn't know what to do all of a sudden. Should I keep kneeling, should I put my arms around him, should I put my hands on his face, should I be undressing him?

His hands brushed over my shoulder, then cupped my face and tugged me even closer to him. 'You're so beautiful,' he murmured. 'You're so perfect and so beautiful.'

He kept kissing me as he tugged off my T-shirt, unhooked my bra. I lay down to take off my jeans and knickers, while he quickly undressed himself. After I was naked, lying on my mattress, I cringed a little. I cringed and curled into myself, trying to hide, obscure my body, in the low-light of the room. What would he think of me? What would anyone think of my body, seeing it like this for the first time?

Heath, naked now, sat back and looked at me. I curled even more into myself, using my arms to cover my breasts and stomach. My stomach was not flat – it was generously rounded; my breasts were not perky – they were full and flopped unceremoniously to each side of my body; my hips were not slender – they were threaded with shiny stretch marks. My shiny black pubic hair was not neatly styled or shaped, my thighs met in the middle. I was curvy, I was a normal weight and shape, but right then, with someone seeing me naked for the first time, I was nervous about my body. Unsure. Even slightly worried. Did I match up to the Heathettes? I couldn't. How could I? They were girls (several of them first-years) who took care of themselves. Who may or may not have styled their pubic hair, but sure as hell wore make-up, followed fashion, made sure they looked impossibly good all the time. I wore make-up when I had to – to the graduation ball, for example – but I and my skin were more comfortable without it. I liked my looks, I liked my body, I was who I was.

And who that was, was me. No more, no less.

'Don't do that,' he whispered, just as I decided not to do 'that', and moved my arms away. He sighed then groaned loudly as he took in the sight of me.

'You're even more perfect than I could have imagined,' he murmured before lowering his head and running his tongue over my nipple. Pleasure like I'd never known before bolted through me and I gasped. He moved to the other breast, ran his tongue over that nipple, too, and I gasped again.

As I recovered from that, he slipped his fingers between my legs and then inside me. 'Oh,' I said, surprised by how good it felt and how wrong it felt as well. Should I be doing this? Should this be happening?

Heath pulled away and stared into my eyes, smiling as he pushed his fingers deeper, and my body reacted by moving towards him, moving upwards, trying to get more of him inside me. I wanted him to touch me as deeply as he could. He groaned at the same time as me and my eyes slipped shut as his fingers continued to move inside me and my body craved more and more of this. This was new, there were no real words to describe the feelings coursing through my veins, setting fire to all my nerves.

'Do you want me inside you?' he asked quietly.

Biting down on my lower lip, I nodded. Yes, I wanted him. I wanted him so much. He pulled away, left the bed and went to his bag, flipped it open. While he frantically rummaged inside for a condom, I pulled back the covers and climbed in, the cold cotton a sudden thrill on my skin before I snuggled down.

Heath pulled two condoms out of his bag with such triumph, it was almost like he'd been on a mining expedition and had struck gold. He came back to the bed. 'Are you still all right with this?'

I nodded again, almost drunk with desire now. Him going to get the condoms hadn't made me change my mind, it had made me more sure that I wanted to do this. That I needed to do this. Heath sat back on his haunches, stroking his erection and staring down at my body. Still staring at me, drinking me in as though he couldn't believe he was actually here with me, he tore open the condom wrapper, then slowly rolled it on. Heath reached out for me again, this time he took hold of my thighs, opening my legs.

He moved himself between my legs, the tip of his erection resting

88

against me. He leant down, brought his face close to mine. Kissed me deeply, I kissed him back. He stroked my face as we kissed, I stroked his. I gasped as he suddenly entered me, arched my back, groaned as he pushed deeper.

He broke away from our kiss, his lips millimetres from mine, he whispered: 'Are you OK? Do you want to carry on?'

'Yes . . . yes,' I breathed, 'yes.' And pulled him closer, folded my arms around him, wrapped my legs around him and cried out in pleasure as he thrust deeper and harder into me.

I didn't know it would be like this. That I could feel like this. That I could be as close to someone as this. My fingers dug into his back, wanting him nearer, needing these feelings to completely envelope me. Responding, Heath pulled his face a little further away so he could look into my eyes as he did what I wanted, until he was moving with me, moving deeply, bringing us so close nothing and no one could ever come between us.

## Headingley, 1999

'I'm scared to talk in case I ruin it,' Heath said as we settled down together afterwards, both of us so hungry I almost let him not wash his hands before he ate. Almost, but not quite.

The house was eerily quiet and echoey as I went to the toilet down the hall, so I dashed back and leapt onto the mattress, scrambling to get under the covers as quickly as possible. Heath drank more of the fizz than he ate, while I ate more than I drank.

'I loved seeing you like that. I loved being the one who did that to you,' he said after a huge gulp of fizz from the Incredible Hulk mug. 'I want to keep doing that to you for ever.'

I almost choked on the piece of pizza I had just swallowed and had to wash it down with the warm wine.

'That was fast ruining, even for me.'

'You haven't ruined anything. I just—'

'You just did it with me because you don't think you're going to see me again. You got your jollies and—'

'Don't say that,' I admonished. 'Come on, H. That was incredible. It wasn't my jollies. Or anything like that. I had . . . I couldn't think of a better first time or a better person for it to be with. It was . . . I've never really known what to think about when I think about sex. You can see it simulated on TV and movies, you can read the descriptions in a book or magazine, but I didn't know it could be like that. So . . . so freeing but also like it's tethering me to another person. To you. Is sex always like that?'

Heath put down his cup, and snuggled down in the bed, facing me. 'Thing is, sex is like pizza – good any time you can get it. But it's not like that all the time and certainly not with everybody you sleep with. I've only had sex like that with one other person and that didn't last long. She . . . It didn't work out.'

'Someone at college?'

'No, before college.'

'Why didn't it work out?'

'Not really something I want to talk about right now. Especially not when we've just gone to bed together for the first time.'

I snuggled up closer to him, resting my head on his shoulder, stroking my fingers down his forearm and back up again. 'Tell me,' I encouraged. 'I want to know.'

'Ah, look, it wasn't the best scenario. I was fourteen and she was older. A lot older. She . . . she was my science teacher. We . . . looking back, I can see it was wrong on so many levels. But she was everything to me. She taught me everything I could ever know about love. The sex with her was mind-blowing. She was so nice to me, because, you know, it was my first time and I was worried that she wouldn't enjoy it because I had no clue what I was doing. But she reassured me. Helped me. And it was mind-blowing, like I say.'

'So why didn't it work out?' I asked quietly, because I was shocked. Shocked that he was sleeping with his teacher. His teacher! What was she thinking? Obviously, she wasn't. Obviously, she was a predator and other not very nice things. But Heath had clearly loved her. He clearly still had a lot of feelings for her; I couldn't trample on that by showing my horror at how he was manipulated by this woman. Abused by her. He was under the age of consent, she was older and in a position of power. None of that should have happened, none of that should have been carried forward and acted on by that person.

'What, you mean apart from the obvious abuse of trust and position as a teacher, as well as the illegality of it and general immorality of a much older person having sex and a relationship with someone so much younger who is under the age of consent? You mean why didn't it work out apart from that?'

'I wouldn't have put it like that.'

'I know you wouldn't and that's one of the reasons why I love you. But let's be honest, just because the sex was incredible and I was completely in love with her, doesn't mean it wasn't abusive. And that's why I'm studying Psychology – I want to work out why I got sucked in and I want to help other kids like me not to get sucked in.'

'God, I'm sorry.'

'No, don't say sorry. I don't feel abused. I don't look back and feel anything bad towards her or our relationship. She was amazing to me, she treated me so well, never did anything awful or manipulative or in any way emotionally abusive or threatening. She wanted nothing but the best for me. It was just the situation that was messed up because it should never have existed, if that makes sense?'

'Yes, yes it does. So what happened?'

He was silent for long seconds, staring into the distance. 'I . . . Look, she'd done it before, had relationships with teen boys in her care. So when her husband found out about me, he killed her.'

I sat up. '*What?* I mean, what?'

'It was grim. Really grim. He's in prison for it now. Thankfully they didn't have any children, but I still get completely freaked out and want to throw up when I think about it.'

I was speechless and we fell into silence for long minutes. 'Did you have to give evidence and everything?' I eventually asked.

'No, he confessed. He went to the police and confessed right after he did it. He did name me, though, so I was forced to change my name. Well, use my middle name. Heath is my middle name. Sawyer is my mother's maiden name – I started using them when we moved to a new area just outside London and started at a new school. It wasn't actually that long ago. And, like I say, I still want to throw up when I think about it.'

I cuddled up to him. Heath was not who I thought he was. Not at all. He was so much more. He had been in so much pain. I couldn't imagine how it must have felt to lose someone you love in those circumstances. 'You must have been in so much pain,' I said to him, stroking his face. 'So much heartbreak. I had no idea.'

'Heartbreak. Never thought of that. It was so loud at the time and I always think of heartbreak as quiet, private.' He kissed me gently and quickly. 'I do avoid thinking about it, though. And that's why I could accept you didn't want me. I've seen where jealousy and obsession can take you. What it can do to your mind.' He pressed his lips onto mine again, a bit firmer this time and for a bit longer. 'Is this going to be a one-off, Cleo?' He spoke hesitantly, the worry tremoring lightly through every word.

'It kind of has to be, doesn't it?' I replied. 'Tomorrow we go off to our new lives. We all have good intentions of keeping in touch, but we never do it. Let's just accept this for the amazing interlude it is and move on.'

'You don't even want to try to see each other in London?'

'London's a big place. A HUGE place. You know that. We're both going to be so busy. I think we need to accept this is, unfortunately, a one-off thing.'

'I don't agree.'

'Fair enough.'

'I think you'll come back to me. In fact, I know you'll always come back to me. But OK, we can accept this as a one-off thing.' He twirled one of my plaits around his finger. 'I think, though, if tonight is all we've got, then we have to make the most of it . . . if you know what I mean.'

'I do know what you mean and, on this, I think we both agree.'

Before we fell asleep, one thing he said floated back to me among all the things we'd talked about during the evening: 'You'll come back to me. I know you'll always come back to me.'

There was something in that which sounded terrifyingly true.

# Part 2

Part 2

# 8

## West London, 2000

'I really don't know why you're putting yourself through all this stress,' Heath told me.

I'd just put down the phone to an estate agent who had told me I hadn't been successful in my application for a houseshare. A houseshare! It wasn't even that nice, just convenient because it was in the right area. I needed somewhere to live that would be easy to get to college from, as well as to and from work. Travelling halfway across London every day from my parents' house was slowly killing my soul.

I lay back on his bed, my arms thrown out to the side, my eyes closed, my mind racing as it tried to work out what I was supposed to do. Living with my parents was not it. At all. I could tell they weren't exactly thrilled by me being there, either. They were torn between enjoying having another adult in the house who was paying them a nominal amount of rent and having to navigate the fact that whenever their daughter was out of the house and didn't come home, she was probably having sex or drinking or behaving in heathen ways. Efie, who had finessed her place in the house since I (and our older sister, Adjua) left, was not happy having me there, either. She'd got our parents to a place where they barely noticed if she was there or not, but since there was the possibility of two of us being there, one of us being there or neither of us being there, our parents were always on alert – waiting for someone to appear. Which led to questions that Efie did not like answering.

More than once recently she'd asked when I was moving on, like it wasn't my childhood home, too. Not that I liked being questioned by my parents, either. Every day was a step closer to one of us losing the plot and saying something unforgivable.

I was loving my Masters. I found the stuff I was learning about magazine and newspaper publishing so fascinating, being given the space and structure to write was incredible and I was on track to get some work experience soon on a national newspaper magazine. All of that was good. But each element came with something fraught. Especially my fast-approaching work experience. Having to travel there, travel to lectures some days and then travel to the bar where I worked evenings was going to break me, I knew it was.

Heath's head suddenly appeared above mine, he turned down the corners of his mouth. 'Awww, poor sad starfish,' he cooed. 'I don't like to see you like this. And I honestly don't know why you're putting yourself through this.'

'I need somewhere to live,' I said miserably.

Heath came back to the other side of the bed and climbed on top of me. With his nimble fingers, he started to undo the small white buttons on my black denim shirt. 'Just move in here,' he said. 'There's plenty of room. You can even have your own room.'

'Here' was the palatial Victorian mansion flat he'd bought in Hammersmith with the help of his parents. They'd given him the money for a large deposit so he could benefit from his inheritance now rather than at some unspecified point in the future and he had put it to excellent use. It had been run-down when he first got it, but he didn't care because it made his life a lot easier with being able to travel easily to his work/training place in Chelsea, and he'd been extra smart future-proofing it by buying a place with three giant bedrooms. The proportions were extremely generous and all the rooms had high ceilings, large windows that let light flood in. He was slowly restoring it to its previous glory with a modern twist. I would have loved to live in a place like this. If one came up for rent in my price range, I wouldn't think twice about moving in. But . . .

'No,' I replied. 'Thank you, but no.'

Last button undone, he splayed open my top, exposing my black lacy bra. I watched him swallow with naked lust, and I felt him shift on top of me as though equal amounts of pleasure and pain were pumping through him. 'Why not?' he asked, his voice suddenly dusky and breathy. He ran his hands slowly over my breasts, his fingers pausing to tease my nipples.

'Because it would feel like we're moving in together when we're still . . . doing whatever this is.'

'There's so much space, we wouldn't be on top of each other. You can have your own room, we can be flatmates.'

His fingers were undoing the metal buttons on my jeans and he couldn't see the irony of what he was pretending. 'Heath, I can't do that. I can't live with you.'

'Why not?'

'It's . . . you're too intense, as Trina once said.'

That stopped him undressing me. He sat back on his haunches, frowning. 'Trina said that? I thought she liked me?'

'She does like you. She adores you, in fact. She was a Heath fan from way back, and she was a Heath-and-Cleo supporter well before I would even consider it. But even she can see that you're too intense, especially when it comes to me. I don't know why, but you are. It wouldn't be fair on either of us if I moved in.'

'I can be less intense.'

I took his hands, pressed them between mine. 'Sweetheart, I don't want you to change who you are for me. You are you and that's wonderful. But you have no real life outside of us. You don't mention any friends, so I'm guessing you don't really have any. You've got this great job and you're meeting new people all the time but you don't go out for drinks with them or anything. I mean, are there even any Heathettes on the scene?'

'Why would there be Heathettes – stupid name by the way – when I'm with you?' His face twisted then. 'Hang on, are *you* seeing other people?'

I sighed internally.

Slowly but deliberately, he tugged his hands out of my hold. 'Are you?' he asked again. The huskiness was gone, replaced by what could only be described as a slow-burning anger.

'Not exactly.'

'What does that mean?'

'It means someone who I work with in the bar asked me out and I thought about it. I said no eventually, but I didn't rule it out like I would if I had a proper boyfriend.'

He was off the bed then. Standing a little way away, staring at me. *Glaring* at me. 'How many people have you slept with?' he asked tightly.

'Why are you asking me that question?' I replied, sitting up slowly and concentrating on doing up my buttons. Doing up my buttons meant keeping my head lowered and not having to face this music. Its tune was not sweet, its melody was not soothing, its lyrics would only burn.

*Your own fault for getting involved with someone so intense,* Trina would have said.

'Cos I want to know,' he replied in a deadpan voice.

'You said, when you went to Australia for those three months, that we weren't together,' I prefaced. 'You said it. Not me. I didn't. You.'

'I know what I said,' he stated in the same deadpan voice. Or was it the same? Were those little beads of aggression pushing through? 'I also know that since I was your first, if you say you've slept with any-one other than me, then you've . . . we'll come to that when you answer this question, I suppose. How many other people have you slept with?'

Heath was good-looking in a way I wasn't moved by. What I liked about Heath was nothing to do with his looks. It was his mind, his humour – when he relaxed – his companionship, his good heart. When we were together and he was relaxed, it was so comfortable, soothing almost – but with the added bonus of mind-blowing sex.

'None,' I said, looking him directly in the eye so he would know I was telling the truth. So he would have no reason to doubt that. It was easy to do because it was true.

'None?' he queried, obviously not believing me.

'None. I haven't slept with anyone else,' I stated again. Then I took a deep breath. 'But I did kiss someone. A guy from the college who I met on a night out. We were both very drunk and he kissed me and I kissed him back.'

'But you didn't make love to him?'

'No,' I replied straight away, immediately, again so he would know I was telling the truth. 'No. No. No.' I fixed Heath with my gaze again. 'And we weren't together. *You* made sure of that. Which is why I haven't asked what you got up to while you were in Australia.'

'Nothing. I got up to nothing. Not even vaguely tempted to because all I could do was think about you. And I said we weren't together because I wanted to prove to myself and to you that you cared enough about me to be faithful even if you didn't have to be.'

'How can I be faithful to a guy who basically dumped me before he went off to a country chock-full of the type of women he usually goes for?' I fired back at Heath, the hurt from his words still burning through me. 'I'm sorry I failed your little test, Heath, maybe next time let me know I'm going to be examined and I'll revise a little harder.'

'Don't try to turn this on me. You were the one who said we should leave that last night in Leeds as a one-night stand.'

'And you were the one who agreed. And then changed your mind and begged me to go out with you. And then six months later, "I'm off to Oz for additional training and to see my family over there, don't wait up for me, think I might test out my dick while I'm there, see you later, Cleo, you loser."'

'Come on, I didn't say that.'

'No, you didn't, but as good as.'

Things were getting heated and I knew I should calm down but I didn't want to. He'd humiliated me. That was the bottom line. After the night in Leeds, we'd parted on good terms, and then he had called me and called me. Every night for two months he called me, begged me to keep seeing him, to give us a chance. I relented because, truth was, I missed him. I was also surprised because I could feel something. I understood what the big deal was about sex now and I missed the connection I had with him through sex. And then, six months later . . . 'You said, "I don't know if this connection between us is strong enough to last three months apart, so I think it's best we split up while I'm away. It's best that I keep my options open in case I get the chance to explore new pastures. It's not like we're that serious, is it?"' I tried to rein in my anger, the furious tears it brought up. 'That's what you said, wasn't it? *Wasn't it?*'

He nodded but said nothing, maybe because he could see the anger and the humiliation. Maybe because he could see the hurt at hearing those things before he got on an aeroplane and left me.

'How many times did you kiss this guy?' Heath eventually asked. 'After the first time.'

'Two more times.'

'And you honestly didn't make love to him?'

'I honestly didn't. I think I did it because I missed you and I was convinced you were having fun with someone else. I didn't like feeling like that.'

'And you haven't seen him since?'

'No. He's not on my course. And we don't go drinking in the student bar any more.'

'Fine,' he said. 'Fine. If you're not still seeing him—'

'I was never seeing him, Heath, and at the time I wasn't seeing you. In fact, I'm not sure if we're seeing each other now, since we haven't had "the talk" and you haven't taken the "we're not together" edict back. Which all adds to the reasons why I can't move in here. Not even as a flatmate.'

'All right,' he said, deflating slightly. 'When you put it like that, I can see that I was out of order. And a little controlling. I'm sorry.'

'Apology accepted,' I replied. I could tell he wanted me to apologise for kissing someone else, but I wasn't going to. He made the rules and if he didn't like it when I played by them, that was not my problem.

When he realised I wasn't about to apologise, he dropped his gaze with a wry smile on his handsome face. 'Do you want another beer?' he asked.

'Yes, please,' I replied.

He kissed me quickly and lightly on the lips before leaving the room. I flopped back onto the bed.

All right, I was probably playing with semantics to get out of telling him all of what happened with the guy, Ethan, that I kissed. We went back to his room on campus, we'd kissed some more and then he'd gone down on me. It was his 'thing', he loved to do it and . . . well, I was single. I'd been told so by the guy I wasn't even properly seeing. So yes, I'd let him do that to me and I had blissed out and I'd willingly got him off manually. But there'd been no intercourse, no lovemaking, just sexual contact. All three times.

Semantics. Twisting, using, *abusing* words to suit your agenda. To suit the narrative you wanted to create. To save yourself the pain of having the same conversation over and over. Because I knew Heath. I knew how possessive and territorial his love could be. And the thing is, I had done nothing wrong. And because I had done nothing wrong, I didn't have to tell him about it. Not if I thought it would hurt him.

I wasn't being dishonest – I was using semantics to save us both a lot of pain.

Because Heath and I couldn't go on like this.

He was too intense for me. He was too intense for us to stay together. I had to end it.

'There you go,' he said, holding a dark, sweating bottle of American beer.

'Cheers, m'dear,' I replied.

I had to end it sooner rather than later. For both our sakes.

# 9

'Change of plan.' Franklyn is upon me the moment I walk through the front door. I haven't even had a chance to put my keys back in my pocket before he is there, right in front of me. It's been a long day, working in the HoneyMay Production offices. I've made more progress, but I'm still at the wanting-to-cry, throw-my-computer-and-drink-sugary-coffee stage. And I still have many long nights ahead of me. I didn't manage to get through to the solicitor, either.

I had been planning on coming home, having a long shower and then climbing into bed to start working again.

'Change of plan,' Franklyn says again.

'OK,' I reply and draw back at his general personal space invasion.

'Lola isn't coming this weekend,' he says quickly.

'Fine.'

'She's here now. Her mother had an emergency and she couldn't take her with her, couldn't leave her there alone, either, because of the school summer holidays, so she's here.'

'OK, fine,' I say cautiously, not sure what the problem is.

'You're cool with it? Yeah? No worries?'

'Of course. This is your home, which means it's her home and you can both come and go as you please. Thought you knew that.'

'Yeah, but don't want to be taking the proverbial, and all that. Especially with all that mess you got going on.' He lowers his voice for the last bit.

'There's no mess, Franklyn. We've sorted it all out.' The heat of humiliation at how he told us off at dinner two nights ago rises through me. I can't look at him right now.

'Yeah, all right. Problem is, though . . .'

*I might have known*, I think. 'Problem is . . . ?' I supply to his sudden silence.

He lowers his voice. 'I may have a "mess" sitch without the "mess" going on myself. Brighton's been all right to me, you know.' He nods appreciatively. 'I thought I was free till the weekend and made "plans" for the next few days, if you know what I mean?'

I know what he means, so I nod.

'So . . . ?' he whispers leadingly.

'So . . . ?' I reply.

'Come on, C, you gonna help a brother out or what?'

'Course. You only had to ask,' I say.

'I was asking.'

'That wasn't—you know what, never mind. What time are you going out?'

'Half an hour ago.'

'And where's Wallace?'

Franklyn's face – my husband's face – draws in suddenly and he looks uncomfortable. His body shrinks slightly, he looks awkward, as though he wishes the background would claim him, would allow him to suddenly and inexplicably blend in so he doesn't have to deal with this. He steps away a little. 'You know Wallace,' he adds, as though that's going to explain everything.

'Yes, yes, I do. But I don't know where he is right now. Especially since you won't be here to help me take care of Lola—'

As if my speaking of her has conjured her, she appears from the turn at the end of the corridor. 'Auntie Cleo,' she says with a huge grin.

I'd forgotten how much I like to see her face, how I miss her like an echo of my heart, how I always love to see her warm brown skin, her beautiful big eyes, her full, plump lips that are always ready to twist into a smile and her shiny black hair that has been plaited into two large cornrows that go down to her shoulders.

'Niece Lola,' I reply, matching her tone.

'On a scale of one to a million, how badly have I messed up your evening plans?' she asks. She has the measure of her father so knows that he's got plans that don't involve her.

'About a minus fifty. I had no plans except work this evening, so you being here is the best thing.'

'I can help with your work,' she says confidently. 'You can count on me.'

'Don't be bothering your auntie now,' Franklyn says to his thirteen-year-old. 'Just go to your room and read after dinner, all right? You know what time bed is.'

'Oh shush, You've got your plans, we've got ours,' I say to my brother-in-law. 'Don't mind him, Niece Lola.'

'OK, OK.' Franklyn nods approvingly. 'I'll go and finish getting ready.'

'You do that,' Lola and I say at the same time.

Franklyn goes off to get ready without telling me where my husband is.

## South London, 2003

My desk seemed to be a fairly accurate indicator of my internal world right now. Four glasses of water at various heights, depending on how much had been drunk, sat in a row at the back of the desk like football players waiting to defend against a free kick. My *Star Trek* novelty mousemat was askew, having not known the touch of a computer mouse in years. The computer mouse could be found on the other side of my desk, the little rollerball out of control and basically useless. A packet of mints lay in front of the desktop keyboard, opened and slowly being consumed whenever I remembered it was there. A couple of Sharpies, lids firmly on, lay next to the mousemat, keeping it company like silent sentinels. In front of the glasses of water were three over-sharpened pencils that looked ready to start a fight their cuts were so severe. A nearly empty tube of hand cream stood upright near the corner of the desk where the desktop computer cable snaked up from the wall plug. A book of stamps peeked out from under the keyboard, while tangled headphones languished over my monitor. This was my desk, my mess, my life, really – things butting up against each other, misplaced, out of place, but still existing and not doing anyone any harm.

I had just left a full-time job and was back freelancing for women's magazines. I'd essentially got the job working for a small but popular magazine so I could have a steady income and get the money to buy a flat in South London. South-East London – the other side of the city to where my parents lived and where I grew up. I'd gone back to freelancing so I could do my other job, the one no one was paying me for – write a book.

Writing books and writing a movie had always been my dream. And, I'd realised recently, no one was going to come and give me a publishing deal, no one was going to ask me to create a TV show or movie for them. I had to do it and then try to get the book published, I had to write it and try to get a TV show or movie made. This was the dream.

And this was me living the dream. With my messy desk and messy flat and bucketloads of self-motivation. I stared at words on the screen. They'd made sense when I wrote them a moment ago. They were right and appropriate and perfect for what I was trying to say. Reading them over now, I was . . . *confused*. Why did I think that word was right? Why did I think that sentence meant anything? Why did I think I could put enough words together to create an actual book?

I let my head drop onto my desk, avoiding the Sharpies and mints and over-sharpened pencils. I stared at the window that had its cream cloth blinds down, and tried to make out the shapes from the world beyond them.

The simple answer was that I was having troubling creating an actual book. Writing one was significantly harder than reading one. Writing one was immensely more difficult than editing an article and finding the right headline and voice for that particular publication. Finding the right characters, tone and take-your-breath-away plot while sustaining it for more than three hundred pages was way more difficult than anything I'd attempted so far.

I was loving it, that was undeniable, but it was *HARD!* I'd honestly thought I'd finished this book. Now I was rewriting it. When I rewrote one part, though, another part would need to be fixed. Once I fixed that, another part would have unravelled and would need restitching. It was never-ending. At least that's how it felt at three a.m. on a Saturday morning when I was seriously questioning every single ability I previously thought I had.

Thing was, I'd been avoiding a truth, and with every passing day that truth was doing more and more to make sure I paid attention to it. The truth did not like to be ignored so was asserting itself in every way possible. The truth?

I had to start again. I had to rip it up (metaphorically) and start again. New characters, new plot, new setting, new writing. New book.

What a revelation to come to at three a.m.!

*Ring-ring-ring!* cut into the middle-of-the-night quiet of my flat and I nearly leapt out of my skin. My mobile phone was on the other side of the room, but I didn't need to see the lit display to know who it would be. My gaze went to the large white-and-black clock face on the wall above my printer. It was indeed three a.m. So it was definitely going to be him.

He did this: got drunk, called, begged me to give him another chance. He hadn't called in nearly five months, though, so I'd thought it was properly over, that he was finally over it.

I was obviously wrong. I sighed heavily. I knew I shouldn't answer his calls. Answering his calls was part of the problem, probably, but I couldn't help myself. I couldn't not answer because the simple truth was I didn't want Heath to suffer.

Knowing that I had to train myself out of this, I crossed the room to my phone. This was going to get me into trouble – being too nice, being too available; my innate need to help and comfort. It's what got me into this situation in the first place. What would my life have been like if I'd just told Heath no and hadn't tried to help him? Would I be picking up the phone in the middle of the night, raising it to my ear and saying, 'Hello?'

Silence.

Silence.

Silence.

'Hello?' I said again, slightly perturbed.

'It's me,' he said, but his voice did not sound like his. It sounded flat – no, no, it sounded devastated. 'I didn't know who else to call. He's gone. My dad's . . .' Silence again. 'My dad's gone. Heart attack. Massive. Nothing anyone could do. He's gone.'

'Where are you?' I asked, already moving towards my bedroom to get changed.

'Home . . . Mum's at the hospital . . . Can't drive, Cleo. Can't move . . . He's gone. He's gone.'

'I'll be there soon,' I said. 'We'll go to your mum's together, all right? Stay there. Try to keep warm. I'll be there as soon as I can.'

'Thanks. I knew you'd know what to do. Thanks.'

## *Richmond upon Thames, 2003*

Since his father's death, I'd somehow become a part of Heath's family. I was involved in all the decisions and drove him and his mother to various appointments because they were both still too shaken and shocked; unable to do anything without prompting. They moved like zombies in their own lives, listless and virtually lifeless, and they both looked to me whenever a decision had to be made. I did the best I could, choosing food, picking hymns, explaining forms that needed to be signed, sometimes putting pens into their hands so they could do the signing. At night, when I'd helped his mother to bed, I sat up with Heath, holding him when he cried, pouring him drinks when he couldn't do anything but stare into space.

They needed me and there never seemed to be a moment when I could back out and leave them to it.

And now I stood at the door of the big church just around the corner from their house, handing out the order of service to black-clad mourners as they entered. I was in automatic mode – removed enough to not feel anything, present enough to offer small, sympathetic smiles to the people who arrived.

'Babe,' Trina's husky voice said right beside me.

When I looked up and it was actually her, I couldn't restrain myself and threw my arms around her. Hugging her was beautiful. The knots of tension and adopted grief melted away and I could suddenly remember what it was like to breathe without a tight band around my chest, how pleasant it was to move my face to make a smile. 'Thank God you're here,' I whispered into her hair.

'SBBF at your service,' she whispered as she clung just as tightly to me. 'And if you don't acknowledge the multilevel, elite punning going on there, I will truly believe I raised you wrong.'

I clung even tighter to her. Trina was exactly what I needed today.

Trina, Heath and I sat in Heath's parents' plush living room. After the wake, which had been in a church hall, a few people had come back to the house to stand around in groups, drinking whiskey and talking in low voices. Eventually they'd left and I'd helped Heath's mother to bed as usual. She never spoke as I stood facing the door while she changed and dressed in her nightclothes, never said a word when I pulled the blanket up over her and snapped off the bedside light. I touched her cheek as usual and then shut the door carefully behind me. I knew she didn't speak because she didn't know what to say. She couldn't work out the point of words, of existing, now that he had gone.

By the time I returned to the living room, Trina and Heath had tidied away the glasses and napkins and had set the dishwasher going to clean away all traces that other people were ever there. Heath and Trina sat at opposite ends of the large leather sofa that faced the television, while I sat on the sofa in the bay window. We sat in silence for a long time, taking it all in, processing it in our minds.

'This is like old times,' Heath eventually said, breaking the silence. 'The three of us sitting here is exactly like old times.'

'For it to be like old times, you'd have to be sat over there staring at this one,' Trina quipped. Her time in Leeds had started to make inroads on her London accent. Her children with Steadman – eighteen months and three – both had adorably strong Yorkshire accents.

'True,' Heath replied with a vague smile. Today had been good for him, I realised. It seemed to have snapped him out of the daze he'd been in and he'd begun to communicate and engage with the world, talking to people, remembering his father. He'd undone the top button of his midnight-black shirt and the matching tie was also loosened. He still had his jacket on, though, meaning he hadn't completely relaxed. 'But I became one of you eventually.'

'Eventually,' Trina said. 'And you were most welcome.'

'Yes, most welcome,' I intoned. While it'd been good for Heath, the funeral had taken a huge toll on me. I was slowing down, my ability to keep going and keep them going these past few weeks finally running out. I felt like I'd been whacked with a lorry, and I wanted nothing more than to lay my head down on the sofa arm and go to sleep.

Trina rested her head back. 'Is this it, then? We're only going to be seeing each other at funerals from now on?' she said sadly.

'Hope not,' I replied, fighting against the tiredness that kept shutting my eyes. 'All the movies and books I've read and watched have led me to believe that our twenties and thirties are going to be all about weddings and births. Not funerals. I will be seriously pissed off if that's not the case. I can take most things, but not being misled about the number of wedding outfits I'm going to need in my twenties and thirties.'

'Same. Same. So, when can I expect the invite to your wedding?' Trina said idly, her eyes closed, too. 'Am I bride or groom in those circumstances? Only kidding, course I'm bride cos I'm the brides-maid! Or is it matron of honour since I got married first?'

An awkward silence blew into the room and expanded, almost immediately filling the whole room with an uncomfortable, self-conscious quiet. I'd told Trina we'd slept together that last night in Leeds, I'd told her that he'd persuaded me to go out with him, I even told her that we'd essentially split up when he couldn't come to her wedding because he was in Australia. I'd told her we'd got back together on his return and then had needed a bit of a break but were still in touch. But I hadn't told her when that had become me actively avoiding him so he could move on. I was circumspect about Heath whenever Trina asked what was going on, which she probably took to mean I didn't want to jinx things by chatting about it but we were together. Me ringing her to tell her about Heath's dad must have con-firmed that assumption for her.

'What? What have I said?' she asked, lifting her head. 'Why are you both acting like I've just let one off in polite company?'

'I've, erm, I've got a girlfriend,' Heath said, uncomfortable enough to fiddle with his collar and shift in his seat.

Trina's whole body sat bolt upright. At the same time, my eyes widened in alarm. 'You've got a girlfriend?' Trina asked, frowning at him like she wasn't sure what she was hearing right then.

'Yeah,' Heath replied.

'One that's not Cleo?'

'One that's not Cleo,' he confirmed.

In response, my best friend's face scrunched up in disbelief and disgust. 'Did you know about this?' she asked, rounding on me like I had done something wrong.

I sat back in the sofa, pinned by the ferocity of her glare. 'No,' I said, 'I knew nothing about this.' Alarm bells were clanging all over the place right now. If Heath had a girlfriend, what the hell was he doing spending every second of the past two and half weeks with me? He'd even persuaded me to let him climb into bed with me a couple of times. Nothing had happened, except him resting his head on my shoulder and then leaving before either of us fell asleep. But if he had a girlfriend, what the hell did he think he was doing?

'How long have you been seeing her?' Trina asked, rounding on him now.

'Erm . . . I suppose about six months . . . to a year?' he offered, his voice getting quieter and quieter with each word until 'year' was barely a whisper.

'A year?!' Trina screeched quietly so as not to disturb his mother. 'And you honestly didn't know about this?' she asked me.

I shook my head. 'Nope.' I did not know. I would not have entertained drunk, late-night calls pleading with me to let him come over to talk, begging to make love to me one last time, practically crying to come over to hold me, if I had. I would not have considered possibly going back to him the last time he begged me five months ago.

'So where is she?' Trina asked, back on his case. 'What does she look like? Who was she today? And why isn't she here now, throwing down a couple of drinks with us?'

Heath slid down so much in his seat he was virtually horizontal as he tried to hide. Neither Trina nor I said anything as we waited for his response. 'I didn't . . . I didn't think it was appropriate,' he finally said. 'She didn't really know my dad. She only met him a few times. It wouldn't have been appropriate.'

Trina scrunched up her face even more as the disgust deepened. 'Why you lying, homeboy?' she said, her Trinidadian accent suddenly out in full force.

'What makes you think I'm lying?'

'Did Cleo even meet your pa? Even at graduation?'

The answer was no and we all knew it, so Heath retreated into silence.

'So why you lying?'

He sighed, rolled his eyes to the heavens. 'She has an issue with Cleo.'

'I've never met the woman,' I said in protest, in case Trina thought I was one of those 'I don't want him, but no one else can have him' types.

'The issue being . . . ?'

'She thinks I'm still in love with Cleo. She thinks if Cleo gave me any indication at all that she was interested, I'd be back with her like a shot.'

'So far, no lies detected,' Trina replied.

'And she went to issue an ultimatum about the funeral but I intervened, told her not to make any bold statements or ultimatums because when it came down to it, I wouldn't choose her. She decided not to come to the funeral.'

'You mean, you told her not to come,' Trina corrected.

'No, I told her she was welcome to come. I would love to have her there, but I also said Cleo would be there as my main support and that was that.'

'That's pretty harsh, Heath,' I said, shocked at him. 'Actually, it's quite cruel.' I'd never thought of him as cruel.

'What am I supposed to say to her?' he snapped in return. ' "Yeah, I'll give up one of my closest friends for you, woman-I've-been-sticking-my-dick-in-for-a-year?" '

Trina and I both drew back. 'That's actually disgusting, Heath,' Trina spat at him.

'Really disgusting,' I added. 'I hope you never speak about me that way.'

Heath raised his hands and flopped them down in frustration. 'My dad's just died. I am not being . . . I'm being a bastard. All right. I wouldn't ever say that to her. Or about her in front of anyone else, only you two. I hope you know that. I'm just broken. *Broken*. I can't get my head around losing him like that. One minute there, the next minute gone.'

I remembered suddenly what he would say on the rare occasions I could get him to open up about his first lover, his science teacher who had been murdered by her husband. What always came through clearest in everything he said was how it horrified him that people could simply stop being. That they could be there one moment and then gone the next. This must be a reminder of that. Of the fragility of life. How suddenly it could be taken away.

'Fuck,' he said, rubbing his eyes. 'I'm going to have to finish with her, aren't I? It's not enough that he dies, I'm going to have to give up someone I actually quite like.'

'Don't do that,' I said.

'Yeah, don't do that,' Trina added. 'Not for Cleo. Not when she has a boyfriend.'

Heath snatched his hands away from his eyes, then slowly slid up until he was sitting properly again. 'You've got a boyfriend?' he asked.

I nodded slightly.

'Why didn't you tell me?'

'You didn't ask,' I replied, now feeling really uncomfortable.

'And he hasn't minded you being with me the past couple of weeks?'

'Why would he? We're just friends and you're going through a terrible time so you've needed my help.'

My ex-lover, one of my best friends, returned to staring at the black TV screen, then slowly started to rub his eyes again.

'Don't go there, Heath,' Trina warned suddenly. It was such a warning, I had to look at her as well. 'Don't start losing your mind over Cleo again. I love the woman, absolutely love her, but she is not worth losing your sanity over. What would you say to one of your clients about this? Wouldn't you tell him to stick with the woman he's with? That while he might not be wild about her, not to make any huge sudden changes while bereaved because that would be clouding everything? Let the dust settle. Give yourself a break.'

'Since when did you become a psychologist?' Heath asked.

'No psychology qualifications needed, just a pure and total love for the two of you. I don't want you to mess up your friendship by going there when neither of you are ready or free.'

'You're right,' Heath said eventually.

'Course I am. Always right, me. Heath, babe, break out the good rum. Let's toast your old man in style.'

Once I'd watched his black-suited form cross the corridor heading for the kitchen and we were alone in the room, I leant towards Trina. 'Why did you tell him I had a boyfriend?' I whispered. I kept my eyes on the doorway so I could see when Heath was on his way back.

'Because he's cracking up as it is. You can see that. Last thing he needs is to get back to where he was with you. You as well, you need to not get sucked back in. He's too intense anyway, imagine what he'd be like now.' She shook her head. 'Nah, he needs a break, you both do.' She was right, of course, but I didn't like lying. It would be all too easy to catch me out, which would cause so much more hurt and upset.

When Heath came back, he carried three heavy cut-crystal glasses and a bottle of dark amber liquid. He crossed the room, handing a glass to Trina as he passed her, then instead of returning to his seat on the sofa with her, he came and plonked himself down beside me. Close. Far too close.

He held out a glass to me and as my fingers closed around it, Heath didn't let go. Instead, he tugged it towards his body while staring straight at me. His eyes, those hypnotic green eyes, held mine while our bodies were connected by the glass.

'Hi,' he whispered softly.

'Hi,' I replied just as softly.

I lowered my gaze and smiled, accepted the glass.

Trina's warning was too late. Heath was right back there. And for some reason, it looked like I was there, too.

# 10

'I have to tell you, Niece Lola, I like you helping me with my work like this.'

We sit on the sofa, feet up on the two large round poufs covered in Kente material that my mum got for us the last time she visited Ghana. We have crisps in large bowls resting on our stomachs and big glasses of pineapple and soda water sweating on the side table. And we're watching her school nativity videos, of which we have many, and ranking them in terms of cuteness, accuracy and overall production values. So far, Reception's version is kicking every other year's ass.

'I also approve of this activity,' she says sagely. 'I approve of checking my cuteness through the ages. It's a trip.'

'It sure is.'

'So you and Uncle Wals are over for real?' she says without warning. It winds me, to hear someone else say it.

'What makes you ask that?'

'You grown-ups, you honestly think me and my age mates don't know anything, huh?'

'I guess so.'

She gently puts her hand on my arm, makes her face serious, concerned and understanding. 'You want to talk about it?'

'No, sweetheart, I do not want to talk about it. What I do want to talk about is how it's possible for your extra-cute Reception Joseph to become bad-boy shepherd number three in Year Three.'

'It's OK,' she says, nodding sagely and patting my arm like she would an elderly aunt's, which, it pains me to admit, she probably thinks of me as, 'you're still at the pain stage; you're not ready to talk about it so you're deflecting, changing the subject. All very normal. When you're ready to talk, I'll be here.' She picks up her glass and takes a huge drink, smacks her lips and then says again: 'I'll be here.'

*I'm sure you will*, I think. *I'm sure you will. But no one can help me right now. No one can be there for me.*

## Leeds, 2003

When I was in college, I contracted pneumonia.

Obviously, I didn't know it was pneumonia and thought a couple of Lemsips would sort it. It was only when my mum threatened to get on the train to Leeds that I went to the doctor. Who told me I'd been partying too much. I duly relayed this to my nurse mother who told me that she would see me in five or six hours so she could take me to A&E.

At which point Trina called a taxi and we used what little money we had to get to Jimmy's (St James's Hospital), which was right in the centre of Leeds. After waiting a lifetime, I was told that it wasn't a cold, that it wasn't too much partying, it was pneumonia. Quite a serious case and I was so ill I had to be admitted to hospital straight away to have intravenous drugs pumped into me. My mum was, as always, proved right (like all of us didn't know that already), and I got a five-night stay in hospital as well as weeks off college recovering.

Since I'd left Jimmy's – in a car that Heath borrowed from a friend – I hadn't been back. Until that day. When I was running through the corridors, trying to find Trina.

She'd been mugged.

She'd been stabbed.

No one could convince me she was all right until I saw her myself. The corridors all looked the same – the same bland colour on the walls, the same bland colours on the rubberised floor, the same slightly earthy disinfectant smell crawling up my nose whichever corridor I ran down. I could hear my feet as I turned corners, trying to follow the directions I'd been given but not having a clue where I was going.

I rounded a corner and suddenly there it was in front of me, the gynaecology ward, the only place they had room for her, apparently. I slowed down before I approached the wooden-coloured doors, rested my hands on my thighs, tried to heave air into my lungs.

When I called him and told him, Heath had wanted to come with me but couldn't get the time off work. I was back working full-time and had told my boss on the phone it was an emergency and hadn't bothered to find out if it was going to be a problem me taking time off. I literally couldn't care about anything except getting to Trina.

I asked the nurse behind the large circular counter where I could find her and she looked as though she was going to tell me about visiting hours. But she must have seen the terror etched into my features, which had been there since I got the call, so directed me to the room she was in. 'But keep it down,' she said.

The room had six hospital beds, with a large picture window taking up the wall opposite the entrance. I spotted Trina straight away – she was in the bed nearest the window, and I had to stop myself running the short distance to gather her in my arms. Restraining myself, I pulled the curtain around, giving us privacy, then sat down.

'Babe,' she said as soon as we were sealed in, 'you didn't have to come. That's why I told Steadman not to tell you. I knew you'd do something like this.'

'Oh get lost! Like I'm not coming.'

I moved in to hug her and she flinched, scared that I might hurt her. I froze, then backed away, sat in the chair. 'What happened?' I asked her. She was connected to a drip, the canula taped in place on the back of her hand. Her shoulder-length relaxed hair was swept back off her face, emphasising the beautiful shape of her features – her amazing large brown eyes, her full, bow-shaped lips, her broad nose; she was a real beauty, my friend. The thought that someone could hurt her terrified me. What if that had been it? What if I'd never got the chance to see her again? Tears sprang to my eyes.

'What are you crying for, you silly mare?'

'Because I can't believe someone could do this to you.'

'All right, yeah, you have my permission to cry.'

'What happened?' I asked again, dabbing at the corner of my eyes with my sleeve.

'I don't even know,' she replied. 'I mean, you know me, I'm no hero. Someone comes up to me and asks for something, they're getting it, no arguments. I'm in the car park at work, it's divorce season – the amount of people who are trying to hide assets at this time of year is no joke! I'm opening my car door, box of stuff in one hand, bag over the other shoulder, and then someone's behind me. I drop the box in fright.

'First of all, I thought he was going to . . . and I freeze. Couldn't move. And then he says, "Give me all your money." So I lifted my arm, managed to get the bag off, and dropped it for him. But he wasn't interested in it. He kind of came closer and I felt him pushing something in my side. Then he says, "Keep your mouth shut," spins me round and then . . .' She stops talking and her whole body tenses up. She holds herself rigid as, I imagine, she is reliving the moment.

'It's OK, it's OK,' I soothe, stroking her forearm, gently taking her hand.

'It happened so fast. The next thing I knew I was lying on the ground. I didn't really see anything. He picked up my bag, took my purse and then . . . this is the weird bit . . . he took out my mobile phone and dialled 999.'

'What?'

'Yeah, he dialled 999, said, "Ambulance," gave them the name of the car park then shoved the phone – still connected – in my pocket.'

'What? Why?'

'No one knows. The police reckon whoever it was just wanted to scare me but they're not sure. Obviously the police have only bothered to try to work out what happened *after* they checked I'm not a drug dealer or "lady of the night".'

We both kissed our teeth in unison at the idea that they had to check she was legit before they bothered to think about investigating what happened to her.

'So they think someone just wanted to scare you?'

'Yeah. Scare me not kill me. I mean, where they stuck the blade in avoided major organs and didn't do that much damage. They were try-ing to put the frighteners on me.'

'But who would do that?'

'Who knows? I don't work on that many high-profile cases but there are a few of the more "delicate" cases with some well dodgy people in our offices at the moment, so . . . But then, I'm quite junior, why tar-get me?'

'Maybe it'll draw too much attention if they go for someone higher up, so they went for someone who wouldn't have a crime against them investigated as much? But targeting a junior person would still have the result of putting everyone in the business on high alert.'

'That's basically what the police said. So it was nice of them to tell me that I wasn't going to get the full-fat investigation, just the skimmed one.'

'This is so awful,' I said, still holding her hand. 'I'm so sorry this happened to you. I feel so powerless.'

'Same.'

'Look, when you're better, do you and the boys want to come down and stay with me for a while? I know it'll be tight, but a change of scen-ery might do you some good.'

'I'd love to, babe, but we're going for the completely permanent change of scenery.'

'Don't understand?'

Trina sighed and carefully lifted her hand to brush across her face. She might have started relaxing her hair and wearing it off her face because of work, but her nails were still next level – right now, red-and-white candy stripes. 'This is the final straw for Steadman. He's been going on about us moving to Barbados *from time*. He's got a house, his folks are there. He wants the boys to get a proper education and be surrounded by people who look like us. My parents are back in Trinidad now, so it'll be easy to see them. It was mainly our jobs keeping us here – but he's got a job in local government there if he wants it. Now this has happened, he just wants to go. There's plenty of jobs for accountants there – even UK companies want people to work there. So we're packing up and heading off.'

'No. No. You can't.'

'We are. To be honest, Cleo, I don't think I'll ever feel safe again here.'

'But I'll never see you.'

'You barely see me as it is. I mean, it's always births, deaths, marriages, which won't change, will it? I'll always come for that.'

'But you won't be here,' I whined and, rather pathetically, started to sob. *Urgh, stop it, Cleo!* I told myself. *Stop it.* I had no idea why I was suddenly so upset, suddenly so bereft. I hardly saw Trina, I spoke to her regularly, but it was maybe once a year we actually physically met. How was this going to change anything?

'I'm touched, babe, truly. I'll miss you, too.'

We chatted for a while longer, but I could see she was growing tired and wanted to sleep. 'I'll see you tomorrow,' I told her and pressed a kiss on her forehead.

I waited to leave her room before I started to cry for real. This felt so significant. Like it was a milestone moment in my life, even though it was nothing out of the ordinary. Friends leave you all the time. They get married, they have children, they get new jobs, they move to different countries, they even move into spaces in their lives where you don't fit any more. Things change, friendships are altered in so many different ways. I knew that. I lived it.

It's just this . . . this felt horribly final. Like I might not see her again.

Like, when she and her family left, the waters would close behind them and I would never be able to see where they went, never be able to be with them again. And that was something I couldn't cope with.

## Leeds, 2003

'How is she?' Heath asked. He was on his way up to see Trina, having managed to move his appointments and meetings around after all.

'Fine,' I mumbled into the phone.

'Is she not fine? You sound really upset. Was it worse than we thought? Is she going to—?'

'No,' I cut in before he said *that* word. I couldn't stand to hear that word right now. 'Nothing like that.' Although it was a bit like that. She was being taken away from me, but not in the way he meant or I was allowed to properly grieve. It would sound pathetic to say it out loud: *'My best friend is getting on with things, she's going to get a better quality of life for her and her husband and children, living on a Caribbean island, and I'm upset about that.'*

'What is it, then?'

'Nothing,' I replied.

'Open the door,' he said.

'Pardon?'

'I'm here, open the door.'

I stumbled off the bed and almost tripped over my feet, running to open the door to room 313. And there he was. Heath. My whole body sagged with relief when I saw him and I had to hold on to the door so I didn't fall over.

He smiled at me and said: 'I was going to go to my room but you sounded so sad, I thought I'd better check on you.'

I stepped aside to let him in and he dumped his overnight bag and bag on the floor by the door. He immediately kicked off his shoes, then went straight to the bathroom to wash his hands. I stood outside the bathroom door, wringing my hands and hopping from foot to foot, like a child waiting to see Father Christmas.

'Come here,' he said and enveloped me in a hug. That was one of the best things about Heath, his ability to almost hug away the pain. 'It's going to be OK,' he whispered into my hair. 'It's all going to be OK.'

He pulled away slightly and stared into my eyes. 'Is there something I should know?' he asked gently. 'Should I be going to see her while I can?'

'No, nothing like that.' Before he could say anything else, before I could think it through, I pushed my lips on his and closed my eyes.

For the first time ever, Heath pulled away first. And then stepped back, right out of reach. '*Cleo!*' he said, as though he was in agony, as if what I had done had caused him real, physical pain. 'I'm still with Abi. You told me not to finish with her.'

'Yeah, well, I didn't know my best friend was going to get stabbed and decide to move halfway round the world because of it, did I?'

'So it's not actually me you want, it's—Wait, she's what?!'

'Trina and her family are all shipping out as soon as they can.'

'Oh. *Oh*. Didn't see that coming.' Heath looked desolate for a moment, too. 'But that doesn't change the fact that you don't really want me, you're just using me to make yourself feel better.'

'I don't believe you've still got a girlfriend,' I said to him, suddenly seeing him so clearly. This outrage of his? It was fake. It was a shield to hide behind in case I rejected him again. 'You finished with your girlfriend the day after the funeral, didn't you?'

His eyes flashed with an emotion I couldn't place, something I didn't think I'd ever seen before.

'Didn't you?'

'You know nothing about it,' he replied, his voice quiet but angry, almost dangerous.

I was angry, too. Angry at Trina for leaving, at the person who attacked her for pushing her to leave and at myself for being so pathetic about it. My reactions were completely out of proportion to what was happening, and it made me wonder again if I was broken somehow. Because I seemed to go from not feeling very much to feeling way too much in a short amount of time. Maybe this was all part of what I used to believe was wrong with me – I couldn't access my feelings properly. Or correctly. In that moment, though, I simply wanted to feel something else. To do something else other than focus on what I was losing.

Staring right at my ex-lover, scared but defiant, I took off my T-shirt. Stood in front of him, topless, braless, showing him my body. I was pretty certain he still wanted me – if he didn't, he wouldn't have lied about still being with his girlfriend; if he didn't, he wouldn't be staring at me like he was now I had quite plainly signalled what I wanted.

I walked back into the main room, which was compact and cosy (the most my budget would allow), the lighting low because I had been ready for bed. Still watching him, I sat on the edge of the bed and stared at him. Defiant. Terrified.

He was immobile and rigid in the archway beside the bathroom as he stared at me, obviously not believing what I was doing. Obviously torn about what to do in response.

It was his choice. He could walk away, go back to his room and tomorrow act like none of this had happened. He knew I'd go along with that, that I would be able to pretend in that way.

He *could* do that.

Or he could almost howl in anguish. He could come towards me, practically tearing at his clothes to get them off and throwing them aside as though he never wanted to see them again, while I lay back on the bed. Once he was naked, he could pull down my pyjama bottoms, discard them in the same way he did his clothes. He could push open my legs and snarl as he entered me so roughly I cried out a little. He could keep eye contact with me as he thrust inside me, his face a mixture of ecstasy and anger; joy and rage.

'I don't want to be like this,' he declared as he gripped my thighs tight so he could get as close to me as he could, fill me as much as possible. 'I don't want to love you.'

'I know,' I replied breathlessly because he was on the edge, right on the cusp, of hurting me. I didn't want him to stop, though, this was what I wanted. 'I know.'

'I don't want to love you,' he said louder as he rammed even harder into me. 'Not when it makes me so crazy. I don't. I don't.' His grip on my legs increased.

He was hurting me now, and while part of me wanted to tell him to be a bit more gentle, the other part of me felt like I deserved this. I deserved for him to hurt me, just like I was hurting him. 'I know,' I whimpered through the pain. 'I know.'

'You make me crazy, but I love you. I love you. I love you.' He kept repeating it, until his words ran together and became moans, his thrusts became slams of unbearable agony, his grasp was so tight, I thought his fingers were going to crush my thighs.

While he orgasmed loudly and angrily, I had the sensation of orgasming but I didn't know where the pain ended and the pleasure began.

Almost immediately Heath withdrew, let me go and then collapsed on the bed beside me. He pushed the heels of his hands into his eyes and started sobbing, the sound of his desperate tears filling every part of the room, smothering all sound and all air.

# 11

Franklyn isn't back for breakfast. Neither is Wallace. I had gone to text my husband, ask him where he was, ask if he was OK, ask when he might come back, but I'd stopped mid-word, reminded myself that I was the one who'd suggested we keep our distance. Knowing that with Wallace, once I made keeping our distance concrete by putting it into words (twice), there was a real chance that he would take off – go stay with friends, check into a hotel or even sleep at his office to give himself space. His ability to just take off and shut me out used to drive me crazy.

The first time, we'd been together properly about six months and everything was heightened, tense, febrile. I had been constantly terrified he would find out the truth about me and would leave, and he seemed to be permanently waiting for me to say something he could take the wrong way. So when I made a joke about him not knowing that you had to periodically clean out dishwashers, things escalated to the point where he was screaming at me about being condescending and I was shouting back that there were a million things that I did in his flat that he didn't even notice, so if I was condescending it was because I was exhausted from doing all the hard work in the flat and our relationship. In response, he'd glared at me as though he could see every terrible thing I'd ever done, like all my previous crimes were crawling all over me, turned around and left. Then didn't call or message for four days.

I had gone to my flat and spent those days pacing, wringing my hands while willing myself not to be sick. I'd been so grateful when he'd turned up at my door four days later, that I'd thrown my arms around him and burst into tears of relief. We apologised to each other for the argument and the things we said, but we never addressed the walking-out. He did it again, of course, a few times, but it stopped stressing me out as much. And when we bought a place together, he pretty much stopped it altogether. Until now.

Lola drowns her pancakes, soft and fluffy and the size of saucers, in organic maple syrup, the bottle held high above her plate. 'You'd better eat all that,' I tell her as I flip another pancake. 'That's about four pounds fifty worth of maple syrup you've got right there. So don't be letting me catch you leaving one drop to be washed down the drain. You eat it all.' I watch her pull the tip of her index finger through the brown slurry, picking up a thick covering of syrup and raising it to her lips.

'No worries with that one, Auntie C.' Her small pink tongue slowly licks away the syrup. 'And no offence, but you're not even one little bit scary. My mum is terrifying. My Pops can be as well. Obviously both my grandmas are top. Even Uncle Wals is scarier than you. You're right down the bottom of the list.'

'Thanks.'

*Knock, knock, ring ring,* goes the door. I shut off the heat beneath the pancake pan, put down the spatula and scowl at Lola as I head for the door.

On the other side of the door is not the postman, as I was expecting. The two people who stand there are, in fact, a policeman and a policewoman. Both are in plain clothes, but both are so obviously police they may as well have been wearing uniforms. 'Are you Cleo Pryce?' the woman asks.

*Erm, yes,* I reply, nervously. I'm thrown. Then I'm scared. I wasn't expecting Thursday morning to begin with a visit from the police, especially not when my husband isn't here. My eyes dart from one face to the other. Is this a death notification? Have they come to tell me I'm a widow?

Neither of them speaks, but they both look at me as though waiting for something and I realise that I haven't actually spoken. In the place of words, I nod.

'My name is Detective Constable Amwell,' the man says, showing a card with a crest and his picture and some writing I'm too shaken to decipher. 'This is Detective Constable Mattison.' She repeats the warrant card gesture. 'Can we come in and ask you a few questions?'

I look over my shoulder towards the kitchen. I wouldn't want them in here normally, but I especially don't want them around with Lola here. I look at their faces again. They don't look like they're doing a death notification, they don't look like they're about to tear my world apart.

'It's not the best time,' I reply. 'I'm in the middle of breakfast, my thirteen-year-old niece is staying. Can we do this another time?'

'Not really,' the policeman says. 'We're from the Surrey and Sussex Major Crime Team. We're investigating a murder.'

'Murder? What have I got to do with murder?'

'We would really prefer to come in to have this conversation,' the policewoman – Detective Mattison – says.

'Like I said, I've got my niece staying. I'd rather she didn't hear any of this, especially if you're going to talk about murders.'

'We can always run you down to the station with your niece, where I'm sure someone will be able to look after her while we talk to you, if you prefer?' Detective Amwell offers.

*Oh come on,* I almost scoff in their faces. *Who would choose that option? No one, that's who. But well played, officers, well played.*

While the officers wait in the living room, I tell Lola to stay in the kitchen, to eat her breakfast, to turn on the television and find something to watch with the sound up. But most of all, I instruct her very clearly to stay away from the living room.

'So, what can I do for you?' I ask them pleasantly, even indicating they can sit down if they choose to. They choose to, and both sit at the very edge of the seats, looking supremely uncomfortable. That's something, I suppose, that they're not totally chill about being here, which hopefully means, after this, they won't be back.

'How well do you know Mr Jeffrey Burrfield?' the policeman asks.

Jeffrey Burrfield? *Burrfield* . . . It doesn't take long for two parts of my brain to connect via my memory. 'The solicitor?'

'Yes. He worked out of offices near Brighton Race Course,' Detective Amwell replies.

'OK, well, then I don't know him at all. I mean, I've spoken to him on the phone and I've met him once in my life . . . And what do you mean, "worked"?'

'We mean Mr Burrfield has been murdered,' the policewoman says. 'And you may be one of the last people to have seen him alive.'

## Leeds, 2003

*Morning-after pill.*

This was on my mind the whole time we talked to Trina. I wondered if she could tell what Heath and I had done the night before from the moment we walked in. She confirmed she knew by shaking her head despairingly and saying, 'You two, I swear,' when he went to get us a coffee.

*Morning-after pill.*

Trina told him about her plan to leave and it had a worse effect on me than yesterday – I felt like my heart was being clawed out by a vicious, flesh-eating monster. I felt like I was being suffocated. I felt like I was going to crumple into a pile of tears and bones and flesh, hollowed out by the reality of this situation. I loved Trina. I always knew I did. But did I tell her that? Or did I think I had plenty of time to do all that? The truth was, I took Trina for granted. I expected her to always be there. I expected to be able to pick up the phone and tell her something had happened and for her to be there if necessary. I expected her to text me and say she needed me and for me to go dashing to her side. I thought I'd be able to arrange to come and visit whenever I wanted so I never did.

Our friendship would always be there, but it wouldn't as well.

This iteration of it was over. Over. Gone. Dead.

Not taking full advantage of the gorgeousness of my friend, the huge benefits she brought to my life, was what was making me feel and act like this.

*Morning-after pill.*

'I'm not as OK with this as I should be,' Heath said to Trina. 'I'm not sure I can cope with more change. Admittedly, we hardly see each other, but I know you're there if I need you. Like she is.' He nodded his head towards me. His face relaxed into a smile. 'We've come a long way since I used to stare at your mate across the common room.'

'We certainly have,' she replied. She moved her gaze to me. 'You're unusually quiet.'

*Morning-after pill.*

She was staring at me in that way where her eyes slowly drilled into my mind and soul, laying bare all the thoughts that I tried to keep hidden. Did she know how guilty I felt about not being a more engaged and present friend? How much I wanted to rewind and get a proper chance to spend time with her? Did she know that I needed to take emergency contraception because of the violent way Heath and I had fucked last night? 'Just managing my devastation as best I can,' I said pathetically.

'Honestly, you two, it's like I live with you. What's going on?'

'I just wish I'd spent more time with you. The last few years have been too busy, too full of other things and not enough of you,' I confessed. 'I feel so devastated, like my heart is broken or something.'

'Same here,' Heath said.

'I'm not f-ing dying!' Trina replied. 'I'm still going to be in touch with you. I'm telling you, you two drama queens need to fix up. And I mean in more ways than one.'

She was telling us about ourselves without actually telling us about ourselves. And she was right. We did need to fix up. We had to sort ourselves out, stop living encounter to encounter in this vague state. *I* had to get a grip.

*After I got the morning-after pill.*

We said long goodbyes. Tear-soaked and messy. Trina, despite being all 'this is what I want, you two need to fix up', cried the most. We couldn't really hug her because of her wound, but we held hands, cried, cried some more, left with tears streaming.

On the pavement outside, Heath and I stood next to each other, scrubbing our faces dry.

Last night, after his epic, heart-rending cry, Heath had got dressed in a tense, regretful silence I didn't know how to penetrate, then left my room without saying another word. I'd climbed into bed, pulled the sheet and duvet up over me, holding on to the smell of him on my skin, letting it soothe me into sleep. While he'd been crying, I'd tried to comfort him and he had jerked himself away from me, not wanting me to even touch him, let alone comfort him. And this morning, he'd turned up at my door to go to breakfast like nothing had happened. He didn't mention it. Neither did I. We ate breakfast like normal and acted like the night before never happened.

'Do you know what our problem is?' I asked him.

'No, what is our problem?' he replied in a monotone. He was cut off from me now that we'd fulfilled our obligations to be normal together in front of Trina. That done, he could escape from me.

I moved to stand in front of him, pushed my bottom lip out, put my head to one side. 'No, what is our problem?' I said in an approximation of his gloomy voice.

He pulled a small smile across his lips – amused by me but not wanting to be. 'What is our problem?' he said in a more normal tone.

'We are two of the most miserable people on God's green Earth.'

'No lies detected, as Trina would say.'

'Let's do something about it.' I took each of his hands in mine. 'Let's stop being such miserable bastards. Let's fix up and be together, properly. Let's do lots of fun things together. Have a laugh. See where it takes us.'

'You mean it?'

'I do.'

'I like the sound of you saying those words to me.' He grinned, relaxed into his features and body for the first time in what seemed like an age. He let go of my hands and gingerly, as though I might freak out if he wasn't careful, slipped his arms around my waist, drew me closer to him.

Quickly, so I didn't have time to think about it and therefore change my mind, I linked my arms around his neck. I was going to do this. And if I was going to make this choice, take my life in my own hands, then I had to do it properly, completely. 'OK, let's start thinking of things we can do together inside and outside of the bedroom – yes?'

'Yes,' he said.

'First of all, though, I need to get hold of the morning-after pill.'

Heath pulled me even closer, his eyes scrutinising my face, and I could see how much he was trying to stop himself from smiling, trying to rein in his happiness in case it scared me off. 'How about you don't?'

'Don't get the morning-after pill?' I replied.

'Yes. Let's leave it up to Fate.'

My heart panicked, scrambling to get out of my ribcage while my stomach immediately filled with lead. Was he out of his mind? Leave it up to Fate if I got pregnant, if we became parents?

'Are you mad?'

'Are you seriously asking a psychologist that?' Heath brought his face near to mine. 'Yes, I am.' He smiled the most beatific grin. 'And I know you are, too.'

# 12

The police officers words and questions swirl around and around my mind as I show them out.

'Why did you visit Mr Burrfield's office?'

'I had an appointment. I'm getting divorced.'

'When was the last time you saw Mr Burrfield?'

'When I left my appointment. About two thirty p.m.'

'Have you had occasion to go back there at any point since then?'

'No.'

'Are you sure about that?'

'Yes, I'm sure. He said he was going to expedite my divorce papers because . . . well, doesn't matter why, but he said I would hear from him. He was meant to call Tuesday but didn't. I did wonder why and I tried calling him a few times but realised he was probably busy so didn't think too much about it.'

'He died not long after you left his office.'

'What?'

'The evidence suggests he died sometime after six p.m.'

'Right. Right. Poor man.'

'You haven't asked how he died and how we know it's murder.'

'Haven't I?'

'No, you haven't.'

'Am I meant to?'

'Most people who are surprised by the news that someone they know was murdered ask what happened.'

'Oh, OK. I am surprised by the news but I'm not sure I want to know. Especially if it's gruesome.'

'Gruesome. You could call it that.' Detective Constable Amwell looked around the room, paying particular attention to the pictures on the walls and mantelpiece. 'What is it you do for a living?'

'I'm a writer.'

'What sort of things do you write?'

'I write books, mainly, and a couple of things for television.'

'Anything we might have heard of?'

'Erm, probably not.'

'What name do you write under?'

'Erm, Cleo Forsum.'

'Cleo Forsum. Forsum. Cleo. Oh yes, I know where I've heard that name before. *The Baking Detective*, right?' DC Amwell said.

'Ah yes, *The Baking Detective*, I know that one,' Detective Constable Mattison said.

As acting went, theirs was terrible. They obviously knew who I was when they rocked up to my door. Why wouldn't they when it's part of their job?

'Oh yes, the one with the lass who makes cakes and solves crimes because the police are so incompetent at their jobs. That one?' Detective Constable Mattison added for good measure, just in case I had any doubt they knew who I was.

'I wouldn't put it like that.'

'But it's quite gruesome, which is why I'm confused about why you would find this too gruesome to ask about when you write the most horrible murders. How you come up with those things I'll never know. And why you wouldn't ask how Mr Burrfield died seems an even bigger mystery. Unless you already know what happened,' that came from Detective Constable Amwell.

'I don't know anything about his death. And the television show is a collaboration. I write the first draft and someone comes and edits it. Then it's re-edited and rewritten. Sometimes I have to sit on set with them while they're shooting to make the script fit what they've managed to capture on camera. Which means, I write a very tame first version. Most of the time, other people write in the gore. Which is why I can't watch or hear about it in real life.'

'Most of the time? Not all of the time?'

'Yes, most of the time.'

They both stood at the same time. 'Mrs Pryce, we may need to come back and question you further. Once we've had some of the items that were found at the crime scene tested, we'll return to speak to you.'

'Right. Well, I doubt I'll know any more. But fine.'


'*Items that were found at the crime scene tested*' keeps spinning around my head like a racing-car driver going for the ultimate win on a smooth, clear track. It sounded like they knew the items were mine. It sounded like they were trying to lead me up one path just so they could catch me out in a lie. That's what working on the show has taught me, what the police advisors have constantly told me: the police will ask you leading questions, they will wait for you to lie yourself into a corner and then they will hit you with the evidence – sometimes physical, sometimes digital – that you are lying to them. Unless you're particularly hard-faced, this will always catch you off-guard so you either start confessing or lying even more. Either way, they've got you.

What possible evidence could they have against me?

I didn't do it. I have done other things – heinous things, *criminal* things – but not this. So how would they get evidence? And, more importantly, what is it?

Lola is sitting in the same position as when I left the room, but the stack of pancakes is only half its original height, a children's TV movie is noisily playing out its story on screen.

Before I can return to my place tossing pancakes in front of the cooker, Lola sets her big browns on me, adopts a sympathetic expression and says: 'So, Auntie C, your divorce lawyer got murdered. That's pretty tough, huh?'

## West London, 2006

'Hi, honey, I'm home,' Heath called from the front door.

'Oh yes you are,' I called back.

He appeared in the kitchen doorway and my heart leapt in my chest. I was always excited to see him nowadays. Since our trip to Leeds, since Trina left and I had made a commitment to give things a proper try, my feelings for him had been transformed. And he was just everything to me.

I put my hand on my hip and raised one arm in the air. 'I have a new outfit.' I was wearing one of his work shirts that skimmed my thighs and a pair of knickers. Nothing else. 'What do you think?'

'I think . . . who are you and what did you do with the real Cleo?' he joked.

143

'Fine,' I huffed. 'If you don't like it . . .'

He was across the room in an instant, slipping his arms around me. 'I like it, I like it.' He kissed me slowly, deeply, and I felt myself melting in a way that shouldn't be possible for a grown woman living in the real world.

We'd had so much fun in the last three years. We had cheap meals in out-of-the-way cafés, we had picnics in various parks around West London, we took day trips to the beach in Brighton, we had Sunday lunch with his mum, Friday-night dinner with my parents. We watched TV in bed, eating pizza. Sometimes he would meet me after work and we'd attempt to walk home until we got tired and he'd use his birthday money to get a cab home. We talked and laughed. And we had so much sex. Made so much love. Fucked all the time.

Our bubble, this world of two we had created, seemed to be everything I didn't know I wanted. I didn't mind the daily grind of getting up and going to work in a magazine in Central London with odious bosses and their dubious work practices, I didn't mind the not having much money and having to budget all the time, I didn't mind paying bills and missing trains and standing in the cold and not having the extravagant lifestyle someone my age was always being promised in the TV shows and movies I watched and the books I read. I didn't mind because Heath was living it with me. He earned twice what I did, but London was expensive, so even pooling our money meant we had to be careful a lot of the time.

Heath broke away from the kiss first, dropped another peck on my nose, then my forehead, before lifting me up to sit me on the marble worktop. I was able to look down on him slightly from that point with the kettle on my right and the wooden knife block on my left.

'So . . .' Heath began.

My heart sank. Of course. Of. Course. Things had been too good for too long. Of course something had to go wrong, my little loved-up bubble had to burst. 'What have you done?' I asked tiredly.

'Why are you saying that?'

'Because I only ever get "so . . ." in that voice when you've done something that I'm not going to like. Just tell me quick and then I can get pissed off and then we can move on.'

'I hate sometimes how well you know me,' he said. 'I love it, too.'

'Out with it.'

'Look, I might have done something that you would not approve of. But I've done it and that's that.'

'Waiting dot com.'

'All right, I've booked us a week's holiday in Las Vegas.'

My eyes nearly jumped out of my head but I was too shocked to speak.

'Do you hate the idea? Do you? Look, I've saved up, I've saved really hard. I've even managed to get us business class. Yes, that's why we've not been doing anything that costs money for the past few months, but I wanted so much to surprise you with this. What do you think? Do you hate it? I can't really get a refund if you do, but I'll do my best. If you hate it.'

I looked around our flat. And it was our flat now. I'd driven us back to his flat when we came home from Leeds and I never really left again. Sure, I went back to my flat in South London to get clothes and stuff, to pick up my post and clean out the fridge, but it essentially became a case of moving two or three bags at a time until he said we should hire a van and go and get the rest of my stuff.

We had some of my furniture (my bedside table and my desk), a few of my furnishings (some of my floor cushions and rugs) and he was always saying I could decorate the flat how I chose. Heath was constantly telling me that more than anything he wanted it to be my home, so if there was something I didn't like, I should change it.

He'd started saying that more regularly when, right after I properly moved in, his ex-girlfriend Abi had turned up in the middle of the night.

According to Heath, she hadn't officially moved in, she'd hung on to a copy of a key he'd let her borrow one time and just began to let herself in. When he broke up with her – the day after his father's funeral, as I'd guessed – she'd been devastated. He'd promised her he wasn't back with me – there'd been more than three months between the funeral and Leeds, so he wasn't lying – and she'd promised to return the key.

Late one night, she'd decided to surprise him, to see if she could rekindle things. She'd got almost all the way to the bedroom before he had intercepted her. Instinctively, I'd stuck my head under the covers, then when I heard their voices in the corridor instead of the front door just opening and closing as she left, I'd pulled my head out, got out of bed, then crept to the door to listen.

*Didn't lie to you . . . only just happened . . . I didn't take anything from you.*

*Knew you were a bastard . . . can't trust you . . . thought you loved me . . . thought we'd be together for ever . . .*

*Never promised you anything . . . your feelings overwhelm me . . . please don't say that . . .*

*I loved you . . . would do anything for you . . . hope your tart is worth it . . . I'm the best thing you threw away . . .*

On and on they went, until she attempted to come and have it out with me and Heath had to block the doorway. Abi left without her stuff, without leaving her key, but with using her fist to punch the framed certificate hanging on the corridor wall, breaking the glass and probably her hand, too. 'Change of locks in the morning, then,' I'd said, when he had double-locked the door and climbed back into bed. What else was I supposed to say? He hadn't exactly covered himself in glory in all of this. Yes, he had finished with her long before we got together – but he had been trying to get with me during the time they were together. He had introduced her to his parents but kept her a secret from his friends in case one of them told me. Not exactly the actions of a gentleman. And, to be honest, even in my loved-up state when it happened, and my more balanced state now, how he treated her did give me pause for thought.

Looking back, how he treated the Heathettes gave me pause for thought, too. Oh they'd all been up for it and most of them were friendly with him afterwards, but he'd told me more than once that he screwed them mainly because I wouldn't screw him. (He'd admitted once when drunk that he would often imagine he was with me when he was with them. I'd been so disgusted rather than flattered by him saying that that he never repeated it.) The whole thing with the Heathettes was messed up. Yes, it was a consensual environment, but not a particularly healthy one. It was no wonder some of them used to glare at Trina and me – even when they extracted themselves from the pool of Heathettes, we would still get evils from them. I didn't see that at the time because I was right in the middle of it, but now I was dubious about the things my boyfriend did in the name of love and sex.

Sometimes, in my more secure moments, I looked around our home, as lovely as it was, and wondered where he and Abi lived out the many little moments of their lives – where they ate, where they chatted, where they made love, where they just were. And I'd remember the note I found that had fallen behind the hall radiator: *Out late tonight. Love you. Abi x*

Sometimes, I looked around our home, as lovely as it was, and wondered what it must be like for Abi to know that the thing she feared most – Heath leaving her for me – had pretty much come true.

And sometimes, I looked around our home, as lovely as it was, and wondered if I shouldn't feel a little more guilty about how long it took me to get here with Heath and what could have been avoided – all those people's feelings that wouldn't have been hurt – if I hadn't resisted him for so many years.

'You hate it, don't you?' he said to the silence created by my meandering into the world of what-I-should-haves. 'You really, really hate it.'

'I don't hate it,' I finally reply. 'I don't hate it at all. I'm just a bit . . . wowed, is all. I mean, what did I do to get so lucky?'

He kissed me, gently and carefully. 'You didn't get lucky, I did. Every day I can't get over how perfect you are and the fact that you love me . . . I honestly feel like the luckiest man in the whole wide world.'

# 13

Grown-ups are wild. Really wild.

Lola often wonders how any of them ever get anything done with their wild behaviour. Like Auntie C.

Auntie C is safe. Other people would call her cool, but she is safe. You know you can have a good time with this auntie.

Lola's family is sad. They've been sad for as long as she can remember and she absolutely knows why. Her Uncle Sidney. She'd never met him, not even when she was a baby, because he has been locked up pretty much her whole life.

It'd taken her a while to find out what it was that made her family sad, but by the time she was eight, she'd found out that her Uncle Sidney was a murderer. He had killed someone a long time ago and was going to spend the rest of his life in prison. She found out by listening to the Growns, by making herself invisible and quiet; unnoticed and near-silent. None of them knew that she knew, but she did. And she kept it to herself. Who was she going to tell? None of her her-age mates would understand, and this was not stuff for her socials. Yes, some of them uploaded some out-there stuff but they did not have the range to

149

understand this. They did not even have the start of an inkling of an idea.

The world is an odd place, Lola has decided. She decided that a long time ago. Really odd, so the best way to deal with it is to keep quiet. Find out information by never reminding people that you are there. That's why she likes Auntie C. She gives Lola space, she allows her to be invisible, but at the same time, she notices her and engages with her.

And when she arrived, when she got with Uncle Wals, Lola had been tiny. The tiniest, only about three. Maybe even two. But even at that age, she could feel the sadness that hung over their family, that followed them like a permanently raining cloud wherever they went, whether they were together or not.

Then Uncle Wals brought Auntie C home. And suddenly their family got less sad, more open, *normal*. A new normal that saw her grandmother laugh sometimes, her grandfather actually talk, that made Pops stop raging at the world so much, and that saw Uncle Wals smile. All the time. He'd always been her favourite uncle, the fun one. When she found out what had happened to Uncle Sidney, she realised Uncle Wals was trying to be two uncles at once. He wanted to be Uncle Sidney in her life as well as Uncle Wals.

Uncle Sidney had been his hero, she'd once heard him say to Pops. And Uncle Wals would always refuse to believe that his hero had done such a thing. He refused to believe that he would break into a woman's house, rough her up and then strangle her. (She'd found that out from the internet, not from listening. No one talked about it in such detail.) And because Uncle Wals refused to believe, he tried to fill the hole in their family's life.

He was good at it, too. But always so sad. Even when he was

laughing and joking, there was a sadness that tugged at him, weighed him down. Until Auntie C arrived. Then there was fun. Real fun.

## East London, 2012

'I do not know why he is bringing someone here,' Donette said tartly. She wasn't the most social of people at the best of times, but for the last three years, which had been swollen and bloated with the arrest, the trial and conviction of her son, her beloved first-born, Donette had decided to cut herself off from the outside world. She only went to church, nothing else. She didn't even bother with prayer group any more because it was full of gossips. Grown women who had nothing better to do than stare and whisper, side-eye and stir. Sidney, named after her favourite actor – Sidney Poitier himself – was innocent. She had never doubted that. He was kind, he had been brought up kind. He had been brought up to respect women, not do the things she'd heard in court. That was not her son. And no one could tell her otherwise.

Her life wasn't so bad without those snakes and vipers with their forked tongues and poisonous words in it. And what was her life without her Sidney, anyway? He told her, constantly told her, that she should get on with her life, forget about him, live for him. But how could she? How could she live with this injustice? And now Wallace was reminding her that life carries on by saying he wanted to bring a girl home with him. It was obviously serious, since he wanted to bring her to meet them, but it made her feel ill. Unsettled. The nausea had arrived the moment she watched Sidney taken away in handcuffs, and it hadn't left her. But the feeling was worse now. Franklyn had been married and had given her a grandbaby, she had accepted those were the normal processes of life. But things carrying on now? Wallace potentially marrying? She wasn't sure. She wasn't sure at all. 'Why is he bringing her here?'

'He wants to show her off,' Tobias replied. 'That is a good thing, you know? It is a good thing.'

Tobias didn't have much to say. He had lost his wife when he lost his first-born son. He mourned the loss of both of them daily. He read his paper, completed his crossword and calculated how to fix his family. They had grown up blessed and then the blessings had disappeared. Vanished overnight. Leaving in its place this hollowness. This hollow of pain and nothingness. He sometimes felt he had been thrown into a deep, blue hole, the type people found in the middle of the ocean. No way to know how deep it goes, and no way to come back up to surface for air. He was there, trapped in something that looked beautiful from the outside – children, nice house, sturdy body, healthy family, good job he would soon be retiring from – but also a trap that was drowning him. Drop by drop, drip by drip, drowning him.

All of them froze when they heard the key in the door. Wallace hadn't lived there in years, but of course he had a key, it was still his home. Amalola scrambled up off the floor and climbed onto her mother's lap, not sure of what was coming next. Whatever it was, she knew it was big from the way her grandmother had been quietly remonstrating, the way Grandpop was trying to calm her down. Her mother's arms came around her in the protective loop she always just expected to be there and Pops put his hand on her ankle, a gentle, calming touch.

'Hello? We're here,' Uncle Wallace called from the corridor.

'In here, Bruv.'

There was a delay, a pause as they all listened to two pairs of hands being washed in the downstairs toilet. Even at three Amalola knew that if you came into her Grands' home, you have to take off your shoes, you have to wash your hands. It was just what you did.

Uncle Wallace, dressed in smart black trousers and button-up denim shirt and black socks, appeared in the room first. He was smiling, his handsome face lit up like all his dreams had come true at once, but even Amalola could see he was nervous, too. Worry tugged at the corner of his eyes. He was scared of introducing this person to his family; terrified of how they would receive her. 'Her', the person the Grands and Growns had been talking about, appeared next. She was smaller than Amalola expected, not nearly as tall as her mother. She was wearing jeans, which made Amalola frown. She'd been forced into a pink dress with matching pink ribbons in her bunches; everyone else was smart. But this lady, this 'her', was wearing smart, navy-blue jeans, a plain white long-sleeve T-shirt and a shiny red belt. She had hair down to her shoulders and the biggest smile. Her face almost glowed with that smile.

Uncle Wallace called everyone by name as he introduced them to 'her'. And then he repeated their names before saying, 'And this is Cleo.'

Cleo's smile, if possible, got wider with every introduction. 'It's so nice to meet you all,' she said. 'Wallace talks about every one of you all the time. Oh,' she added, before holding out the glass box with a white plastic lid in her hands, 'I brought you this, Mrs Pryce. I'm of Ghanaian heritage and you can't come to see someone important without bringing them something. Wallace said none of you really drink, so I took the risk of making you something. Deep-fried okra and black bean balls. I hope you like them. Wallace is an amazing cook and he said you taught him to cook, so I know it's a risk, like I said, but these are my favourite and my mum's favourite and I thought you might like them, too.'

Instead of accepting the proffered box, Grandma Donette's face seemed to harden. 'It was my son Sidney who was the cook. He had the gift. He taught the other two. Made sure they knew how to look after themselves.'

'Her' immediately dropped the smile from her face and her eyes went to the rectangular mountain range of photos that were crammed onto the mantelpiece, to the large canvas picture of the three brothers that hung above the fireplace. The oldest brother was at the front of the picture in the middle, a twin on either side. They were in their twenties, all handsome, all confident. 'Her' eyes lingered on the photo before she returned her gaze to Grandma Donette. 'Yes, Wallace told me. He said you and his brother taught him to cook.'

'You told her?' She glared at her son. 'What did you tell her for?'

'Of course I told her, Mum. Why wouldn't I? We've nothing to be ashamed of. Neither has Sidney. Sidney is innocent.'

'You hear that, girl?' Grandma snapped at 'Her'. 'My son is innocent. He didn't do anything. Not one little thing. Do not come round here looking for gossip. You will not get any!'

'I know he's innocent,' she said quietly. 'I knew Sidney a little bit before. And I went to his trial. And what I didn't know, Wallace has filled in. But I know Sidney is innocent. I've always known he's innocent. And nothing anyone says will ever convince me otherwise.'

Amalola felt her mother's body relax and her father's hand, which had suddenly felt heavy and tense on her ankle, lighten again. In fact, everyone in the room seemed to relax, let out a collective breath.

Amalola stared at 'Her', knowing that she was going to be welcomed into their family now, and that she would be around for a while. And Amalola didn't mind that at all.

11 AUGUST, 2022
CLEO & WALLACE'S HOUSE, HOVE—BRIGHTON BORDER
LATE NIGHT

Lola didn't like the fact that Auntie C was leaving. Lola knew that the moment she was gone, the happiness in their lives would be gone, too.

She'd been racking her brains, really thinking about what she could do to get Auntie C to stay. Uncle Wals was the real deal, as well. She'd seen how sad he was all the time now when she last came to visit. He smiled, tried to be normal, but she'd felt it. Grown-up wildness. Grown-up inability to keep it together. She'd seen the look in Uncle Wal's eyes before – in Pop's eyes and in Mum's eyes when they started to split up.

Uncle W and Auntie C were breaking apart but, because they were grown, they had to pretend they knew what they were doing.

The Growns *never* knew what they were doing.

They just pretended they did until it looked like they did.

Like her parents. Even when they had been arguing all the time, she knew they wouldn't if they didn't still care for one another. It was when they stopped shouting, stopped caring if the other was there or not, that she knew it was over. All the plans and thoughts and every-thing else she'd been devising to try to save their marriage were useless because they just did not care about each other any more.

Auntie C and Uncle W hadn't got there yet, but for any plan she might come up with to work, her uncle needed to actually be there. So far, he was Mr No-Show.

When Auntie C returned from talking to the police, she was shaken. And scared. Ever since Lola touched down in their house she'd noticed the look in Auntie C's eyes. She knew her Pops wouldn't really have noticed, and Uncle W must not have because she knows he would not leave Auntie C if he knew.

Because of grown-up wildness, none of them could see that behind the smiles and the acting normal, Auntie C was terrified.

# 14

## *Las Vegas, 2006*

'Cleo Forsum, I have been waiting for this moment since the moment we met. I know, I know, you're a magazine editor and you'll want to take that second "moment" out and replace it with another word, but I can't think of a word that would encapsulate that past and this present as much as "moment". It sounds a fleeting thing, but it is full, burgeoning, overripe with so much – with memory, with love, with experience. The "moment" I met you is something I will never forget. This moment right here is something that has been ten years in the making.

'Will you marry me, Cleo Forsum? Will you make me the happiest man in the world and marry me?'

This was our second night in Las Vegas. We'd got our bearings, we'd conquered jet lag and I was just about getting used to how *on* everything was here. The whole place seemed to be filled with bright lights and noise and motion; constant mental, emotional and physical energy. Everything sounded different, felt different, *tasted* different. It was like stepping into a slipstream of light on another planet.

There'd been a mix-up with the rooms – something to do with there only being one room of the type Heath had booked left and it was a smoking one, so we were given a suite. A junior suite but still, it was a giant junior. It had two large rooms, a kitchenette in the living area and a huge pink marble sunken bath in the bedroom area. It all added to the otherworldliness of being here, it all made everything not at all real.

To add to the surreal illusion of the life we had stepped into, my boyfriend was down on one knee. Asking me to marry him.

Heath wore a smart black suit with white shirt and gold tie, I was dressed in the floor-length gold dress that had been my bridesmaid dress for my older sister Adjua's wedding. (He hadn't actually gone to the wedding because we weren't together at the time, but he'd appreciated the hell out of it when he persuaded me to try it on for him one night.)

*Is this why he suggested I brought this dress with me?* I wondered as I stared down at his upturned face. *Because he was going to do this?*

I couldn't speak. I couldn't really think, but I certainly couldn't speak. Every time I went to open my mouth, I stopped myself because I knew some version of 'HAVE YOU LOST YOUR MIND?' would come screaming out and I didn't want to ruin our holiday.

Objectively, why wouldn't we get engaged? We both had good jobs (it wasn't my dream job, but it paid the bills and it allowed me to write in the evenings), we had a nice home, we enjoyed being with each other . . . the only reason not to get married would be me being in my head again. Me regressing into that state of not feeling and not understanding feeling. That place I thought I'd put behind me when I stepped out of the hospital in Leeds and chose Heath.

'Go on, then,' I said to him.

'That's it? "Go on, then"?' he teased. 'No, "I love you and I've waited so long for this"? No, "this has made me the happiest woman alive"? None of that? Just "go on, then"?'

'Sometimes it's like you haven't even met me before,' I laughed.

Heath stood up and reached into the inside pocket of his suit jacket, pulled out a black velvet ring box. 'Usually, I would have waited for you to choose this, but you'll understand why I didn't wait when I say what I say next.' He stopped talking. And waited. He didn't open the ring box. In fact, he did nothing at all except stare down at the box, looking bereft and – fleetingly – a little scared.

'What have you done now?' I asked, wondering why something that was meant to be amazing was suddenly looking like it might mutate into something horrible.

His gaze moved up to meet mine, and he smiled sadly. 'I forget you know me,' he said. 'I've done something. At the time I thought it was romantic and amazing: now I think you're going to freak out and it'll ruin everything – not just the holiday.'

'I hate things like this, can you just tell me what it is so we can deal with it?'

'I . . . well, when I said will you marry me, I meant,' he paused, grimaced, 'will you marry me *now*?'

'Excuse me, what?'

'I kind of, well not kind of, I actually did . . . I booked the wedding. It's in about three hours. We have to go and get the marriage licence at the Clark County Marriage License Bureau, taking all our ID and everything. Then we come back here, you get hair and make-up done if you want, then a limo will pick us up and take us to the chapel to get married.'

He was speaking words but I couldn't really understand. Well, I could understand, I was just a bit frozen and shocked, so it felt like I couldn't understand.

I stepped backwards and was grateful that the bed was right there, so I could sit down. Which I did, heavily.

'I knew I shouldn't have done this,' he was saying. 'I just thought it'd be romantic, our little secret. It wouldn't actually mean anything other than here. We don't have to register it at home, which means it's not legal over there. But I thought, I don't know, I just wanted to be married to you. To be your husband. These past couple of years, they've been amazing. And I wasn't just saying it earlier, I have been waiting for this since the moment I met you. Back when I used to stare at you.'

*Your feelings overwhelm me*, that's what he'd said to Abi. I knew what he meant. 'Heath, your feelings are too much for me sometimes,' I confessed. 'Way too much. This is madness.'

'I know. But wouldn't you love the glamour of it? Being able to tell people you got married in Vegas? And, you know, wouldn't you like to be married . . . to me?'

When I didn't reply, Heath said, 'That wasn't a rhetorical question, would you like to be married to me?'

'Well, obviously, I just said yes to your proposal.'

'So if you do want to be married to me, why not now?'

'Because we have no one here – your mum, my family, no friends. We're supposed to do it in front of everyone. Marriage is about standing up in front of the people who mean the most to you and declaring that this is the person you've chosen. It's not about slinking off to do it in secret.'

He threw himself down onto his knees in front of me. 'And we can. That will be our official wedding, the proper one with all the bells and whistles, the one that legally counts back at home, but this will be for us. Just you and me. It's always best when it's just you and me, isn't it?'

That, I could not argue with. When it was just us, in our little bubble, things were better. Easier. More fun. But that wasn't real. We had to live with and encounter and engage with other people.

'My mum would never forgive me if she found out about this before we were properly married,' I said to him. 'I mean, she's already decided how many trips we'll need to look at wedding dresses, who she wants to make her formal Ghanaian outfit, who's going to do the food. To be fair to her, she had all that down when I was single, but she will not be happy.'

'We only tell her after the real, formal wedding is done and dusted.'

'And maybe not even then,' I mumbled.

'That sounds like you might want to do it,' he said, a grin developing like a photograph across his handsome face.

'Yes, I think I might, actually.' My own matching grin developing, too. 'I think I might.'

## Las Vegas, 2006

'I, Cleomara Amma Forsum, take you, Alfred Heath Sawyer Berland, to be my wedded husband. For better or worse, in good times and in bad, in sickness and in health, for richer, for poorer. I promise to be loving, faithful and loyal to you, till death us do part.'

# Part 3

# 15

The conference room in HoneyMay Productions is large and plush, and on a different floor to the open-plan office and the place where I usually work. It has a military-grey carpet and comfortable white leather padded seating placed around a long smoky-glass table. Its white walls are graced with silver-framed posters of their most successful programmes, and large picture windows showcase the beautiful vista, which is a water-coloured beauty of greens, browns, creams and reds. Out there everything is sumptuous and deep and teeming with life, while at the same time being serene, peaceful.

Inside this room, tension hangs heavy and low in the air, like a razor-sharp executioner's axe about to fall. There are fourteen of us in this room, all sitting around the large oval meeting table, facing Harry Andrews, Chief Executive Officer of HoneyMay Productions. He sits at the head of the table like an overbearing patriarch, an image made worse by the large screen behind him via which, I guess, they hold remote meetings. In front of everyone else, are printed-out sheets of A4 paper, most with highlighter marks or brightly coloured sticky notes inserted at various points of the script. I am the only person with just a notebook and a selection of pens in front of me. It looks and feels like I'm the only person not to get the memo about reading and annotating the scripts before this meeting.

It feels like an ambush.

When I'd arrived at ten to two for the two o'clock meeting, everyone was already there. They had all picked a seat and had left me the chair closest to Harry Andrews. Dread had filled my entire being at that point. And I'd had to shake myself a few times to walk confidently to the seat. I'd lowered myself into my designated chair and had taken out my notebook and pens. And when I'd looked around, no one would meet my eye. Not the senior script editor, Anouk, who I worked quite closely with. Not Dianne, the head of production, who I also spoke to a lot. Not Sandy Burton, the Chief Operating Officer. Not even Gail, Clarissa or Amy, who had gone out of their way to be nice recently.

That axe, the one hanging over us, is obviously only hanging over my head.

I have stopped trying to get someone to look at me, and I am now facing Harry Andrews, the big boss, because he is clearly about to speak.

'First of all, Cleo, I'd like to say a big thank you for your work on the last episodes of *The Baking Detective*,' he says. 'And thank you for allowing us to see what is coming with the script for the extended final episode.

'And, having read it, like we all have,' he indicates to the people who are blanking me around the table, 'I'd like to ask what the fuck this is? I mean, I know you're having some kind of woo-woo break, but what the hell is this shit?'

I'd known I was about to be told off. I'd known that I was in trouble.

But I thought he was going to keep it polite. I didn't think he was going to swear at me.

Around me, collectively, I feel people silently gasp in shock and then cringe in horror. This is clearly not what they were expecting, either. Everyone knows his reputation: that he is hard-nosed and tough; that he expects the best from you whether you are sitting at your desk or ill in bed, but I don't think they expected him to blow up at someone outside the kingdom he presides over.

I stare at Harry Andrews, the chinned wonder, as I like to think of him. He wears his longish-on-top salt'n'pepper-coloured hair swished off his face, he makes sure he never uses the top three buttons of his expensive shirts so everyone is treated to the sight of his chest hair peeking out the top, and he always has an expensive watch on his wrist – I've yet to see him wear the same watch twice. He reminds me so much of another terrible man I encountered when I worked in magazines. Another awful human who couldn't help himself when it came to behaving badly.

'What were you thinking?' Harry Andrews doesn't normally come to these meetings, doesn't taint the writers' room with his presence, but, like everyone else, he hasn't been happy about my decision to end one of his most successful shows. When Dianne was still talking to me, she'd let slip that he went straight to get legal advice when I first broached the idea of ending the show after this run. And came away pissed off that there was no way to overturn the contract. If I said we were done, then we were done.

Harry Andrews isn't used to being crossed, he isn't used to being challenged, he isn't used to not getting his own way.

He's never actually confronted me, though, not until this moment – when he is going all out. He's being ridiculous, of course, since what is filmed and shown is rarely anything like my original scripts. They are similar, sure, in the sense that the murder happens when I wrote it, the killer is often who I'd carefully plotted them to be, and the characters I'd conjured up for any particular episode often keep the same names and traits I gave them. But collaboration often means several other people would work on and rewrite the script until it fit with the narrative about the show they wanted. Even if I watched and rewatched the aired episodes, read the shooting scripts, hell, even discussed it with the script editors, whatever I produced never went untouched, never went completely unrewritten.

'Look, I understand you're not in the best place' – he waves to the area near his head, his tanned, lined face almost cracking with the effort of not shouting – 'but did you have to let it show in your work? You're killing off—'

'I'm not killing her off,' I say meekly, although I feel anything but meek right now. I have myriad feelings swirling in and around me right now, but none of them is timidity.

'Of course you are. After all we did for you, we let you work on the show when, frankly, you have no business being involved in any of it. You have held the show back with your inexperience, but we were always too polite to tell you the truth. Which is why we're all here in this situation without a decent script that we can even start to pull together.'

I scrutinise the people around the table, watching them all stare downwards. No one wants to be here for this. No one wants to witness this, knowing they could be next. I'm pretty sure this is also why the other people who work here have been 'off' with me – in my absence, he takes his anger out on them.

Harry Andrews slaps open the script, jabs his finger at a part of the page. 'I mean, who is this Tally person and why is she in a coma? What sort of nonsense plot device is it?'

'It was in the pilot,' I say. 'One of Mira's friends from a long time ago who was left in a coma by someone that Mira is always hunting.'

Andrews snorts his disgust, a thick, phlegmy sound that turns my stomach. 'And where does this nonsense about a secret wedding in Bali come from?'

'It was hinted at in the pilot and mentioned throughout.'

*Snort.*

'And what is this bollocks about her best friend languishing in jail for a crime she didn't commit?'

'Again, that's been in there since the first episode.'

*Snort.*

'And what's this shit about the cakes being a replacement for the gaping hole inside her where children should be?'

'She hints at it throughout the whole show. I was just finally putting it to rest—'

He sneers at me, then turns his anger and rage on everyone sitting around the table. 'And you lot let her get away with this shit? For seven years? Seven years of this drivel!' He picks up the script, only to throw it down, it seems. 'We let you have your funny ways. We let you get involved in casting the show with an ethnic main character and her family, even though we knew we would be limiting its success domestically and internationally. No one really believes in that casting, but we played along, we let you do what you wanted and *this* is how you repay us. With some bullshit about best friends in prison with miscarriages of justice. Who gives a shit about her whiny best friend? No—'

'Oh!' I gasp suddenly, interrupting him mid-flow. 'Oh.' I gather up my pens and shove them to the bottom of my cloth bag along with my black notebook. 'I have to go.'

Alarm mixed with shock rises like a mushroom cloud over the room. I'm guessing it's less to do with me being upset and needing to exit, and more to do with them all knowing that if I leave, they're going to get it.

'Go?' snaps Andrews. 'Go where?'

'Erm . . . well . . .' I make a show of looking at my watch, I'll be three hours early to meet Lola from her art class, but they don't know that. But why lie? At this stage why lie to these people? I'm free now. The things that bind me to this place, these people, actually this society, are fast disappearing – what do I need to stick to the rules for? Why do I need to hold my tongue and play nice to keep the peace when, very soon, that peace will have absolutely nothing to do with me. 'I need to be somewhere else,' I say to him. 'Somewhere other than here.'

'We're really behind on this script, Cleo, we'd really appreciate it if you stayed,' Sandy Burton says, a plea in her tone and phrasing, but not in her words. 'Really appreciate it.'

'Yeah, well, should have thought of that before someone got mouthy and rude . . . and none of you spoke up.' I say this once I am on my feet.

Everyone is looking at me then; Andrews is shocked into silence. Probably the first time someone has stood up to him.

'You know, I remember when half of you were liking and sharing and putting up "me too" posts. I remember all your "times up" solidarity hashtags. I even remember when your social media feeds were wall-to-wall black squares and inspirational quotes about doing better. And you think I'm going to sit there and take this nonsense from you?

'Why would I? When it's not me, it's all you. And I am removing myself from this. When everyone is ready to play nice or just not behave like utter *trash*' – I look at Andrews – 'I'll be back and we can work on the script.'

By the end of my speech, my voice is breathy, making me sound close to tears. But I don't care. That is nothing to care about. All that matters is me removing myself from this situation at this time.

The big frosted glass door to the conference room is heavy and as I approach it, I can't remember if it swings inwards or outwards or both. I can see myself making a complete show of myself, I can see me stalling as I try to escape and completely embarrassing myself in the process. As I get to the door, I push at it and it thankfully yields to my touch so I can leave with dignity.

It wasn't the harsh words about my writing that did it. It wasn't the swearing and the berating, either. It wasn't even the way he rubbished every single thing about the show. It was what he said about Mira's friend being in prison.

*Who cares about that?*

Me. I do. That's why I wrote it. I wanted to give myself hope.

Hope that I would one day get Sidney, Wallace's brother, out of prison, since I'm the person who put him in there in the first place.

## Central London, 2007

'Cleo, can you stay a few minutes, please?' Ivan Carlton, my new boss at the magazine, called from his glass-walled office.

I was on my way out of the door with Samantha-Louise and Wendy, two work friends who knew how to start the weekend with a good drink and all the best magazine-world gossip, when his deep, commanding voice had floated out to me. I was tempted to pretend that I hadn't heard, to carry on gathering my belongings and speeding the hell out of there.

'It won't take long,' he added a tad louder, obviously guessing I was working up to ignoring him.

Wendy grimaced first, then Samantha-Louise. Our new editor came to us with a bad reputation for having an eye for the ladies and a mind for the vicious. Our previous editor had been a horror, but we could handle her. She wasn't pleasant, but she didn't care enough to make anyone's life a misery. This guy . . . Always there early and would shoot pointed looks and make barbed comments if you arrived after him; most nights he was there late and made it known without saying it directly that he expected you to stay as well. In his first meeting addressing the team, he had told us that he was on a mission to upgrade our career expectations of ourselves. He wanted only go-getters on his team and if you thought you could coast on his watch, you could think again.

What his upgrading your career expectations actually entailed was to bring you into his office several times over the course of two weeks to demoralise you by making you detail to him what you weren't very good at, make you then question and eventually doubt anything you did think you were good at. Then, at that point, when you were low, he would tell you what he thought you should be doing with your life. All the while not letting you get on with the job you were hired to do, and then remonstrating in meetings about work not being completed on time.

It was clearly my turn in the hot seat.

'Good luck,' Samantha-Louise whispered as she headed for the door. 'We'll be down in the Wellington. I'll get you a double.' She turned to look briefly at what awaited me. 'I'll get you a triple.'

'Cleo . . .' My very important boss moved from behind his desk to the front of his desk, to where I'd taken a seat. Casually, he leant his bottom back on it then raised his leg to rest his foot on my chair, right next to where I was sitting. It had the unfortunate effect of giving me a too-close view of his crotch area. And with his proclivity for extra-tight trousers, nothing was being left to the imagination. I averted my gaze, burning up with embarrassment. 'I have really good news for you,' he said. 'The board are expanding the team. They want to branch out into special projects – one-off specials and the like.'

I nodded and quietly said, 'That sounds great.'

'We're considering you to head it up.'

That made me lift my head, catch sight of his 'area' and lower my head again. 'Me?'

'Yes, you. They weren't sure, of course, because you don't seem to be the most *experienced* of girls.' The way his mouth slimed out the word 'experienced' made every nerve in my spine shudder. 'But you know me, Cleo, a friend to all. I told them, "Hey there, dudes, even little Black girls deserve the chance to shine." I also told them I'd be there, an experienced, safe pair of hands to guide you through. I could tell that swung it in your favour. So, what do you say, partner?'

*What do I say? About having you breathing down my neck for every moment of my working life? To you expecting me to be forever grateful? To the prospect of you dismissing everything I've done in my working life and pretending I only came into existence when you arrived?* 'This sounds like a great opportunity,' is what I said. 'I'll have to think very carefully about it.'

'What's to think about? I would have thought you'd be jumping at this opportunity. If you turn it down, though, the powers that be are not going to be happy. They're not going to be happy at all.'

'I'll have to talk it over with my husband,' I said, chickening out of telling him where to go. 'It's a big thing to decide.'

'Husband? I thought you were single?'

'I mean my partner. We've been together so long I call him my husband,' I replied. I was always calling Heath my husband in my head; this was the first time it'd slipped out to someone else.

'I thought you were enlightened, Cleo. I thought you were an independent lady with an open mind. Is that you or are you a woman shackled by a man, chained to his side and only allowed to do his bidding? Cos if that's the kind of gal you are, then I'm thinking this . . . this won't work out.'

I didn't even know where to begin with all that he had said: the evocation of slavery, the sexist tropes, the subtle hint of the sexual harassment to come. There was no way Human Resources would take any of this seriously – it wouldn't even be my word against his, it would be 'nice, forward-thinking "feminist" man gives inexperienced Black girl a chance and this is the thanks he gets'.

This was a no-win situation for me. Truly. If I worked with him, I had a whole world of subtle racist, sexist, patronising comments to endure before he tried it on, but if I didn't work with him, I was pretty sure he'd make my life unbearable anyway.

I pushed my chair back before I stood up. I didn't want to be too close to him. 'Thank you so much for offering me this opportunity,' I said, still avoiding looking directly at him. 'I'll let you know what I decide in a few days.'

'You do that,' he said tersely. 'You think very, *very* carefully about your position here.'

## West London, 2007

Heath found me in the bedroom on the bed, staring up at the ceiling.

I'd been there since I got in. He hadn't rushed back because he thought I was going out for a few drinks with the girls from work; he had no idea that instead I'd left the office and come straight home. On my miserable journey back to the flat, I'd been trying to work out the best thing to do about my job. I *liked* working on the magazine. I would *love* to be a special projects editor. I was excited about what career doors it could open. It could even be the gateway job to a deputy editor position. It was just, I was less a fan of setting myself up for being harassed either for working with Carlton or for thwarting his efforts to have another minion under his direct control.

*I have to get a new job*, I'd pretty much decided by the time my husband leant over me.

'Uh-oh, the sad starfish,' Heath said, turning down his lips in sympathy. 'I haven't seen you in a while. What's happened?'

I took him briefly through it. 'Ah, babe,' he said at the end of it. He slipped his hand up my top and stroked across my stomach, immediately soothing me. 'This is a shit situation.' He kissed my forehead. 'If I was your psychologist, I'd be telling you to figure out how to stand up for yourself and to maybe consider why you weren't able to do that in the moment. If I was your jealous, out-of-control husband I'd go kick the living shit out of him. As the man I hope you think I am, I'm going to suggest you start looking for another job as soon as possible.' He kissed my forehead again. 'This is so unfair, you work so hard at that job. Maybe you could speak to the people above him about the position without him.'

'I wish! Not the way those places work, unfortunately. And anyway, there are all sorts of rumours about him and how he has "connections" not only on the board but elsewhere. They always make it sound like he has gangster affiliations. Gangster mates or not, though, I try and go above him, he'll do his best to break me. As it is I've got to be careful in case he slags me off and my name becomes mud in the magazine world. I've seen it happen to writers and editors more experienced than me.'

'Well, if it becomes unbearable, you can quit your job and write that book or movie you've always wanted to. I'll support us both.'

'Yeah, maybe,' I said despondently.

'Oh come on, babe, don't let it ruin your weekend. We'll come up with a plan that will sort all of this. And I fully mean it about supporting you while you write your book. I have my inheritance. You don't need to stay miserable in that job.'

'Thank you,' I replied. 'Thanks for being so supportive about this.'

'You're welcome . . . how about some nice sex to cheer you up?' He waggled an eyebrow suggestively at me.

'Hey, I actually called you my husband when I was talking to him. Had to correct myself, but it felt so natural to say it.'

'Glad to hear that. But what I really want to know is, yes or no to cheer-up sex?'

'Yes,' I said, pulling him close, enjoying the sensation of his weight on top of me, the smell of him filling my senses. 'Of course, yes.'

# 16

'Have you heard from your dad at all?' I ask Lola as we drag our groceries up the garden path. On the way back from the summer holiday art class she is now attending practically every day, we stopped to get a few bits and pieces from the local supermarket. That had ballooned into near enough a weekly shop because we had no idea what to have for dinner.

Even though I'd told her I was staying at home today, she still went to art class. I had spent most of yesterday – the day after the disastrous meeting with Harry Andrews and HoneyMay Productions – with my phone off, and logged out of my email. No one at HoneyMay Productions had my home number, thank goodness. My agent did, though, and she rang a few times to say they were having meltdowns. Everyone was sorry I'd misunderstood what was being said, everyone wished I hadn't left so suddenly because we could have thrashed things out, everyone was super-stoked about the extended final episode and how I was going to write it to make sure it went out with a bang. Yeah, sure. In other words: *Is she going to tell anyone that the head of a company that has had its fair share of 'me too' controversies and bigotry accusations is still publicly humiliating people who work for him? Or is she going to do what most people are forced to do by circumstance and wanting to pay bills and just shut up and put up?*

I'd almost told Antonia the truth. She was always on my side, always supportive – even when she didn't understand what I was doing – so I almost said that I had bigger problems than Harry Andrews and his lack of redeeming features. That what I was actually working on, the reason why I was dismantling my life, was so much more important than an inadequate man who had never been punched in the face for the things he said and did. But I didn't confess, didn't let her in, because I adored my agent, she didn't need to be involved in this mess. What I did say, though, was that I would love – for once – for people like Harry Andrews to get their comeuppance. For him (and others like him) to face real-world consequences for the things they did and said, not just get away with other people making apologies and everyone turning a blind eye to what they did. Antonia agreed and said we should let them stew for a bit, not give them a definitive answer about what next for a couple of days.

Today I woke up ready to fight the world. Ready to march down to HoneyMay Productions and deliver a very real, very unmissable lesson to Andrews et al. I'd funnelled that fierceness into the script, using my anger and regret that I hadn't said more as fuel for the words that appeared on my screen. By the time I came to meet Lola, most of the rage was there on the page, expressed in the most vicious murders the Baking Detective had had to deal with to date.

'Yes, Pops has been texting me non-stop,' Lola says to my question. 'He's having a break with a "friend" in Portugal. He keeps calling her a "friend" or a "mate" like I don't know he's got a girlfriend. He knows I know what sex is, right?'

'I presume so.'

'Mum's got someone else, too. She's a little less shifty about it because I'm there all the time and it was Pops who left.'

I've had a suspicion about why Valerie made Franklyn leave, even though it was him who walked out – she was the instigator because she'd finally had enough and had given him an ultimatum. All I have is suspicion, though, since Valerie won't speak to me except to ask after Lola when she's here, and neither Franklyn nor Wallace have entrusted me with that information.

'Pops wasn't happy when he found out that'd she'd been dating,' Lola continues. 'I heard her saying on the phone that he thought she'd just wait around for him to come back when he was ready. Have you got someone else?'

I stop midway up the path and turn to my niece, who is, disconcertingly, nearly as tall as me.

'That's a very good question,' the police officer from the other day asks over Lola's shoulder. 'One that I'd like the answer to as well.'

The male police officer smiles at me, waiting patiently for me to answer Lola's question it seems. Further behind him, I spot the female officer getting out of a grey car. She has on a beige mac over her black trouser suit, just like he has a beige mac over his black trouser suit. *Twinnies!* I used to think whenever I saw Wallace and Franklyn together or looked at the big portrait of them at their parents' house. (Trina asked me once if I was physically attracted to Franklyn as well as Wallace and I told her the official answer was of course not, because they were different people, but the reality was, if I was slightly too far away, I would mistake my husband's twin for him and would have a moment of lust before I realised who he was.)

Lola, who obviously remembers the police officer's voice from the other day, twists her face into the image of utter defiance before she turns to glare at him. There is no love lost in the Pryce family for the police, that's for certain.

'Can I help you?' I say pleasantly. It's not for him to know that my heartbeat has shot up, nor that adrenalin has flamed heat all through my body.

'We just have a few questions,' he says.

I shove my hands into the pocket of my black jacket, searching for the familiar jagged, metallic edge of my keys. Once my fingers touch them, I pull them out. 'Lola, take my keys and go inside, please,' I say to her. Even though all I can see is the back of her head, I can still feel the distaste with which she is looking at this man and woman.

She doesn't move, doesn't even give any indication that she has heard me. 'Lola,' I repeat, a bit more sharply. 'Take my keys and go inside. Now. *Please.*'

Silently kissing her teeth, she spins to me, takes the keys and marches to the front door. I listen to her opening it, the rustle and clink of the bags, the brushing of her coat, the bleep of the alarm and then the sudden silence as she shuts it off. She doesn't shut the door all the way, I realise when I turn to check if she has properly gone inside.

The female police officer has arrived now, and is standing at her colleague's shoulder. They look, for a moment, like the cover of a DVD for a TV drama that wasn't picked up after the first series. *Two dedicated detectives, united in their fight against crime. Will they be able to put aside their differences to solve their most difficult case yet?* The urge to write blurbs for real-life situations had been with me long before I became embroiled with working with television people. Long before I wrote novels, even. I remember doing something similar in school and my teachers not appreciating my ability to hone down the bones of a situation while wildly exaggerating other parts. (*Romeo & Juliet* may well have been the peak of my brilliance – *Two teenagers, two families, and a load of misunderstandings that will echo through the ages.*)

'You had some questions?' I say after a quick peek over my shoulder to see if Lola is listening again.

'May we come in?' DC Mattison asks.

'I'd rather you didn't,' I reply to her.

'It would be better if we came in.'

'Pretty sure it wouldn't.'

'Have it your way, Mrs Pryce. By the way, is your husband in?'

'No.'

'Will he be back soon?'

'I don't know.'

'I suppose you wouldn't, considering you went to see a divorce lawyer.'

The policeman still has a smile on his face. It is pleasant and non-threatening, but I know all about pleasant, non-threatening people. How they can smile while gently gutting you, carefully cutting you up, slowly bleeding you to death. 'How are you holding up?' he asks kindly.

I must look thrown at that question.

'After finding out that you were the last person to see a man alive before he was murdered? A man who was helping you,' he supplies. 'It must be pretty traumatic for you.'

It's not, because . . . 'I try not to think about it.'

'I can understand that. Especially since Mr Burrfield was injected with a muscle relaxant before he was smothered. And his body was staged in a way that would make it look like he was working.'

With every word, a chill of familiarity flows its way through my body. Alarm and horror follow that chill and I think for a moment I'm going to fall over. *Familiar.* Too familiar.

'Does that mean anything to you?' he asks.

'Should it?' I ask casually.

'That was how one of the episodes of your show started. A solicitor ended up dead, murdered by someone connected to one of his clients because he knew too much about them. The baking lady worked it out over the course of an hour.'

'Right,' I mumble.

'Me, I don't watch anything outside of the news, it was DC Mattison who worked it out. Big fan of the crime-solving baking lady as it happens.'

'A recent fan,' she says. 'I don't generally like TV shows that paint the police as so stupid that an ordinary member of the public has to solve crimes for them. Especially murders. But I'm kind of changing my mind about your show. So imagine my surprise when I saw that episode and there were so many similarities.'

'Imagine,' DC Amwell says. 'Quite the coincidence.'

'I suppose so.'

'Did your husband know that you were seeing a solicitor?'

'No. No one knew. No one knows that we're getting divorced, apart from his brother who lives with us. And I didn't tell him I was seeing a solicitor, either. I didn't tell anyone.' Not anyone I could tell the police about, anyway.

'Coming back to the question asked earlier – do you have someone else?'

I don't have someone else in the way they mean, which means I can answer honestly when I say: 'No.'

'Very well. We'll leave you to your evening.'

'That's it?' I ask before I can stop myself. Sometimes I am not smart. Sometimes I am just damn stupid.

'Did you think there would be something else?'

'No, not really. It's just, last time you said there was some evidence?' Not smart at all.

'Oh yes, the evidence,' the policeman says. He nods. 'The evidence.' He turns a little to his partner. I wonder for a moment if they're together. If I should rewrite my blurb for them to involve an ill-fated romance? 'We'll leave you to your evening,' he says without elaborating on the evidence. *This is all a tactic, all a tactic*, I say to myself. The police plant something in your mind but take their time to explain it to you. That way you're always on edge, always wondering what they know so you're more likely to slip and tell them something that will show your guilt.

*I mustn't fall for it. I mustn't.* 'OK, thank you,' I reply, because I don't know what else to say.

I pick up the shopping bags, heaving them up into my hands. I make sure to turn before they walk away. I have to reclaim a little footing in this situation. I have to reclaim as much footing as I can.

### North London, 2007

'Welcome, welcome to Jump-Start: Do You Have The Write Stuff?'

Work was hell, but I had decided to focus on the good things in my life. My husband, my family, my writing. Those were the things that were keeping me going.

With Heath's encouragement, I'd signed up for this course and tonight was the first night. There were twenty of us right now, but I guessed that number would fall away. I'd done short courses in the past – 'How To Write A Soap Opera', 'Comedy Writing For Beginners' – and the numbers always fell as the weeks progressed. People found that the course wasn't for them, the commitment wasn't for them, just writing with others wasn't for them. I wasn't sure if it was for me, but it was something to do. It was a way to get feedback. It was a way to meet people who were interested in writing in the same way that I was.

'You will get out of this as much or as little as you wish,' the teacher explained. 'But we have a few rules. What's discussed in here stays in here. I know it can be tempting to tell others about the things you hear, but it's not fair on your fellow writers. You all need to feel safe enough to read out your work and talk about your writing without worrying that other people will hear about it. Other rules are you only offer constructive feedback. Remember that your consumption of someone else's fiction writing is subjective – if you don't like something, feed that back but only in a constructive way. Nothing is wrong, it's just not to your taste. If you think it could be written better by altering structure or changing form, fine. If you think it's something beneath you or your intellect, show yourself the door before you inflict those thoughts on anyone else.'

I liked the teacher. She was smiley. And experienced. And she had a good measure of people. I was going to enjoy this course. This would be my chance to explore my storytelling abilities. I had wanted to make up stories since I was a teenager. Probably younger. The only thing I liked better than reading stories was making them up. Writing was my escape, my comfort. It was also going to be my future. I knew it. Once I had finished this course, I was going to make sure I had all the tools to start and finish a book. I was going to get myself into a routine so I wrote no matter what else was going on in my life.

This course was going to be my next step to actually doing it. To actually writing that book I was always talking about and had seriously attempted a few times.

'Welcome to the stories of your life.'

# 17

*This is not good*, Lola thinks. *This is not good at all.*

Lola honestly thought that last time was an anomaly – something she would tell Mum and Pops about at some point and everyone would snarl about the police having nothing better to do than hassle innocent people, and they would, ultimately, put it out of their minds.

But it looks like they're targeting Auntie C. Why? From what she heard listening at the door, it sounded like they thought she had something to do with the death of the solicitor. Well, yeah, it was a bit weird, her being the last person to see him alive and, yeah, it was even more weird that he was killed in the same way that she wrote about on her TV show. But that didn't mean anything, did it? *Did it?*

Out of all the people she knows who are grown, Auntie C is one of the least likely to be involved in something shady. She is always so nice about everything, but not in that way it makes you side-eye and wonder what exactly she's hiding. She just seems to like people and want to help them.

But since her parents' split, Lola has to admit to herself that she doesn't trust people as much as she once did. It's nothing personal, it's just that people are messy. Humans are complicated. Growns like to

186

create drama and pretend it's all a surprise when the drama blows up in their faces. That's what she learnt from her parents' relationship – they ignored each other, they acted as though the world only revolved around her and their work and their home and not the other adult in their life. They acted like that and then were surprised when they stopped caring what the other one did, to the point where they didn't even notice the other one until it was time for them to leave.

Lola had tried. Really tried to get them together, to get the three of them to spend time together as a family – games nights, movie afternoons, just eating meals without the television – but neither of them would commit to it more than once or twice. And she watched her family disintegrate.

And that disintegration led to her not trusting people – Growns – to do what was best for them. Even if it was staring them in the face.

Is this the start of a similar process with Auntie C? She's already split up with Uncle Wals. That is big chaos, mega drama, from someone who has never shown such urges.

When Auntie C returns to the house with the remaining shopping bags in her hands, Lola is standing by the kitchen door, arms folded across her chest, an unimpressed look on her face.

'Why were they back?' she huffs.

'Because that poor man was murdered in the same way as one of the TV show episodes,' Auntie C replies. 'But you know that since you were listening. I don't know why they needed to tell me that, though, but they did. I'm sure it's a coincidence he died that way, but the police obviously don't think so.'

Lola is floored by Auntie C's honesty. She was not expecting that! She was expecting to be brushed off as usual. 'For real?' she says.

'Yup.'

'Do you think they'll be back?'

'I hope not, but I suspect so.'

'What can you do about it?'

'Nothing,' Auntie C replies, hefting the bags into the kitchen and dumping them on the floor. 'There is literally nothing I can do except wait for them to catch the person who did it, I suppose.'

She sounds distracted, worried. *I suppose you would be*, Lola thinks. Knowing that Uncle Sidney is in prison for something he didn't do has made Lola very aware of injustice. Of things going horribly wrong without you realising anything was even amiss. Is this what is going to happen to Auntie C? Is that why she is so scared all the time?

'Why you standing there like that?' Auntie C asks when she returns from washing her hands in the under-the-stairs bathroom.

'Do they think you did it?' Lola asks.

'Did what?'

'The police. Do they think you did it, with the lawyer man?' She makes a slicing movement across her throat, then closes her eyes with her tongue stuck out.

'To be honest, I don't know. I hope not, because I obviously didn't do it.' Auntie C goes to the kitchen sink, grabs the dishcloth from its bowl of bleach, squeezes it out before going to her shopping bags. 'Well, don't just stand there, wash your hands, get changed, come and help me put this stuff away. We haven't even thought about what to have for dinner. Cough, takeaway, cough.'

Lola shakes herself, forcing herself to come out of her physical and mental trance. She isn't sure why Auntie C is behaving like nothing is wrong, when clearly *everything* is coming apart right now, but does suspect things are about to get a whole lot worse for Auntie C. And for herself.

# 18

## Central London, 2008

I uncapped my coffee and my eyes slipped shut for a moment while I inhaled the aroma.

There was nothing like a good hit of coffee to get me going of a morning. Sometimes I wished I was brave enough to go back to the days of publicly dunking and drowning chocolate in my coffee, that would make things more interesting. But that was then, this is now. And I wasn't allowed to do that sort of thing. It was painful for anyone watching, for one. So I just stuck to my five sugars no matter the size of the cup. Still, maybe it was something I should try, since I was constantly searching for things to get me through the day. Ivan hadn't got any better. Since I'd turned down his 'very kind' offer to be harassed by him while working as his minion, he had become pretty much unbearable.

And no matter how much I searched, how hard I looked, there were no jobs out there for Cleo. Heath had been encouraging me to quit anyway, but I didn't want to. I'd always worked so I didn't like the idea of being reliant on anyone else for money. Money is power and much as I loved Heath, much as I trusted him, I was never going to willingly give anyone that much power over me.

Our office was a medium-sized, irregular-shaped octagon with the desks packed quite close together, but there was space for us to hold meetings at one end, and a cupboard for stock. The editor's office was a glass box at one end where the windows were. We had posters up on the wall, music played constantly, we had a good vibe. Obviously Ivan had done his best to try to kill the fun atmosphere in our offices, but we were hanging on, we were still finding ways to be a team. I was the first in today, which was unusual. Ivan had spent a lot of time commenting on my 'timekeeping' – meaning he expected me to be there an hour before work officially began – and I'd had no choice but to comply. I was often minutes after him, but today he wasn't here. I could drink my coffee in peace.

'Cleo, Cleo, Cleo!' Samantha-Louise came skidding to a halt by my desk, which was in the corner by the window.

'Samantha-Louise, Samantha-Louise, Samantha-Louise!' I replied as she bobbed down, her ankle-length black dress flaring out around her. She used a perfectly manicured finger to push a lock of shiny black hair behind her ear.

'You'll never guess what's happened,' she said breathlessly.

'You're right, I'll never guess, so please tell me.'

'Guess.'

I grrrred at her. I hated people doing that. It got my back up like very little else. Samantha-Louise knew that but she still did it.

'All right, all right, Ivan has been attacked.'

'Pardon?'

'Ivan, he's been attacked. Late last night!'

'What? Really? *Really?*'

'Apparently he was knocking off one of the big boys' wives. You know, one of the people on the board. He was literally dipping his dick somewhere he shouldn't have been. Well, obviously that wasn't going to go unanswered. Someone or someones – they think it might have been two of them – jumped him as he got home last night.'

'Bloody hell, really?'

'Yup.'

'Is he OK?'

'No, he's not OK. He is very definitely not OK.'

'What do you mean?'

'Oh God, it's awful. They properly did him over.' She put her hand on my knee to steady herself. 'They think he won't walk again.'

'What?'

'When Jessie from marketing was describing all his injuries, my jaw was on the floor. It's just this list of . . . ruptured spleen, broken kneecaps, crushed spinal cord . . . on and on the list went. They were not messing around. Jessie said they think he's lucky to be alive.'

'Bloody hell. And they really think it was cos of who he was sleeping with?'

'Uh-huh. Or all those rumours about his gangster buddies might be true and they've turned on him? It could be that?'

'But that's . . . that's like something out of a TV show or movie. Do you know whose other half it was?'

'Take your pick. Apparently, there were quite a few. And that's how he got the best positions and got to do whatever the hell he liked – the women he was sleeping with had their husband's ears and would talk him up, make sure he was protected.'

I shuddered. 'I can't imagine *wanting* to do it with him, let alone actually doing it, let alone actually doing it more than once.' The thought of that honestly turned my stomach. 'But for that to happen to him . . . It's horrific.'

'I know!' Samantha-Louise stood up, waggled her legs to see if she could get them moving again. 'I wonder who they'll put in to cover for him?'

'Anyone has got to be better than him.'

'Well, yes, for you it will be a million times better.'

I said nothing. Apart from Heath, no one knew the true substance of the conversation I'd had with Ivan a few months ago. It wasn't hard to see that he hated me, that he picked on me, but Ivan was clever enough to make it seem like it was a result of me not delivering, not because he was a vicious, nasty little man.

Samantha-Louise said, 'You think no one noticed? Oh, we noticed all right. A couple of us tried to talk to the board about it but we were shut down. Now we know why – he was protected. In so many ways.'

'Oh, Samantha-Louise, that's so sweet, thank you.' I was genuinely touched by that. I had no idea anyone had tried to help me. 'I'm so touched.'

'Fat lot of good it did. But look, when none of us expected it, a big old dose of "what goes around comes around" arrived to sort it all out.' She shrugged in an exaggerated way. 'Not saying he deserved it, but here we are.'

Yes, here we are.

The thought of Ivan stayed in my mind all day. For things to get better for me, they'd got a whole lot worse for him. Not what I wanted. Not what I wanted at all.

# Part 4

# 19

'Stop changing the subject, Cleo, I'm not going to let it go. Have you got a will or not?'

My big sister, Adjua, was lecturing me about my future. Had actually rung me up specifically to do so. She was the oldest by five years (ten years older than our younger sister) and she had always inhabited the role of super-daughter with ease and without resentment. She had got good grades (to be fair, we had as well) but she went to university to do a proper African-daughter's degree – in Accountancy and Business Management. She met a nice man just after college whose parents came from Ghana as well, and she waited until she got married to have sex and then have children. (We knew the no-sex-before-marriage line was absolute bull – but if you knew my sister, you would know that it *felt* true and that was more than good enough for my parents.)

In being herself, and doing it happily, Adjua took the heat off me and Efie – our parents were happy that they had a daughter doing things the 'proper' way so they rationalised away my Psychology and Media degree, and by the time it got to Efie, she was allowed to study English Literature without anyone raising an eyebrow. The pay-off, of course, was that Adjua regularly felt duty-bound to try to drag me into being a grown-up. Today, it was a conversation about wills. I'd tried many, *many* ways to derail the conversation – music, TV, dinner arrangements, what her children wanted for Christmas and birthdays – and we always ended up back here.

'No, I do not have a will,' I said. 'I do not need one.'

'Please, under which rock has your body been living? You need a will. Everyone needs a will. Especially if you're living with someone.'

I stood up, my eyes wide. She was a cool, swotty sister, but she was also the tattle-tale sister. She was going to tell on me. And she didn't even know that Heath and I were married – in name only, and in another country so technically it didn't count – but it would *so* count to my folks. 'Who says I'm living with someone?'

'Your address, your phone number, your boyfriend answering said phone number, your boyfriend having dinner with your parents most weeks.'

'Don't tell Mum and Dad,' I said quietly. Although why I was whispering, I wasn't sure.

'You think they don't know? You honestly think they believe you sleep in the spare room and live as dating flatmates? How stupid do you think they are? How stupid are you? You're a grown woman. Of course they know. You're meant to be the cleverest of us three – don't tell Efie I said that – and you are spectacularly thick sometimes. But, again, no distractions. When are you getting a will sorted? Your boyfriend has one.'

'How do you know that?'

'He told me.'

'When?'

'At one of Mummy and Daddy's dinners.'

'He just told you that? Out of the blue?'

'No, I asked him. Why wouldn't I? He's involved with my sister, I need to know what kind of person he is. "Has Will" puts him into the "Serious Person" category. "Does Not Have A Will" puts him into the "Wasting My Sister's Time" category. He passed. With flying colours. Even went as far as to tell me that his flat and pretty much everything goes to you and a bit goes to his mother if he dies.'

'Really?'

'Absolutely. He is a Serious Person. Now you need to be a Serious Person and get yourself a will. And make sure you leave me your ring collection and your handbags.'

'Oh Efie bagsied those years ago. As well as my first editions, my vintage leather coat and my designer make-up box.'

'And you just gave her those things?'

'Why wouldn't I?'

'The utter disrespect of this.' I could hear her shaking her head. 'Whatever, I suppose. But get a will. The next time I speak to you, I expect you to have a will or at least to have started the process.'

'And if I don't?'

'Well . . . Maybe the stress of you not having a will makes me tell Mummy and Daddy you're not sleeping in the spare room at Heath's house, maybe it doesn't. Who knows? Who knows indeed?' To my silence, she added, 'Speak soon, love you, bye.' And hung up.

I stared at the phone. I had to get a will. Or my sister would tell on me. The thought of that was terrifying.

I had no idea where to start. But if Heath had one . . . in fact, I remembered suddenly, I knew he had one. A while back when I was rifling through the drawers of his desk, looking for where he'd hidden one of my birthday presents, I'd come across an envelope with the words '**In The Event Of My Death**' typed on the front.

I hadn't been brave enough to open it, especially since his death or anyone else's death was something I didn't like to think about. And I couldn't say anything to him about what I found because of the whole 'shouldn't have been looking for your present' situation. But if I was going to have to do this will stuff, then I'd take a sneaky peek at Heath's to see what sort of thing I should be writing.

All right, it was a pretty flimsy excuse for being nosey, but it was a valid one and it would get me into that envelope with *some* legitimacy. If he caught me, I could say that to him.

Yes, opening the envelope and reading its contents wouldn't actually be the end of the world. It would help me. It wouldn't do anything but help me. Would it?

# 20

*West London, 2008*

*The front of the envelope read:*

**To Be Opened By
Cleo Forsum
In The Event Of My Death**

*The note inside said:*

In the event of my untimely demise, darling Cleo, I would like you to have this. I started writing it for myself, but it is for you, too. It is the truth of my life, *our* life, to date. Please know that in all of this, I love you.

I love you.

I have always loved you.

And I would do it all again for you.

# 21

## Clinical Psychological Assessment Report

## ON Mr X

### (continuing)

---

**EVALUATION COMPLETED BY:** Dr A H Sawyer Berland, Clinical Psychologist

**TIME PERIOD:** Ongoing

**REFERRAL HISTORY:** Mr X self-referred after another recent bout of debilitating stress, anxiety, negative self-thoughts and repetitive intrusive thoughts.

**CURRENT SYMPTOMS:** Mr X has a long-standing history of his current symptoms but states a current stability with them, however this current state has been achieved and maintained by strenuous effort. Mr X is concerned that his current efforts may not be sustainable. He first began experiencing the symptoms highlighted in this assessment after the murder of his teacher and lover (Mrs L) as a teenager. Mr X has reported historic and current problems with concentration, stress and negative self-thoughts. He was sent for psychological assessment and counselling following the death of Mrs L.

**SIGNIFICANT MEDICAL HISTORY** *(Including incidents of psychological or psychiatric interventions, substance use and abuse, etc):* Mr X has no remarkable medical history. Previous psychiatric history is explored below. Mr X has never used tobacco but has abused alcohol and recreational drugs, particularly in the aftermath of the death of Mrs L.

Mr X does not currently abuse or consume recreational drugs but does drink alcohol in moderate amounts. Mr X is otherwise fit and healthy although does occasionally suffer from debilitating headaches.

**SUMMARY OF PREVIOUS INVESTIGATIONS AND FINDINGS:** No previous neurological or neuropsychological evaluations.

**DEVELOPMENTAL HISTORY:** Mr X has stated he was top of his class throughout his education and was moved out of year to challenge him from age 10. He was regularly bullied and physically assaulted by other school pupils. Mr X reports eventually becoming numb to these assaults and by the age of 14 was able to stand up for himself, which resulted in the bullying and assaults ceasing.

Six months before his 15th birthday, Mr X came to the attention of the new science teacher at his school, Mrs L. She took him 'under her wing' as he describes it since he showed a real aptitude for science. Within weeks the relationship became emotional and then sexual.

Mr X describes the relationship as loving, fulfilling and nurturing. He talks openly about Mrs L being gentle with him and states he had feelings of deep attachment to Mrs L, feeling incomplete and desolate when not with her. Mr X also states in his time with Mrs L he felt he grew as a person and genuinely felt his future was with Mrs L.

The relationship came to an end when Mrs L's husband found out about the affair and became so enraged he killed her. Mr L is currently serving a life sentence for manslaughter with mitigating circumstances having immediately confessed to the police about the crime.

Mrs L's death had a profound effect on Mr X. He confesses to feeling stuck in the moment of realising she was gone. He regularly replays moments from their relationship and takes comfort in them. Mr X's parents, although horrified by their son's relationship with Mrs L, were supportive after her death and moved out of London and changed his name to give him the chance of a normal life. Mr X found moving to university in Leeds a welcome relief from his past.

In his first year of university Mr X met Miss C. He was immediately drawn to her physically, emotionally and mentally. Despite the connection he felt with Miss C he remained only a friend until the end of university. On the final night in Leeds, Mr X and Miss C consummated their relationship.

Mr X reports this as being one of the happiest moments of his life. He had not felt complete until that night. Although Miss C was determined they remain just friends, Mr X relentlessly pursued Miss C until she agreed to start seeing him.

This stage of their relationship was the happiest Mr X had been since the death of Mrs L. After Mr X was given the opportunity to work in Australia for three months, he decided to test his relationship with Miss C by ending it. On returning to England, Mr X discovered that Miss C had been unfaithful, claiming to only have kissed someone else. Not long after this revelation, Miss C ended the relationship.

Mr X became extremely depressed and entered into a period of intense therapy and CBT to try to break what he had come to accept was an addiction to Miss C. Mr X began a relationship with another woman who he came to be fond of and this did help to mitigate some of the effects of not being with Miss C. He admits that during this time, he did attempt to rekindle his relationship with Miss C but she would not give him another chance.

When his father died, nearly three years after his break-up with Miss C, Mr X turned to her for emotional and practical support, something she provided without hesitation. At his father's funeral, one of their friends from university – Miss T – lied to him about Miss C having a boyfriend, in an attempt to keep him and Miss C apart. Miss C had mentioned before that this friend had once said Mr X was 'too intense'.

After his father's funeral, Mr X ended his relationship with the other woman, realising he only wanted to be with Miss C. He also became fixated on Miss T, the friend who had tried to keep him and Miss C apart. Feelings of rage, anger and revenge started to grow in Mr X. He tried the techniques learnt in CBT to try to dampen the feelings, however they became overwhelming and

Mr X decided to confront the friend. Unfortunately, upon seeing Miss T, Mr X was overcome with such anger and rage that instead of verbally confronting the friend as planned, Mr X stabbed her.

Mr X was horrified by his actions and went to visit the friend in hospital with the intention of seeing her before turning himself in to the police. However, an unintended consequence of the incident was for Miss C to decide she *did* want to be with him, properly. With the prospect of finally having a relationship with his perfect woman and the possibility that she might become pregnant with his child, Mr X did not go to the police. He instead committed himself to being Miss C's ideal partner to atone for what he did.

The next few years passed without major incident and Mr X even managed to convince Miss C to marry him in America. The couple kept this wedding a secret, further cementing in Mr X's mind that things had worked out for the best.

Unfortunately, during what was a happy period, Miss C was sexually and racially harassed by one of her work line managers. Mr X watched as his wife became more and more withdrawn, depressed and despondent. All the things that had made her happy became meaningless.

Mr X reports experiencing deep feelings of anxiety, worry and terror that Miss C would become lost to him. To solve the issue, Mr X began to investigate the man in question. He followed him a few times to find out where he lived. He discovered that the man was having various relationships with married women. When he had the information he needed, Mr X approached the man to ask him to lay off his partner. The man mistook the approach for an attack and Mr X was forced to defend himself in the ensuing fight. As they fought, Mr X gained the upper hand. When that happened, Mr X lost control and recognises he went too far in punishing his wife's tormentor.

When Mr X heard that the man he'd fought with would probably never walk again as a result of injuries sustained during the attack, he admits to not feeling as sorry as he probably should have. It didn't seem to be such a bad thing to do when the man had almost taken his wife away.

After the man was dealt with, Miss C was promoted and returned to her happy self. Mr X felt vindicated about his actions.

Mr X is currently on an even keel, although he is plagued by headaches. He also experiences bouts of anxiety and worry over Miss C falling out of love with him, leaving him or finding someone else. He often experiences other physical symptoms including palpitations, stomach cramps and shortness of breath.

**IMPRESSIONS:** It appears that Mr X is suffering from Limerence, as characterised by Dorothy Tennov (1979). Further work by Albert Wakin and Duyen Vo (2008) lends credence to this observation since they characterised limerence as having intrusive, obsessive and compulsive feelings and thoughts about one particular person.

Mr X has all the markers for limerent behaviour, that is, being in a constant state of addiction to another person, namely Miss C. It is likely that he had similar feelings towards Mrs L, however her death ended any uncertainty about their relationship.

Although Mr X has arguably achieved his goal of entering into a long-term relationship with his Limerent Object (LO), the imbalance in their relationship serves to maintain the uncertainty element, which is thought to sustain and perpetuate limerence. In other words, because there is always the chance that Miss C will end the relationship as she has done in the past, Mr X still feels in a constant state of flux when it comes to their relationship.

While Mr X has achieved his goal of being in a loving, committed relationship with his LO (Miss C) he continues to experience the sometimes debilitating effects of limerence. Mr X is aware of the unhealthy nature of his obsession, pointing to his last relationship where the woman he was involved with seemed to feel, in part, about him the way he feels about Miss C.

He is aware of the unhealthy nature of his ex-girlfriend's behaviour towards him, although he can see that his feelings and behaviours towards Miss C are far more extreme, but he has been unable to curb them. He is also aware that should Miss C discover the true nature of what he has done for and because of his feelings for her, she would most likely end the relationship.

On many levels, Mr X has been tempted to confess his actions to Miss C to bring about the end of the relationship so he can put an end to the limerence. Mr X is hopeful that should the relationship end comprehensively, that would end the uncertainty of their situation and would allow him to move on. However, he is aware that is part of the limerent thinking process and knows that should Miss C end the relationship or were the relationship threatened in some meaningful way, he would not be able to control himself. He would do anything to bring her back to him.

Mr X is scared of his feelings. From his past actions (stabbing his friend, hospitalising Miss C's co-worker) Mr X knows that he will go to extremes to preserve his relationship with Miss C.

**RECOMMENDATIONS:** Mr X should seek further psychological and possibly psychiatric help. He reported that CBT helped in part previously, particularly with the intrusive and obsessive thoughts about Miss C. Although he has been resistant to medication, this may be the solution to his mental and physical anxiety issues, as well as helping with the intrusive and obsessive thoughts about Miss C.

Despite his fears, Mr X should consider sitting down with Miss C and telling her the truth. He should only embark on this course of action, though, when he has secured the recommended psychological and psychiatric help to mitigate his reactionary behaviours. Once on an even keel, Mr X should tell Miss C the truth about what he has done and the true depth and strength of his feelings in order to rid himself of his guilt and in the hope of creating a more equitable relationship, which may help to 'cure' Mr X of his limerence.

**CONCLUSIONS:** In conclusion, Mr X should continue in his attempts to free himself of his limerent behaviours. He should follow the recommended advice to try to mitigate his current mental and physical symptoms and, in the long term, work out how to tell Miss C the truth.

# Part 5

# 22

I'm glad, when I settle down at my desk in my office, that Lola has opted to go to the summer holiday art class again. I'm not sure if she loves spending her days working on art, she's bored by my company or simply doesn't like the general emptiness of the house when I'm working, her dad's away and her uncle is who knows where. (I've emailed and texted Wallace asking if he's OK and have had nothing in return. I've been avoiding ringing his work because I don't want them to gossip about him or our relationship.) The house is quiet with only Lola and me in it. Now that I've had my 'calmed down' talks with HoneyMay Productions – first through Antonia, and then via Zoom with Sandy Burton, Chief Operating Officer, Dianne, the head of production and Anouk, the show's main script editor – I'm back working on the scripts.

Every one of the women on the call intimated, but didn't dare out-right say, that they knew the scripts weren't as bad as Harry Andrews had made out. He was, they hinted, just staking his claim as worst manager ever because all attempts to get me to change my mind had failed. So while we all knew there was nothing terrible about my work, the 'tweaking' was extensive.

When I first came to this type of writing, fresh off the high of having *MY* novels on shelves, in shopping baskets, in people's hands, I knew it would be difficult. But I honestly thought formatting and learning to use scriptwriting software would be my biggest hurdle to TV screen success. Turns out it was my descriptive style of writing (there was too much of it); it was my constant need for a backstory to explain a frontstory (the less of *that* there was the better). And, of course, it was my need to have people who looked like me visible and whole and properly formed. This had caused the biggest problems. The response to my characters was generally: 'Well, we don't *really* do that round these parts, so could you preferably look the other way while we do things like we've always done, but if you can't look away, could you just not make a fuss while we try to cut that particular character, or try to cast the role with a white person or try to define them by the racial abuse they've received?'

How we all laughed when I – and Antonia – said no in as many lovely, calm, understanding, collaborative, writerly ways as possible so I didn't get labelled as aggressive Black girl lashing out cos she's out of her depth!

'Laughed, I tell you, laughed,' I would rage to Wallace at the latest microaggression, which didn't seem that micro, truth be told, I'd experienced. He would wrap me in his arms, he would kiss the top of my head and he would ask: 'What can I do to help?'

'Just listening is enough,' I'd say, not knowing what to do with all my feelings. They frothed and foamed like fast-boiled yam – ready to spill over at any time. But I knew I had to keep hold of my feelings, cling on and keep them in check and find ways to deal with what was being thrown at me.

Girls and women like me deserved to be on the screen, we deserved to be 'every woman', we deserved to solve crimes while creating the most extravagant cakes the world had seen outside of a white tent in a field.

'Do you think my work is trivial?' would inevitably be where I went to next. 'Do you think me writing basically frothy books and similar TV shows is shallow and trivial and I shouldn't be surprised when people look down on me? Do you think I should be trying to write literary books that add to the weight of intellect from Black people out there?'

'No, no and hell no! Other people do intellect because it's their jam,' he would say, stroking my cheeks and kissing me again. 'You do you. Cos you is the other type of intellect – the fun, the light, the gripping, the real. I mean, who knew you could stop a criminal with the top layer of a wedding cake and some well-aimed macarons? No one, until you wrote it.' He pulled me even nearer, bringing me to my favourite place in existence – so close to Wallace I was far away from anything awful going on in *the* world and *my* world. When Wallace held me this tight, my past seemed a reality away, not something that sat on my shoulder at every moment of every day.

'It was a celebration cake,' I reminded him, 'but you know, effective weapon in a fix.'

'One of the best things about being with you is that I'm allowed to watch those programmes. Never would have sat down and watched them before, but now I have to, to support my wife. How cool is that? And I'm allowed to "notice" another fine-looking babe. It is all good from my ends. All. Damn. Good. And I know I'm not the only other person out there thinking that. You make us visible and show we're possible, that we deserve to be in every space. You can do no wrong in my eyes.'

Of course we were having two different conversations, but the guilt always lessened a little when he said that about me doing no wrong in his eyes. Always. Because my guilt, my mammoth, colossal guilt, was insurmountable sometimes and it seemed like Wallace was the only one who could ease that burden.

# 23

My eyes are tired and my fingers are stiff from spending most of the day 'tweaking' the script, which despite what I tried to convince myself of, totally turned into rewriting large sections. It just made sense to do so. I always kid myself that pulling out one loose thread here or there won't cause the whole structure or significant parts of it to collapse. I'm always proved wrong.

When I check the clock, it's time to pick up Lola from holiday art class. She doesn't technically need picking up – she travels miles and miles on her own to get to school usually, but it's nice to have a built-in break that forces me away from my desk for a significant amount of time.

My velvet jogging bottoms and velvet hoodie land unceremoniously on top of the washing basket where I sling them before I pull on my outside clothes of dark blue jeans with yellow stitching and dark grey sweatshirt. Wallace's sweatshirt, of course, because I need something of him close to me right now.

Keys and mask in pocket, I hit the set button on the alarm and open our purple front door and find myself face to face with the two detective constables – Amwell and Mattison. Mattison and Amwell, actually, since she is on the left today. A small 'Oh' of surprise escapes my lips as I stop short. I hadn't heard from them in two days and I'd actually begun to fool myself into thinking they wouldn't return. That they'd realised the 'evidence' was nothing to do with me and, despite the coincidence of how he was killed, I had nothing to do with Jeff Burrfield's murder.

'Looks like you're going out, Mrs Pryce,' Amwell says.

'Yes, I need to pick up my niece.'

*Beep, beep, beep, beep,* reminds the alarm as it waits for me to complete the circuit by shutting the front door. 'We need a word,' Amwell says.

*Beep, beep, beep, beep,* the alarm warns. If I don't shut the door soon, it will start to screech that something is wrong.

'I'm pretty sure it'll be more than "a word" but I don't want to be late for Amalola, so you'll either have to walk with me or you'll have to wait till I come back.' They both look uncomfortable while, *beep, beep, beep, beep,* the alarm insists. I force them backwards by stepping out and shutting the door behind me. The alarm immediately sets itself by becoming silent. 'So, what's it going to be – coming with me or waiting here?'

They look at each other and then at me. They're kind of expecting me to stay because they've asked, but neither of them is going to voice that. I move towards the gate. 'We really need a word, Mrs Pryce.'

'I know, but I need to be walking, so you'll have to come with me.'

They follow me down the path and then when we hit the pavement, Amwell comes out with: 'There's no easy way to tell you this, Mrs Pryce, but your employer, Harry Andrews, has been viciously attacked and left for dead.'

That makes me miss the step I was about to take and I have to reach out, my fingers scraping painfully on the exposed red brick of the wall surrounding our rocked-over front garden to steady myself.

Amwell adds: 'Mr Andrews is in critical condition; it's thought he won't last the night.'

Adrenalin suddenly spikes in my veins, fills my stomach and I think I'm going to throw up the emptiness of that stomach and pass out, possibly at the same time. 'What happened to him?' I manage to push out, aware that I am losing time and I will soon be late to pick up Lola.

'We believe he was run over and then his body moved to the seafront where he was thrown off the seawall onto the pebbles below to make it look like an accident.'

The adrenalin spike is almost a tsunami this time. That's how another one of the episodes of *The Baking Detective* started. A vile man who was shown shouting at his employees, who'd been implicated in many incidents of 'me too'-type behaviour, got his comeuppance in the first act. He was run over, then his body was taken to the seafront and he was thrown onto the pebbles – to make it look like an accident. This was after the freelancer whose contract wasn't being renewed told him where to go when he tried it on with her. It turned out to be his wife and girlfriend working together, but the poor freelancer spends much of the story in prison, wide-eyed and terrified about her fate.

This can't be happening.

I had a fight with Andrews, I walked out, he turns up close to death.

'Oh, I see you've recognised that this is almost the exact same way a nasty boss was killed in your show,' Mattison says, some satisfaction in her voice. 'Is it true you recently had a run-in with him?'

'No it's not true. I had a *meeting* with him and some others at HoneyMay Productions earlier this week. I didn't have a run-in with him – he shouted at me, I left. I haven't seen him since.'

'But there was bad blood between the two of you?'

'I don't carry bad blood for someone like him.' I wave my forefinger in the direction of my face. 'It gives me wrinkles.' The red-orange bricks of the wall that I am still heavily resting on is rough under my fingers. I let it go without thinking that through, and wobble a little as I stand upright. 'I have to go. I'm already late and I have to go.'

'Very well, we'll return to speak to you either later this evening or early tomorrow.'

'Do you have to?' I reply. 'I mean, what else can I give you? I don't know anything about his attempted murder, I haven't spoken to him since that meeting. I don't know when he was attacked exactly, but I've been here most of the time because I have a thirteen-year-old to look after. That is literally all I know.'

'But don't you think it's a bit odd that two people have been attacked and – in the case of Mr Burrfield, lost his life – in a way that you allegedly made up.'

'I didn't *allegedly* make it up. I *did* make it up for the show,' I say. 'And I could only do that because it's the sort of thing that could happen in real life, especially to people like my main character.'

'Are you—?'

'No,' I interrupt firmly. 'No, I've told you I have to go. I'm late for my niece. I have to go.' Without waiting for a reply, I turn to face the direction I was leaving in and move off at speed. At such speed I can pretend I didn't hear Mattison's voice say, 'We'll see you later to talk about the evidence we've found.'

### North London, 2009

I headed for the tube with my woollen hat on my head, my gloves on my hands and my scarf wrapped twice around my neck. I'd also buttoned up my coat right to the top before I left the old school building and stepped out onto the pavement. I still felt cold. Since . . . Since 'the discovery', I always felt cold, no matter what. I was always wanting to throw on a jumper or a coat or two, always wanting to pull on gloves and a hat. I could never get warm.

Truth of the matter was, finding out who Heath was had frozen my core and I was probably never going to feel warm again.

I didn't know what to do.

That was what it all came down to. I didn't know what to do. Did I go to the police? Sure, and tell them what? *My partner – sorry, husband – is so in love with me, so obsessed with me, he hurts people who he thinks might take me away from him. How do I know? I read something he wrote, which sounds like total fantasy but I know is the absolute truth.*

'Yes, that will work, Cleo,' I mumbled. 'They'll definitely be all over it. Right away.'

I'd opened the envelope carefully so there was no sign that I'd read it, and I'd put it back in exactly the same place where I found it. And then I had called my parents and asked if I could stay. I had texted Heath and told him my parents had asked me to come over as they needed me. And I'd spent the whole night wide awake, trying to work out what to do.

By the time I reached home the next day, I had forced myself to switch into pretend mode, where I acted like I did before I made 'the discovery'. I played out my memories of what being 'normal' with Heath was like. It was all I could do.

The last thing I wanted to do right now, though, was to go home, see Heath, slip back into pretend mode, but as I rounded the corner, the bright lights of the Tube station and its surrounding shops came into view – people moved towards it like they were drawn by a large powerful magnet, other people moved away from it like they had been spat out – I knew that was what I was going to have to do.

'Bad break-up?' the voice said beside me.

I was so mired in the horror of my husband, I didn't even jump when the man spoke. I simply looked in the direction of the voice, wondering if I understood the words he'd spoken?

'Bad break-up?' I repeated as a way of helping me to decipher his meaning.

'Are you going through a bad break-up?' he asked kindly.

'No, why would you ask that?' *I WISH I was going through a bad break-up*, I thought. *I wish Heath had left me. I wish my relationship status could be registered as heartbroken and alone.*

'When you started the writing class, you were all "rom-com" and "contemporary classic", now it's all "death, destruction and dystopia". Don't get me wrong, I like it. I like your writing no matter what you turn your hand to, but I can't help but worry you're going through something. Possibly a break-up.'

'Not a break-up,' I said. 'Unfortunately not a break-up.'

'Rah, that bad?' he replied.

'Worse. So much worse,' I said and, to both our horror, burst into tears.

\*

The kind gentleman was called Sidney. He stood patiently in the middle of the pavement while I cried, and then gently steered me towards a late-night café bar that was worryingly empty considering how close it was to a Tube station. Worrying because it must be terrible to be that deserted when there was such high footfall in that area. Not that I cared.

Sidney had the kindest brown eyes; I noticed that about him as he ordered two coffees from the man behind the counter. We sat at a table from where you could see the door. The gloom inside the café bar was more 'trying to save on the electricity bill' than 'trying to create an atmosphere' but I didn't care either way. I was only there because Sidney had guided me there – the lighting wasn't important.

'I'm used to making girls cry, but I've usually done something,' he said, affecting what sounded like a Ghanaian accent. 'My powers, they're getting strong, you know. Now I say less than ten sentences and the girl are a-crying.'

I managed a weak smile. 'I'm sorry,' I said.

'Nah, nah, it's good. It's all good.' After a lengthy silence that was pockmarked by the noises of the man making coffee, Sidney told me, apropos of nothing: 'You remind me of my sister.'

I blinked at him, not really able to speak, so he continued: 'Every week I think that. Every week I think, "I should tell her she reminds me of my sister". Never seems to be the right week. But it is this week: you remind me of my sister.'

'That's nice. Well, I hope it is. Where does your sister live?'

'Nowhere, I don't have a sister.'

'You don't have one now or you've never had one?'

'I've never had one.'

I stopped staring gloomily at the cracked, tiled tabletop and squeezed my face up at him. 'How can I remind you of a sister you never had?'

'I don't know. I just look at you, listen to you, and you remind me of my sister I never had.'

'Do you have siblings?' I asked. 'Obviously not a sister.'

'I have brothers, twins. Identical twins. Although they just look like the cheap bootleg versions of me. Even my mum admitted that.'

That made my body spontaneously relax – my shoulders unwind, my jaw unclench – enough for me to laugh for the first time in an age. 'No way did your mum admit that!' I giggled.

'She did, though? She said it was uncanny that they looked so much like me from the moment they were born.'

'And you took that to mean they were bootleg versions of you?'

'*Cheap* bootleg versions of me. Yes.'

The man brought the coffee and I noticed straight away the crack in the wall of my cup, the chip in the rim of Sidney's. I was starting to understand why it was empty. Despite the general grubbiness of the place and the specific squalidness of the cups he had brought over, we thanked him genuinely enough to illicit a smile from him before he blended into the background again.

I tore open five packets of sugar and poured them into my mug of coffee.

'You want some coffee with that sugar?' he asked.

I shook my head, helpless. 'It's my only vice. Coffee with five sugars. I can't stop.'

'Fair play,' he replied.

'Your stories and pieces are really good,' I said to him. 'Always so different to what I expect.'

I'd been right about the course, Jump-Start: Do You Have The

Write Stuff? – it was the perfect escape from everyday life, while providing me with the discipline and regular deadline I needed to actually get words on a page. Since I'd started it before I found out who Heath was, Sidney was correct in that what I used to write was lighter.

Now the set exercises were used to examine my feelings, to explore the turmoil that raged constantly in my head, to navigate my dilemma. Because it was not a case of just leave him. It wasn't theoretical what Heath would do if I left him, it was fact – he would hurt whoever he thought was trying to take me away from him.

'What do you expect?' Sidney asked.

'Oh, I don't know. I suppose, when you write women, you don't focus on their looks and their physical attributes. You make them full, rounded humans. It's like you realise women aren't a separate species and you write them so well.'

'Wondering very hard if I should be offended by that,' he replied. He was grinning when I looked at him, though, so I knew he wasn't in any way offended.

'It was a compliment, why would you be offended?' I ribbed him back.

'I use my writing to try to explore what I'm feeling,' he said. 'I try to get into the heads of other people so I can see things from their point of view.'

'Think most writers are meant to do that, aren't they?'

'They are meant to, but do they? Nah. You can tell. You can always tell when a writer doesn't care. All the words, no matter how pretty, no matter how clever, if they don't come from the heart, they mean nothing. They fall flat. You can always tell.'

'I've always thought that. So many times I've read something that is beautifully written, incredibly clever, and it will get all these plaudits, and it'll just leave me cold. Stone cold because it felt like it didn't matter to the writer. And then I'll read something that people say is "trashy" or a "guilty pleasure" and it will touch me. It will move me or will reflect my experience or will help me make sense of something. I love reading because of that. I love writing because I get to do that, too. I get to write stuff that could one day touch people.' I haven't yet found a book that will help me to deal with what I found out about Heath and our relationship, which was why I'd been experimenting with the things I created.

'Writing is my therapy, too,' he said.

'I didn't say it was my therapy,' I replied.

'Nah, you're playing yourself. It's your therapy, Sis.' Sidney picked up his coffee, noticed the chip in the rim of his cup, rolled his eyes and kissed his teeth, put the cup down again. 'I also have a lot of issues to write out,' he said.

I sat back, openly shocked that he would say that to a total stranger.

'What's wrong with your face?' he asked. 'I told you you're like the sister I never had, why wouldn't I tell you that? I have issues. Big issues. Things I can't talk to people about. I put it all there on the page.'

'What's going on the page?'

'Me. Who I am. Who I am not. How to figure that out.'

'Crossroads time?' I asked.

'Criss-cross, cross-criss roads time.'

'I suppose I'll get to read all about it.'

'I'll tell you all about it. I ain't stingy like that.'

I grinned at Sidney, the tug of familiarity that I'd felt when we walked into this café now a definite pull. I liked him. I hadn't felt this drawn to a person since I met Trina on the first day of college. There'd been an instant familiarity when I'd opened the door to her knock on the first day and she told me that she was my next-door neighbour. 'We can be friends or we can be enemies,' she informed me. 'I haven't got time for anything in between. What's it to be?' I'd been impressed by the way she'd laid it out – we could be mates or not, she wasn't going to entertain lukewarm behaviour. And I'd felt an instant attraction to her, a knowledge that she was going to be my friend. Same with this man. I knew he was going to be my friend.

'Come on then, Sis,' the man opposite me said, 'who is this man giving you trouble and when are we leaving the dutty jancrow?'

# 24

'Any news on your divorce lawyer who was—?' Lola makes a slicing motion across her neck with her hand, then sticks her tongue out at the corner of her mouth.

'Don't do that,' I say, shuddering and wondering if the police will be waiting for me when we get home to talk about the latest murder I'm linked to. That would make it three (if Harry Andrews dies). How is that possible? Most people aren't even linked to one, but me . . . three. And two of them in the past few days. 'What sort of news were you expecting exactly?'

She shrugs her shoulders. 'I dunno. But you've got that look on your face and that vibe about you that you had the other morning when the police turned up. So I'm guessing you've had another "encounter" with the Five-Os.'

'Can you just concentrate on being thirteen and leave the rest of the stuff about the adult world and crimes to me?'

She clucks her tongue reproachfully. 'Not my fault you brought the detective brain to my door,' she states. Lola's picture from art class today is an illustration. It is Takashi Murakami style – lots of bright,

226

geometric flowers, drawn overlapping and sitting next to each other on a white background, and then furnished with faces. Some smiling, some sad, some weeping, some scowling, some confused, some sleeping. Each one different – *unique* – from the others on the page. Lola understands emotions. She gets people because she can read the nuances of their expressions. Also, she's great at eavesdropping.

'I didn't bring it to your door. I'm pretty sure you're too young to watch the show, and I know you're definitely too young to read my books. Any detective brain you have is entirely down to how your parents chose to parent you. Not my fault.'

'Good one, Auntie,' she laughs. 'Speaking of parenting—'

'How's your mother?' I ask to disrupt the conversation. This is not something I want to be talking about at all, but especially not with her. She's far too young for me to bring her into this. Far too young.

'Oh, not good. Grammy – her grandma – is not getting well as quickly as they thought she would. She's there supporting Granny – her mum – and doing everything she can. She sounds exhausted.'

As we navigate our way through the streets, heading, without really talking about it, to the convenience store in the opposite direction of home, meaning we'll have to do a huge loop to get back, I hear the sadness and worry in her voice. She misses her folks. I know she does. I am a poor stand-in, particularly without Wallace around. 'Do you want to go and be with her?' I ask. 'I can drive you over to Essex, no worries.'

She scrunches up her face, screws up her mouth, then shakes her head. 'No. I want to see her and all, I want to see them all, but I'm best out of it. If she doesn't have to worry about me, she'll be happier.'

'Less stressed, possibly, but not happier. Who could be happier without your lubbly, dubbly face?' I say to her in baby-talk voice, knowing it will make her smile.

'You're one of the kindest people I know,' she says to me. She speaks so sincerely, a little ball of emotion gathers itself in my throat. Unexpected. No one is thinking of me like that at all right now. 'It's a shame you and Uncle W couldn't make it work.'

'Uh-huh,' I reply non-committally. *We* could make it work. *I* couldn't, though. I was the problem. Me and all the things I did to get here.

'How come you two didn't ever give me a cousin?' she asks. The row of shops where the supermarket sits looms ahead of us.

'You shouldn't ask people that, you know?' I chastise gently.

'Uh? Why not?'

'Because . . . so many reasons. Mainly, because it's none of your damn business. But it's . . . You never know what someone is going through. If they want to have children but can't. If they don't want to have children but know if they say it out loud people will think they're weird so they keep quiet. If they're working things through with their partner and one of them is refusing to take that step. On top of that, they'll often have well-meaning family members asking them all the time about it. It's stressful. They don't need someone else – often someone they don't know very well – adding to that stress by asking those types of questions. But mainly, you shouldn't ask those questions because it's none of your damn business.'

'Ah. Right. Safe. Safe. So why did you and Uncle W never give me a cousin?'

We arrive at the supermarket and I'm not even sure why. We bought a load of food the other day that we haven't even begun to get through. But whenever I open a cupboard, the snacks don't feel good enough. Their brightly coloured packets don't sing to me in a way that they should. In the fridge, the succulent fruit just doesn't know how to hit the spot, the carrot sticks aren't what I need, the ice cream isn't the right flavour. It's the same for her, she doesn't find the right snack to hit the spot in the cupboards and fridge and freezer at home. We need to find that flavour combination, the perfect salty-to-sweet-to-texture ratio that will make us feel better. Not that I can eat.

'I get the impression that even though I've just told you all that stuff, you're just going to keep asking, aren't you?' I reply as we stand outside the entrance.

'Yup.'

'OK, then I guess I have to answer as honestly as I can.'

'Go on, then. Why didn't you and Uncle W give me a cousin?'

'It's none of your damn business,' I reply. 'And I'm going to keep saying that until you stop asking.'

## West London, 2009

'Are you falling out of love with me?' he asked.

It was the middle of the night and we were, on either side of the bed, both wide awake. Wide awake but spinning in our separate orbits, nothing at all linking us physically together. The further time moved me on from that moment of discovery, the more time I spent away from the flat and from Heath. I worked late – often offering to cover for other people if they were busy and something needed to be done. I would meet Sidney at our grubby, dingy café and talk to him about nothing much or writing. Sometimes I would sit alone in bars, nursing a drink and staring into space. Anything to stop myself being around Heath.

But just because I removed myself, that didn't stop us being linked, connected, married. I would come home to my dinner on the table, dried out and sad-looking. I would find little notes saying 'Love you' or 'Miss you' left on my bag before I went to work. I would notice how his breathing would deliberately slow when I slipped into bed because he was pretending he was asleep.

I didn't know how much longer this could go on, but obviously not too long because we were here, him asking me this question.

*I was torn.*

It was like there were two different people called Heath. Heath who I loved and Heath who I suspected of all those horrible things. Because how could I believe them? How could someone I knew honestly do those things? The way they were written down, written in the third person, often made me question the reality of what I'd read. Because, come on, didn't I spend every hour I could creating fiction? Making things up? Didn't I spend a lot of time imagining things? What was to say Heath didn't do that, too? Sidney was a hedge fund manager, and he wrote fiction. There were people on our course from all walks of life – doctors, solicitors, accountants – making things up. Writing disturbing things in the third person, using their own lives, their own stories as a backdrop. What if Heath, a psychologist, had used the things that had happened in his life to explore his fantasies? To rework fact to fit the fictions that would make him feel strong and in control of his life, then laid it out like one of the reports he wrote for his patients? I did that all the time. In my stories, I rewrote conversations and scenarios, sometimes from long ago, so they went the way I wanted them to go, not the way they did go. What was to say that Heath wasn't doing that with the document I saw?

My gut. That was what told me it was true. My knowledge of him. My feelings for him. His feelings for me. His never-been-hidden feelings.

I kept going back in my mind to the hotel room in Leeds. The violence with which we'd had sex. The furious, burning, eventually explosive anger that he'd displayed as he moved inside me. His desperate declarations that I made him crazy, his painful proclamations that he didn't want to love me but he did, his grief-stricken crying afterwards. I just knew that Heath had done those terrible things he wrote about and I knew with the same certainty that it was my fault.

I shouldn't have been his friend. That's what his report, written about himself in his capacity as a psychologist, had said. That's what everything I've since read about limerence and obsessive, addictive love says. The limerent object (me) needs to show no interest in the limerent (Heath), to give them no hope whatsoever of a relationship, so they would have a chance to move on. But being disdainful and horrible doesn't come easily to me. Does it come easily to anyone? Most of us are nice, aren't we? As a default we are nice to other humans.

Even if 'we' as a collective aren't, I am. And how could I know that my inability to be nasty straight away, my tendency to be nice first, would lead to this? Would drive a man to do this? And even now, knowing what I did, I couldn't cut him off. I couldn't just discard him.

'Are you falling out of love with me?' Heath asked again. He sounded so fragile, this man who had stabbed our friend, who had taken away another man's ability to walk. This psychopath I had married.

'No,' I replied. 'I'm not falling out of love with you.' Semantics. I was engaging in semantics. I wasn't falling out of love with him. That sounded gradual, slowly eroded; that sounded like I might still be in love with him.

I wasn't falling out of love with him – I *was* out of love with him.

It'd happened in the exact moment I realised who he truly was, what he'd actually done. But that was the active part of loving him. The residual love I had for Heath, the part that was latent and passive, that would probably always be there in some way, would never properly leave me. How could all those happy years, joyous times, be lost for ever?

And even if I was falling out of love with him, how could I say it, knowing what he was capable of?

'I feel like I've lost you,' he said.

I couldn't say anything to that.

'I feel like every day you slip further and further away from me. You're never here, I never see you, you never want me to touch you if we are here at the same time. It's like you've gone but your body is still here sometimes. It's like you're in a coma.'

'What . . . what would you do if you found out someone wasn't who you thought they were?' I asked him.

'I don't understand the question,' he replied, but the timbre of his voice told me he understood the question but was hoping he could deflect me away from pursuing it.

'What would you do if there was someone you loved – loved with all your heart – but then you found out that they were not who you thought they were. That they were capable of terrible things. What would you do?'

'We're all capable of terrible things. That's part of what makes us human. That's part of what makes walking away from others so difficult. We spend a lot of time categorising people, while forgetting that very few of us sit in these categories neatly and stay there – we all fit into multiple categories. And in the capable-of-terrible-things category, very many of us fit.'

'But what if those terrible things aren't just theories, what if they're real? What if they've actually been carried out? What would you do?'

'I . . . I don't want to lose you, Cleo.'

'What would you do?' I repeated.

232

'Tell me what's wrong and I can fix it.'

'What would you do?'

'Look, we can start planning the wedding if you think we've waited too long?'

'What would you do?'

'We can start planning to have a baby?'

'What would you do?'

'I would love to make a baby with you.'

'What would you do?'

'I was so disappointed after that night in Leeds when you didn't get pregnant. And I've had this fantasy ever since that you would get pregnant. That I'd get to call you the mother of my children. I want nothing more than to be the father of your children. Why don't we start planning for a baby?'

'What would you do?'

'I don't know! Stop asking that! I don't know what I would do! *I don't know!*' Heath hadn't raised his voice to me in an age. It was only when he did it then that I noticed I was scared by it. *I can't believe I've lived with you all this time and I haven't known who you are*, I thought. *I can't believe that I didn't know.*

Heath was horrified by how I flinched, the fear I showed. 'I wouldn't ever hurt you, Cleo,' he said, moving closer to me. I flinched again when his arm slipped around my waist and his whole body moulded itself against me. 'I would never hurt you,' he whispered in my ear, kissed my cheek. 'I could never hurt you.' He moved as close to me as possible. 'I could never hurt you. Whatever else you believe, whatever you think and feel, please, please know that I could never hurt you.'

'I know,' I mumbled. Because in all of it, I knew that was true.

Heath would never hurt me.

# 25

The police officers are waiting outside my front door, which means I have to let them in. The fact they stood here and waited for me to return means they must have something big on me. But what that is, I can't imagine because I didn't do it. Any of it. Not even Harry Andrews who, I admit, I would have loved to have seen get his comeuppance. And Mr Burrfield was helping me. Why would I hurt or kill him?

But these officers are not here for laughs, they are not here because things 'may' be connected. They have evidence that links me to all of this. 'I take it you've been hanging around because you think your "evidence" somehow links me to the two horrible crimes you told me about?' I say to them. Lola stared them down until they reached the safety of the living room.

'I wouldn't say that,' he says. 'If we had evidence that links you, we would have to arrest you. We're simply, at this stage, trying to decipher what seems to be your very strong connection to the two crimes.'

'Mrs Pryce— Or is it Ms Forsum?'

'Either is fine.'

'We'd like an explanation from you about the evidence we found,'

234

DC Mattison says. 'We found your pass at Mr Burrfield's murder scene.' On the footstool where Lola and I had rested our slippered feet, she places an evidence bag in which is the white rectangle and long blue thread of a lanyard. The pass is facing upwards and there's a little rectangle with my serious, I-don't-like-taking-pass-photos face on it. My first name – Cleomara – is lower case except for the capital C and is in a smaller font size than my surname – FORSUM – which is all in capitals.

My missing pass. The source of 'Philip' the security guard's power over me before it had been deftly curtailed by Gail, the production assistant. '*Shoulda just given her the pass*,' Anouk had said to him. Maybe if he hadn't, maybe if he hadn't shrunk at Gail calling him pathetic and petty, I would have looked harder for the pass. Would have noticed sooner its proper absence in my life. What difference would that have made, though? I was hardly going to know it had been left at a murder scene, was I?

'I must have dropped it when I was there,' I state.

'That's what I said,' Amwell says, like he can't believe he and I said the same thing.

'Yup, that's what he said . . . And then, just to be sure, I checked it against the log at HoneyMay Productions. It's a very basic system – nothing too sophisticated. But it does tell us what time people tap in and tap out.'

I know what she's going to say. If I was watching this on television, I would know what she is about to say. If I was writing this for television, I would know what she is going to say. Especially when she reaches into her inside pocket and unfolds a piece of paper. I do my best to not look like I am expecting her to start reading.

'You returned to the building that afternoon at two thirty-seven, where you tapped in. You went to the toilet at four seventeen. Returned to your desk at four twenty-three. You tapped out to go home that evening – everyone presumes – at five forty-nine. Basically, Mrs Pryce, it looks like you didn't drop your pass when you say you were there. It looks like you dropped your pass sometime later.'

'It's a little obvious, don't you think?' I reply, because what the hell else am I going to say? This is pretty much a bang-to-rights scenario. 'Me murdering someone and leaving behind evidence with my face and name on it? I mean, who does that? Only a stupid person, that's who.'

'I think you'll find that most people aren't as clever as they often think they are,' she says. 'The television shows glamourise these things, but very often it's the stupid people – as you call them – who think they can get away with murder.'

'They always have an overinflated sense of their own intelligence and guile,' Amwell adds for good measure.

'I won't lie, in a sick way I'm impressed by the way you've both just called me stupid right to my face, but I won't take offence since I didn't do this. I don't know how my pass got there, except the possibility that someone is trying to set me up? And I have no idea who that could be.' That last sentence is obviously a lie. Of course I know who. There is actually a list. But I'm betting that the person at the top of the list is not the one the police are looking for. I'm betting, in the privacy of my head, that this person is doing this because I am not dismantling my life as it is fast enough, so this is a motivator.

'We might be inclined to believe you, if . . .'

I almost fall for it, almost ask 'if what?' but I don't. I keep my mouth shut.

'If we hadn't found what seems to be one of your earrings snagged on the shirt of Mr Andrews.'

This is not good. Someone is deliberately trying to frame me for these heinous acts, but not doing a very good job of it. Almost like they don't want me to be arrested for the crime but they do want me to be always on edge. Always waiting for the act that will leave no doubt in the police's minds that I am the culprit. There's only one person who would think like that. Who would actually do that.

'Honestly?' I say to the police officers. 'You think I would make the same mistake twice? So quickly?'

'The earring was found inside his jacket, which makes us believe that with everything going on, the killer didn't notice her earring had got caught on his clothes while she was trying to move the body to make it look like an accident.'

Unlike the pass, I hadn't noticed any of my earrings were missing. I take them off and put them on so many times during the day, who knows where they are? I also have many pairs of hooped earrings. 'I'm sorry, but once is stupidity, twice is incompetence. If I was leaving my belongings all over crime scenes, I'd have no business writing crime stories, let alone committing them. And anyway, how do you know it's my earring? Out of the millions on Earth, how could you possibly know it's mine?'

'It might not be, that is true. But it's the same earring as the one you are wearing in the picture on your pass, and in most of the pictures we have seen of you.'

'Again, it's probably one of thousands of the same earrings in Brighton, let alone the UK.'

'That's true. Which is why we'd like to take a DNA sample to compare it to the DNA we found on the earring.'

'Yes, sure.'

'You will?'

'Sorry, I said that in the wrong tone of voice. I meant, "Yeah, right, sure I'll do that. In which reality?"'

Their immediate response is to stare at me in shock. They just called me stupid, but now they're clutching pearls because I snapped back at them? Of course I wouldn't be doing this if I wasn't in my current situation. If I wasn't almost one hundred per cent sure that it was my earring, I would be cooperating all the way. My knowledge that someone is setting me up is making me behave like a wayward teenager. 'In all seriousness, I was told by an actual crime scene investigator that the police rarely carry out forensics on small items, especially fingerprints. Possibly DNA, too. It's a lot of work for pretty much no real chance of getting the DNA material required. So, no, I will not be giving you my DNA so you can run it through your computers to see if I'm connected to any other crimes. I mean, I'm not, but I'd really rather you didn't play fast and loose with my genetic data.'

While they look at each other, wondering what I have to hide and how they can get me to reveal this thing I have to hide, I am thanking – in my head – Kathryn Bendelow, a crime scene investigator who gave me that titbit of information. After she read my first book in the *Baking Detective* series, she'd said how much she enjoyed it – then told me off for hanging a huge plot point on the collection of fingerprints from a small keypad. I'm grateful to her for that now. *So* grateful. 'Like I said, someone is clearly trying to set me up.'

'Why would someone try to set you up?' Amwell asks in an 'OK, I'll bite' type of voice. He's indulging me. Not sure I want to be indulged in this, really. There really is only one person who would want to set me up.

I look from one police officer to the other, not really sure what I can say without explaining it all. And I'm not doing that. If it was just about me, then I'd probably start blabbing. But what I do now will have reverberations, ripples, that will move through everyone in my life. From Wallace to Lola; my mother to my younger sister, Efie. No one will escape the tidal wave that will wash over my life and everyone in it, and it will leave them devastated. I can't tell them. I can probably never tell them.

I shrug that I don't know, so I'm not verbally lying. 'But seeing as I didn't do it, and I don't know how my pass got to a crime scene, nor how my could-be earring got to that other crime scene, that's the only explanation.'

'It really would clear your name quicker if you would just give us some of your DNA.'

I slap my hands on my thighs dramatically, and stand up. My joints creak and I find it hard to move quickly sometimes, but right then, I am sprightly. 'Thank you for your visit, officers,' I say when they don't move. 'And thank you for your patience in waiting for me to return from picking up my niece.' Still they do not move. 'I have to get on. I have a person to feed, work to do. Thank you. I'll show you out.'

They don't say anything more, not even an ominous 'we'll talk to you again soon'. I'm not sure what they expected from me but from the hangdog expressions on their faces they clearly haven't got it.

Lola hasn't even bothered to pretend to not be listening. She leans against the corridor wall, glaring at the retreating forms of the police officers. When I shut the door behind them, she turns her beady, unimpressed gaze on me.

'Why are you looking at me like that?' I ask.

She shrugs. 'I'm just trying to work out if I can see you trying to off some dude or two.'

'And?'

She stares some more, her brown eyes moving up and down my body. Then she stands up straight, unfolds her arms. 'Nah, can't see it.' A little shake of her head. 'Can't see it. I don't get psycho vibes off you. You aren't a killer.'

You never know, I should say to her. You never know who a real psychopath is until they sit opposite you and tell you that they've killed someone because of you.

## North London, 2009

Sidney was there in our grimy café when I arrived. He always was. He was Mr Punctuality. Always on time. One of the quirks of his personality that I appreciated.

I shed my coat and sat down opposite him. The horrible, gloomy little café by the Tube station had somehow become 'our place' despite me constantly staring and shuddering at the chipped, stained mugs, the cracked tiles of the tabletops, the grungy-looking walls. It was my worst nightmare, really, this place, but it was out of the way; Sidney and I could stay there as long as we liked without being bothered by the owner, and we had enough room on the table to spread out our notebooks and printed sheets.

We had decided to make our meetings constructive so had taken to working together, dissecting sections of work, verbally working through tricky parts, nervously giving and receiving feedback. Sidney had his work out already, the pages annotated with red and blue biro marks from where he was editing, greeting me like a familiar old friend.

He'd loosened his blue-patterned tie, undone the buttons of his gold waistcoat, and the jacket of his royal-blue suit was draped over the back of his chair. His sleeves were rolled up to show he was really serious about getting down to editing. 'How was work?' he asked as I reached into my bag to get my notebook and pens out.

'Same old, same old. How was your work?'

'Great. Was only mistaken for the other Black guy five times today. Think that's a personal best. In a couple of years, they may realise there are two of us.' He opened his hands in a shrug. 'We can only dream.'

I grinned at him. He made me laugh so much, the way he took on the world. The way he didn't engage with any of its bullshit. 'And what about . . . ?' What about the decision he'd been avoiding? Sidney was stuck. Scared. He'd been exploring a serious decision he had to make through his beautiful writing, so I knew that beneath the carefree attitude and easy smile, he was wrestling with himself, with his demons. 'Too hard today,' he said. 'Too hard all week.'

'Do you want to talk about it?' I asked.

'Not right now.'

'All right, but you have to deal with it.'

'I know, Sis, I know. What about you?'

'What about me?' Suddenly, the large, muck-filled crack in the table tile was very interesting. The most interesting thing on Earth, in fact.

Sidney put down his pen, sat back in his seat. 'Are you still sleeping with him?' he asked.

My stomach dipped at that question. Bloody Sidney with his giving a damn about me. 'If I say yes, will you think less of me?' I asked quietly.

'No, course not. At least you're getting your *tings*, I suppose.'

'It's not even that,' I said. 'I'd think more of myself if it was just about that.' Mostly, it was fear. Fear that if I didn't sleep with him sometimes, he'd start thinking he was losing me, and then would look around for the cause and would hurt someone else. Sidney would be prime suspect, even though I hadn't really told Heath about him, but so would Samantha-Louise and Cynthia and Wendy at work. So would this café owner, I suppose. Not my family, I suspected, because they weren't new elements in my life and they were nothing but lovely to and about him, but I didn't know how Heath decided these things, how deeply he thought about it.

I had told Sidney that my partner – I'd almost slipped up and told him Heath was my husband – had warned off a couple of people who he thought were going to take me away from him. I hadn't actually told him the details because they were too horrific to share with anyone, even Sidney. I said the crazy thing was, he didn't care about me having friends, about me going out drinking or clubbing or even on holiday with other people. He didn't care if I spoke to people, didn't make a nuisance of himself if I was out without him, he didn't show up to places where he knew I would be with others. None of that classic abusers' behaviour. It was only when he thought our relationship was threatened that he would act.

Because of that, every so often when Heath would touch me or kiss me, I would go along with sex, and I would take as much pleasure as I could from it so he wouldn't think I was faking it and then become a danger to other people.

'Give me your hand,' Sidney said.

I did as a I was told, looking him in the eye as I did so. Sidney's hands engulfed mine easily, even though I had large hands for my relatively short stature. He slowly, soothingly, rubbed his hands over mine and held me close. 'You need to leave him,' he stated. I began to withdraw my hand but he wouldn't let me go. 'I am serious here, you need to leave him. You can't keep letting him fuck you to stop him harming—'

'That's not what I'm doing,' I protested. 'I didn't say he harmed anyone.'

'You didn't have to. No one is as scared as you are unless something serious has happened.'

'I'm not scared.'

'No, you're literally petrified – too frightened to do anything. But, Sis, you need to leave him. Leave London, leave your job if you have to, but you need to get far, far away from him. He's dangerous. I don't like the thought of him fucking you on top of everything else.'

'It's not like that,' I protested again. I wasn't simply saying that, either. Sometimes it wasn't about fear. Sometimes it was like I hadn't found out about Heath. Sometimes it was like my memory about what he'd done had been erased and everything was normal between us. Like a few nights earlier, he'd come to bed an hour or so after me, and after climbing into bed, he'd cuddled up to me. Floating somewhere between sleep and consciousness, I hadn't immediately tensed up and then frozen at his touch. Because of that, because I hadn't gone rigid, he kissed the back of my neck. When I hadn't flinched at that, he'd kissed my neck again. When I didn't object, he'd moved his hands down into my checked pyjama trousers and kissed my shoulder. And when that wasn't rejected, he whispered, 'Can I come inside you?' and I'd said yes. I hadn't minded at all, him gently pushing me onto my front, taking my pyjamas off and then entering me. I moaned softly with every stroke, every 'I love you so much' he'd breathed in my ear, and I'd buried my face in the cool sheet covering the mattress as I'd orgasmed to stop myself being loud. I'd even felt a deep pleasure rippling through me as he came, too. That hadn't been awful. That whole

243

thing hadn't been terrible or abusive. It didn't even feel like I'd done it because I was scared and wanted to keep him on side. It felt like normal sex between two people who loved each other; it felt like sex with the man I loved.

'Most of the time, things are fine,' I explained to Sidney. 'Most of the time things are completely normal.'

'That's because you've normalised living in terror. You've normalised being hypervigilant and scared all the time.'

Hypervigilant was the type of word Heath would use. 'I'm not—'

'You need to leave him,' Sidney said decisively. 'And soon. The longer you live like this, the harder it'll be for you to see the reality of the situation, which means you'll end up staying because you'll think it's not too bad or you'll go back once you do leave because you'll remember it wrong. You need to leave him.'

'What about you and your situation?' I said to him, not wanting him to get away with this if we were going to deep-dive into our situations.

'Sis, don't try and deflect. My situation isn't going anywhere. Yours is more urgent.'

'He would never hurt me. He would never lay a finger on me.'

Sidney kissed his teeth and cut his large brown eyes at me. 'Like you don't know there are more ways to hurt a person other than physically,' Sidney said, calling me out. 'You studied Psychology! You know there are so many ways to hurt a person.'

I said nothing.

'You have to leave him,' Sidney said, as though that was the last word on the matter.

I knew I did. I knew I had to leave. But like he said, I was petrified.

# 26

*Entertainment * Trending*
**Harry Andrews**
Trending with #TheBakingDetective #LifeImitatesArt #metoo

By the time Lola and I have had dinner (with me forcing as much rice and stew down my throat as I could to make it look like I'm eating) and we have got ready for bed, news of Harry Andrews's attack is all over social media. Trending in lots of places.

I scroll through the various feeds, my scrolling getting faster and faster, the words and images popping out at me like lightbulb flashes on a camera.

The first thing I did when I saw his name up there under the trends tabs was lock my 'Cleo Forsum' account. When I first got my book deal, I claimed my real name on every social media site, then jumped through various hoops to get blue-ticked. Whether I became success-ful or not, I did not want anyone pretending to be me. Under those accounts, I posted information about the books, I posted info about the TV show and nothing else. I did not want to engage with anyone, to invite people into my world where they would go digging up my past. I also have another account under the name Meliza Green and a couple of numbers, so I can access 'members only' content on those sites.

HoneyMay Productions locked their blue tick account, too, as have almost all their employees. Not having access to these accounts hasn't changed anything: the wild theories roll on, the memes, the testimonies, the digging-up of old articles, past transgressions. A lot of it leaves me out of it and focuses on Andrews himself and his reputation. People haven't figured out yet that he was almost killed in the same way as an episode of *The Baking Detective*. All bets will be off then.

I gorge myself on stories and posts and comment videos – scrolling, scrolling, scrolling, clicking, clicking, clicking, guzzling, guzzling, guzzling like a pig at fattening time, until I am bloated and swollen and absolutely stuffed with Harry Andrews. And his murder. His attempted murder.

When I can't take any more, when I feel ready to vomit at any moment, I throw my phone down and it bounces on the bed before landing face up.

'*Why are you doing this?*' I want to scream at him. '*I promised you, and you promised me. You didn't have to do this.*'

I pull my knees up to my chest, wrap my arms around them and rest my forehead on my knees.

The phone, which is still lighting up with notifications about Harry Andrews, bleeps with a text message. I'm sure Efie, who lives on social media, will have seen the news and will have told Adjua, who will tell my parents. So they will be on the phone soon, telling me to disassociate myself from the show, telling me to stop writing those books about killing people because they bring nothing but trouble, telling me to move back home where it's safe.

I pick up my phone to switch it off, and the text message catches my eye. It's not from one of my family, it's an unstored number. I know the number, though. I learnt it off by heart so I wouldn't need to store it. So I wouldn't have to risk anyone, especially Wallace, seeing it and asking questions.

Furious and scared, I open the message and read:

° Do I have your attention yet?

## North London, 2009

The ticking of the clock in my favourite terrible grungy café was making me anxious.

I didn't know why I could hear it, since I was pretty sure the owner hadn't changed the batteries in the white-faced, black-numeraled, dust-covered unit in years (the hands moved, but never continuously, and it rarely showed the correct time). But I could hear it. I was sitting at our usual table – we could pretty much sit wherever we wanted since virtually no one came and stayed – in my usual seat with my back to the door.

I was waiting.

Waiting.

Sidney was late.

And he was never late. Ever. There were several things I'd got to know about him in the past few months of us being friends and his punctuality was one of them. He'd told me his brothers had often ribbed him for it, wondering why he needed to be so uptight, so controlled. 'Says a lot more about them than you,' I'd laughed. 'Although you do seem a bit uptight about it!'

Without having to check if the grunge café owner would mind, I took a packet of Maltesers out of my pocket, tore off a corner and squeezed out a shiny brown sphere. I dropped a Malteser desolately into my coffee, wishing Trina was here to object and point her finger and tell me what I was doing was disgusting. Everything had seemed simple back in college. So simple and easy. And I hadn't even realised that things could get so complicated. I watched the little puddles of oil from the chocolate rise to the top of the drink.

I heard the café door open and almost collapsed with relief. I turned towards the door, ready to mock scowl at Sidney for being late, ready to laugh at him for not being Mr Perfect Punctuality. The smile withered and died on the vine of my lips, and my heart stopped beating in my chest.

Heath.

Not Sidney.

Heath.

I turned in my seat, so I was back facing the wall. Now my heart was thumping, each beat like a punch against my ribcage. It didn't take long for my husband to pull out the chair opposite me – Sidney's chair – and sit down.

I couldn't speak first. He shouldn't be there, he was out of place and maybe if I didn't speak to him, he wouldn't stay.

'I'm sorry, your friend Sidney isn't coming,' he eventually said. As always, Heath spoke quietly, his words considered, his tone reasonable. And that was what was terrifying about him. His rational, reasonable demeanour. 'He is otherwise engaged.'

'What have you done to him?' I asked after bracing myself. He stabbed Trina, he paralysed Ivan. What did he do to Sidney?

'I haven't done anything to him.'

'We were friends. We were only ever friends, never anything else. Just friends.'

'I know,' Heath replied. 'That's why he's still breathing. If it was anything more, then . . . let's just say he would not still be breathing.'

'Just tell me what you did to him.'

'Nothing. He's fine – for now.'

'What have you done to him?' I asked again, the terror mounting. I couldn't stand for another person to be hurt because of me.

'I haven't done anything to him. I'm saying he's fine for now because' – he checked his watch – 'I'm guessing he's just going through the first round of questioning. How he'll fare in police custody is anyone's guess.'

Terror, pure, undiluted terror, moves through me like a waterfall. 'Wh-Why . . .?'

'Why has he been arrested? No idea. I just heard . . . Oh, you don't want to know.'

I swallowed, curled my fingers into the palms of my hands to steady myself. 'Tell me. Please tell me.'

He skewered me to the moment with his green eyes, held me secure. 'I heard it was murder. I heard an ex-girlfriend who dumped him had been murdered. I heard the police had an anonymous tip-off. I heard there was quite a bit of evidence against him.'

'No. I don't believe it. Sidney wouldn't hurt anyone. Much less ki—' I stopped speaking when I realised what Heath was telling me.

'Much less?'

249

'Much less kill anyone.' I hoped I was wrong. That Heath wasn't saying what I thought he was saying. That he wouldn't.

'Are you sure he wouldn't hurt anyone?' Heath said. 'Are you sure Sidney didn't hurt, say, a man who loves his wife more than anything and has spent years trying to give her everything she's ever wanted? Who has only ever wanted to be with her. From the moment he met her, he knew she was his destiny so he waited patiently for her. He waited for her to be ready. And even when she left him, he waited *again* for her to be ready because he knew with absolute certainty that she would always come back to him. What about that man who has always loved his wife, and has never stopped wanting to be with her? Did Sidney hurt him by befriending that man's wife and encouraging her to leave? Did Sidney do that?'

I could hear my breath. It was impossibly loud. I could feel the tears on my cheeks, they were hot and they were slow-moving. I could feel the trembling, it was shaking my entire being. 'Please tell me you didn't.'

'Didn't what, Cleo? What didn't I do?'

'It wasn't his fault.'

'Whose fault was it, then?'

'Mine. It was my fault.' I still couldn't breathe. The breath kept racing in and then dashing out, nothing would stay, nothing would allow my chest to relax. 'He didn't do anything.'

'He tried to get you to leave me.'

'He didn't do that.'

'Yes, he did. He told me he did.'

'*He* told you?'

Heath sat back and, for the first time in an age, I saw the anger that I knew simmered below his surface, sitting there on his face, in his eyes. 'I had a talk with him, man to man. I wanted him to know that you had a partner who loved you very much. Who wouldn't give you up without a fight. He told me he had no romantic or sexual interest in you. He told me that you were like a sister to him.' Heath's lips twisted with his rage and he glared at the tabletop. 'He could have left it there, but he didn't. He told me . . .' His gaze was back on me then. 'He told me that you were scared of me and what I might do to the people you love. Did you say that to him?'

I shook my head.

'He said you were scared of me. And he said you had to leave me. And he said he was going to help you to get strong enough to leave me. Imagine, he just said that to me. Right to my face.'

'Did you really kill someone to frame Sidney to stop me leaving you?' I asked. It was ridiculous now I had said it out loud. No one would do that. No one could do that.

I met Heath's eyes.

'Did you?' I asked him.

'I didn't do anything. He, on the other hand . . . All the evidence points to him being a very bad man. A killer.'

No, Heath couldn't have done that to Sidney. He couldn't. He just couldn't. And there was no way that anyone who knew Sidney would think he did that. No way. 'I'll go to the police,' I told him. 'I'll go to the police and tell them the truth about Sidney.'

'Tell them what, exactly?'

'That you set him up. That it was you who did it.'

'Be my guest. But you don't even know who was murdered or how, or if I have an alibi for that time. Or even when it was. You don't know anything about it. But feel free to go to the police. I'm pretty sure they won't just dismiss you as some crazy lady trying to involve herself in an investigation while trying to cause trouble for her lover.

'And, of course, if you don't have such proof now and you went to the police, I suspect that if at any point you *did* find proof that your friend Sidney was innocent, they might not believe you a second time. Cry wolf and all that.'

'Please don't do this to Sidney. He doesn't deserve it. Please.' Sometimes bargaining works. Sometimes you can negotiate your way out of a situation. And sometimes you know that begging is the way forward. 'Please, Heath. Please. Don't do this.'

And sometimes you know that nothing will work. The cards are played, the die is cast, the move is made and nothing can change that.

While I wiped waterfalling tears away with shaking fingers, my husband shook his head. 'Cleo, it's already done. I couldn't stop the motion of this – even if I wanted to.'

I covered my mouth first, then my eyes and then my whole face as my body rocked back and forth.

There was nothing I could do. Nothing.

Poor Sidney. Poor, poor Sidney.

# 27

Lola knows that Auntie C isn't asleep. She can hear her moving about above her. She should be creeped out, sleeping down here on her own when Pops isn't here, too, but she isn't. It makes her feel grown-up. Not in that messed-up way of being Grown, but the 'I have my own space and I can do what I like with it' kind of way.

This is what it'll be like when she finally leaves home. Obviously the décor will be a bit more peng than this, it won't be old. It'll have her touches, her flare, but a space like this to hang out in would be ideal. She'd have Kente cloth curtains at her windows, though. She won't have a sofa bed like this one, nice as it is, she'll have a large corner sofa, covered in the softest grey material, like the ones in the expensive furniture store she passes on the way to school. She'll have a chrome reading light that stands like a sentinel behind the sofa, and she'll have all the cushions. *ALL* the cushions. A nice footstool like the Kente one in Auntie C's living room will stand in front of her sofa, a big cream rug will cover most of the floor. It'll be so soft her toes will disappear into it. On the walls, she'll have her own framed artworks, the ones she likes the best, not necessarily the ones that look the best.

253

Lola has plans for her own place and this summer she had been planning on asking Pops if she can make some of those changes to their little flat in Auntie C and Uncle Wals's house. But that was before all the Growns started having crises or sex. Or both.

She can hear Auntie C moving around above and she's not surprised. Lola had gone on to socials intending to only be on there for a few minutes to see what everyone was saying before she went to sleep, and then she'd seen the stuff about the man who was killed. Almost killed, although lots of people had him as dead already. They were talking about *The Baking Detective*, they were talking about the man being trash, others were talking about what an amazing man he was.

It is messing with her mind. She'd wanted to message her best friend, but his mum was über-strict and he was only allowed his phone to go to and from school. And now, part of her wants to post something on socials instead. She could overlay a vid of her looking knowingly into the camera with the words:

*When the feds talk to your auntie about a murder that's on everybody's lips . . .*

Like she ever would! But it feels like there is pressure in the air, all around her. She needs to do something to get rid of it. Maybe she *should* go back to stay with her mother? Or maybe she should text her Pops and tell him some bad stuff is going down and she wants him back? Or maybe she should not let her imagination run wild.

Lola throws back the covers, slides out of bed into her slippers. Pulls on the grey dressing gown she leaves here for when she visits. Lola grabs her phone to use as a light. She gets to the bottom of the

254

stairs when she remembers her book and has to go back for it and her glasses case.

She tries to be silent as she climbs the stairs. She's wrong about sleeping in the flatlet alone. It's starting to creep her out. Auntie C said she could sleep in the bedroom next to hers, but she'd been all 'no way, give me my space'. It's like living in the desert now. She's about to sneak by her auntie's room when she changes her mind. She taps quietly on the space between the wooden panels and waits. And waits.

She taps again, quieter, not louder.

The door opens and Auntie C's face appears in the gap. 'You OK?' she asks after clearing her throat.

'I'm OK,' Lola says. 'Are you OK? You look so sad. Do you want a hug?' She doesn't wait to get an answer, she just pushes open the door and wraps her arms around the older woman. Auntie C's body tenses then relaxes as Lola clings on to her. Eventually her arms come up and encircle Lola.

'Thank you,' Auntie C says. 'Thank you for caring.'

# Part 6

# 28

I let myself into the flat, knowing Heath would be at work.

I'd borrowed my dad's car because it was bigger than mine and I'd taken the day off work to come back and pack up my stuff. I was taking as much as I could now – anything that wouldn't fit would have to stay, because I was not coming here again.

I hadn't seen Heath since the day in the café. I'd sat and cried, feeling utterly powerless, completely defeated. I wasn't sure what I expected him to do, but what he did do was sit and watch me, occasionally say he was sorry it had come to this, and didn't try to stop me when I got up and left. Since then I'd stayed on Samantha-Louise's sofa, and had ignored his messages, which were always: 'I love you. Please talk to me.'

Now I was getting my stuff and I was moving in with my parents for a little while. They were obviously overjoyed that I was coming back (again), but I couldn't uproot the tenants in my London flat because my life had gone wrong.

Disabling the alarm, I shoved my keys into my pocket. What had happened at the police station the day before was still circling my head like water down a never-emptying drain. They'd taken time from their

259

investigation to speak to me, obviously thinking I was coming to give them more dirt on Sidney. When I told them that he hadn't done it, the police officers – plain-clothes detectives – had exchanged looks then both stopped short of rolling their eyes in frustration. Still, they hadn't thrown me out, they'd sat and listened to me.

'Are you able to provide Sidney Pryce with an alibi for the time of the crime?'

'I don't know when the crime was, but I haven't seen him in a couple of weeks, so no, I can't provide him with an alibi.'

'Did you know the victim?'

'No.'

'Did you ever see Sidney Pryce and the victim together?'

'Not that I know of.'

'What exactly are you doing here, Ms Forsum?'

'I know he didn't do it. He didn't.'

'How do you know?'

'I know who did do it.'

'Who?'

'Erm . . . erm . . .'

'We don't have all day, Ms Forsum.'

'It was my partner. He . . . he didn't like Sidney being friends with me so—'

'He didn't like you being friends so he killed a woman?'

'Yes.'

'Do you have any proof of this?'

'He told me.'

'He told you.'

'Yes.'

'Your partner, who didn't like you being friends with a man, told

*you that he killed someone so he could frame that man, which would*
*stop you from being friends with him?'*

'I know how it sounds, but I'm not lying. I'm not making it up. I
know he did it. He's done stuff like this before.'

'He's killed someone before?'

'No, he's . . . he's hurt people before. He stabbed my friend and he
beat up my old boss.'

'And he told you this as well, did he?'

'Not exactly. I found . . .'

'You found?'

'I need you to believe me. Sidney didn't do this. He wouldn't. He
just wouldn't.'

'Thank you for coming in, Ms Forsum, we'll keep what you've said
in mind.'

I stopped at the cupboard in the corridor to grab a couple of my holdalls, then headed for the main bedroom to start with my clothes. I had
too many clothes and I didn't have the luxury of taking them all, so I
had to be ruthless. And I had to be quick, because I had no idea when
Heath would be back. I did not want to see him. Ever again.

I started with my underwear, emptying the drawer out and shoving
the mostly black bits of cotton and nylon and lace into the nearest hold-
all. I would normally fold them up, but no time. Next, I opened my
wardrobe in the alcove, started to unhook armfuls of clothes on hangers and dumped them on the bed. I emptied out the drawers at the
bottom of the wardrobe of my socks and tights and other items I'd
shoved in there because they didn't really have a place anywhere else.

From the top of the wardrobes, I got down more holdalls, and then
went into the walk-in cupboard between the bed and window to grab a

couple of suitcases. I was moving at speed because I really needed to get out of there.

My body stopped short and the breath caught in my chest when I walked out of the cupboard to find Heath leaning against the bedroom doorframe, arms folded across his chest. All at once, anger, fear, dread, hurt, heartbreak, sadness, terror, anger, anger, *anger* flared up through me like a volcano erupting.

Pretending he wasn't there, I moved towards the clothes on the bed and started pulling items off hangers, vaguely folding clothes before shoving them into one of the suitcases.

'I know you're upset,' Heath began.

I was quickly running out of space in the suitcase because I wasn't folding properly and because I had a lot of jumpers. Maybe I should just shove them into black bags, wedge them into the car around everything. Maybe I should leave the other suitcase for my books and notebooks and other stuff? I had so much stuff. A whole flat-full, a whole lifetime full. Too much to give me a quick getaway.

'I know you're upset,' he repeated, 'but please talk to me before you do this. Before you throw away our life together.'

That almost worked. That almost made me talk to him. But I resisted, carried on packing because I needed out of there without getting sucked into his orbit again.

'I'm sorry,' he said quietly. 'It wasn't meant to go this way. I just need you to talk to me.'

I threw down the black dress in my hands. 'You killed someone, Heath! Killed someone! You ended their life! Because you were jealous. Not because you were scared or in fear for your life, not by accident – you did it on purpose. You *murdered* someone. *MURDERED* them.' That still horrifies me. Every part of me still painfully vibrates with that knowledge. 'And then you fixed it so someone else is going to prison for your crime. And no one will ever believe me if I try to tell them the truth. What am I supposed to talk to you about? What is there to say?'

'Cleo, I did it for us. For you.'

'Don't you dare, don't you dare try to put this on me. Don't you dare make me a part of this. This is you. This is ALL you.' I started packing again, speeding up because I had to get out of there. Fast.

'NONE OF THIS WOULD HAVE HAPPENED IF YOU HADN'T CHEATED ON ME!' he yelled suddenly.

That made me stop again, that made me look at him. He was dressed for work in his navy-blue chino trousers and white shirt. In the past week he'd cut his hair, but he hadn't slept – I could tell by the paleness of his features, the dark shading under his eyes. Good. He should never sleep again, because I sure as hell was never going to.

'I have *never* cheated on you.'

'You were going to go on a date with someone else when you were with me.'

'No, Heath, some guy asked me out and I said no. Years ago.'

'It wasn't just that, though, was it? If you hadn't cheated on me, we would never have split up and none of this would have happened.'

'I have never cheated on you.'

'You said you kissed someone but—'

'I HAVE NEVER CHEATED ON YOU!' I screamed at him.

'YOU DID!' he shouted back. 'When I went to Australia.'

'We were not together then. You finished with me specifically so you could go on holiday and do what you liked, screw who you liked. That's what you told me.'

'You knew I was committed to you. You knew I was totally in love with you. I finished with you to see if you felt enough for me to stay faithful. And what do you know, you didn't.'

'Whatever your reasons, you finished with me and caused it. And I can't believe you're using a kiss to justify all this.'

Heath walked into the room, his contrite demeanour gone, vanished in his righteous rage. 'It wasn't just a kiss, though, was it, Cleo? It wasn't just a kiss with some random man in the pub, though, was it? It was so much more. More than once, he went down on you, gave you multiple orgasms.'

That stopped me, that caused me to screw up my face in confusion. How did he know? How *could* he know? I had never told him. I'd never told anyone. 'How do you know that?'

'He told me. *Ethan.*' Heath spat his name out like something disgusting he'd been chewing on. '*Ethan* told me how he had you writhing and whimpering in pleasure every time you lay down on his bed. How you clung to his head, how loud you were when you came, how you couldn't get enough of it. Insatiable, he said.'

I took a step back in shock. 'How did you know who he was?'

'I found him. I talked to every guy in that college bar until I found him.'

'You did *what*?'

'I knew you were lying to me, saying it was just a kiss. So I found out. I kept going back to that bar, talked to every man it could be until I found him. And he was more than willing to tell me all about it. I mean, come on, Cleo, couldn't you have found someone more discreet? He left out no details. He told me EVEYTHING! How you were practically begging him to stick his dick in you that third time. How you were so pathetically grateful that he allowed you to give him handjobs and how you loved him coming all over your stomach. How you were so desperate for him to stick his dick in you, you would have done anything for him. He told me. *EVERTHING. Every. Single. Thing.*'

My heart started to race, my mouth suddenly dry. Heath was a proper psychopath. How did I not see this before? How did I not realise he was a psychopath before he murdered someone? Before he broke a man's spine? Before he stabbed my friend? How did I not notice that? *He had always been like this.*

'What did you do to him? To Ethan?' I asked quietly.

'Nothing he didn't deserve.'

I closed my eyes, took several deep breaths. 'What did you do?'

'I only beat him up a little bit. Reminded him he shouldn't talk about women like that. It was disgusting, the way he was talking about you. He shouldn't have done that.'

'*You asked him.*'

'He shouldn't have done that. He would have been fine after a couple of days.'

My mind raced back suddenly to the man who had asked me out. He was a DJ and regular at the bar I worked at. He suddenly stopped talking to me, having been fine with me turning him down, he started to cut me dead if I tried to speak to him. Would avoid being anywhere near me. 'Did you . . . I can't even believe I have to ask this, but did you do the same with the guy who asked me out? Did you ask around until you found him and then beat him up?'

'I didn't touch him. I spoke to him, man to man. Explained you had a boyfriend. He was fine about it. Which was why I had to speak to "Ethan". Find out the truth about what you'd done with him.'

Heath hadn't started with stabbing Trina, like I thought. No, he had started with threatening a man, then beating another one up, then it was stabbing a friend, then it was breaking a man's spine. Increments. Heath had moved in increments along the road to murder. Every step had made the next step easier. Each movement along that road had made murder possible. And I hadn't seen it. I hadn't seen any of it.

I thought I could keep him under control. I thought that by sticking around, acting as though we were still a proper couple, I could stop him from doing anything else. But that was outside of my power. I could see that now. Heath was out of control. He always had been. He could keep a lid on it for long stretches of time, especially when I didn't do anything to threaten the equilibrium of our relationship in his head, but we were always going to end up here.

The man I loved had always been walking along the road to murder – I just hadn't realised it wasn't an 'if' but a 'when'.

'I can't talk to you any more,' I said quietly. 'I need to finish my packing and then I need leave. I can't talk to you any more.'

'Don't leave,' he said quietly, no longer the raging monster. Now he was normal Heath. 'Let's sit down and talk it out. We can work it out. Please don't leave me.'

Dangerous. All my reading had told me that leaving someone not even as extreme as Heath was a dangerous time. And the actual physical deed of exiting was the most dangerous time of all. He always said that he would never hurt me. Did I really want to test that out?

'Heath,' I said calmly, 'I need some time to think all of this through. You murdered someone. I need time to work through that.'

'I can help you with that. We can talk through it. We can work it out.' He was sounding desperate and that would make him even more dangerous.

'No, I need time alone. I'm just going to stay with my parents for a bit, I'm not setting up home by myself. I just need some space.'

'I don't want you to go,' he said, lowering his head and crossing his arms across his chest again. 'Space means we're splitting up.'

'It doesn't. It means I need to work things out in my head before I decide what to do. If you're always around me, it'll drive me away.'

'I'll stay out as long as you need – I won't come near you, but don't leave.'

'If I don't leave now, I will never stay with you,' I stated, sounding like it was an option, like I could ever stay.

'OK,' he conceded eventually.

'I need to pack now. Can you just give me some space to do that? Please?'

'I feel like we need to—'

'Please, Heath, I just need to get some space to pack. We can talk when I'm settled at my parents' place. OK?'

Again, he conceded. 'OK.' Then added: 'You'll come back to me. I know you will,' before he left the bedroom. Those words again. They'd unsettled me when I first heard them ten years earlier, but now they opened up a whole new chasm of horror inside me.

I never, ever wanted to come back to him.

Never.

# 29

### *Trina calling . . .*

Flashes up on my mobile. As Wallace mentioned last week, Trina has
been calling and texting and emailing for the past few weeks.

It goes against everything in me to duck her calls, but I can't speak
to her. Despite what I said to Wallace, I can't speak to her. She's my
best friend and it would be virtually impossible to talk to her right now
and not tell her I am leaving Wallace. As it is, I've done well to keep
my other plans from her to this point. I know what she will say if I tell
her even the smallest part of what I'm doing – I know she'll work it out.
She'll know this is all to do with Heath.

The phone keeps ringing, and I keep staring at her face attached to
her name and number in my phone. She's giving the camera a sultry
but almost smiling look, like she's reminding the camera of the secret
they share. She sent me the picture to use as her contact pic saying,
*'Felt super cute, think you should look at this every time we connect.'*

Despite us being in touch usually three or four times a week over
the years, I still haven't told her what Heath did to her. I can't. It would

terrify her, and it would probably lead to her never feeling safe and never trusting anyone – including the people closest to her – ever again. I am also pretty sure that if she ever found out about it and then realised I knew but kept it to myself, that would be the end of our friendship. But I can't tell her. How can I? How can I tell her that because of me, Heath had put her in hospital? That he had sat there in that hospital talking to her two days later like normal? How can I tell her that and not have her lose her mind?

'How's Heath?' Trina had asked me about a year into mine and Heath's blissful love fest. She'd seemingly called up just to ask since I hadn't mentioned much about him in our other calls. Once invited to, I'd had no trouble gushing about the loved-up bubble we'd been living in. 'Well, I suppose I did tell you to fix up' she'd replied. 'And you did.'

Years later, when I messaged to give her my new number and address after our split, Trina had called me straight away. I couldn't answer the phone, though. Couldn't talk to her and explain what had happened because it would have to include telling her that he'd stabbed her and I couldn't even form those words. Instead, I sent her a message saying we'd split with no way back and I couldn't talk about it right then. Like a proper best friend, she'd taken me at my word and didn't ask about him again.

When I told her about getting together with Wallace, she'd tentatively asked about Heath and I said I hadn't heard from him and we'd changed the subject. I'd expected Trina to ask about Heath again when I told her I was getting married, but she didn't. I wasn't sure why, but it'd been years since we split, so I assumed it was because we were all meant to have moved on.

The phone continues to tell me that one of the people I love most in the world wants to speak to me. And I want to pick up the phone to her,

I honestly do. But there are too many other things going on right now. If I stop to speak to Trina, if I indulge myself by revealing all, I'll end up stuck and scared, instead of just scared.

I let the phone ring out and let the answerphone kick in.

I will have to speak to her at some point. Just not now.

Just not right now.


## Central London, 2011

I'd almost forgotten what he looked like in real life. Almost.

The Heath that haunted my dreams, that I often saw on the street or in restaurants or public transport, was the one I last saw properly in his West London flat. The Heath in front of me had aged. As had I in the interim. I stopped taking his calls by the time Sidney's trial started six months after his arrest, and I certainly hadn't seen him. He sent me the odd text, just asking how I was, reminding me he was there if I wanted to talk. Often saying he was my friend first and foremost so if I needed him, he'd be there.

The Heath I was sitting down with had cut his blond-brown hair very short, practically shaved on the sides. His face was slightly more angular, his green eyes were bright and keen as usual, but underneath them they were smudged with grey. His usually healthy pinkish skin was pale, he'd lost weight. He would have looked normal – good, even – if you hadn't known him before. He was wearing his wedding ring on his hand, I noticed as I sat down. We'd never worn our rings on our fingers, only on chains around our necks. I'd put my wedding and engagement rings into one of the holdalls I'd used for moving and hadn't looked at them since. He was probably wearing his ring now to make a point.

'Thought I'd be immune to you by now. You know, absence makes the heart grow stronger for someone else and all that.' He gave a small, soundless chuckle. 'No such luck.'

I managed a smile. I wanted something from him, so I couldn't be how I wanted to be. 'Not sure what to say to that,' I replied, the most neutral thing I could come up with.

'Sorry, I didn't mean to make you uncomfortable.'

'You didn't. I just wasn't sure what I was meant to say. I've never split up with anyone before. Well, I have, but that person was also you, so . . . not sure how I'm supposed to respond to the things you say.'

Heath nodded, refocused on the table for a moment. 'So we are split up, then? It's not just a pause.'

'Who has a nearly eighteen-month pause in a serious relationship?' I replied. This had already gone wrong and I hadn't even been trying.

He manifested that small wry smile of his. I used to think that smile was kind of sexy, kind of cute. Now I knew it preceded him deciding to do harm to someone. It scared and chilled every part of me to see it. 'If we've split up, I suppose you're seeing someone else, then?' he asked quietly.

'You would suppose wrong. There is no one. Not even any new friends. I freelance now, so I go to my job and I come home. I see my parents every six weeks or so. I sometimes see my older sister and her family, I sometimes hang out with my younger sister. Nothing more. I don't even do the writing course any more. There is no one else.'

'I didn't want it to be like this, Cleo,' he said quietly, his voice full of genuine regret. 'I didn't want you to shrink your world. I know how much you love people and being around them. I didn't want you to have no one.'

*What else am I meant to do?* I wanted to ask him. *How else am I meant to deal with the guilt of Sidney, the fear for everyone else?*

'I don't have no one. My life is my life.' I shrug. 'It's different from before, that's all.'

'Cleo, could you look at me for a minute?' He sounded so earnest, I steeled myself then fixed my gaze in his direction and eventually managed to force my eyes to look him full in the face.

Our eyes met across the space.

And that was the thing about it all. Even knowing what I knew, despite having incontrovertible proof, you couldn't tell that he was a killer.

He didn't look like a killer.

He didn't have dead eyes, or eyes that were twin pools of evil nothingness; you couldn't look into them and see he was without a soul.

My husband was a psychopath, a killer, and you couldn't tell by looking at him.

He sighed. 'I've missed you. I don't mean just in a big way. I mean in the everyday little things like you grouching about me not wiping down the kitchen table properly, or getting into bed and it being warm because you were there.'

I stared at him, our life – the silliness, the laughter, the lovemaking, the friendship, the togetherness – flashing through my mind. We'd had a great time together, we'd had the best relationship, and through it all, he'd been this monster.

'Do you miss me?' he asked when I didn't fall into the pit of reminiscing with him. 'Have you missed me?'

In response I sat back and stared at my hands. I had learnt my lesson. I could not give him any hope, not unless I meant to go back to him and all of that.

'I'll take that as a no. Why did you want to meet, Cleo?' he asked.

'I want to ask you something.'

'Ask away,' he replied, even though he was visibly disheartened.

'Please just think about it when I ask. Just think about it before you give me your answer. And I will give you anything you want in return.'

'Anything, huh?'

'Yes. Anything.'

'Intriguing. As I said, ask away.'

I took a deep breath, steeled myself. Then asked. Found the words to ask him for the one thing that I wanted more than anything.

He listened. He thought about it. Not for very long, but he thought about it. Then he said yes. And I knew before he said the words what he was going to ask for in return.

# 30

Since the text message, I've realised that no one around me is safe. I thought we had an agreement, a promise, but obviously not. He is circling closer. Giving me a chance to do as I promised before he comes for those close to me.

That makes me put aside my pride as well as my worry that people might talk and I call Wallace's office number. They often open on weekends, especially if they have a big campaign on. I have to know he is safe, that he is somewhere I can get in touch with him if I need to. And it isn't like I'm going to announce our divorce on the phone. I'd been hesitant because I knew there would be eyebrows raised and lips twisted and looks exchanged at me calling the office number instead of his mobile. It'll be hard enough for him soon when they find out he's about to become single. I know quite a few people who would be happy to find out he's back on the market. But, as with a lot of things it seems, I don't like to think about that. I dial the general office number and am relieved when someone answers. I ask to speak to him and when he picks up the phone and says, 'Hello' in that softly gruff voice of his, I close my eyes. I keep them closed as I wait for him to say, 'Hello?'

again, so I can feel the word move from his lips through the phone and then diffuse into me, before I hang up. He is fine. Nothing has happened to him, nothing is happening to him, I can tell by his voice. The biggest threat to his happiness and welfare is me splitting up with him without a proper explanation.

I suspect he still doesn't believe I will go through with it. I suspect he thinks – probably quite rightly – since I can't really offer him a proper explanation, that I am just having a 'moment' and I will call the whole thing back on again. I have been wavering. I can admit that to myself. I have been dragging my heels, especially with the divorce part. It has taken me weeks to tell him. And then time to get a divorce lawyer sorted.

That is why my attention needed to be 'got'. Why my mind needed to be focused.

The morning papers are filled with stories about Harry Andrews. His brilliance, his downfall, his rehabilitation that allowed him to rise from the ashes unscathed. I haven't seen any mentions of Jeff Burrfield's murder. He obviously isn't noteworthy enough to make the pages of national newspapers. Which leads me to believe he was probably a nice enough man who did enough good, who lived an OK sort of life. He didn't really bother anybody and, ordinarily, nobody would have bothered him if I hadn't picked him out of an online search for divorce lawyers.

Jeff Burrfield would be alive today if he hadn't decided to take on my divorce case. That makes me inordinately sad. Poor Jeff Burrfield. He didn't deserve this. At all.

I'd almost messaged Gail, Amy, Anouk and Clarissa to find out how they are coping with having a colleague so publicly attacked, and with the attention that is now on HoneyMay Productions. But thought it best to leave it. If I want to help them, then I should finish the scripts so everyone can move on from the stage where a lot of the focus is on me.

I text Franklyn to ask when he might come home, and found out that he has indeed gone to Portugal as Lola said. I ask if he'll be gone for one or two weeks and he asks if Lola is OK. When I confirm she is fine, and ask again when he might return, he says, 'Soon' then stops replying. Valerie had the patience of a saint, I decide.

I don't want to, but I have to call Valerie. I have to make arrangements to get Lola away from here. I do not want anything to happen to her, especially not because of me.

'I can't talk right now, Cleo,' her tear-stained voice says when she answers after three rings.

'OK,' I reply quietly.

She must hear the tremor of worry in that one word because she says, 'Is Lola OK?'

I know Valerie is going through the worst possible time, that she is slowly losing one of the people she loves most in this world, that it will mean her life will never be the same again, but I do not want Lola here. I do not want something to happen to her.

I need to tell Valerie that. Some version of that anyway.

But I can't. She sounds so broken, so upset, I can't add to her worries. 'Yeah, yes. She's fine. I told her I'd check in with you, see how you are. She misses you. And she worries.'

'She's a good girl,' Valerie says. 'I miss her. But I don't want her here to see Grammy fading away and my mother falling apart. I remember being around adults when they were going through something like this when I was her age and it really messed me up, you know?'

'I can imagine.'

'I know I haven't really spoken to you or Wallace since the split, but I know you take good care of Lola and I'm grateful. Especially at a time like this.'

'It's no problem. And Franklyn does most of the caregiving. Wallace and me are just here for back-up. Although if you tell anyone that, I'll swear up and down it's just me, of course.'

That makes her laugh a little, the sound bereft and tear-soaked. 'Thank you.'

'It'll be OK, Valerie. It doesn't feel like it right now, but it will turn out OK. You won't be the same afterwards, but none of us stays the same. We may try to, we may pretend to, we may even try to change reality, but life and time change us. And at the end of it, we're OK. You'll be OK. But I'm sorry you have to go through this to get to OK.'

She sniffs and I can hear her cradling the phone between her chin and shoulder so she can grab a tissue and wipe her nose. 'Life's hard sometimes,' she says. 'Whenever I forget that, it feels like something comes along to remind me.' She wipes her nose again. Sniffs. 'Look, I have to go. Give Lola a hug from me.'

'I will. See you.'

She hangs up first. And I sit with my phone to my ear. 'Actually, Valerie, I think it's best I bring your daughter back to you because my ex is a psychopath and he might try to harm her to get to me,' I say quietly into the phone.

It doesn't sound *so* outlandish when I say it out loud. Not when you think about it. When you think about it, it sounds utterly delusional.

I have to keep Lola with me at all times. That's the only way I can know she's safe.

I place my phone on my desk, not even tempted to open the documents I need to work on.

How is he doing this? That's what keeps coming to mind. How did he get my pass, get my earrings? Is he following me? Must be, to know who Jeff Burrfield was. But to go into my bag, get those things out . . . I actually haven't checked if anything else is missing. But how would I know? If he's got my pass and earrings, then how am I going to know if there's a pen with my fingerprints missing? What about the random receipts that live at the bottom of my bag until VAT and tax time? What if he's got one of them?

But my bag hasn't been out of my possession for longer than going to the loo at HoneyMay Productions. Could he have slipped in there and stolen stuff then? But he'd need a pass. And anyway, the police said I used my pass to go to the toilet.

It must have been in the street. I was all over the place after seeing Jeff Burrfield. I kept stopping and staring. I kept zoning out right in the middle of the street. Lots of people brushed past me, bumped into me while trying to get on with their lives. One of those bumps must have been when my possessions were lifted.

I still don't get why, though.

This was all part of the plan. I am going as fast as I can. I thought he understood that. Why would he do this?

I replied to the text message last night with:

 • *Please don't do this. I'm going as fast as I can.*

But had no response.

I'm not sure what to do now. Do I just walk away from my life, leave things unfinished? I want to tie things up, though. End things with my work, speak to people who have been in my life for so long, make my family understand. But that delay is dangerous now. It is creating opportunities for people to get hurt. It is drawing the violence closer and closer to me. I won't be hurt in that way, I never am; it's everyone around me who suffers from the fallout.

Maybe I should just go to the police and confess. To everything. Tell them about everything that has gone before, including confessing about my other husband.

# Part 7

# 31

The wait to enter the area where I visit him always felt too long.

Too long, too much. The atmosphere was fraught, fizzing, almost popping with the energy of those of us who were in limbo. I didn't know how the others in there did it, but I always felt as though I was counting down time until I got here. I was only allowed to come every other week and even though I wrote to him in between, I could only truly relax when I saw him. When he walked through the doorway and I knew I had sixty minutes where he was safe and in sight and with me.

He wasn't the person I once knew any more. He moved with only vague familiarity, because he had been diminished since he came here to first await trial and now with serving his sentence. He had lost weight, his muscular body slimmed down; his face was gaunt, especially now that he had shaved his head, and the easy smile he always had for me and the world had left him. He smiled but it was not the same. I couldn't stand it. I could never stand it. I would fix my face so I could sit opposite him, I would will away my tears, I would wait until I got to my car before breaking down. Going there was one of the hardest things I had to do; living there must have been impossible.

As Sidney lowered himself into the seat opposite mine, I did my usual

283

checks. *Face: Does he look like he's been beaten up, been in a fight, been crying, been sleeping? Hands: Is the skin split from fighting, are his nails ragged from biting or picking; are his wrists obscured because he has them bandaged up? Legs and feet: Is he walking carefully from being in pain, does he flinch from his trousers touching his legs because he has been self-harming again? Torso: Has he lost more weight from not eating, has he started to bulk up again, is he sore from getting into fights?*

He seemed fine. He walked normally, he didn't appear to be in pain, his face was clear, same with his knuckles.

'Did I pass?' he asked.

'Pass?' I replied, knowing exactly what he meant.

'Inspection. Did I pass your checks so you know I'm not getting my raas kicked and I ain't putting the beat down on anyone? Do I get a pass?'

I kissed my teeth and cut my eyes at him.

'Give me your hand,' he said.

I relaxed, actually felt my whole body unwind as he took my hand between both of his. The warmth of his touch spread through me and our eyes met across the gap. I had something to tell him, something that would change everything. But he was clinging to me, I was holding on to him, so I let us hold on to this closeness and the simple, nourishing joy of being together that bit longer.

'He said if I go back to him, he'll give the police the evidence to set you free,' I stated.

Sidney's hands immediately tightened around mine. 'No.' Nothing else, not one more word. He was emphatic and clear with that one word.

'I have to,' I stated. 'I can't stand for you to be in here a moment longer. It's killing you and it's killing me to see that it's killing you.'

'No.'

'It's not so bad, you know? He does love me. He would never hurt me. I can go back and he'll get you out of here. And I know he'll stick to his word because he's like that.'

'No.'

'It will be fine. I will be fine. I'm treading water right now. I can't do anything because I just . . . why should I get to do anything when you're in here? Why should I get a life when your life is being eaten up one day at a time in a secure institution? I can't do anything. I'm stuck. And if you're free, I'll be able to move on.'

'No.'

'My life will be fine with him. Like I say, he loves me. He will never force me into anything.'

'I said, no, Cleo,' he said sharply, firmly. 'You're not going back to him.'

'The thing is, Sidney, I am. You can't stop me. I have to. I'm only telling you because you won't see me again. I didn't want to just not turn up one day. But you'll be out, you can start your life again, and I can get rid of this guilt.'

'I haven't been through all this for you to go back to him, Cleo.'

'It's because you're going through this that I have to do this.' I tightened my hold on his hand, put my other hand on his. 'I have to do this.' I'd thought it through and thought it through and this was the only way. I couldn't live with this huge ball of guilt that was jamming up my body any more. I had to do everything I could to get him out of there. Nearly two years of this was enough now. I had hoped, during the first stages, in the six months leading up to his trial, they would find out that he was innocent and would let him go. I had prayed during the trial that the jury would see that he was innocent and let him go. And now, over a year later, with no chance of appeal because there was no new or compelling evidence . . . 'I have to do this. I want you safe. I want you free. You can't stop me.'

'You're my sister, Cleo. I would do anything for you. I would do time for you. Don't go back to him.'

'I have to.'

'All right, all right. Don't do anything in a rush. Come back for the next visit and we'll talk again.'

'I'm not going to change my mind, you know?'

'Oh, I know. I know the stubbornness of Cleo.' He smiled, almost like he used to before his arrest. 'Come back for the next visit. Say goodbye properly. This can't be it.' He shook his head. 'Nah, this can't be it. I need time to prepare. Yeah? Yeah?'

'Sidney—'

'Yeah?'

'OK, I'll be back in a fortnight. But don't think you're going to stop me by delaying the goodbyes. I'm going to do it.'

'Oh, I know you are, Sis.' He gave a little laugh. 'I know how it goes with you – ain't nobody telling you anything.' He chuckled. 'About anything.' He chuckled some more. 'Ever,' he said in my voice, with the accent on point and everything. His shoulders started to move up and down as he laughed a bit more. 'Ever. Ever. *Ever.*'

'Yeah, all right, Chuckles.'

'Ever,' he laughed, still in my voice. '*Ever.*'

It was the last 'ever' that did it – I started laughing, too, remembering that there was a time when we would do that. We would giggle and laugh at not very much because that's what people did, that's what life was about. Not everything had to be heavy and difficult; sometimes you could just laugh for the sake of it.

'Look at you, laughing and that,' Sidney said in my voice.

'You were laughing, too,' I countered.

He nodded and grinned at me. 'Come back next time, yeah? Don't do anything until next time? For me?'

I sighed in frustration, at how easy it was for him to manipulate me. 'All right.'

Loud, intrusive, *rude*, the buzzer sounded, signalling that it was time for me to leave. And the panic spiralled up inside me. I hated this bit. I hated it so much. I hated leaving him. I hated not knowing what was going on with him until the next time. 'Stay safe, OK?' I said frantically. 'You stay away from people who are trouble. Keep yourself to yourself as much as possible. Stay safe. Take care of yourself.' The tears were rushing to my eyes, to the cracked surfaces of my feelings, the ragged edges of my emotions. 'Be careful. It's only for a little while longer. Please, just be careful.'

'I'm fine, Sis. Just go and I'll see you next time, OK? I'll see you next time.'

I slammed my teeth down together, curled in my lips to stop myself crying. It felt like this was the last time I would see him. It felt like I had left it too long to fix this. Like I should have gone back to Heath and got him out of here a long time ago.

## HMP Holcomb, London Outskirts, 2011

Late.

I was *late* getting to HMP Holcomb – my car, which had always been the most well-behaved vehicle I'd ever owned, was playing up first thing, the traffic, which had never been a problem, appeared from nowhere to gridlock my journey out of town, the queue to be searched seemed to stretch on for ever, the search itself took another for ever. Everything seemed to be working against me. By the time I got into the room, I was a couple of minutes behind and distressed that they were a couple of minutes with Sidney I would never get back. Especially since this was the last time I was going to see him.

I'd been devastated the last time I left here. Devastated and terrified. I thought I wasn't going to see him again. I feared something would happen to him before I had the chance to put things right.

I sat at our usual table in a fluster and didn't even notice for a few seconds that Sidney was already out instead of in his cell waiting for me to arrive.

'Here she is, Miss Punctuality,' Sidney joked.

'Oh don't, I'm so sorry. Everything was conspiring against me today! The last time I see you and I'm late. I'm sorry.'

'Don't say sorry, none is needed. I know you're good for it.'

I did my usual checks and he looked OK. He looked good actually. My heart lifted – I was doing the right thing. He knew he'd be getting out of here soon, so he was doing better. The knowledge of coming freedom had revitalised him. Imagine how relaxed and happy and content he would look once he was out of here.

'Cleo . . .' he began and my recently lifted heart dipped, fell straight down like a rock dropped into a large, deep pond – no trace of it at all after the initial ripple. He was about to tell me something awful. 'Cleo, I'm being ghosted. Transferred. Somewhere up north. It won't be so easy for you to come and see me as often.'

'Well, no, that can't happen. You'll be getting out of here soon so there's no point in them moving you. I'll talk to them. Let them know that there'll be some new and compelling evidence soon, so you'll obviously get fast-tracked through the appeal process. They need to know to keep you here until you're set free. That's all there is to it.'

'Look, C . . . stop! That's not what I need to talk to you about.'

I couldn't believe this was happening. It wasn't fair. None of it was fair, but especially not this.

'I need you to do something for me,' he said.

'I am, I'm going—'

'C, listen, OK? Just listen. I need you to take care of my family for me.'

'What?'

'When I'm ghosted, they won't be able to see me as much, if at all. That's going to be hard on them. It's going to be hard on all of them. I need you to take care of them. Go see them. Cheer them up. Make them happy.'

'But I won't need to because—'

'I'm not letting you go back to him, C. That's just not going to happen. If you even try, I will confess to doing it. I know enough about the case now, I'm here already. If you go back to him, I will make sure that I never get out of here by confessing.'

'But—'

'This is the only way. I'm not letting you go back to that life. But I am asking you to do this thing for me. I can do all the bird in the world if I know you're taking care of my family. Especially my brother Wallace, you know? He's been feeling it the most. I just need you to take care of him. Them. All-a them.'

'It's not fair of you to ask this of me. I can get you out of here. You can take care of them yourself.'

'No, C—' Sidney stopped talking when someone arrived at our table. Assuming it was a guard coming to tell me to pipe down because

I was getting heated, I ignored them. Until the person sat down. Outraged, I swung towards the seat – and was taken aback to find not a guard, but a good-looking man who seemed uncannily similar to the other good-looking man on the other side of the table. He was wearing dark jeans, white open-necked shirt and a black jacket, he had close-cropped hair, the slightly longer top styled like ripples on water. He held two squat, beige cups filled with warm tea (warm so it can't be used as a weapon). Confused, he handed a cup to Sidney before focusing on me.

'Hi,' he said simply.

'All right, Wals, this is Cleo. I was just telling you about her.'

Wals, or Wallace, lifted his chin in a hello gesture.

'Cleo, this is my brother Wallace.' I returned his greeting and said nothing more. His brother! I had seen his name on the Visiting Order when I'd received it in the post last week and had been stressing out about meeting him. All of that had been forgotten in getting here late and now Sidney being moved.

'I know you,' Wallace said suddenly, waggling his finger at me. 'You were at the trial. Every day. You sat on your own. Crying a lot. So you're the Cleo Forsum that was listed on the Visiting Order?'

'Yes,' I mumbled, ashamed that he had spotted me in such a vulnerable state. Even more ashamed that I hadn't jumped up and screamed and screamed that Sidney was innocent until people took notice.

'I've told you about her before? She's an old friend. My baby sis,' Sidney explained with a swell of pride. 'She's the sibling I never had.'

Wallace's head whipped round to glare at his brother. 'What you talking about, man? You've got two brothers. I'm one of them.'

'Yeah, well, I was always trying to trade you in for a better option. Ask your mother, she'll tell you how I came up with the idea of writing adverts in the back of the local paper to give you both away to loving homes. I had it all sorted then I called up and found out they charged by the word to place the ads. Your mother wouldn't give me the money, so we had to keep you.'

'What you talking about?' Wallace asked. His face was creased in an endearingly annoyed way.

'Ask your mother, she'll tell you,' Sidney repeated. 'I kept asking her for the money. By the time I was old enough to get a paper round to pay for it, I'd changed my mind and decided it was all right for them to keep you.'

'Man, that's cold. That's . . . cold,'

I smirked incredulously. 'That is *really* cold,' I laughed.

'What you piping up for? I said you were the sibling I would have picked if I had the choice.'

Wallace curled his lips into his mouth to stop himself laughing. Sidney was deploying his superpower of drawing people in with humour and then getting them to open up or do what he wanted. That was why I couldn't imagine what he and Heath had been like when they were talking.

'I wanted you two to link up,' Sidney said, serious suddenly. 'As I've just told you both, I'm being ghosted. I need you both to take care of the family. I know me being here has caused everyone too much stress, so I need you to make it right. I trust you two to make it right. Take care of the family. Take care of each other.'

How could I be with his family knowing that he had been taken away from them because of me? How would I explain who I was to his grieving, traumatised family?

Wallace looked as ambivalent at the prospect of this as I was. And he knew the people involved. An awkward silence swept over us, neither Wallace nor I willing to commit to this. I was still convinced that I could get Sidney out of prison, that there would be no need for any of this to happen.

Sidney's face was creased now with wrinkles that made him look so much older than thirty-seven – when I first met him, I struggled to believe he was over thirty, now he looked old enough to be my uncle. Patches of dry, cracked eczema had started to collect on his cheeks, and he looked like he never slept. 'Are you two going to help me out or what?' he said. 'Can't trust anyone else with this. Only you two.'

'It ain't that simple, Sides man,' Wallace said. 'What am I supposed to do to take care of the family that I ain't tried in the two years? Everyone is broken. This has broken them. There's no fixing that while you're in here.'

'Don't give me that. Despite everything, despite being the smallest kid in your year, who was it that went on to represent the school in that Maths tournament and beat everyone there by a mile? Despite being the smallest child in your year, who was it that got a scholarship to Oxford and Cambridge? Who was it that's been promoted more times than anyone at that place you used to work at? And that's from starting as work experience! And you,' he was talking to me now, 'who is still one of the most wanted freelancers in the magazine business? Who was rejected by every single literary agent in the country and still got back up, still wrote another book and has now got an agent interested? And that's despite everything that you've had going on!' He opened his hands and I realised my checks hadn't been thorough enough – the knuckles of his right hand were puffy, slightly swollen. He'd been in a fight and he'd hit someone. Or it'd got too much and he'd hit a wall to let the pain out. Either way, I had to get him out of there.

'Listen, you two, you can do anything, you know that. Wals, lean on Cleo. She'll help you. She's a good kid. She'll help you.'

*Will I? How am I going to do that?*

'You'll know what to do,' he said to me, reading my mind. 'You can steer him in the right direction. What to say to them. What to get them to do. I'm not saying rock up to the house or anything like that, but help Wals out. He'll need someone to talk to after he's tried to gee up the family. And you always know how to make people feel better. Just be his friend. Be there for him like you've been there for me.'

Be there for them like we tried to be there for each other, he was saying. We leant on each other, we'd tried to help each other and this is where we'd ended up. His life destroyed. His family's life destroyed.

*I have to do this.*

If he wasn't going to let me get him out of there by going back to Heath, this was the only thing I could do. I could help his brother to help his family. I could try to indirectly ease their pain. I could do whatever it was that Sidney wanted. I owed him that much.

'OK,' I said to Sidney with a nod of understanding that also signalled I wasn't going to return to Heath. Not yet, anyway. I would help his family and then see where things lay. 'OK.'

His smile, full of joy and gratitude, relief and happiness, was enough to make his brother draw back. He stared at his older sibling for long seconds, suddenly realising how much this meant to him. How important it was that we did this; that Sidney needed us to step up for him in any way we could.

'OK,' Wallace said reluctantly. 'OK. I'll do whatever it is that you want and need me to do. Of course I will, Bruv, course I will.'

# 32

'I think you should come and meet my family. Properly.'

Wallace and I had exchanged numbers outside the prison the last time we saw Sidney and we'd spoken quite a bit on the phone. He'd wanted to meet, but I couldn't risk that. I wasn't sure if Heath would still be watching me; as it was I had changed the locks on my flat twice since we'd split up and then a third time just for luck. I'd changed my phone number, bought new handsets for the landline and, as well as a new mobile handset, I'd bought all the anti-spy software I could get for my computer. I was pretty certain that he'd found out about Sidney by simply following me, but I couldn't be sure of that, so I made my life as anti-spyable as possible. Meeting Wallace in a public place, having him come to my flat, going to his place in Brighton were all no-nos. The phone was the safest way to communicate as far as I could work out.

'Not a good idea,' I said to him. I was flat on my back in my bed-room where I'd come to lie down after the last phone call I'd received. I was still in shock about that call.

'Look, Cleo, I don't feel right about everything you're doing and my folks don't even know you exist.'

'I'm not doing it alone, you're doing it as well.'

Most of our chats were businesslike, making plans. We'd brain-stormed what we could do and were going through the logistics of it all. We had a list and we were working our way down it.

'You're going to be putting money into this, they should at least meet you.'

Truth was, I wanted to meet them. I wanted to hug his mother and tell her how sorry I was. I wanted to hug his father and tell him how sorry I was, too. I wanted to take both their hands and say thank you for raising such a thoughtful son. I wanted to speak to Sidney's sister-in-law, who everyone in the family had a lot of time for. I wanted to play with his niece, see if she had the same voracious love of books and Lego and cooking that my nieces did. I wanted to stand in between Wallace and Franklyn and see who was more like a cheap, knock-off Sidney. Truth was, I would have loved to see the Pryce family up close. Truth also was, I couldn't be among them without admitting who I was.

And who was I?

I was a woman serving her penance by trying to repair the family I helped to break.

'You're putting most of the money in; I'm just putting in a bit of cash and time.'

'Were you fucking my brother?' he asked suddenly.

'No. No. He told you, we're like brother and sister.'

'Yeah, Sidney always has a lot going on. He rarely tells me every-thing. I wasn't sure about what your situation was. Why you're so keen to help out.'

'He asked me to. He was there when I needed him: I need to do the same for him.'

Wallace was quiet for a time and, in the hush, I fancied I could hear him thinking, trying to work things out. 'They'll like you. Come and meet them.'

'Just rock up and say what, exactly?'

'That you're my girlfriend. We can tell them you know Sidney, but we'll tell them you're with me. That'll give you some kind of standing.'

'I don't know, it just sounds like a really complicated way for you to ask me out.'

'No, no! Why would you think that? I'm not putting the moves on you. No way—' Wallace spluttered and I burst out laughing.

It was good to do that, it was incredible to do that. The sound had become so alien to me, something that had been quite far from my life. The more I laughed, the more it felt like sparkles were dancing in my chest.

'I'm messing with you,' I said breathlessly.

I heard him smile down the phone, and remembered the delicious way his full lips moved, the dreamy way his eyes would look at you, the floaty way his voice could make me feel. 'You've got to meet them,' he said. 'It's what Sides would want. If you come as my girlfriend, you can duck out whenever you want and we can say we've split up. If you come as a friend and then disappear, that will hurt them.'

He was right about one thing, it was what Sidney would want. 'All right. You've convinced me. I'll come meet the folks at some point.'

'Good,' he said. 'We'll have to meet up beforehand, you know that, don't you?'

'Why?'

'Because people aren't stupid, *my* people aren't stupid – body language. They'll be able to tell we aren't really together if we don't move like we've ever been alone in the same room.'

'I suppose you're right. We can meet up.' The thought of that excited me and I was happy for a moment or two, before the sceptre of Heath shimmered into view and cast its pallor over the idea. 'At some point.'

'I've got some brochures. We can have a look then start booking things.'

'Yeah, cool. Anyway, look, I've got to go.' I had to get off the phone before I started to think stupid thoughts.

'Safe. Speak soon.'

I dropped the phone on the bed beside me and stared up at the ceiling. I'd wanted to tell him. Well, Sidney would have been my first choice, Heath would have been my second if we were back then. But Wallace would have been my choice for the reality I was living in. Before Wallace had called me, my new agent, Antonia, had been on the phone. She'd sold my book.

A publisher had read my story of a cake-maker who kept stumbling across sometimes gruesome crimes and somehow managed to solve them, and they had loved it. And not only had they loved it – because honestly, publishers seemed to be very free with their love for something but very cautious about the following-through – they wanted to publish it.

As is.

That was the big thing about this book deal. They wanted my book as it was.

We'd had near-misses before because the deal always came with 'helpful' suggestions for little tweaks, such as changing the main character to a white woman or introducing a white boss or co-worker who eventually unravelled the mystery or exploring 'the Black experience' with a shiny new subplot of the racism that becomes an uplifting 'learning moment' for the white person, or even just making the main character a 'proper' Black woman by sprinkling in liberal doses of 'sass'. (Couldn't wait to tell Trina about that!)

None of that with these publishers. They read my story. They liked my story. They wanted to publish my story.

I'd gone into the bedroom to lie down because I wasn't sure my legs would hold me up. It didn't seem real somehow. I'd finally got there.

I stared up at my postcard from Brighton I'd stuck up on the ceiling. I'd got the postcard when I was in sixth form and had gone to Brighton on a protest march. I'd been wide-eyed at the water being so close to the city, and I'd decided I wanted to live there one day. But then it was college and then it was Masters then it was work then it was Heath and then it was Sidney. No Brighton.

When I moved back into my flat after I left Heath this time, I'd stuck the postcard on my ceiling to remind myself every morning of the Brighton dream. It had the pebble beach, two deckchairs facing the water, the Palace Pier in the background. It was tatty and worn around the edges, the vibrant colours had faded, but looking at it always evoked a feeling inside. A yearning. A longing to be by the sea.

With this book deal, I could move to Brighton. I would need to sell my flat, not simply rent it out, but if I did that, I could get somewhere to live in Brighton *AND* still help out Sidney's family.

The sparkles in my chest started up again, but this time in my stomach, too.

If I moved to Brighton, that would be a huge step in moving on from Heath.

I could reinvent myself. I could leave all of that behind. Well, not completely because I would still be involved with the Pryces, but I would be even further away from Heath. And that . . . that would be incredible.

Before that, though, I was just going to lie on this bed and enjoy the fact that I was about to become a published author.

# 33

## East London, 2012

'So this decorating your parents' living room idea, whose was it again?'

'Pretty much yours,' Wallace replied.

His parents' furniture – covered in beige hessian painters' dustsheets – had been pushed to the centre of the room. We'd laid newspaper on the floor, we'd moved ornaments outside into the corridor, and we'd set up the pasting table as well as laid out all the brushes, Stanley knife and spirit level. We hadn't even opened the wallpaper paste to begin mixing it up and it felt like we'd done a day's work.

'I think I probably meant to pay someone to do this. Wallpapering is one of the most thankless tasks in the world. We should be paying someone to do this.'

'We already paid for my family to go to Togo for a month, do you really have decorator money?'

It had taken us six months to execute our plan to lift the spirits of his family. For years, Sidney had been quietly topping up his parents' income, paying for any extras, but they would not take any money from Wallace or Franklyn, so we'd been working on what to do to help them out. When I wrote to Sidney to tell him we'd settled on sending them away to visit family in Togo for a month so we could decorate their house, he'd been pleased and had told me that he knew he could rely on us to sort out his family. And his palpable relief through his words on the page made me feel better, too.

The Pryces still thought I was Wallace's girlfriend, and after his mother's initial frostiness – she properly hated me – they had begun to accept me. Valerie told me that their mother was like that with everyone and that she'd been like that since before Sidney's 'troubles', as everyone referred to it. 'Pay her no mind,' she told me. 'She'll get used to you. I think she's a bit . . . Wallace has never brought a girl home before. I think she thought he'd be the one to not bring her the stress of another woman. So don't mind her.'

Despite my worries about getting involved with anyone, Heath had stayed away and it was nice coming to see the Pryces, sometimes going for a drink with Valerie, chatting to Wallace's dad about politics and crosswords. Being with them, doing stuff that made their lives easier, also lessened my guilt. And every good thing that happened to them made Sidney happy, which, ultimately, was the point of all of this for me.

Wallace was also happier. He laughed, he joked and he didn't seem so uptight. One night, as he drove me home, he told me that this was the first time in adulthood that he didn't mind spending time with his family. They didn't row as much, they relaxed a bit more. But, obviously, they weren't cured. Nothing could replace Sidney, but things were easier for them.

'I will ask you again, do you have decorator money?' Wallace said to me.

'I do not have decorator money.'

'Well, then, you have decorator time,' he told me.

'But I don't have decorator energy,' I wailed. 'I can't go on.' I threw the back of my hand against my forehead and swooned. 'I just can't go on.'

Wallace dashed to my side, took hold of my shoulders. 'Pull your-self together woman,' he ordered. 'You've got a job to do.'

'I don't know if I can, sir, I don't know if I can,' I replied, still swooning.

'Dammit, you can! I haven't trained you this hard and this long so you can give up now.' In one move, he scooped me into his arms, held me close. 'You can do it.'

'I can't do it!'

'Yes! Yes! I know you can.'

'Thank you, sir, thank you.'

Wallace had been my fake boyfriend in front of the Pryce family for four months and this was the first time he'd touched me when we were alone. He would hold my hand or rub my shoulder or sit close to me on the sofa in front of the others, but alone, never. Alone, it was as if we were completely indifferent to each other.

Right then, now I was in his arms, Wallace didn't seem indifferent to me, and he didn't seem to mind holding me. He didn't seem to mind staring at me, taking in my face with his big brown eyes, his face softening into an affectionate gaze the longer he looked at me. I barely noticed that he was ever so slightly holding me closer, bring-ing my body nearer to his.

'You're so beautiful,' I said to him, placing my hands on his chest.

'Isn't that meant to be my line?' he joked.

'Nah, you snooze, you lose, buddy,' I replied.

'I'll remember that,' he said, grinning at me now. 'I will definitely remember that.'

When our lips came together, it was the most natural thing ever. Our mouths moved together, our bodies found a space together and we kissed as though we'd been doing it since the dawn of time.

# 34

## Brighton, 2014

I prised open my eyes, which felt heavy and sticky, and then immediately clamped them shut again. Everything was too bright on the other side of my lids. Way too bright. I moved my hand to rub at my face and that didn't happen, either – my arm was too heavy to lift.

*What's going on?* I wondered. My whole body felt like it had been encased in lead and my nerves felt like they'd been simultaneously blunted by sandpaper and set on fire by it.

The last thing I remembered was . . . Wallace and me eating dinner at a fish and chips restaurant on the seafront. The April air was a touch on the wrong side of cool, but we'd sat outside anyway so we could listen to the waves caressing the shore in the dark and have the smell of the sea air swirling around us. This was one of my favourite restaurants in Brighton and I loved coming here whenever we could. As the evening progressed and the temperature continued to drop, I had felt a bit woozy, light-headed, but I hadn't thought much of it. And then . . . And then . . . ? Nothing. Nothing else was there.

I tried again to open my eyes, edging my eyelids apart this time to let the brightness in slowly.

302

'Hello, you,' Wallace said.

With effort and bracing myself against the pain, I turned towards his voice. 'Hey.'

His face creased with a smile tinged with relief and sadness.

'What's happened?' I asked. Heath. It had to be. He'd done something and now we were paying the price.

My boyfriend took a deep breath, exhaled at length, clearly steeling himself to tell me something awful. He took my hand between his, a warm gesture, a movement of comfort like his brother used to do. I wanted to scream at him to just tell me what was wrong, but I also didn't want to know. Because if it was Heath, then I'd have to deal with him pushing more damage on this family; him inflicting more pain when he had already done enough.

'Cleo . . .' he said gently, 'you had an ectopic pregnancy. The fallopian tube ruptured earlier at dinner and you passed out.'

I closed my eyes as I replayed what he said. Tried to process the words and the feelings that were coming with them. 'Oh,' I eventually said. 'I . . . erm . . . I didn't know I was pregnant. Well, ectopically pregnant. I didn't even actually know if I could get pregnant – ectopically or otherwise.'

'Big thing to take in.'

'Yes. How do you feel about it?' I asked, wondering if I was about to deal with the case of the incredible disappearing Wallace. He didn't give the impression of being someone who would run away, but I knew none of us are necessarily who we seem.

'I don't even know. But I *do* know I've never been as terrified as when you passed out. Right in front of me. Mid-sentence.'

'Sorry about that.' I grimaced. 'Did I break anything when I went down? Or did I just faceplant in my chips?'

'Bit of both, really – you went into your chips then took the plate and other stuff down when you fell off your seat.'

'Oh jeez. Obviously we can never go back there ever again.'

'Obviously.'

'How are you feeling about this? Cos I am quietly freaking out here. I mean, I love you, but I don't know what I would have done if it'd been a viable pregnancy. I know it's probably odd, but I've never really thought what I would do if I got pregnant by you. What about you?'

'I don't know. It's a lot to take in. Haven't processed it fully yet. I was more worried about you. But if I think about it, you know, it would have been cool. Me and you and a baby? Cool, yeah.' He caressed my hand some more. 'And I love you, too, by the way. Can't believe you said it first.'

'You snooze, you lose, buddy,' I joked, my voice still dry and sticky.

'You say that too many times, so you know what? All right, two can play that game: Will you marry me?'

Even in my fragile state I was able to do a double-take. 'What? We have literally just done the "I love yous".'

'No snoozing or losing.'

Another out-of-the-blue proposal. At least this time I didn't have to worry about the wedding being in three hours. No, but I did have to worry about already being married. But was I? Properly married? Heath had said we were only married in name outside of America, and I'd believed him. But at the time I'd had no reason not to believe him. I mean, we never registered our marriage here so did it mean anything? I remembered a few years back that one of the Rolling Stones had argued in court that he and his ex weren't technically married because they'd done it abroad. They'd got an annulment rather than a divorce on that basis. They didn't do it here, so the court didn't recognise their marriage. So, while I may not be legally married in the UK, I was, for all intents and purposes, still married in the US. So if I ever went there with Wallace, it would mean I was a bigamist, I suppose.

I had to speak to Heath.

That thought turned my stomach. We'd last spoken when he said he would get Sidney out of jail if I went back to him. He didn't even bother to get in touch when I didn't contact him again, so I was pleased and relieved that he seemed to have let go.

But I would have to speak to Heath if Wallace and I were to actually get married. He had the certificate, I would need his cooperation to get divorced in America. Could I do that without triggering him into harming someone?

This was just a proposal, though. It didn't really matter if I was married in America at this moment, did it? It didn't matter if I might have to talk to my ex to get properly divorced. Saying yes to Wallace in the here and now had nothing at all to do with all of that.

'I often think about Sides introducing us,' Wallace said. 'I think he knew we'd get together.'

He was right, of course. I'd asked Sidney in a letter right after Wallace and I first kissed if he was all right with me being with his brother, considering how dangerous being involved with me could be. And Sidney had written back saying he'd been disappointed it'd taken us so long. *You and Wals are meant to be.* 'Yeah, I think your brother is quite astute like that.' *And you'll be fine. He hasn't been in touch all this time, has he? You and Wals can handle him, as long as you stick together*, Sidney had added.

'Not hard to be astute when he finds me the perfect woman to fall in love with.'

*Perfect woman.* Those words turned my stomach. Whenever I heard them, they would remind me of Heath's obsession. We're supposed to want to be the beautiful heroine that someone falls in love with. We're meant to inspire armies to march, for people to lose their minds, for people to want to do anything for you simply because they love you; are obsessed by you.

Being the object of someone's obsession is a horror I would not wish on anyone. I have read so many books, watched so many shows, where the beauty of the heroine inspires all around her to lose their minds, to do anything to be with her, to almost cease to be if they aren't with her. It's applauded, it's valued, it's held up as the ultimate example of love.

And it creeps me out now.

To have someone love you, be obsessed with you, do anything to be with you, is terrifying. And dehumanising. Heath thought I was the perfect woman. *His* perfect woman, and in that, I stopped being human. I stopped having nuances, layers, imperfections and *flaws*. I became the vessel into which all of his ideals and dreams and unrealistic expectations were projected. And when those expectations weren't met, when the flaws began to show through, the cause of them had to be eliminated. When my flaws – the things that could potentially take me away from him – became apparent, they became the excuse Heath used to hurt people. To *kill* people.

'I'm not perfect,' I said to Wallace. 'Far from it. I am so far from perfect. I'm just an ordinary woman.'

'I know that. I just mean—'

'I'm just an ordinary woman who just so happens to have bagged herself a wonderfully ordinary, caring, loving man,' I interrupted. I did not want to hear another good thing about me right then. Not when I didn't deserve it.

'Does that mean you will marry me?' Wallace asked.

I would have to work out how to find out if my wedding, conducted by a James Brown impersonator in a purple chapel in Las Vegas, meant anything outside the borders of the country of which I wasn't a citizen.

But I could still say yes to Wallace right now. All that wedding stuff was far, far in the future. In the present, I could just say yes and enjoy the moment.

'Yes,' I said with a grin. 'Yes, I will marry you.'

# 35

*Brighton, 2015*

In the bridal suite in The Brighthelmstone, a thirty-room boutique hotel at the very edge of Brighton, my younger sister, Efie, and Trina and I were in various stages of getting ready. Efie had her red silk dressing gown on over her underwear, waiting for the very last minute to put on her gold bridesmaid dress; Trina had her make-up on and her bridesmaid dress on, but still had royal-blue curlers twisted into the tips of her shoulder-length hair, while I was still in my dressing gown with hair rollers in and not a scrap of make-up.

My mum and Wallace's mum hadn't been happy that we were not getting married in a church, but they liked each other so much – especially since they both came from neighbouring West African countries – they decided to let this slide and allow us to instead get married in the function room at The Brighthelmstone without too much comment or disapproval.

My mum, incredibly striking in her purple-with-gold-flowers-Ghanaian-lace two-piece and matching headwrap, had nipped downstairs to talk to my older sister about something.

Efie stood beside her open make-up case, ready to start on my face.

'While Mummy is out of the room,' she said, 'tell me quick – are you sure about marrying Wallace?'

'Of course,' I said. 'Why wouldn't I want Mummy to hear that?'

Using light, expert touches, my sister dabbed foundation under my eyes with a little round sponge. 'Cos of Mr Wuthering Heights? You were with him for years. Years! What happened there?'

Immediately, in the mirror, my eyes went to Trina, standing at the back of the room beside the bathroom door. She held my gaze, the understanding of all those years with Heath in our lives passing between us.

'We split up,' I said to my sister. 'Ages ago.' In the mirror, I watched her use a large sponge to smooth foundation over the rise of my cheeks, down into the hollow. 'People split up all the time, Efie. And their naughty little sisters don't bring up their exes on their wedding day.'

'Just checking we aren't going to be having some dramatic entrance at the last minute,' she replied. 'Cos that man – nice as he was – was intense.'

After a brief raise of her eyebrows, Trina took a 'you have no idea' sip from her champagne flute, which told me she felt entirely vindicated for saying that years ago.

'Don't think I haven't noticed the knowing looks going on between you and Miss Trina,' Efie said. 'I'm right, though, aren't I, he was proper intense?'

'I'm saying nothing,' Trina replied before clamping the champagne flute to her lips and sipping Prosecco as though that was the only thing stopping her from saying all the things she'd wanted to say for years.

'Don't get me wrong, he was a nice guy, I liked him a lot, but *intense*. Whew! The way he used to stare at you like he might die if he looked away . . . It was a lot.' Efie stepped back and narrowed her eyes as she scrutinised my face. 'Wallace is nothing like that, thankfully.'

'That would be because they're different people,' I said. I hadn't wanted to think of Heath today. I hadn't wanted to think of him at all, but obviously I couldn't avoid it in the run-up to today. I'd been sick with worry that it would come out that I'd been married before, that I'd said 'I do' and 'till death us do part' to someone else. I'd gone several times to contact him, to find out what we would need to do to get divorced, but I couldn't do it. I couldn't face speaking to him and potentially unleashing him on my life and the Pryce family again. I had searched as much as I could for my name and Heath's name and any online documentation about that night in Las Vegas but I couldn't find anything. Alfred Heath Sawyer Berland and Cleo Amma Forsum had never been married as far as anything official online was concerned. And when the official searches on my name were conducted so Wallace and I could get our licence, they all came back clear, too. Which meant that Heath was telling the truth – getting married in Vegas didn't count here. Emotionally, it counted, of course, but legally it didn't. Legally I was free to marry Wallace.

I was free to marry the man I loved.

Deftly, my sister began shaping my eyebrows, using a thin black pencil to measure the distance between the centre of my nose and the start of my brows on either side, then the arc between the edge of my brow, the edge of my eye and the edge of my nostrils. She hadn't finished torturing me, though. 'I often debate which of them would be better between the sheets,' she said.

Trina almost choked on her drink, coughing and spluttering, while I squeaked in surprise. Why I was surprised by this revelation, I had no idea – this was my sister all over. She hadn't ever met a raw nerve she wouldn't twang for fun. 'Oh, don't pretend you haven't ever wondered, Miss Trina,' she said.

Appalled, truly repulsed, Trina replied: 'That is almost as disgusting as when your sister used to drop Maltesers in her coffee. Actually, no, it's worse than that. And just for the record, no, that has never crossed my mind.'

Oblivious, Efie continued: 'Wallace is who I would normally go for. He has *everything* going on. But that intensity in Heath . . . yeah, that could make for some good times between the sheets. That guy had all kind of kinks oozing out of him. He would see to me, all right.' Her gaze wandered off for a moment, as though she was actually imagining climbing naked into bed with my ex. 'Oh he would really see to me.'

'This is officially the worst conversation a woman could have on her wedding day. Literally the worst,' I said.

'Oh, hush, let me do your lips.'

'No, I won't hush, not if you're going to keep talking about *that*,' I told her. 'I'm going to tell Mummy when she comes back, if you carry on. And I'm going to tell her how you had sex with your first boyfriend in their house, see how you like that.'

'All right, all right, no need to get out of hand,' she laughed. 'No more talk about jumping the ex. No more talk about the hot, hot pepper sauce he could pour all over this body and—'

'That's it!' I screeched.

'Jokes! Jokes!' my sister cried, massaging clear lip softener onto a thin brush. 'I'm just trying to give you jokes!'

'Yeah, well, you wouldn't be crying jokes if I said something like that about one of your exes,' I snapped.

'Thought you only went with humans, though, Cleo,' Trina said.

That broke the atmosphere that had been ramping up and we all collapsed into giggles.

As I laughed, I did the best I could to scrub from my mind every single thought of Heath like I would scrub at a stain that was fresh enough to be completely removed. I wanted to walk down the rose-petal-covered aisle downstairs, to take the hand of my waiting fiancé with a cleansed mind, a sanitised history. I wanted to truly move on.

I loved Wallace and I didn't want our wedding day to be in any way about my other husband.

# 36

**Brighton, 2015**

*Dearest Cleo,*

*Babe, I'm a coward. I wanted so many times to tell you this, but I could never find the words or the opportunity. But now you're happily married to the most wonderful man, and I'm most likely on the plane home when you read this, I can tell you.*

*It was Heath who stabbed me.*

*In the days after the attack, when we were packing up to leave, I had lots of nightmares and flashbacks. Post-Traumatic Stress. But with every one of them, I began to remember more and more about what happened. And then I remembered the scent. My attacker's smell. And then I realised it was the same one I'd smelt on Heath when you both came to see me in the hospital.*

*I thought I was going crazy at first. Honestly, I thought I was losing my mind. So I left it. By this point, you and he were seriously together and I'd told you to fix up, so I knew you probably wouldn't believe me. What was I going to tell you, anyway? That I suspected our friend of almost killing me? I had no proof, he just smelt the same? And what would I do with this thought? Go to the police? Even if we hadn't left the country by then, I'm pretty sure they would have laughed me out of the place.*

*Then, I had a nightmare that was so vivid, so clear, and I finally got a proper look at him. I mean, I did that night it actually happened, but everything felt blurry and unreal. But that night, that dream, showed me his face, and even though he had a balaclava on, I saw his eyes. Heath's eyes.*

*That was it. I finally accepted what my mind had been trying to tell me – it was him. He had done it.*

*Without thinking, I rang you, didn't I, on your house phone. Well, it was his house phone of course. And he answered.*

*I almost hung up, but then I thought, I need to know if I am crazy or if I am finally remembering what happened. So I told him it was me and then I said, 'Why did you do it, H?'*

*And he went silent for a really long time and then he said, 'I'm sorry. I'm so, so sorry. I can't stand the thought of losing her. I love her so much. I'm sorry. I'm so sorry,' and then he hung up.*

*I think he did it because I lied about you having a boyfriend. He probably hated me for that, for trying to keep the pair of you apart. He's . . . I'm not sure what is wrong with him. Or why he latched on to you so strongly for so many years, but I am glad you're not together any more.*

*I am glad you have married someone who adores you but isn't obsessive with it. I am so grateful that you're happy. Seeing you with Wallace has made me understand what you were talking about back in the day. I remember you said something about not really feeling anything for anybody, not really feeling that connection and wondering if you were broken. I did think you had that with Heath, but seeing you with Wallace now makes me realise that you've finally, truly found it. It's equal, how you and Wallace feel about each other. You're right there with him, you're so happy that you glow.*

*I wasn't ever going to tell you this, by the way, but Steadman said I had to. He said I had to tell you so that you would* never *consider going back to Heath.*

*In case you did know, and you haven't known how to tell me – which I can imagine you would be tearing yourself up and down about – it's fine. I wouldn't know how to tell you in your shoes, either. I don't blame you for any of it. I only blame him.*

*Please try to put Heath completely behind you, my darling. Please move on with this wonderful man you have. Please don't ever let Heath into this new life you have. This life you have is glorious. Protect it at all costs.*

*Thank you for asking me to be your bridesmaid/matron of honour.*

*With all my love,*
*Trina*
*x*

Trina had slipped the envelope into my hands as we hugged at the airport. I didn't ask what it was because I knew she wouldn't tell me: 'If I was going to tell you, I wouldn't have written it, would I?' she would have said.

With the bathroom door locked, I read her letter over and over. Each time a little more teary and a lot more horrified. A small part of me thought that maybe I was wrong, that there was no way he would do it. Because to have stabbed her instead of just going to confront her like he claimed in his 'report', he would have had to have taken the weapon with him. He would have had to have planned it. He would have had to have set out to hurt her. Heath went there to harm Trina, knowing he could have killed her.

Slowly, I folded up the letter, returned it to its envelope. I had to do what she said – I had to move on with Wallace. Put Heath behind me. Even if, every so often, his words about me always going back to him did rear up in my head.

# Part 8

# 37

> ° We need to talk. Face to face.
> Meet me at the corner of your road
> outside the house with the yellow
> door in 10 minutes. Come alone.

Ten minutes doesn't give me much time to do anything. I suppose that's the point. I can't get the police involved. I can't go and check out the spot beforehand. I am at a complete disadvantage. And I can't come alone. I can't leave Lola in the house on her own. I just can't. But I can't bring her along to meet him, either. I'm sure Valerie and Franklyn would be fine with me rocking up to meet a murderer with their thirteen-year-old in tow.

I'm pacing the kitchen, trying to work out what to do about this text. Lola is in the living room finding something for us to watch to go with the popcorn and crisps. I was so grateful when she decided to start sleeping upstairs. It meant I could put the alarm on to cover the downstairs of the house at night, and I could feel a little safer knowing she was nearer. How can I start to put her in danger now?

319

*Nine minutes.* What am I going to do? If I tell Lola I'm just nipping out to the shops, she'll probably want to come with me. If I tell her I'm going to meet someone, she'll definitely want to come with me. If I tell her to barricade herself in the bedroom while I turn the alarm on downstairs, that will terrify her. She'll never feel safe again in this house. Is that a bad thing? Maybe I should insist she goes home anyway.

If I scare her now, though, without foundation, she'll never get over it. It will stay with her for life. I remember reading *The Rats* by James Herbert when I was around Lola's age. It terrified me so much I could barely sleep. It genuinely scarred me for life – I can't even watch them on television without screaming for it to be switched off. I will never be all right with rats and that was just a fiction book. Imagine being told by a trusted adult to barricade yourself in somewhere in case someone tries to grab you. You would never relax again. And thirteen is too young an age to develop this kind of fear. Especially when you've been overhearing – through every fault of your own – about murders your aunt is possibly involved with.

**Eight minutes.** *What do I do?*

I can't take her with me, that's clear.

If I leave her here, I'll tell her to go upstairs, get into my bed, find us something to watch, put the downstairs alarm on. I'll just frame it as something I would normally do if I was just nipping out. I won't get her to barricade herself in and I'll just be super chill about it. She'll understand why I would do that. That shouldn't scare her too much. Should it?

**Seven minutes.** Part of me doesn't want to go. What good would it do to see him or speak to him? I thought we'd sorted all of this out last time I saw him. I thought we'd agreed. But I should have known he wouldn't stick to it. What psychopath ever sticks to an agreement that doesn't favour them? I don't want to go, but I have to go. Not only because he's demanded it, but also because I may be able to get him to back off. I'm as sure as I can be that all the attention from the attempt on Harry Andrews's life is not what he would want. Heath has never been one for attention. Especially since what happened to his first lover generated so much attention that he had to change his name and his family had to move.

**Two minutes.** Lola is installed in my bed. She has snacks, she has the TV remote and instructions not to litter my bed with popcorn or crisps. She also has the house phone, her mobile and instructions to stay in my room until I return. I've shown her how to disable the alarm if necessary, but it shouldn't be necessary because she is going to stay put. I also told her to call 999 if she's at all scared but I wouldn't be long so she'd be fine. My final instruction was to prop the dining chair I brought upstairs under the handle of my non-locking bedroom door. That had made her raise an eyebrow, but I told her to do it and not to argue. Once I leave the room, I stand outside and wait for her to do as I've instructed. I try the handle as soon as she's done it, the door doesn't open. Good. This is as secure as I can make her. I won't be gone for long, either.

**One minute.** I check several times that I have my keys in my pocket, that I have my purse, that I have my mobile. I push my black hat on my head and slip on my black longline cardigan. I push my feet into my trainers in a way I know would have Wallace raging. The disrespect I show my trainers has always – and will always – aggravate him. He is a trainer lover and the way I don't care for my everyday shoes breaks his heart – so much so that he regularly takes them off me to clean and update the laces on my most abused pairs. With one last look up the stairs, I type in the code to set the alarm for the lower part of the house and rush down the corridor. The alarm *beep-beep-beeps* for ten seconds when I shut the front door before falling silent. With my heart in my throat, I start off down the road to meet Heath.

# 38

## Richmond upon Thames, 2022

*Tap, tap, tap* on the driver's side window of my car.

Despite my best efforts, despite hanging around right at the back of the church and leaving as soon as the congregation got to their feet for the last time, despite positioning myself behind other black-clad mourners at the crematorium so no one could see me from the front rows, despite slipping out of the heavy mahogany door as soon as the blue curtains closed behind the coffin, I still found myself in this place. This place where he was using the knuckle of his forefinger to tap, tap, tap on my car window.

Heath's aunt, Lynda, had contacted me. She'd left several messages over the course of three days with my agent, Antonia, asking me to call her. I hadn't. I'd always got on with Lynda and did feel bad about ignoring her, but I wasn't stupid – I didn't want to get sucked back into Heath's world, even obliquely. The final message, the one that got me to engage, had said she wanted to talk to me about a death in the family.

My heart felt like it had stopped when Antonia said that. Heath. I thought for a moment it was Heath and Aunt Lynda was unwittingly ringing to tell me that I was a widow without knowing that he and I had got married. When I called her back, she'd told me Heath's mother had passed away. I'd been relieved for a moment, then felt awful because I shouldn't be relieved that a woman who had always been nice to me had died, when her son, the psychopath, was still alive. But, I admitted to myself with my eyes closed and the phone pressed to my ear, if Heath had died, that would be the end of my hope – my continued hope – that he would go to the police and confess to murder so they would let Sidney out.

'My sister was very fond of you,' Lynda had said, her voice catching. 'She never forgot how kind you were to her and Heath after her husband died. She wanted you to come to her funeral. I will, of course, understand if you'd rather not, but I wanted to make sure that I did as I promised and told you. She left you something in her will, as well. I'm not sure what yet. But I will let you know when I find out.' Lynda paused, as though wondering if she should keep talking, then obviously decided she should by adding: 'She never really got over you and Heath breaking up. She thought the world of you. She was so proud of your success, and she loved to read your books and watch your television show.' We'd chatted a while longer and she continued to lay on the gentle pressure like thick layers of jam until I agreed to take down the funeral details and to think about coming.

Once out of the crematorium, I'd hurried as quickly as I could around the corner and along the road to where I'd parked the car. I hadn't looked back in case someone saw me – in case *he* saw me and called out to me. I'd pulled my coat around myself like a Victorian lady hurrying along to try to escape the attentions of Jack the Ripper, and still . . .

*Tap, tap, tap*, again.

Without looking in the direction of the tapping, I reached for the door handle and popped the car door open. In response, Heath stepped back, waited for me to climb out. I gathered my long black coat around me – I didn't normally drive in this coat, but I'd wanted a quick getaway.

We stood a couple of metres apart, looking each other over.

I had an image of Heath in my head. It was always post-makeover. Neat clothes, dancing eyes, short, carefully styled hair. Easy smile. That Heath wasn't standing in front of me. I'd forgotten how time changes us; it ages, deepens, alters us. Our bodies are time machines, and they wear the ravages and caresses of each part of our journey.

Time had painted white strands into Heath's blond hair. It had firmed up his tall frame. It had pressed creases into his skin. But it was grief that had concaved his cheekbones, that had colour-leached his skin, that had smudged dark circles under his eyes. He had looked the same when his father died.

'Thanks for coming,' Heath said.

I nodded, not sure how to speak to him. Ex. Psychopath. Murderer.

'I didn't think you would. Aunt Lynda said you probably wouldn't, but I'm glad you did.'

Another nod from me.

His face relaxed into a familiar smile, one I was so used to seeing, that I was thrown for a moment, thought I was way back when he could smile like that and I would like it. I would love it. 'Honestly, I thought after all these years I'd be immune to you. I thought I'd see you and I wouldn't feel a thing . . . but no such luck.'

'Where's your wife?' I asked him.

'Right in front of me,' he replied.

'Oh, for . . . where's your partner, your other half?'

Immediately he lowered his head, stuck his hands deep into his coat pockets, hiding something – hiding *from* something. 'I . . . erm . . . well, she didn't come. It wouldn't have been appropriate.'

'In what way?'

'She's still got an issue with you.'

'Why would she—? Oh right, you got back together with Abi.'

'Yes.'

'You just never learnt to move on, did you, Heath?'

'It wasn't intentional! We bumped into each other not long after it was clear that you and I were properly over. We'd always got on so . . .'

'Well, erm, good for you. I hope you've been very happy together. Not sure why she still has an issue with me when you've been together for years.'

'She's always felt . . . Mum adored you. Always. She never stopped hoping . . . She regularly asked after you, and more than once asked why we couldn't try again.'

'In front of Abi? That's horribly cruel.'

'No, Mum would never do that. She liked Abi . . . but she wasn't you. And then Aunt Lynda kind of let it slip in front of her that Mum asked for you to come to her funeral and that she'd left you something in her will. And I don't know, Abi took it as well as anyone would, I suppose.'

I closed my eyes and shook my head in despair. I felt sick, physically nauseous for that poor woman. 'She must have thought it was déjà vu. I hope you reassured her that you weren't going to dump her straight after the funeral again.' It was a statement, because only a psychopath wouldn't reassure the woman he's in love with that he wouldn't hurt her in exactly the same way he hurt her last time, for the very same reason. Only a psychopath.

Heath said nothing, instead he lowered his head again.

'You didn't reassure her,' I stated. It was weird how I kept needing more and more proof that he was a psychopath. He killed someone to get rid of my friend, what more proof could I possibly need? 'That poor woman. I don't even know her and I feel sorry for her.'

'How could I reassure her when I knew what would happen the second I saw you again?'

'I suppose this isn't history repeating itself, is it? I mean, *if you dare do anything to anyone I care about—*'

'I'm not going to do anything to anyone.' He is fierce, like he has to say this loudly and clearly so we both believe it. 'I'm better. I don't do that sort of thing any more . . . I've had therapy, I've been on medication for years. I'm on an even keel.'

I wasn't sure if I should believe him or not. But what difference did it make? It wasn't as if an apology could make up for the things he had done. 'Good for you.'

'Although . . .' His voice petered out and I knew he wanted me to pick up the thread, but I wasn't going to. This wasn't a normal conversation where I had to follow his cues. This was something that was very rapidly messing with my mind.

When he realised I wasn't going to engage, he said: 'Although, what I said all those years ago still stands.'

I knew what he was saying, of course I knew, but I still wasn't going to engage. 'You said a lot of things over the years.'

He stood up properly then, moved his shoulders back, strengthened his stance. 'If you come back to me, I will give the police evidence that will clear . . . your friend.'

I couldn't believe he'd actually said it out loud. What about Abi? What about me? What about the life I had? The people in it, the ones I cared for? What about them if I decided to do what he'd just suggested?

'He didn't want that. He didn't want me going back to you.'

'But he wanted you to shack up with his brother instead?'

I said nothing, even though I involuntarily shrugged a little.

'He *did*?' Heath was incredulous. 'He set you up with his brother and you just went along with it?'

'I didn't go along with anything.'

'Are you sure? Because from where I'm standing it looks a like he got you to do penance by taking on his loser brother,' Heath said. 'Win–win for him, I guess.'

'Wallace is not a loser. He's the absolute opposite of a loser. Sidney thought I would get on with him, that his brother would get on with me, and it turns out the attraction was mutual.'

'So it's just attraction? Nothing else?'

'What is it you expect me to say to that? I mean, of course it's more than the instant attraction we both shared. It's an easy relationship, always has been. We "get" each other, our thoughts and values are aligned. We balance out the excesses in each other's personalities, we have fun, we talk, we adore each other—'

'Who's being cruel now?' Heath virtually snarled, his whole face and body aflame.

The worst part, of course, was I wasn't even trying to be cruel. He had started it by being snide and I had answered to stop him diminishing the man I loved and our relationship. But, if I was being honest with myself, I had enjoyed the look of horror and pain on his face. I had indulged in making it clear that the things wrong with our relationship *were* unique to our coupling, *I* wasn't broken, *I* could love and be loved in a healthy way. I didn't mean to be cruel, but I had been . . . and I had almost enjoyed it. I refocused my line of sight on the small row of shabby shops I could see over his shoulder. Like most things, most people, this bank of shops had seen better days, but despite the worn posters and peeling paint, the dirtied windows and fading signs, they stood proud and strong.

'Just don't trash-talk my husband,' I said quietly. Before he could say anything else, I added: 'And I mean my real husband, not you . . . Look, I should go and you should get back to your guests.'

'All right, "Sidney" didn't want you coming back to me in exchange for setting him free, but what about you? Didn't you want to clear his name? Get him out of prison?'

'Of course I did,' I replied through tight lips. 'It's all I thought about.' *It's all I think about.*

'Well, I can do that. I can do that.'

'How can *you* do that? He hasn't been able to appeal all these years because we need new and compelling evidence. And there is nothing. It'd have to be pretty spectacular—'

'I've got video,' he cut in.

'Video?'

He nodded once, twice, three times then added: 'I watched him arrive and leave and she was very much alive. They had sex. Which was why they thought she'd been . . . interfered with.'

His phrasing made me look at him. He'd killed someone – in the coldest of blood – but couldn't say the word 'rape'? 'That all came out at the trial,' I replied. 'I'm pretty sure, even with video evidence of him coming and going, they'll just say the time of death was an estimate and will adjust it to suit.' I refocused on the shabby shops, standing like ageing soldiers in a sea of progress, clinging on to who and what they were, despite everything changing around them. 'To get out, there would have to be new and compelling evidence. That's why his applications to appeal have been turned down all these years – no new or compelling evidence.

'So, unless you have something else that's not a full confession, let's not talk about this, all right? It stresses me out. More than stresses me out. It rips me apart.' The guilt sat like an anvil on my chest. Every day. I had not forgotten, I had not 'moved on', I had not walked away without a backward glance. But Sidney would not see me. He would not send me Visiting Orders. He would see Wallace – and only Wallace – *sometimes* but that was it. He wanted us all to get on with our lives, as though that was ever a possibility. Like I ever could just go on and not think about him every day. Not curse Heath for doing this, not curse myself for causing all of this.

'I've . . . I've got . . . I've got another video . . . of . . . of me doing it.'

It's like the sensation of someone reaching into the cavity of my chest with a giant fist and squeezing my heart, causing my whole body to freeze in horror. I couldn't look at him as I asked through numb lips: 'You've what?'

'I filmed myself . . . I tied her up so I could set the camera . . . I filmed myself. So I could never forget what I did. I knew that I would be able to pretend away what I did, so I had to have a permanent reminder. Despite the balaclava and gloves, you can see in the video that it's not him, that it's a white man.'

'Was she scared?'

Heath stared as though he'd forgotten how to speak.

'Was she scared as you did it? Was she begging for her life while you filmed yourself killing her?' I had to know. I had to know if he had been getting off on this snuff movie all these years; had he been feeding his psychopathy with this ultimate act of power and dominance. '*Was she scared?*' I hissed to his continued silence.

'No,' he said quietly. 'No, I don't think she was. She wasn't aware of very much.'

'You're just saying that to make yourself feel better,' I spat.

'I'm not. She and Sidney had been drinking heavily, which is why they got into an argument. You could hear the slurred shouting in the street. That's what the neighbours said – they could hear shouting. Then it looked like they smoked a lot of weed. And she took sleeping pills. They were on her bedside table – open. She took more than she should. Only a couple more, but it was enough to mean she barely stirred when—' Heath stopped talking, as if realising what he was saying, *explaining.*

'When you put your hands around her throat. Is that what you were going to say? So why the pillow over her face? Just to make sure?'

He hung his head, stared at the pavement. I stared at the pavement, too, my eyes suddenly overbrimming with tears. Like they did whenever I thought about this. I could be fine, or happily laughing and joking, or about to fall asleep, and then it would come storming into my brain: *a woman is dead because of me. Because a man loved me so much, he killed someone to try to stop me from leaving him. A woman is dead because of me and her whole family are devastated. And they all hate the wrong man, they all hate someone who is completely innocent.* And my eyes would well up, and I would feel winded because my heart would feel like it was being squeezed, just like my husband squeezed the life out of a woman he didn't know.

*I have to get my hands on that video*, I decided. *I have to get it to the police and get Sidney out of prison. That's all I can do. I can't bring her back, but I can help set Sidney free.*

'I know what you're thinking,' Heath said, suddenly able to face me again. 'You're thinking you need to get your hands on that video. You can't. You'll never find it. If you tell the police about it, it'll be like last time, they'll never believe you because they'll never find it. I hid it somewhere where no one who isn't me will find it.'

'What do you want, Heath? In return for the video, what do you want?'

'What I've always wanted: you. I want you back. You come back to me, I'll give the tape anonymously to the police . . . And you agree not to tell them it's me.'

I opened my mouth.

'And I know if you promise me you won't then you won't. And, like last time, I have a rock-solid alibi.'

I swallowed at the immobile lump that was closing up my throat, then tried to moisten my lips. 'How would it even work, this coming back to you? I mean, do you think I'm going to live with you? Have sex with you?'

'Of course. Look, we always gelled in the bedroom, you can't deny that. Even when you didn't love me any more you still enjoyed making love, I could tell. If you come back to me, we could be happy again, I know we could. We could get married – publicly this time. And we could have a baby. I know we're both getting on, but we could try. People older than us have babies. You haven't had one with this other bloke, so that might mean you don't want a child. Which is cool. I'll go along with whatever you want.'

*Except give the tape to the police without wanting me in return*, I almost said. Instead I asked again: 'Why do you want me back, Heath? You must know that if I come back to you because you've forced me to, I'll never be able to love you like you want me to. I'll never be properly with you, so why do you want me back?'

332

'Because I love you.'

'This isn't love. I don't know what it is, but it's not love.'

Heath squeezed his hands together, his fingers finding tight housing between the fingers of the other hand, as though in desperate prayer. 'I've told you before, I don't want to love you. I've tried not loving you. And it works for a while. Sometimes, like when I was on medication, it worked for a long while, but it doesn't last. None of it lasts because my default setting is loving you. I was made to love you. And it is love. It *is*.'

'If you loved me, you wouldn't be doing this to me.'

'I don't want to love you,' he offered pathetically.

'I don't want you to love me, either,' I stated, before opening my car door and climbing in.

The reason – the real reason – I didn't want to come to the funeral was because I knew, without any doubt, that it would lead to this. I had known all those years that I had been living on borrowed time. That what I was doing would come to an end and I would have to go back at some point and pay my dues again – this time with Heath.

I had done what Sidney wanted, I had helped his family. With Wallace, I had helped to redecorate and repair their home, we'd got them on to as a sure a financial footing as possible, that allowed them to make trips to Togo whenever they wanted. We had got them a house built just outside Lomé, so they could take as many breaks as they wanted. We had repaired as many relationships in their family as possible, we had tried to light up their life. But Sidney's parents were getting on, his remaining grandparent may not have much longer. It was time for Sidney to come home, to make their family complete.

I had been living on borrowed time all this while and now it was time to pay it all back.

Sitting frozen in my car, I pressed my hands over my face so I could hide, even from my ghostly reflection in the windscreen. I didn't want to go. I didn't want to give up Wallace.

He was the complicating factor in all of this. I loved him. The thought of walking away from him, leaving him, was mining new depths of pain inside that I didn't know it was possible to feel.

I had been in agony for years over what Heath had done because of me – I could never forget, I was always trying to find ways to get the universe to forgive me by doing everything I could for Sidney's family, but I was selfish, too. I had fallen for Wallace, I had taken his love when I had no real right to love anyone. Not when 'love' had driven Heath to remove someone from the world. Wallace had eased my pain when I didn't really deserve to feel anything other than torment. And now I had to leave him.

Not only that, I would have to hurt him, too. I would have to walk away from him without telling him properly why. How could I tell him why? How would he understand that I had let his brother languish in prison all this time when doing this one thing would set him free? My relationship with Wallace would have to come to an end, and the thought of that was torture.

The other car door opened and I felt Heath climb in, shut the door behind him, sealing us in together.

'I can't do it straight away,' I stated.

'How long?' Heath asked quietly, almost as though he couldn't quite believe what I was saying to him.

'I have to get divorced,' I replied. 'And I need to quit my job—'

'I don't want you to do that. You love that job.'

I swallowed the bile-tinged words that wanted to spew out of my mouth. 'I have to end my old life,' I stated. 'I can't do that stuff any more. I have to start over if I'm going to do this with you.' That was why I had been so adamant in the contract negotiations about being able to permanently end the series; I knew this day would come.

'Would you like us to leave and go somewhere no one knows us?'

'Yes. That would be for the best,' I mumbled.

'All right. I'll start looking. Anywhere in particular you want to go?'

'I don't care.'

'I'll find us somewhere, somewhere really beautiful, where it can be just the two of us.'

'Fine. Good. Yes.'

I flinched when Heath put his hand on my head then ran it down to my shoulder and rested it there. I almost told him not to touch me, but stopped myself. What was the point? I was going to be with him soon enough. Why pretend that I wouldn't let him touch me in that time? I'd have to do whatever it took to stop him hurting anyone else.

'It's going to take a while,' I said. I briefly covered his hand with mine then took his hand off my shoulder and lowered it for him. I couldn't stand for him to touch me. Not when I was still married to Wallace.

'How long?' he asked again, then held his breath. Waiting for me to reveal myself as a liar and time-waster. Someone who was just stringing him along until she could dupe him out of the video. I couldn't do that. I could never risk anyone getting hurt by him again. I was going to do this. I was going to go back to him so he wouldn't harm anyone again.

'I have to give the TV company notice and I have to find out about getting divorced. Six months, I reckon, tops. I'll do my best to make it sooner, hopefully no more than three months.'

I finally lowered my hands from my face and turned to him to make sure he knew I was serious. I was doing this for real.

'I do . . . I do love you,' he said. 'I have since the moment I met you. And everything I've done is because I love you.'

I stared at Heath, not sure what to say. Being loved by someone was meant to be good, not this dangerous, not this toxic, not this awful. 'I'll get in touch nearer the time,' I said.

'Will you really?'

'Please don't hurt anyone or do anything before then,' I responded.

'I don't do that any more.'

'I promise you, I am going to come back to you. Promise me you won't hurt or do anything to anyone before then.'

'I don't do that any more,' he insisted.

'Just promise me.'

'I promise.'

'Thank you. I need to get back,' I said to him, facing the windscreen. 'I'll see you in three months, if I can, six months if not.'

'We're going to be so happy together, I promise you. We're going to be so happy.'

With a pounding heart and knots where my stomach should be, I drove home, ready to start the next stage of my life.

Without my job.

Without my home.

Without my family.

Without my beloved Wallace.

# 39

It's quiet around here at night. After about nine o'clock most people seem to bed down; although lights are on, there's very little sound to disturb the smooth softness of the cool night air. A few streets away a dog barks, which causes another couple of dogs to bark in reply. I'm aware of the sound of my footsteps as I hurry to get to the end of our road. It's quite a distance to the meeting place and I have to pick up pace to make sure I get there for the allotted time.

The house with the yellow door has a very large gravel driveway because it's the biggest house on this street and contains five good-sized flats. There's a green electrical box on the pavement, but the street light is a couple of houses down and does nothing to shed light on this area.

He's not here.

I expected to see him standing here as I was rushing down, then I expected him to step out from the driveway into the street when I stopped. No.

He's not here.

I look around, searching the shadows, squinting at trees and parked cars and darkened doorways. He's not here.

337

I raise my phone, flick on the light, shine it around to see if its bulb can shed any type of light around so I can see where he might be hiding.

*He's not here.*

*He's not here, he's not here.*

*He's. Not. Here.*

I turn to face the direction I've just come.

*He's not here. So where is he?*

# 40

*There's someone in the house.*

Lola can feel it.

*There's someone who shouldn't be here in the house.*

She'd heard Auntie C set the alarm and it hadn't been turned off, so there shouldn't be anyone in the house.

Lola drops the fistful of popcorn she'd been about to stuff into her mouth back into the clear plastic bowl then sits very still, listening. The TV isn't on very loud, she's watching a movie with the subtitles turned on so she can hear the creaks of the house, she can hear any sounds from outside. And she can also hear the things that shouldn't be there. Nothing for a moment. Nothing, just the dog barking over the back somewhere. And then . . . the soft thud of a footstep. And another. The rustle of material as someone moves slowly and stealthily down the corridor. Towards this room.

*Someone is in the house.*

She looks over at the door and her eyes widen in shock and fear as she realises that she didn't hook the chair back into place under the handle after she returned from getting her book and glasses from the room next to this one.

*Was the person in the house, then? Waiting. Waiting to come out when Auntie C was far enough away?*

Another soft thud of a footstep. And another.

They're going to be here soon. Very soon.

Her eyes scan the tangle of bedclothes – the flowery duvet, the soft furry beige blanket and the cushions – for her mobile or the house phone. Auntie C had made her hold them. *'Keep them in your hands until I get back,'* she'd said. Lola had done what she was told – until she went to get the book and her glasses. Then she'd just put them down and now they're lost to her.

*Soft footstep, soft footstep.*

Oh God, what should she do?

She looks at the window. Can she climb down and not break her damn neck? No. There is no way of pretending she can.

Should she hide?

Hide. Yes. Hide. Her eyes swing wildly around, looking for a place to hide in this room. Nothing comes to mind except in one of the wardrobes or under the bed. Neither are good hiding places.

Should she put the chair under the handle again? Yes, that's a better idea. Much better idea.

Yes, yes. Seal herself in, find her mobile, call the feds.

Lola slides out of bed, trying to be quiet so the person doesn't realise she knows they're there. She eases her feet onto the carpet and pushes away from the bed as quietly as she can.

She can hear her heart beating, although she's pretty sure no one else can, but she's holding her breath any way, just in case they can.

Slowly, carefully, Lola moves across the room, aware that she needs to speed up, the footsteps are almost at the door. She makes a break for it, runs for the door and grabs the chair, ready to swing it into place, just as the door bursts open, knocking her backwards off her feet and bringing the chair down on top of her.

The intruder, dressed in black with a mask covering their mouth and hood up, shoves the door hard, and is in the room before Lola can recover.

All she can do is get out the start of a scream before the intruder rushes her and slaps a gloved hand over her mouth.

*This is it*, Lola realises. *This is the moment I die.*

# 41

*That sounds like a scream.*

I could be imagining it, but it sounds like a scream that's been cut off. But then there are foxes making that kind of noise all the time. They scream when they are mating and I always stop, always sit up, because for those first few microseconds when the sound hits my ears, it sounds like a scream. Just like that noise I just heard. But this came from the direction of my house.

And Heath is not here.

*Why are you standing here? Why are you not running in the direction of the scream?* I shout at myself. And then I am running, dashing back to my house. My feet not moving fast enough, my legs not giving me enough power. I'm getting closer, but not fast enough. Closer, closer, running, running, and then . . . *WEEUWEEUWEEUWEEU-WEEU!* A burglar alarm explodes into the night, warning everyone that something bad is happening. I stop in my tracks, turned to a pillar of salt like Lot's wife – except it isn't one last look that has petrified me, it is the sound of someone breaking into my house.

Breaking in to get to someone I care about. To get to Lola.

I run again, this time my speed coming from the fear and the horror of what is happening. My phone starts to buzz in my hand, ringing me to tell me that someone has tripped the alarm in my house.

I shouldn't have left her. I shouldn't have left her. A car is pulling away from the kerb as I approach, a number of dogs are barking at the alarm disturbing their peace. I don't really slow to round the corner onto the path to find our purple front door gaping open like the mouth of a deeply shocked person. *WEEUWEEUWEEUWEEUWEEU!* The alarm, a terrifying backdrop to the horror clamouring inside me, continues to scream. *WEEUWEEUWEEUWEEUWEEU!*

'No. No. No.' I run into the house, swipe my keys over the alarm keypad to stop the unholy noise and then take the stairs two at a time. My bedroom door is also agape, but it is splintered at the handle, where it wasn't turned before being forced open.

The television is on, the popcorn is all over the bed, the bowl is upturned on the floor, the chair is on its side in the middle of the room. Lola's mobile sits like a black oyster in the shell of the bedclothes. The house phone lies on the floor next to the crisps bowl.

It takes a couple of seconds for the scene to filter properly through my brain, and when it does, I run out, running from room to room, calling her name, asking her – begging her – to tell me that she's here. That she's fine. That he hasn't taken her.

I run downstairs and do the same there, finishing in the little bedroom down the back and top of the house where Franklyn sleeps.

Empty. The house is empty. She is gone.

The car. There was a car speeding away. Maybe she was in it. Maybe she'd escaped out of the house. I run outside, but obviously the car is long gone. If it did have Lola in it, then I missed my chance to stop them.

Shaking, trembling, I stand facing my house.

This can't be happening. This can't be happening. What am I going to tell her parents? How am I going to explain this to anyone, let alone them? Something pings in my mind and I run back into the house and up to the smallest room on the first floor. It's become a dumping ground that we rarely go into. The window is open. A piece has been cut out of the glass so the person could reach in and undo the sash locks.

This isn't Heath. He wouldn't have done this.

Yes, he did that other thing, but this is not him. He might do this to other people, but not to me. Never *to* me.

My mobile bleeps in my hand. A cheery ding among the horror unfolding around me. Because it is still unfolding, it is nowhere near done.

> ° Tell anyone about this and she's dead.
> Just wait for more instructions.
> I mean it. Tell anyone . . . police, her
> parents . . . anyone and she's dead.

Definitely not Heath. I should have known. None of the messages sounded like him. Even at his angriest, his most terrifying, he has never sounded like that. I reply:

> • Who are you? Why are you doing this?

The response is almost immediate.

> ° : ) LOL You've worked it out.
>
> ° Congratulations on not being
> completely stupid. You'll hear

from me. Stay by your phone.
And when the police come by
keep your mouth shut.

• *Why would the police come by?*

° You'll see.

• *What have you done?*

° You'll see. Now, download
the CleanMyGetaway app
and delete all of these messages.
The police won't be able to retrieve them.
Then delete the app.
If you don't, she dies.

I'm about to do as I'm told because I can't risk Lola at all when the phone flashes up with a photo of Lola. She has a large rectangle of silver duct tape over her mouth, wisps of hair are escaping the two cornrows, parted at the centre, that she plaited into her hair earlier. But instead of looking terrified like you'd expect, she is glaring at the camera. She is clearly cussing out the person taking the photo in her head.

I actually smile. *Keep it up, Lola*, I think, *I'm coming to save you. I'm coming to find you.*

# 42

I'm back in the kitchen, pacing. Trying to work out who did this. My phone, permanently cleansed of all the messages from whoever it is, is silent. I am waiting for instructions as to what to do next, but I am racking my brain.

It's clearly someone who hates me.

But someone who hates me and has access to my life. Who has been following me. Who knows my house. Who knows my road. Who knows my work. Who knows my routine.

I have to think, I have to work it out for Lola's sake. I've tidied up as much as I can – straightened up the bedroom, stuck paper over the hole and moved boxes in front of the window so it does not look like someone broke in – in case Franklyn or Wallace comes back. I do not want them to walk into a crime scene. But I do not know what I'll tell them about Lola. Of course I want to call the police. Of course I want to call her parents, but this person has killed before. They have tried to kill again. Harry Andrews is still only hanging on by a thread.

A *BAM! BAM! BAM!* at the front door makes me jump. I stop pacing and stare at the kitchen door, my heart racing from the sudden

346

scare. Actually, my heart has been racing since someone took my niece, but this is an added layer of speeding. *BAM! BAM! BAM!* again jolts me into moving. I go to the front door.

I'm pretty sure I know who it's going to be.

I open the door and there they are. DC Amwell and DC Mattison, backed up by four of their uniformed mates.

'Mrs Pryce,' they both say at the same time.

I say nothing. The urge to blurt out what has happened is too strong.

'We have a warrant to search your house,' Mattison says. She holds out a piece of folded paper, which I do not take. There's more. Judging by the gleam of excitement in their eyes, the barely restrained joy dancing around their mouths, there is more.

'May we come in?' Amwell asks, obviously amused by this turn of events, this shift in the balance of power.

I step backwards. They're going to go into the spare room and find the cut-open window. And they're going to see the damaged door in my bedroom. And they're going to . . . what, ask me questions? I don't even know. What difference does it make to them if it doesn't point directly to the crimes they're investigating me for? My mind is still racing, I'm trying to think who is doing this.

'Is there anywhere we can wait while our officers carry out their search?'

'Anywhere,' I say. I honestly don't care. Whoever did this probably paused to plant something in my house. They're going to find it, they're inevitably going to think I'm stupid enough to actually leave evidence lying around and we're going to do that ridiculous dance all over again.

My lack of resistance takes the shine off things for both officers, I

347

can tell. I listen to the other officers march from room to room, over-turning things, opening things, moving things. Looking and searching for that thing that's going to help them put me away.

I stand in the corridor, watching it all happen, experiencing it like I am far away. I am, I suppose, since my mind is elsewhere.

'You haven't asked why we're here,' Mattison comments. 'How we were able to obtain a warrant.'

'Because you think I killed Jeff Burrfield and tred to kill Harry Andrews,' I state, not bothering to hide how distracted I am.

'No,' Amwell takes great pleasure in saying. 'We're not.'

'We're here because someone tried to kill Sandy Burton. She is in a coma.'

*Wait, what?* 'Pardon? Someone tried to kill Sandy Burton? The Chief Operating Officer of HoneyMay Productions? When?'

'Earlier today.'

'I, erm, I can't take this in. How?'

'Why don't you tell us, Mrs Pryce?'

'How would I know?'

Amwell takes out his mobile and a piece of paper from his pocket. He then makes a big show of typing the digits on the paper into his phone. He then presses the call button while staring right at me. There's a second's lag and then the phone in my hand lights up before it starts to ring. I look down at my handset, a number I don't recognise and isn't stored flashing up.

'Answer it, then,' Mattison says.

I hit the reject call button and sigh.

'Ms Burton was lured to the steep stairs over near Madeira Drive on the seafront, then she was pushed down them.'

Another way someone was killed in *The Baking Detective* show. A woman who was vain and selfish was lured there by a woman who turned out to be her long-lost daughter who'd grown up in poverty while her mother lived a life of perpetual luxury. The woman who was murdered did have a look of Sandy – short-cropped blonde hair, strong features in her face, which she'd had lifted several times, slim to the point of skinny. 'The text message that got her to go over there said . . .' Amwell raises the piece of paper and reads: ' "Having second thoughts about cancelling the show. Would you be able to come and speak to me about it? Can we meet somewhere private, out of the way? Don't want to get anyone's hopes up." Then there are the meeting details.'

'I didn't send that message,' I state through my dry mouth.

'We thought you might say that. Which is why DC Amwell rang the number the text message came from in front of you, so you could receive the call in front of us.'

'No, you don't understand. I didn't send that text message. There's no way it came from my phone. You can check if you want; there's no such text message.' I look desperately from one face to the other. Neither of them believes me. 'I didn't do this. Someone is setting me up. They're trying to set me up. I didn't do this.'

'Cleo Forsum Pryce, I am arresting you on the suspicion of attempted murder.'

*No. They can't do this. Not right now.*

'You do not have to say anything'

*I need to find her before it's too late.*

'But it may harm your defence if you do not mention when questioned something which you later rely on in court.'

*Because if I don't do whatever I'm told, she's going to die. He's going to kill her.*

'Anything you do say may be given in evidence.'

'Please, I didn't do this. I promise you, I didn't do this. And you have to let me go.' *You have to let me go. It's a matter of life or death.*

# Part 9

# 43

'Do you know what I think, Mrs Pryce? I think you think you're a genius. You believe you are so much cleverer than everyone else, certainly the police.' Detective Constable Mattison speaks like someone who has been forced to watch *every* episode of *The Baking Detective* and read *every* book in the series and has hated *Every. Single. Second. Of. It.*

We have been at this for hours. HOURS.

*Aren't you tired?* I want to shout at them.

I slide my arm onto the table that separates them from me, and rest my head on it. I am so tired, but my mind is still racing. It is burning up so much energy from racing and racing, trying to work out who did this. Who has spent so much time doing this to me.

I need to get out of here and find Lola.

'*I* think you married your husband to get close to his brother, because you liked the idea of having close links to a murderer.' I close my eyes. I'm not going to bite. 'But that didn't turn out to be as glamourous as you thought. So you decided to turn your hand to real-life murder. And you thought, by being careless, by emulating the murders in your stories, you would be able to get away with it.'

353

'I think I'd like a solicitor now,' I murmur.

'Pardon?' Amwell replies. 'Did you say something?'

I sit up and sit back and try not to cry. 'Grey is not my colour,' I say of the tracksuit I've been given to wear while they process my clothes. 'But is it anyone's colour?'

'You don't seem to be taking this seriously,' Mattison says.

'I am, I just don't know what to say to everything you've just said. I didn't do it. Any of it. If you check my phone, you'll see I didn't send any messages. You'll also see that it didn't leave my house all of today.' I shrug. 'I didn't do it.'

'Then who did?' Amwell asks.

'I don't know. I do know that I didn't send anyone any text messages to meet up. It must have been one of those phone scam things ... spoofing. Phone spoofing! Where scammers use genuine phone numbers of banks to get people's money. They must have done that. Because once you've been through my phone, you'll see there's nothing there.'

The pair of them simply stare at me, and it's suddenly obvious to me that they *have* been through my phone and they have found no evidence of me sending that text message. And they have probably had preliminary info back to say my phone did not leave my house. Not stuff that will exonerate me, but it does look like I am telling the truth.

'Do you know what I find interesting about your show?' Mattison says.

'That you didn't like it?' I reply.

'No. That the main character is so much like you.'

'Why's that interesting? A lot of writers create characters that are versions of themselves.'

'That's probably true,' she says as she leans on the table, and I can see how the cloth of her suit jacket has become worn and shiny at the elbows. She must sit like this a lot. 'But with you, there are so many similarities. I mean, take the name for example. You actually called her Mira Woode.'

'Yes?'

'Mira. That's basically the other half of your name. Cleomara. "Mara". "Mira". I'm not sure many writers take it to that extreme to name their main character after themselves.'

'I didn't even realise I'd done that,' I confess. *Wow. How narcissistic of me. I wonder how many people have thought I am totally up myself because I did that?* 'I very rarely use the "Mara" part of my name. In fact—' I stop talking as it hits me like a brick in the head.

The other half of my name. The other half of my name means I could call myself Cleo or Mara.

'In fact?' Mattison asks, wanting me to keep going. She feels we've established a rapport now, that we'll keep chatting and I'll relax enough to confess or, at least, give her some information that will help them to convict me.

'In fact I'd like a solicitor now,' I say. 'I don't have one to hand, so if you don't mind getting me the duty solicitor, I'd be very grateful.'

I sit back and carefully fold my arms across my chest. Slide down a little in my seat. That's how Heath used to sit. The more he wanted to hide in a conversation, the lower he would get. Like the first time he told Trina and me about his girlfriend. He'd been virtually horizontal by the time all the details of that revelation came out.

The girlfriend who had an issue with me. The girlfriend who he hadn't reassured before his mother's funeral that he wouldn't dump for me. Oh, but she must hate me. She must hate me so much.

Abi.

Abi. Who has hated me for years.

Abi. Who would love to get revenge on me.

Abi. Who would love to see me arrested for crimes I didn't commit.

Abi. Who knows all about me and my past.

Abi. Who would know Heath's number to spoof it.

In his London flat, not long after we came back from seeing Trina in Leeds, I'd found one of the notes she'd written to him behind one of the radiators. It'd been written on a pink sticky note that had faded and dried up over time. The black biro she'd written it with was now grey, but you could still read it quite clearly:

*Out late tonight. Love you. Abi x*

Abi. I'd thought then how her name seemed incomplete. Almost as if she hadn't finished writing it – like there should be more to her moniker. More to *her*.

But going back to setting me up, how would Abi know my work? How would Abi have access to my security pass? To my earring? Because she is not just Abi, is she? There *is* more to her. More to her name.

She is Abi.

Abi.

Abigail.

Gail.

# Part 10

# 44

24 AUGUST, 2022

## *Abi's Confession*

You know, Heath, I sometimes think of our relationship as a film. Obvious, right, since I work in the visual arts, yeah, yeah, the movies.

I think of our relationship like that because when I step back and think about it, I don't watch it from beginning to end in one go, I have to keep rewinding and forwarding and pausing. Do you want to see? Do you want to see, Heath? Go on, then . . .

**Rewind. Go on . . . rewind . . .**
I watched you. Standing there, huddled together by her car. Both of you in black, both of you so comfortable with each other it was like you had never been apart. Like you had never split up. What about me? What about me, Heath? The world was grey, overcast and subdued and you never even saw me, did you? Standing at the back of the church, standing at the back of the crematorium. I saw who you were looking for first of all in the church, and then at the crematorium. And when everyone left to go back to the hall for the wake, you didn't support your aunt, you didn't support your mother's cousins, you pretty much broke your leg to go see her, speak to her.

I saw you. I saw you trying to get close to her. The long looks, the words I knew you would whisper to get her to lean in close. I saw you get into her car after she was meant to drive away. I saw her bent over, head in her hands, sobbing – I guess that it wouldn't be so easy for her to leave her husband, after all. I was sure you wouldn't do this. That we were strong enough to withstand you seeing her again, strong enough for you not to get cock-drunk on just being near her. But I saw you getting into her car, putting your hand on her. I saw her looking at you. Was that the moment? Was that when she decided it would be you and her again?

You and her make me sick, you know. I mean that literally. I threw up when I saw what was happening. That history was repeating itself. That in your time of need, it's her you want and it's you she comes running to be with. Every. Single. Time.

Why isn't my love good enough for you, Heath?

Why her and not me?

Why?

**Go back. That's it rewind. Further. Further.**

'And this is our new production assistant, Abigail Brewster.' Sandy Burton introduced me to her, this amazing woman of yours.

And do you know what she did? She smiled at me. She smiled at me, she stuck out her hand and said hello. And she said: 'I'm so pleased to be working with you on *The Baking Detective*.' She had no idea who I was. No clue. That's because you didn't even bother to tell her about me, did you, Heath? You just discarded me and pretended I didn't exist. So she doesn't know anything about me. I mean, technically she should be quaking in her pristine trainers at the thought of me coming onto her turf, at what I could possibly do to her. But did she even blink an eye? Did she do anything other than smile sweetly and say, 'Is that a hint of a Yorkshire accent I can hear?'

'Yes, yes it is,' I said.

If she had asked, I would have told her. But of course she didn't ask. Too busy playing the big star. Too important to do anything but make the briefest, shortest of chats with the production assistant.

**Rewind. Go on, rewind.**

There you both are, leaving with suitcases, heading off to who knows where. Together. Always together. You never wanted to go away with me. Not even for the briefest of minibreaks. How I had to beg to get you to come to visit my folks up in Sheffield. *'I'm working, Abi'*, *'I can't get the time off, Abi'*, *'I just want to relax, not sit in someone else's house and drink warm beer, Abi'*.

You didn't want to be with me, to involve yourself in my life. But with her, you were always trying to get in, weren't you? For her, you'd travel halfway across the world at the drop of a hat. And wouldn't you know it, you'd changed the locks! I wouldn't have done anything. I just wanted to have a look, see what she'd done with the place. Have a look at what you had let her do to my home. Why would you change the locks? What exactly did you think I was going to do? I don't know why it upset me so much that you changed the locks, but it did. It hurt. Like everything else, it hurt that you didn't want me. That you discarded me.

**Rewind. More. More.**

Ah, yes, here we are. I ask you on the phone if we could meet. No. You're going to Leeds. I could never get you to come away with me, but you're on the way to Leeds to see a friend who's been hurt. In the middle of the working week. I was in Sheffield, seeing my gran who wasn't well. If I'd asked you to come up, would you? My nan loved you. Would you have come to see her? 'I have to see Trina, she's in the hospital.' And when I say I'll come with you, what do you say? 'No, no. We're not together any more. We shouldn't see each other. It'll make you think we've got a chance to be together when we haven't.'

'Promise me you're not with Cleo. Promise me you aren't leaving me for her.'

'I haven't seen her in three months. Since the funeral. I didn't leave you for her. I'm not with her. I'm not going to be with her. You and me have nothing to do with me and her.'

Liar.

I saw you.

Outside the hospital. You put your arms around her. You pulled her close. You kissed her. You kissed like you'd spent the night making love to her. You think it was nothing to do with me? How you always chose her over me? Nothing to do with me? Really? I knew you were going to be together for a while then. But still, I thought if I could talk to you, if I could come into your flat, get you all loved-up and sexed-up, that you would listen, that you would remember. But she was there. She was living there. And you threw me out. Made me leave. You didn't need me any more.

**Yup, rewind again. That's it, further back. Back. That's it, stop there.**

There you are. The three of you, sitting in your mother's living room, the night of your father's funeral. I came, of course I came. But you didn't notice me. In your fug of grief, you didn't notice me, or even think if I'd like to pay my respects. I did want to so I did. And it was all about her again. Rubbing my face in it. I couldn't believe what you said to me, how you said, *'Don't make me choose between you and Cleo, Abi; I'll choose her, every time.'* You didn't even think about how I might want to be there for you. How I might care. How I would help you arrange things. No, that happens and the first person you call is her. Always her.

I didn't come inside at the wake, I just wanted to pay my respects at the church. I did wait outside for her to leave your house. For them both to leave. I would have come in to comfort you then. But no, she didn't leave. No, she and her friend stayed there. The curtains were open, there was low lighting, but I saw you three. Sitting there like there was no one else in the world. I saw you get up, leave the room, come back with glasses and a bottle. I saw you change seats, sit next to her. I saw you hand her the glass – then hang on to it, so she was connected to you. I saw you look into her eyes. I didn't have to be any closer to see that you were back with her. That she was the one you were going to be with.

I hoped . . . I hoped you wouldn't do it. That you would remember that I loved you. But you didn't even leave it till midday before you were on the phone, telling me it was over. Not even midday. By phone. I suppose I should have been grateful it wasn't a text message or an email. 'I don't see any future for us. You deserve to find someone who can give you the love you want and need.' How dare you say those things to me. How dare you. I had found those things. I had. Why couldn't you understand that I had found that. With you. But then she got in the way. She turned your head. Her. Always her.

**Rewind. More, a little more. No, more, more, more. Keep going, keep going, there. Stop, we're at the beginning.**
There we are. Leeds. First day. Halls. Everyone carrying boxes, bags, suitcases.

I see you. The most perfect-looking man I have ever laid my eyes on. And you are on the next floor. You smile at me. You say hello. I know that you are mine. You speak to me whenever we pass in the corridor, see each other on campus. No classes together, but I don't care. Because I see you all the time. You come to my room sometimes and we talk about books, we listen to music, we talk about everything and nothing. I know one day soon you'll kiss me. You'll kiss me and my life will be complete.

**Fast-forward now, just a little. There.**

Leeds. Here we are. In the canteen having coffee, and there she is. Her. Cleo. She walks in with her friend and she doesn't even notice you. THIS IS WHAT I DON'T UNDERSTAND. She doesn't even notice you. 'Do you know her?' I ask you because you won't stop staring at her.

'I wish,' you say. I am sitting right there and you say 'I wish' about another woman.

She's not even that pretty.

**Fast-forward, just a little. A little more.**

You've changed yourself. For her. She took you shopping and you're a new man. New haircut, new clothes, new confidence. And everyone wants you now. None of them noticed you before, none of them hung on your every word. I did. I loved the real you. But you didn't notice, especially now you were surrounded by these other women. These women who didn't even know you were alive before a haircut and out-fit change.

And even then, even when you were sleeping with anyone who looked twice at you, it was her you wanted. Her you craved.

**Fast-forward. The tiniest bit. Yep, there, stop.**

Do you remember? Easter holidays. You stayed, I stayed. We drank Thunderbird and Stella, and you finally, finally made a move on me. And we finally, finally made love. And it was beautiful, better than I could have expected. My first time was with you and that was how it was supposed to be. We spent that whole holiday together in bed. And it was glorious. Glorious. But when she came back, when the other girls came back, I was expected to share. Share. I wouldn't even have minded so much if you'd acted like it meant anything to you.

But you didn't notice me. Us. The others. You would sleep with us, you would be friendly with us, but it was her you stared at. I could tell you were oblivious to the nasty looks I shot your way when you started to just openly sit with her. She didn't want you, but you still kept sitting with her. You still spent as much time with her as possible. The other women reluctantly put up with it, but I hated her for it. Started hating you a little. Started hating you a lot. So I got myself together. I walked away. Did you even notice, Heath? Doubt it, cos it was all always about her.

I got some self-respect, I walked away. Do you remember when I walked into your life again?

**Fast-forward. A lot more now. A lot more.**

There. Us again. How I walked back into your life. The company I worked for had been hired to film in your building. Remember we passed each other on the way in and out of the building several times before you said, 'Sorry, do I know you?'

And I laughed and said, 'I'm Abi.'

'Abigail? Is that you?' Straight away. Straight away you remembered me. I looked completely different, but you remembered me and my name. 'Wow, that's a blast from the past. It's amazing to see you. How are you?'

We had drinks in Soho that night, we kissed and necked all the way back to your place in West London in the back of a black cab and then screwed all night. Do you remember? I didn't ask about her because she was obviously in your past. We were together after that. Boyfriend and girlfriend. You had no trouble introducing me like that. You even took me home to meet the folks, remember? 'My new girlfriend,' you said, so happy and joyous. Grinning. You were actually grinning. 'This is Abigail, my new girlfriend. Call her Abi.'

I almost feel sick when I think about how happy we were; how complete. We didn't need anyone else. We were happy. Until I see late-night calls on your phone. Calls to her, to Cleo. No texts. Nothing that would leave a proper trail. Just calls. I could tell by how short they were that she obviously didn't want to know. I put up with that because I knew as long as she wasn't interested, you would stay with me.

**Fast-forward over the next bit. We've been there. We've seen how you discarded me. Here, stop here.**

There you are at my door. Begging me to help you. You did something bad, illegal. Cleo drove you to it. (Oh no, you didn't say that, it was just written all over your face.) You did something bad and you need me to lie for you. You need me to say you were with me if anyone asks. You weren't with me, why would you be? You have barely given me a second thought since she walked into your life again. Since you pulled her towards your body and she threw her arms around your neck in Leeds. I stopped existing for you. But of course I'd help you. How could I not? No one asked by the way. But you know that, don't you? You didn't need me for that after all.

**Fast-forward. Yes, yes, stop. Here we are.**

You haven't been with her for ages. I know because I kept an eye on things. She was there, you were somewhere else and you just weren't together. I suppose I should thank you for not coming running to me. For not making me your rebound girl. Because I saw that you went back to your old ways. I saw that you started sleeping around. Looking for love in all the wrong places, using sex as a stop-gap.

At the time, I didn't see it like that. I couldn't work out what it was about me that kept you away. Why didn't you want me? Now that she wasn't an option, why not me? I went with it, though. I had to stop pining for you. I'm a beautiful woman, I have lots going for me. What did I need you making me feel second best for? But here we are. Fate bringing us together again. Me filming in a coffee shop, you coming in.

I saw you well before you saw me. My first instinct wasn't to rush over to you, it was to pretend I didn't see you. Because you are pain, Heath Sawyer. To me, you are pain. You have caused me pain since I met you and at that point I was off the pain merry-go-round, where I wait for you to do something to hurt me. And I followed that instinct, melted into the background, pretended I didn't see you. But you saw me. You saw me and your first instinct was to come on over, to offer me more pain at a cut price. 'Hi, Abi. Haven't seen you in a lifetime,' you said, all smiles. Remember? It was the smile that got me. You were smiling at me like you meant it.

'Heath,' I said. 'How are you?'

'Good, actually. It's great to see you.'

'You, too. I'll see you around.'

'Do you fancy a drink?' you asked. You. Asked. Me.

'No, no thank you.'

'No?' You were surprised, huh? You couldn't believe that I would dream of turning you down.

'No, no thank you. I'm off the pain merry-go-round. I don't need to be unceremoniously dumped for another woman you're not even with more than once to get the message that you're not good for me. Actually, I do need to be, which is why I let you do it to me in college and then as adults. So no, learnt my lesson. The hard way. Twice. Not going to do it again.'

Was that admiration on your face as you listened? I think it was. You were impressed that I had finally grown up. I had finally got a backbone when it came to you. 'Fair enough,' you said. 'I'll see you.'

'You probably won't but I know what you mean.'

And that was it, wasn't it? That was when I got a taste of what it must be like to be Cleo because you pursued me. Pretty hard. Three months of calls, texts, emails and casually bumping into me. Three months before I was convinced that it was me you wanted, her you were properly over, us who were meant to be together.

I didn't even find any calls or texts to her, you were completely loyal. I mean, I didn't completely believe it; I was constantly waiting for the day when you'd start hankering after her, but it didn't happen.

Which is when I got complacent. I relaxed. I allowed myself to believe you wouldn't do it again. She was past. I was present. *And* I was future.

**Fast-forward. Yup, keep going. Keep going. Skip over all of that. Skip over that, too. That's it, keep going. Oh, here we are now.**
That's it. Your mother is dying. She's nice, your mother. Always so upbeat and friendly, even when she is in pain. I liked her, I liked her so much. She was practically my mother-in-law, after all. And she stabs

me in the back. Her witch of a sister, Lynda, sits there and starts to bring *her* up to you. I mean, I know she was allegedly trying to be discreet so she told you when I wasn't around, but I walked in, didn't I? Insisted she keeps talking. 'Your mother said she's left her something in her will. I think it might have been jewellery, but I won't know until afterwards.'

'Her, who?'

Now she's looking embarrassed. Now she's wishing she'd kept her mouth shut. Shutting up is free, I should have told her. She didn't *have* to tell you, did she? But she tells you, and suddenly she's back in your head. I notice you stop taking your medication, I notice you start to get headaches. I notice that you're staring into space. You're playing certain songs over and over and over. We're back there. Where she is the centre of everything. And it's only a matter of time before I get my marching orders.

**Fast-forward, not too much. That's it there.**

There's me, getting a job at her television company. It's a job far below my experience, and when they ask why in the interview, I say I'm suffering burnout, need to take a step back. I am burnt out. Burnt out of the fury of her running my life again. But this way, I can keep an eye on her, keep an eye on you. See if she wants you back. Your mother lasts another six months. Which is wonderful, because I did like her. I liked her a lot.

**And a tiny fast forward to here. The funeral, watching history repeat itself.**

Yes, here I am, watching you talk to her. Watching you come more and more alive the longer you speak to her. Thinking about it now she

369

wasn't even looking like she wanted to talk to you, both of you had non-positive body language, maybe you were arguing about who had stopped you being together, but I knew what was going to happen. You would keep talking until she was back there with you. Until she was staring at you in her car, probably promising to come back to you. Probably helping you to plan your lives together. And then my phone call would arrive. I would be dumped.

**A tiny, minuscule fast forward. Yup. Stop.**
A week after the funeral and I haven't had a phone call. I've been avoiding home because I don't want you to dump me. But you know where I am, you could do it if you really wanted to. And you don't. So maybe . . . just maybe . . . maybe if I got rid of her, you'd stay with me. I mean, not kill her. That would be stupid. That would be setting her up as the woman you never get over. But what if I created an out-of-sight, out-of-mind situation? What if she went away for a very long time?

What if she's in prison for such a long time that you, Heath, are given the time and space to get over her again? I could encourage you back on to medication, back into therapy, give you a proper break from her.

**Again, a tiny little fast forward. Yup. Stop.**
I've been following her every chance I get: learning her routine, learning who her people are, seeing how fucking ordinary this woman you're constantly losing your mind over is. Here I am, waiting for the right time to execute this plan to stitch her up, which is why I haven't done anything yet. But I know the chance will present itself. And it does. When she goes to see a divorce lawyer. Why would I allow her

to be free so she can go after you again, Heath? Why would I? I've been waiting and waiting, but when I see this, I have to move quickly. Improvise. So I go in to where she is working that evening, encourage her to leave with the rest of us, go into the room to help her pack up, pocket her security pass. She doesn't even notice I use her pass to buzz us out. Which is how I am able to 'drop' the pass when I go back and off that meddling lawyer man. I say improvise. I already had three of the four people I've gone after pegged, I knew which episodes I was going to use, he was just short notice.

I wish I could have been there when they questioned her, when she realised he was killed in the same way as one of the characters in her stupid show. I would love to have seen that.

**OK, shuffle forward a little. That's it.**
You know why I had to go after Harry Andrews, don't you? He was trash. I mean, he was already on my list, wasn't he? Only partly because he was constantly slagging Cleo off and I knew it'd only be a matter of time before he said all those things to her face. But he made the list because that place he created is toxic – rotten-to-the-core toxic. *And* he was a total sleaze. *Total sleaze*. I'm not even kidding. He has touched up or threatened for sex every woman who has worked at HoneyMay Productions. Every single one. Yes, including me. Oh, he had it coming. Again, would have loved to see her face when they told her about the way he was killed. Well, almost killed.

**That's it, the tiniest of tiny forwarding. Quick, there. Stop.**
And here we are at what happened to Sandy Burton, illustrious Chief Operating Officer of HoneyMay Productions. Why her? She's a bit stand-offish and looks down on everyone, but I'm sure she didn't seem

so bad to Cleo. Well, she was perfect because she was so awful. She absolutely contributed to the hideous atmosphere at HoneyMay Productions – the woman was totally racist, totally classist, and hated women who were anywhere near as successful as her. She was perfect because she hated Cleo almost as much as I did. A little birdie told me that since Cleo signed the contracts – seven years ago – Sandy had been trying to find legal ways to force Cleo to either keep writing *The Baking Detective* or turn the rights over to HoneyMay Productions. Get this, at one point she was even exploring how to get Cleo declared legally insane. Yes, honestly. Oh, she was perfect. So much motive, so much another person asking for it.

And here we are. In present. Bearing witness to all I've done. The man I killed. The man I tried to kill. The woman in the coma. The little girl I had to take. All done to set *her* up.

All done to finally set you free from Cleo Forsum.

# Part 11

# 45

*It's a good thing I don't need the toilet,* Lola thinks. *Because there is no way she is letting that Woman take her anywhere.*

Lola is not happy. It's not the fact that she's here, who knows where, being held hostage, it's that The Woman got her at all. Her parents have been sending her to martial arts lessons since she was young and she always thought she could look after herself. But as soon as she realised there was someone in the house, it was like all the stuff she had learnt vanished from her brain. And when it did finally kick in, it was too late. The Woman had her hand over her mouth and had picked her up like she weighed nothing.

She'd struggled, really fought, but The Woman had been so strong. So strong. And by the time she'd thrown her in the back of the car, Lola had admitted *temporary* defeat.

She still isn't sure what she wants with her, but she's been cussing her in her head. Who is this person? And why is she always texting? Why did she take a picture of her?

Lola's hands are tied together in front of her and wrapped up with thick silver tape. There is a rectangle of tape over her mouth, too. Lola wishes The Woman would take it off. There are a few things she would like to say to her.

'*Mmmm, mmmm, mmmm,*' Lola mumbles.

The Woman looks at her, eyeing her up suspiciously. She's been looking at Lola like that for a while now. She wasn't expecting her to be so defiant. Most hostages would be cowed, fearful, terrified of what is going to happen to them. This one is bold. And openly pissed off. Not what you'd expect from a teenager in such a dire situation.

She starts mumbling again, trying to speak behind the tape. The Woman picks up her weapon, a large, sharp-looking kitchen knife with a shiny black handle, and comes towards her. She presses the knife right up against her neck and, for the first time, Lola feels fear. It rises rapidly inside her, like a wave of vomit, and she doesn't like the taste of it. But she isn't going to show this person that she is scared.

'If you scream, I will slit your throat. It's really that simple.'

She rips the tape off Lola's mouth in one awful move that makes it feel like her lips have been ripped off. 'Ow!' she says, bringing her bound hands up to her face. 'Rude! And OW!'

The Woman stares at her impassively, obviously not caring that she could have damaged one of Lola's favourite features on her own face. 'What do you want? What are you so desperate to say?'

'First of all, rude! Second of all, what is this place? And then, who are you?'

'My name isn't important,' she replies.

'Erm . . . yes it is.'

'All right, just call me Auntie A.'

Lola screws up her face, like she's just heard the biggest stink joke of all time. Or maybe this Woman *is* the stink joke. 'Not being funny, but you're no Auntie. I'm never putting respect on your name like that.

I'm never calling you Auntie anything. Except maybe Auntie Incarcer-
ated!' Lola begins to laugh, which seems to enrage The Woman. She
doesn't like that at all, and brings the knife, which she had lowered,
back up.

'What am I even doing here?' Lola asks.

'You should ask your aunt that,' The Woman replies.

'I kind of can't, she's not exactly here, is she?'

'Your aunt . . . she has spent the last twenty-five years, ruining my
life. This is a little payback.'

'For real? How has she done that?'

'You wouldn't understand,' The Woman spits.

'Try me.'

The Woman looks at her with disdain and contempt.

'I'm serious, try me. I mean, I think grown-ups are a trip, don't get
me wrong, but I'm always trying to understand them. Like my parents,
they're divorced and I'm always trying to work out why.'

The Woman's face twists with a new emotion. 'What's this, are you
trying to befriend me so I won't kill you? Is that what your aunt taught
you? Befriend your kidnapper and they might not kill you? Well, let
me tell you this, "Lola", I've killed before and I am going to kill you.'

'You have a lot of anger,' Lola replies. 'A lot of grown-up-lady-anger
issues.' Lola is not concentrating or even acknowledging the way her
stomach has started to somersault. She has no doubt in her mind at all
that The Woman is going to kill her. Going to try. That's how Lola is
going to think of it. The Woman is going to *try* to kill her. But she can't
succeed. She *won't* succeed. 'I hope you get some help for it. Soon.'

'You've got a smart mouth for such a little kid.'

'Where is this place?'

'What's it to you?'

'I'm just asking a question. It's a nice place. Looks familiar.'

'It's one of the sets for *The Baking Detective*,' The Woman says in a normal voice. 'HoneyMay Productions decided to buy a place to use for filming when all the lockdowns started. It was easier than trying to hire a studio. They film a lot of stuff here, just change the furniture and décor.'

'Cool.' Lola looks around the living room they are sitting in. It isn't anything like the one back at Auntie C and Uncle W's place, nor the one she stays in with Pops. And it isn't even like the one she imagines she'll one day create. But it is nice. Comfy sofa, nice rug, side table, lamps, bookshelves. Boring but nice. They are sitting mainly in darkness, the only light coming from the mobile phone torch this Woman has lit and put in the corner. 'Does that mean it has a working toilet?'

'Yes, why do you want to know?'

'Why do you think?'

'Hold it.'

'I can't.'

'Hold it.'

'I. CAN'T.'

Sighing loudly and crossly, The Woman picks up the mobile she is using as a light and slots it into her front jeans pocket so the path ahead of them is lit. She marches over to Lola, hoists her to her feet and drags her to the corridor. In the space under the stairs is a toilet and tiny sink. The Woman throws open the white lacquered door and shoves Lola forwards.

Lola turns to face her with her hands out. 'Either you untie me or you take my tracksuit bottoms and knickers down. And I wouldn't do that if I were you.'

'Try anything and I will hurt you.' The Woman uses the sharp point of the knife to pierce the silver tape and then slices through it. The sweet relief of being able to relax her hands. 'Get on with it.'

Lola moves to close the door but The Woman sticks her foot against it. 'Leave the door open.'

'But I can't go if you're watching.'

'Well, then, you won't have the problem of needing the toilet, will you?'

Lola shakes her head. Being kidnapped and held hostage is nothing like it is on the TV or movies. It isn't plotting an ingenious means of escape while tricking the kidnappers into thinking you like them. Not at all. It is on-the-edge women waving knives about and issuing threats and making you wee in front of them. Being kidnapped and held hostage is, in fact, really undignified.

# 46

The duty solicitor did the best she could, but the police were determined to hold me for as long as they legitimately could. But since my
phone came up clean for the text message to Sandy Burton, since the
earring turned out not to have my DNA on it, and since there was
nothing incriminating in my house, they had to let me go.

I know they'll be monitoring my phone, because they are going to
keep looking for something to connect me to those crimes, but that is
the least of my worries. I have to find Lola. I have tons of missed calls
from Valerie and Franklyn. They've obviously tried to contact Lola
and had no response. Her phone is still with the police, taken from my
house when they searched the place.

I stand outside the custody centre looking at the missed calls on my
screen. The messages getting more and more frantic, asking me to call.
And I can't. If I call them, I'll tell them. And if I tell them, Abi/Gail
will harm Lola. I know she will.

I have to work out where Lola is. I have to get home, get changed
and work out where she is.

380

Because I know Abi/Gail will hurt her. Kill her if she gets a chance. I know it like I know how to breathe. It's instinctual.

My phone bleeps with another message. I look down, expecting to see Valerie or Franklyn demanding that I call them. Instead the name by the message box reads 'Wallace'.

Everything inside flips over. I want to open the message, read it, find out what he wants. But I can't. I can't open any messages in case they have read:receipt on and they know I'm reading messages. Right now they all need to think Lola and I are off doing something together. That we're ignoring them together.

As I shut the door of the aqua-green-and-white taxi I've hailed to get home, my phone bleeps again. Thankfully I'd left my keys and purse in my pockets from when I went out to meet the person I thought was Heath earlier.

> ° How was your
> night in a police cell?

She can't know that the police are still trying to connect me to the crimes so will be monitoring my phone. That's the problem with just watching the show and not reading the book – details like this are lost. It would have been too much exposition to explain that even if a person is released, if the police think the person is guilty of that crime they have the power to monitor their texts. If she knew that, she would find another way to contact me, I'm sure. In response, I type:

> • *Where do you want to meet, Abi?*

She replies:

> ° Aww, clever girl, you worked it out.
> Will send you instructions.

She definitely doesn't know my phone is being monitored. I type:

> • Is she all right, Gail?

She replies with three clapping-hands emojis and:

> ° Oh so you really worked it out.
> Well done you.
> I'll let you know where
> to meet in a couple of hours.
> Stay by your phone.
> Remember, tell anyone and she's dead.

# 47

She hasn't fed Lola all day. She's given her a few sips of water from a plastic bottle and that's been it. Lola is hungry. And weary. And bored out of her brain. The Woman had put on the television, but since they only have the free channels, she'd put on CBeebies. Not even CBBC, which has a few shows Lola occasionally watches. No, the baby channel. When she'd complained, The Woman, who is agitated and skittish, constantly checking her phone, had put a rectangle of silver masking tape over her mouth again.

*Dutty Jancrow!* She'd muttered behind the tape. *Dutty, dutty Jancrow.* (She'd heard Pops say this more than once and she knew this woman fit the description and more.)

Pops. Mum. They will have been calling and texting her. They will be going out of their minds with worry because she usually messages them non-stop. She sends them emojis and memes and lines from songs. She sometimes sends voice notes saying nothing much except, 'Love you.' The thought of their worry upsets her. She knows she's their world. She wasn't enough to keep them together, but they both love her. They both love her more than anything else in the world.

She's always known she is lucky that her parents were together for so long and that they are both still involved in her life. So many of her age mates have at least one parent who just doesn't care.

A tear escapes Lola's eye and she does the best she can to wipe it away before The Woman sees it.

The Woman is still wearing the black hoodie and jeans she has been in since the night before, and Lola is still wearing socks and the blue velvet tracksuit she sometimes falls asleep in.

Through the shut blinds and curtains, she's watched night turn to day turn to night again. She's probably going to be spending another night sitting upright on this sofa, drifting in and out of sleep.

The Woman told her that Auntie C had been arrested and they were just waiting for her to be released so they could 'link up'. She hadn't said anything to that because she had tape over her mouth, but if she hadn't she'd have asked The Woman if she knew what 'link up' actually means. And she'd tell her not to say it again. It sounded *painful* coming out of her stupid mouth.

The Woman taps away at her phone for a while and keeps snorting as though disgusted by whatever it is that comes up on the screen. Eventually, she stops tapping, puts the phone in her hoodie pocket, picks up the phone they've been using for light and slots that into her front pocket again.

'Time to go,' she says, grabbing Lola tight around the bicep and dragging her to her feet. 'Time for you to see your auntie. She's literally dying to see you. Literally.'

Lola wants to tell The Woman to never say that again, either.

# 48

While I wait to hear what I've got to do next, I've been trying to work out where she would take Lola.

Abi. Gail. Abigail. Whatever her name really is. The more I think about what she's done – getting a job at HoneyMay Productions so, I presume, she can keep an eye on me, then going on to murdering people – the more scared I am for Lola. The woman is dangerous. That's the thought that has been running like a high-speed locomotive through my brain all day and all night. She is dangerous and she will kill Lola if I don't find them in time.

I've been trying to work out what she will do next. The murders that she copied from the TV show are all Brighton specific. With the solicitor's murder (which she replicated with Jeff Burrfield), he was seen shopping in the Lanes for an anniversary present for his wife and taking a walk along the seafront before going back to his office where he was killed. With Harry Andrews's attempted murder, the evil boss was pushed off the wall that separates the promenade from the shingle after being run down near his office. With the Sandy Burton attempted murder, the shady executive was lured to a clandestine meeting at the notoriously steep and high steps that lead from the Madeira Drive part of the beach up to the street. The other murders in the show – and the books – could technically have been carried out anywhere, but these ones were all about this city.

There are only three other episodes that are like that. There is one where a beach hut is pushed on top of someone, crushing them. There is another where a shady businessman and former politician is fed copious amounts of cake on the ornate Victorian Bandstand. And then there is the cheating spouse who is tied to the base of Brighton's Palace Pier and left there for the tide to come in. That is a particularly brutal one. That is slow and agonising. That is the one I would choose if I had to decide how to torture someone I hated.

I came up with these crimes to have them solved. I always wanted them solved and the right person to go to prison because it hadn't happened that way in my real life. With my books and then the TV series, I have been trying to right the wrong that has followed me for every second of every day of my life.

But if I hated someone enough to do this, I would absolutely choose the slowest death to hurt them.

My phone flashes up with more messages from Valerie, Franklyn and Wallace. It won't be long before Wallace comes over to find out what's going on. I've been getting calls and texts from my mum and my sisters, too. I'm guessing Wallace has been in touch with them.

I'm staring at the phone, watching messages pop up like jack-in-a-boxes, when the one I've been waiting for comes up:

> ° We're waiting for you at
> the Pier. But which one?
> Palace Pier, West Pier or Worthing Pier?

Three choices, only one
chance to get it right. Good luck.

I know which one I would instinctively choose – Palace Pier. The same as the show. But she would expect that. She would want me to go there when she is in Worthing. The decrepit West Pier I would normally discount because you need to swim out to reach it and it is quite far from the shore. Plus it's more exposed than the others so people might see what you're doing. But might she go to where it used to connect to the seashore because she's assuming I would discount it? I don't know.

But I have to get this right. Lola's life depends on it.

I stand very slowly, the weight of this choice bearing down on me.

Into my mind pops the postcard I used to have stuck on my ceiling. The deckchairs by Palace Pier that I bought the first time I came to Brighton as a sixth-former. I used to look at it as a reminder of where I wanted to live, where I wanted to grow old. Now the place in that image, its place in my history, has become part of a terrible choice I have to make. Or is it a clue? The deciding factor in all of this?

I'm shaking so much I have to stop and push my hands onto the wooden tabletop to steady myself. I can do this. I know I can.

I think again of Abigail. Abi. Gail. I think of what she is like, what she has done, why she is doing this. I close my eyes and think of her. And it comes to me. Which pier she will have chosen.

And so I've made my choice.

I hope to God that it's the right one.

# 49

Lola fights. Every step of the way she fights and kicks and wriggles as The Woman drags her across the shingle, the small pebbles flying up in the air or being forced into ridges by her feet trying to stop what is happening to her.

The Woman is strong, though. And she keeps going, making slow progress because Lola is fighting. But it is progress. And eventually, after an age, The Woman gets Lola to the legs of the pier rising up from the water, waiting, it seems, for someone to do what The Woman is about to do. She removes a chain from her pocket, threads it through the tape keeping Lola's hands together, then hooks it around the base of the leg of the pier and locks it together with a padlock.

Lola still fights, but she can't get free. Her socks, wet and heavy, slide and slip in the silt and the pebbles until she has no choice but to give in to the gravity of the situation and not resist when she slips but instead allow her body to hit the water.

Her clothes become soaked almost immediately, the shock of the cold water making her gasp and wince. Her eyes sting with tears and the splash of the salt water, bashing against the pier leg, smacking her in the face. It is pitch out here. Pitch and quiet. She can hear her own breathing above the waves it is so quiet. No one is going to find her here, she realises. No one is going to come.

'It'll be high tide in the next hour or so,' The Woman states. 'That means all of this, where we are, will be under water. Which means . . . Well, sucks to be you.'

*Auntie C will find me*, Lola tells herself. *Auntie C will save me. Auntie C will save me.*

# 50

*Oh God, no.*

I pull up in the car, barely remembering to turn off the engine, take out the key and shut the door. And my heart plummets. I can't see them. I've made the wrong choice. I run along the promenade and road, my eyes searching in the blackness for them. I can't see them. I've chosen wrong.

*No. No.*

*She's going to die.*

*No.*

I won't have time to go anywhere else.

*I should have called the police, not waited for them to decipher what is going on with their monitoring of my phone. I should have called Wallace and told him to go to the other pier. I should have—*

I collapse onto the pavement.

*She's going to die. In a slow, horrible way.*

*And it's all my fault.*

# 51

The water has come in so quickly. When she was first put here, it barely reached her thighs. Now it's up to her shoulders. And rising. Rising.

*Auntie C will save me.*

Another wave crashes over her, and she's floating, her whole head weightless. She's used to the temperature now, but the loud sensation of being submerged, trying to close her eyes so the salt doesn't aggravate them, feeling wet seaweed and litter brushing up against her face, she can't get used to.

*Auntie C will save me.*

The water recedes and for a moment she can breathe. There is air and it is going down into her lungs. She knows that it'll only be for a few moments. The moments of breathing are getting shorter and shorter. The water is at her chin now, lapping up onto her tape-covered mouth.

*Auntie C will save me.*

Another wave, swirling over, immersing her again.

*Auntie C will save me.*

Air. A moment of air she tries to inhale through her nose.

*Auntie C will save me.*

Water. Saltiness. Sinking.

*Auntie C will save me.*

No air. No room to breathe. Nothing. Water, water, water.

*Auntie C—*

# 52

*Get up. Get up, you stupid woman! Get up! Do something!* I hear my voice in my head.

I was so sure. I was so sure. This is the sort of thing she would do. She would come here. She would come to the *other* pier. The original pier in Brighton, the Chain Pier, which is way out beyond the Palace Pier. It blew down at the end of the nineteenth century, but bits of its legs remain, stuck in the sea, too stubborn to go the way of the rest of the structure.

I was sure she would come here. That she would cheat when she made me choose a pier. That she would do all she could to make me lose. It is far removed from the main throng of people. Very few people come here at this time, which would be perfect for what Abigail wants to do.

I get to my feet, go to the railings and look again. Frantically search the dark beach for some sign of life. No, there's nothing there. The remaining legs of the Chain Pier are almost all submerged now. She would come here, I know she would. With difficulty, I climb over the railings – haven't got time to find a gap.

I hit the shingle and immediately start to slide. Rather than resist, I lean into it, allow the motion to propel me down the slope, kicking up pebbles and shells as I go. I get to the bottom in record time, the water racing up to greet me, it seems.

She has to be here. She has to be.

My eyes try to see into the dark water where the remains are. I can't see. I can't see, but I head there anyway, just as a huge wave rolls in from the sea and crashes against the legs of the Chain Pier, displacing all the water there.

Lola.

Lola is there, sagged against the largest leg, which is bent sideways. Her hands are bound, her mouth is covered and her eyes are closed. She doesn't move when the wave hits her, doesn't resist.

'Lola!' I scream and run towards her, the water slowing me down. 'Lola! Lola! I'm here! I'm here!' I'm shouting to her as I run, the sound of the waves swallowing up my words. When I reach her, I see she is chained to the leg. She doesn't stir when I touch her. She is unnaturally still. 'Hold on, Lola. Hold on.'

I can't unlock the chain and the tape will not come apart. I have to think and think quickly. I position myself beside Lola, take her in my arms, hold tight on to her and then as the next big wave hits, I use the movement to pull Lola up and sideways, dragging the chain in the dir- ection of the bend of the leg. The chain moves with us and lets her go, sets her free of the leg.

Using all my strength, I pick her up and carry her to the beach, to the shingle. The tide is still coming in, but I can't carry her far. She remains motionless.

When I place her on the pebbles, I immediately rip the tape off her mouth. Give her a chance to breathe. To take in air. Nothing. She doesn't respond.

I put my ear to her mouth. Nothing. No sounds of breathing, no tickle of her breath on my cheek. I put her head to one side and water dribbles out of her nose and mouth. I move her head to the centre again, pinch her nose and start CPR.

This has to work.

This HAS to work.

*Please, Lola*, I sob in my head. *Please, Lola, please wake up. Please wake up.*

# 53

I'm drizzling my fifth sachet of sugar into my coffee when Wallace pulls out the plastic orange chair opposite mine and sits down.

His face is grave; he looks like he's aged a million years in three hours. It feels like we all have. Franklyn is home from Portugal, Valerie has arrived, as have Lola's grandparents.

They're all furious with me and grateful to me at the same time. They don't know how to feel and neither do I. Wallace's mum, Donette, is the most resolute, though. 'Get that thing out of my sight,' she said to Wallace about me. I didn't need telling twice. I took myself off to the canteen and bought myself a coffee that I over-sugared and drank in three gulps – not noticing its heat – before going immediately back and buying another. This is my fourth one.

'I don't even know where to start,' he says. Anger tightly laces up his beautiful features, like one of his beloved trainers. I can't look at that face when it's this angry, no matter how justified his anger is.

'Is she going to be all right?' I ask quietly. 'How about you start there.'

'Yes. She is going to be all right. They say you saved her life. A few minutes later and . . . we'd all be in a very different place.'

396

Everything had moved at break-neck speed after I got her breathing again. My phone still worked despite being dunked when I went in the water, and the ambulance appeared in no time. We made it to the hospital in no time, too, because we weren't that far away. They said she would probably be fine, but they were going to take her in and treat her anyway. On the way to the hospital I had called Wallace and told him where we were, and told him to tell everyone else. I couldn't speak to Franklyn and Valerie – I was too much of a gigantic coward.

'What the hell is going on? Why would that woman take Lola? Why wouldn't you tell me? Call the police? What is this all about?'

I run my hands over my face, temple them over my mouth as my eyes fill with tears. This is where I rip apart my life. I thought I could control it, that I could manage its dismantling in stages to my design. But it was never going to be that easy, that simple.

'This is all about my other husband,' I tell him.

'Your *what*?' he asks. The edge in his voice isn't anger, it's shock and it's hurt and it's incredulity.

'My other husband. I got married a long, long time ago. But I never got divorced. I thought it wasn't legally recognised over here, which is why I *married* you. But it turns out it *is* recognised here, so I'm still married to him as well as being married to you. I recently found out that I'm probably going to prison for that, which is great.

'I met him at uni and we became friends. Trina knows him. He was obsessed with me. Imagine that, eh? Someone *obsessed* with little old me.' I glance up to see what Wallace is thinking – he still has a look that says he thinks I'm pulling his leg or trying to deflect from earlier events by making up lies. 'His obsession led him to hurt people if he thought they were going to take me away from him.' I have to look away for the next bit. I am a coward and I cannot stand to look at my husband's face when I tell him this. 'He thought Sidney was trying to get me to leave him. He knew we weren't together or anything like that but he still wanted Sidney gone. So he . . . he killed that woman and framed your brother.'

'What the hell are you talking about?' Wallace's voice is now angry as well as incredulous.

'My other husband, Heath. His name is Heath. He said if I came back to him, he would give the police the evidence to get Sidney out of prison. I was going to do it, I swear on my life, I was going to do it, but Sidney wouldn't let me.'

'Wouldn't let you? What the hell do you mean, "wouldn't let you"?'

I chance a glance at the man sitting opposite me and he is glaring at me like he hates me. He should get in line because I hate me more.

'Sidney said if I went back to Heath, he would confess to the crime. He would make sure he never got out of prison. He made me promise to look after his family – especially you. That's why he asked us to go to the prison that time. He wanted to make sure I didn't go back to Heath.

'I wasn't supposed to fall in love with you. But I did. I did and I didn't ever want to leave you. Except I knew I would have to one day. I knew that I'd have to go back to Heath so he would get your brother out of prison. And that's why I asked for the divorce. That's why I ended the TV show – I was ending this life so I could go back to Heath and you could all have Sidney back. But . . . but his girlfriend, she hates me. She blames me for him finishing with her. And she killed my divorce lawyer. And she tried to kill the CEO and the COO of Honey-May Productions so she could frame me for their deaths. And then she took Lola to hurt me. And that's it. That's everything. Except . . . I'm sorry. I should have told you. I was just too scared of losing you, of you hating me, of Sidney actually confessing to the crime. I'm sorry.'

Wallace doesn't speak or move. I don't think he's breathing. Then he gets up so fast he knocks his chair over. I look up at him and he is scowling at me, all his hurt pouring out at me. He picks up the chair, slams it upright and then walks away. I know he's never going to speak to me again.

# 54

'I knew you'd save me,' Lola says when I'm allowed to see her. The family have only allowed this because Lola created such a fuss about wanting to see me, her parents caved. None of them will look at me and they certainly won't talk to me – it's obvious that Wallace has told them the truth.

'How did you know that, then?'

'That's what happens in your books. Someone is in danger, you save them.'

'I don't. The character does. Mira.'

'Yeah, and she's you. You even named her after yourself.'

I shake my head despairingly. 'Seriously, am I the last person on Earth to see that I did that? I honestly didn't notice.'

Lola glances at her parents and uncle, who are standing by the door – Valerie with her arms folded across her chest, Wallace with his arms around himself, Franklyn with one arm around his ex-wife, the other on his brother's shoulder, supporting them both. Lola looks dreadful, of course. But she is alive, she is being monitored and she will get better. 'You are in so much trouble,' she says. 'I feel it's my duty to tell you this.'

400

'I deserve it. I absolutely deserve it.'

'You probably do. But you know, Auntie C, I'mma gonna need to come live with you. Brighton is rad, man. Proper rad.'

'We'll talk about that. Sometime in the future, the far, far future.'

Lola's face creases into a grin. I know she's going to be all right. In all of this, I need her to be all right. And she will be. I know she will. I kiss her forehead and say a silent goodbye. I won't be seeing her again. I know this.

'I'm sorry,' I say to her parents on the way out. I don't linger too long in front of them, I know they can't stand to even look at me right now. 'I'm so sorry.' Neither of them speaks, but they don't spit in my face, which feels like an absolute win.

And right now, I'll take all the wins I can get.

# 55

The last week or so has passed in a dreamlike blur.

I've been sleepwalking through it all: the talks with detectives Amwell and Mattison, who try to be supportive but I'm sure are secretly pissed that I wasn't the killer after all; the interviews under caution about the bigamy; the updates on Abi/Gail/Abigail sightings, which keep coming until they tell me they've got her – four days after she tried to kill Lola. She wasn't very good at hiding and it didn't take too much to find her. It looked like she'd tried to leave the country when she realised that Lola had survived. Amwell told me a few days ago that she wanted to speak to me. 'Why would I do that?' I replied.

'For closure?' Mattison said gently.

'I'm not doing your job for you,' I said. 'I know you want me to speak to her so you can hopefully get her to confess to all sorts. Not my problem. I don't care why she did it. That she did it and did it so many times is enough.'

Enough.

I had finally reached that point, I realised, when I began to pack my things. Wallace didn't come back to the house and I had reached the

402

point of enough. Enough already. Just go back to Heath and be done with it. Just go back to him and set Sidney free.

I walk from room to room after I've finished. I have packed a great deal, but I have marked more for charity. Heath and I are going to go away together. Where it is going to be just the two of us. I've had enough of fighting this, it is time to accept it. And I will be best leaving most of my possessions behind. '*You can't take it with you*,' people often say. I wonder if they realise it also applies when you're simply going away?

When I am packed, when I am finished removing myself from Wallace's life, I move the boxes to the spare room, where the window was cut out. I've had that fixed and I ignored the strange looks from the glazier who measured up and then fit it.

Before I leave the house for the last time, I ring Wallace. The call immediately goes to voicemail. '*Wallace, I'm just calling to let you know that I've packed up my things and I'm leaving the house today. I'm leaving Brighton, too, so you won't see me again. Thank you for the good times. I want you to know it wasn't fake. It was all very real. I adored you so much. All my love, Cleo.*'

# Part 12

# 56

Light is pouring in the large windows of Heath's flat when I arrive. I'd told him on the phone that I was finally free and asked if he still wanted me back. 'Always,' he replied. 'Always.'

He keeps staring at my bags, as if not believing I am actually here and we are actually doing this. 'What happened?' he asks when he has brought up the rest of my bags from the car. 'Why are you suddenly here?'

'You know some of it, but honestly, yeah, we kind of need a lot of coffee to deal with that,' I tell him. I reach into my jacket pocket, taking out a packet of Maltesers *and* a packet of Minstrels.

'That bad?' he asks.

'That bad.'

I make us coffee, I put five sugars in each. I feel Heath's eyes on me as I spoon them in and I can feel him shuddering. 'Shall I start yours again?' I say, laughing. 'It's automatic at this point.'

'No, no, if we're doing this, then I need to take the rough with the too sweet.'

'Good choice, Heath man, good choice.' I finish sugaring our

DOROTHY KOOMSON

coffees. 'Remember how you started drinking this in college to impress me? Your face was a picture every single time you took a sip.'

'My teeth. My poor, poor teeth.'

I laugh at the memory of it. Of us. 'The things you used to do to try to get me interested.' I laugh again, shaking my head.

'Why are you so "up"?' he asks when I take a seat at the table. 'You're not usually so upbeat when you speak to me. In fact, usually you act like you're going to disintegrate if you're near me any longer than you absolutely have to be.'

'Because I want you to do something for me. And once you've done it, I'll be free to be with you. And I won't leave you ever again. I've accepted that, so I'm just . . . When you can see your future clearly, everything seems and feels different. Clearer. Easier. Happier, I suppose. How are you getting on with finding us somewhere to live?'

'I found a nice place up in the Highlands. We can become farmers if we want. Grow our own veg.'

'Yeah, well, I'll have to think about that one.'

Heath takes a big drink of his 'coffee' and grimaces as though he's forgotten what I'd done to the drink seconds ago. I smirk at him and take a sip of my own.

'What's the favour you want?'

'I want you to confess so Sidney can come out of jail.'

'I said I would.'

'I mean today. I want you to record everything that happened, what you did, and then I want to send it to the cloud. Once we've got to our new place, we can send it to the police.'

'But we can record it then, surely?'

I shake my head, sip my drink. 'No. Because I know you'll stall. As time goes on, you'll stall in case I leave you. And you'll find more and

408

more ways to put off doing it, until you never do it. I don't want you to go back on your word. You record it today and I accept we're together for ever. Happily.'

To avoid answering, to think about it, Heath sips at his drink, grimacing each time. 'Oh, for Pete's sake, stop drinking it if it's that bad!' I tell him. 'I'll make you another one.'

He pulls a stoic face and then raises his cup and takes a big gulp. 'There, see. Rough with the too sweet.' He slams his cup down, like a Viking who has just bested a large keg of mead. 'All right. I'll do it.'

'Right now?'

'Right now.'

I take out my phone and hesitate when I see the lock screen – a big picture of Wallace, smiling softly at the camera, at me. I unlock the screen, get up the voice memo app. 'You have to tell them everything. As many details that only you can know as possible. All right? You need to tell them everything so when the time comes, they'll let Sidney out. OK?'

'OK.'

His face becomes serious, his features pinched and pensive. He looks like he's going cry, then looks like he's going to vomit. He pulls the phone towards himself. After hanging his head for a moment, he presses record. And starts to speak. He starts to talk and drags me into the hell he created all those years ago.

By the time Heath has finished speaking, I am sitting on the floor, resting against the cupboard under the sink. Tears are streaming down my face. He comes to join me, handing me my phone. Slowly, because I am still navigating hell, still stepping carefully through the things I have heard Heath describe, I name the file, I send it to the cloud. I place the phone on the floor between us, shaking. Trembling. I can't quite believe what I've just heard.

'Did you kill your first lover, the science teacher?' I ask him. Since I found out what he is capable of, I have wanted to know. This seems as good a time as any to ask.

'No, of course I didn't,' he says. 'I could never hurt her. Just like I could never hurt you.' He pauses, and because I know him, I know that while he didn't kill her, there is something that he did that was terrible. 'But I did tell her husband about us.'

I close my eyes at the horror of this. The set of events that he had set in motion. No, he didn't kill her but he sparked the fire that led to it.

'We were in love,' Heath says. 'We were so perfect and happy together and she wanted to be with me. I know she did. I knew she couldn't love him like she loved me and I knew he couldn't love her like I did. So I went to their house to talk to him, man to man. I told him, I told him straight. And he . . .' Heath's face twists as he remembers that time, the conversation. 'And he beat the crap out of me. He was a grown man, I was young. And weak. It was no match. He kept saying he was done with her. That this was the last time he was going to put up with this.

'I didn't even realise at first that he was saying she'd done it before. She'd slept with her pupils before. I just . . . I couldn't defend myself properly. Once he'd knocked me down, he just kept stomping on me.

'Then he made me wait for her to come back so she could look me in the eye and tell me about the others. About the eight others. How she'd had to move schools three times because of the rumours.'

'Jeez, Heath, that is horrible.' No wonder he is messed up. No wonder.

Heath stares into the void beside me, not seeing anything. 'I didn't care she'd done it before. Because I knew she loved me more than them. She might have done it before but it was different with me. And even though he forced her to tell me that I was just another notch on her bedpost, I knew she didn't mean it. And then he did it. He just killed her, right in front of me.'

I sit forwards, staring at him as I gasp, 'No.' I didn't know that he'd been there, that he'd seen it.

'I couldn't move. I couldn't help her. All I could do was watch while he took her away from me.' He refocuses on me, seeing me again, back in this room now he has visited that terrible part of his past. 'I decided there and then that no one was ever going to take the person I love away from me again.'

I understand now. I understand more about him and why he does the things he does. What I don't understand is the other thing I've always wanted to ask. 'Why me, Heath?'

'Why do I love you?'

'Yes. Why me? I'm nothing special. Not to anyone but me. Why did you do all this? Why me?'

'You remind me of her. You've always reminded me of her.'

'Your first lover?'

He rubs his fingers on his eyes and nods. 'You don't look like her. She was white, she was older than you, obviously, different body shape, everything was different. But when I saw you that first day of college, I just . . . it was like déja vu. This déja-vu feeling.' He forms a fist and pushes it into his chest. 'Here.' He moves it to his stomach and pushes the fist there, too. 'And here.' His kitchen is darkening, the light that was flooding in when I arrived all but gone. 'I hadn't felt anything since she died, not anything. I was so numb and nothing touched me. And then I saw you, and these feelings exploded inside me. And I . . . It was like she was alive again. It was like I was alive again. I remembered what it was like to feel, to want to experience the touch and presence of another person.

'You jump-started my heart again. My life again. And every time I was with you, it was like I got another chance to rewrite the ending of my story with her. But it wasn't just that. It was also like she had been the prelude to you. She'd been around to show me what love felt like. All the bad bits, the painful bits as well as the euphoria of it. And it felt sometimes that I'd had to lose her so I could find you.

'And whenever someone would come between us or threaten to take you away from me, it was like watching him murder her, watching him take her away from me all over again. I had to stop it. I had to do something. Anything to stop someone taking you away from me.

'You were my everything. Remember I said to you about moments and how long they can be and how short they can be? Every moment has been about you since I met you. You are every moment to me.'

'Do you know how f-ing creepy that sounds?' I say to him with a laugh.

He grins at me, wicks away the tears that have started to fall. 'I suppose it does.'

The silence takes over us again. The memories of our time in here crowding in. That was when I didn't know any better and Heath was the reason why I smiled, he was the reason why I felt my heart was full and the world was good.

'You asked me to go to Vegas over there,' I say to him, pointing to the kettle and the chopping board. 'Knowing that you were going to persuade me to marry you.'

'I did,' he replies.

'And you told me that you hated my Saturday soups over there,' I say.

'I did,' he smirks. 'Your face was . . . not happy, shall we say.'

'I could not believe the brass neck of you. Someone spends week after week making you a wonderfully nutritious soup and you had the audacity to say you didn't like it.'

He laughs. 'I had sex in a kitchen for the first time with you over there,' he says.

'The first time, really?'

'Yes. Does that surprise you?'

'You were very experienced, I just assumed you'd done it everywhere.'

'You assumed wrong.'

'Do you remember when that noticeboard you put up fell down in the middle of the night and scared the life out of us?'

Heath laughs. 'Yes! I remember you grabbed the remote control and were out of bed like a shot.'

My laugh bubbles up and out of me. 'I had no idea what I thought I'd do with a remote control against someone who could make such a huge noise! Wasn't thinking rationally, I don't think.'

'Not rationally at all.'

The silence that settles this time is sweet, soft, gentle. It's what our time together was always meant to be like.

'You know I've come to kill you, don't you?' I say to him. I turn my head towards him to find him staring at me like he used to in college – as though I am all his dreams come true. 'Don't you?' I add softly.

'Yes,' he replies. 'I know.'

'And myself.'

'I know.'

'I've kind of reconciled myself with a lot of stuff, realised that I wasn't to blame for the things you did, but I suppose if I'd spoken up

413

earlier, that poor woman might still be alive. Sidney wouldn't be in prison. His family wouldn't all hate me. I wouldn't have brought all this stress and shame to my family's door. That poor solicitor would still be alive. And I couldn't go on, knowing that I'd killed you.'

'I'd tell you not to hurt yourself – not because of me – but I suspect it's too late,' he says.

'It is,' I say with a smile.

'You poisoned the drinks, didn't you?'

'I did. Lethal dose.'

I decided to do this a couple of weeks ago. I had to put an end to Heath and the things he did. Because he may think it would be OK, that he's finished with all of that, but I know him. I know that as time goes on, any interaction outside the two of us, any moment that he feels threatened, he will revert to type. He will start to obsess. He will start to hurt people to keep me. I don't want that on my conscience.

On the floor between us, my mobile lights up.

*Trina calling . . .*

'Talk about perfect timing,' I say. 'The three of us together at the beginning and at the end.'

I can feel the medication taking proper hold now. Before I can't move, I want to say goodbye to Trina. I cancel her call and send a text: 'Love you. Always' I type and hit send.

'Can I get one of them, too?' Heath asks. His voice is blurry, fuzzed by the massive amount of drugs I dissolved earlier and poured into both our cups. It's taste had been hidden by the huge amount of sugar I always put into coffee. 'Can I get a "love you", as well?'

I had loved Heath once. I had loved every part of him. It takes a moment to steady myself, and I still wobble as I move forwards and press my lips onto his. He closes his eyes and leans into the kiss, his hand briefly on my face as we kiss for the last time. Heath breaks away first, his head listing on to the cupboard before his body completely relaxes and he lets go.

I hear his house phone start to ring somewhere. It sounds so far away, I'm not even sure it is his phone. But somewhere there is a ringing sound. Somewhere someone is trying to break through. His features are very blurry, and my mind is finding it hard to keep hold of any thoughts. I know somewhere there's a ringing sound.

'Love you,' I say to him.

*Love you.*

# Epilogue

Trina has small gold glasses sitting on the end of her nose and she is looking down as she fills in a crossword puzzle.

'Am I in hell?' I ask. 'Am I waking up in hell?'

My best friend whips off her glasses and puts aside her paper. 'The disrespect. I save your life, I travel halfway across the world at great time and monetary expense and I get this level of disrespect. It's no wonder you've always stayed an SBBF.'

'Sorry, sweetie. The one who has the dramas is the main character, the one who is married to one man and has the kids and a normal existence is the SBBF.'

'Oh, you, you're something else,' she says. 'Having serious doubts about saving your life now.'

'What do you mean, you saved my life?'

'I called you. I mean, let's all acknowledge you've been ducking my calls from time. But I've been calling you because I kept having these really vivid dreams about you – you were in hell. H was there with you. This last dream really scared me, though. So I called you this time and rather than being blanked, I get a text reply. I call your babes, he tells me you've split up, you've told him all about your other husband who I know, and the things he did. Then he says he doesn't know where you are. Then I call H's flat. I get no answer. I'm panicking now cos that text was basically you saying goodbye so I called the police and created hell until they came to his flat to check if anything was wrong. I thought he'd done for you, too.'

'You should have just left us. Let us die. Everyone would have been better off.'

'No, I shouldn't,' Trina replies, suddenly serious. 'The world would be a terrible place without you. Without both of you.'

'Is he . . . ?'

'No. You were both found in time. But you've both been out for four days now. Well, you woke up before, which is why you're here, but you went straight back to sleep. Anyway, you being out so long was perfect since it gave me the chance to arrive to receive my rescuer flowers.' She places a comforting hand on my cheek. 'He is going to prison, though. For a very long time.'

'So am I.'

'We'll see.'

'What do you mean, we'll see?'

'I mean, we'll see if you getting a full confession that will reverse one of the most heinous miscarriages of justice can be weighed up against some shady wedding business that wouldn't be in the public interest to prosecute.' When I frown at her, she adds, 'We've been talking to a lawyer. Adding in the fact you saved a young girl's life and helped bring another killer to justice . . . I think it's safe to say there is unlikely to be any jail time for you.'

'Who is we?'

'Me, your family, your babes.' She points a perfectly manicured finger to the door of the ward I'm on. I watch Wallace open the door and walk across the ward with two cups in his hands, just like the first time I met him.

'Is he here to shout at me?' I ask.

'No. Sidney explained things to him. Confirmed everything you said. They've started the process of getting him out, by the way. It'll take time, but it's going to happen.' She gathers up her belongings and stands. 'He hasn't left your bedside,' she whispers as she leans in for a hug. 'Sometimes he would sleep outside in his car to be near you.' In a more normal tone, she says: 'I'll give you two some space.'

'Thanks, SBBF,' I say and she narrows her eyes in return.

Wallace takes the seat Trina has just vacated.

We say nothing for a long time, just stare at each other, like two familiar strangers who are unsure what to say, who don't know where to begin.

Eventually, he says, 'I don't want to snooze and lose, so I suppose I should start by saying I love you. Very much. And we can take it from there.'

My face relaxes into a smile. Yes, I suppose we can take it from there.

## THE END

# Acknowledgements

Thank you to . . .

My wonderful family
My incredible and supportive agents, Ant and James
My excellent publishers (who are fully credited at the back)
Graham Bartlett for the research help
My fabulous friends
My beloved MK2
My best girls Jollof and Fufu
You, the reader. As always, thank you for buying my book.
And, to E & G. . . always and forever.

# Author's Note

## *Dorothy Koomson's Big Reveal: Am I Or Am I Not Cleo?*

If you've read *My Other Husband* and you've heard a little about my life, you'll probably be wondering: is Cleo in a very thinly disguised version of Dorothy Koomson?

After all, I went to college in Leeds like Cleo, I write books like Cleo, I started off my career in magazines like Cleo, and I live in Brighton after moving down from London, like Cleo.

You'd be forgiven for thinking I've simply written an autobiography and have scribbled in a couple of murders to throw everyone off the scent.

Well, after lots of protestations that I am not, in fact, Cleo, I'm going to just come at you with a big reveal and say: 'Yes, yes I am Cleo.'

Sort of.

Before we go any further, let me state for the record: I only have one husband. Just the one. Honest.

Although, yes, I did meet him in Leeds like Cleo does Heath, the similarities end there. Doctor K and I didn't go the same college – I met him while he was up there visiting a friend. And he didn't stare at me, I think he barely noticed me. I didn't see him for most of the 90s

# Credits

*Without all these people, there'd be no* My Other Husband.